DAUGHTER OF DARKNESS - PRINCE OF BLOODSHED

Allie Cole

DEDICATION

To those who need to escape in fantasy worlds because it's easier than real life sometimes – I see you.

And to the quiet girl I used to be, who spent her nights staring at the ceiling with stories in her head – Thank you.

PLAYLIST

Wait - M83

Let Me Hurt - Emily Rowed

This City if a Graveyard - Baby Storme

Twisted Love - Aryia

In the Distance - Tony Anderson

Folle - Izia

All of your lies - Morgan Clae

Trustfall - PINK

Can't Help Falling in Love - Tommee Profitt (feat. Brooke)

Loona - Miss Monique

Never Let Me Go - Florence + The Machine

Just a Game - Birdy

My Tears Are Becoming a Sea - M83

IMPORTANT NOTE

Delving into themes of loss and mortality, this book takes readers on an emotionally intense journey, ultimately concluding with a bittersweet ending.

The content can entail some triggering situations for the reader, such as graphic violence, sexually explicit scenes, emotional and physical abuse, suicide, and death.

Please be mindful of these elements before delving into the story.

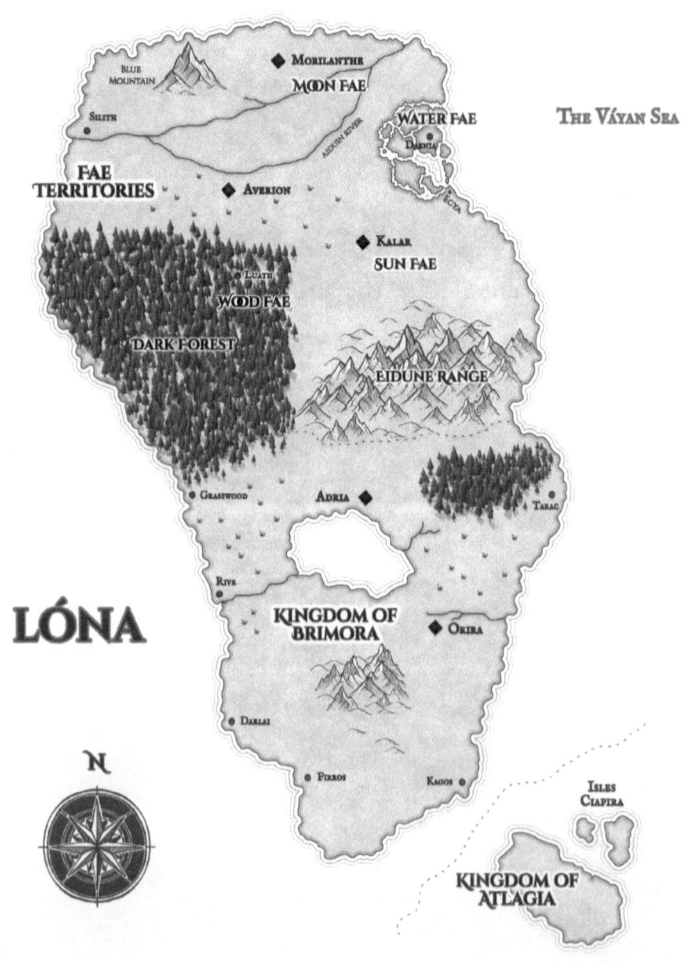

LÓNA
THE VÁYAN SEA
BLUE MOUNTAIN
MORILANTHE
MOON FAE
SILITH
WATER FAE
DAENIA
AIDUIN RIVER
EOVA
FAE TERRITORIES
AVERION
KALAR
SUN FAE
LUATH
WOOD FAE
DARK FOREST
EIDUNE RANGE
GRASSWOOD
ADRIA
TARAC
RIVE
KINGDOM OF BRIMORA
ORIRA
DARLAI
FIRROS
KAGOS
ISLES CIAPIRA
KINGDOM OF ATLAGIA
N

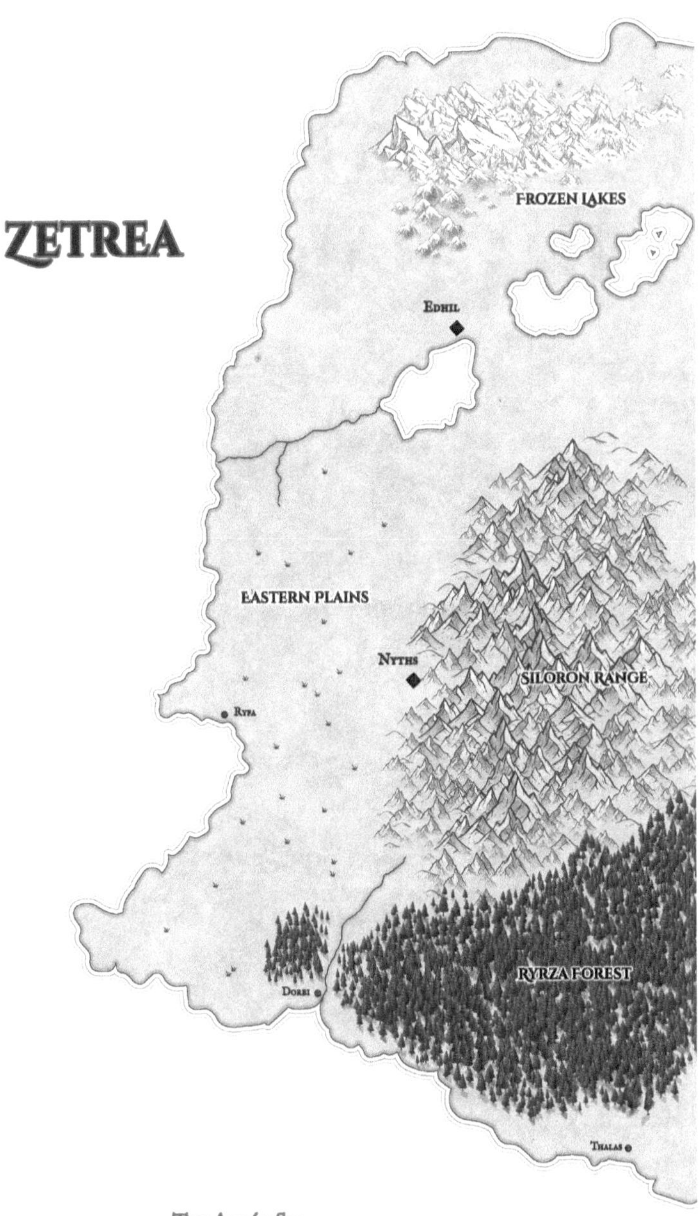

ZETREA
FROZEN LAKES
EDHIL
EASTERN PLAINS
NYTHS
SILORON RANGE
RYFA
RYRZA FOREST
DOREI
THALAS
THE AERÓN SEA

IMPORTANT TERMS AND CHARACTERS

Elanor, Ela, L, or Unifier – Daughter of Tannyll and Aerín

Tannyll – Father of Elanor (D)

Aerín – Mother of Elanor (D)

Azran, Az – High Lord of Lóna, mated to Elanor

Calen, Cal – General of Lóna's army

Vesta, V – Elanor's best friend, soldier in Lóna's army

Morthil, Mor – Head of Lóna's healers

Naar – Captain of Averion, mated to Morthil

Wyn - Twin brother of Varan, soldier in Lóna's army

Varan – Twin brother of Wyn, soldier in Lóna's army

Savage – Fae Wolf, guardian of Ela (D)

Aanor - Queen of Brimora, the human kingdom

Braern – Leader of the rebels in Lóna (D)

Amrynn – Lady of the Moon Fae, Azran's cousin

Irann – Lady of the Wood Fae

Keryth – Lord of the Water Fae

Tharrion – Lord of the Sun Fae

Barus – Intendant to the High Lord of Lóna

Rina – Royal aide

Ilyana – Aerín's caretaker

Ayas – bartender in Averion

Rick – friend of Vesta

Nahtar – Ancient Fae sword, wielded by Elanor

Averion – Capital of the Fae Territories of Lóna

Darkclaws – Bear beast with poisonous claws

(D) - deceased

PART 1

STILL WATERS RUN DEEP

"Who says you're alone?"

CHAPTER 1

AZRAN

The sea breeze whips strands of hair across my face as I go over the plan for the hundredth time. I'm counting the days and hours since I left Averion, determined to return as soon as I can.

Squinting against the briny gusts, I turn my head and my eyes lock onto the one sight that always steals my breath. Elanor's willowy frame leans against the wall of the ship's cabin, her back to me, and a pit opens in my stomach.

The setting sun frames her silhouette in a halo of gold and pink hues that complement the warmth of her chestnut hair. My heart constricts the way only she could provoke, and peace settles through me, the calming eye in the center of the storm. As long as I draw breath, I will cross endless oceans to remain by her side.

If only it were that simple. The hint of a smile plays at the corners of my mouth until the mirage fades away amidst the organized chaos of the shipmates rushing around me. Pain flares in my heart.

If only she could be here with me. My mouth opens but the cry doesn't leave my throat as our mating bond blazes inside me.

I understand now more than ever her reluctance to the bond. When life separated us, it became nothing more than a cage, squeezing tighter and tighter around my heart, crushing my soul, hurting my body and mind. What used to connect us and fill me with pure bliss grows more torturous the further I go from her.

I pinch my eyes shut, hoping to bring the vision back; Ela's hair flowing in the wind, her irises full of life, her smile widening as our eyes lock, but it's her blood-smeared face that appears. That image haunts me, torments me at night, forever taunting me with the impossible.

Fresh nightmares have replaced the old ones, terrifying companions of my nights since Braern's defeat. It's not my enemies' corpses I see anymore. Now, it's hers.

Her victorious smile appears when I close my eyes and her memory tears through my chest as I scream her name into the ether, but no one answers.

Staring at the horizon, where dark waters extend as far as the eye can see, my mind inevitably wanders to my mate. I see her in the shadows. I see her everywhere, expect her to appear by my side and confirm it was all a bad dream.

The ocean spray whips my face and I check the mating bond. A familiar void greets me. My grip tightens on the wooden railing of the boat and the cold wind carries the smell of saline and algae, reminding me how far from Averion I've wandered.

Another zap of pain goes through the bond and I clench my jaw hard to fight the wetness pooling in my eyes. I would have imagined that the longing would recede with each day, but it only amplifies, making her absence the only thing I can think about. Every hour, I check the bond, irrational hope filling my heart, though I know no one has the power to bring her back.

I can only focus on what I have to do. My mission in Zetrea is the last purpose I have left. The threat to Lóna has not been eradicated yet. I have to find out how Braern got hold of the sorcery that decimated the ranks of our army in Adria weeks ago.

We stopped him, but not before thousands died. Cries and wails from the battle mix with other massacres forever engraved in my head. These dreadful memories now harbor Ela's piercing scream, too.

Blood calling for blood, my power flares and my desire for revenge awakens. Strength floods my arms until the wood beneath my palms cracks and I let go. War has haunted my every waking moment since long before this power awoke inside me. It is my burden and calling, in this life and the next.

We raided Braern's base of command after his defeat and confirmed the deadly powder was gone, but we found encrypted letters detailing how to use and command his weapon—an enchantment controlled by an amulet. With the whisper of a few words, a touch of the talisman, the battlefield exploded, killing blindly, unleashing pure wrath and destruction.

A smile tugs my lips at the memory of Ela leading the final attack. Forever a mind of her own, she snuck into the enemy camp at night, set on fulfilling her revenge. And that, she did. My smile widens as I lose myself in her remembrance.

She slayed Braern without a second thought after I snatched his medallion. As his head fell to the ground, she turned to me, unyielding and victorious. She looked at me as if for the first time, with love and pride in her hazel eyes as she embraced her true self fully. I'll never forget that sight.

My heart swells before the image fades and reveals the endless pit inside of me.

I was ready to take that last memory with me to my grave when my consciousness slipped into oblivion, my body torn from Braern's attack, but Ela found a way to save me, trading her life for mine.

I awoke, and she didn't.

My hand brushes Ela's soft cheek one more time, and her face remains undisturbed, frozen in a peaceful state. It's been weeks, but I keep caressing her pale skin, hoping this time will be different. This time she will hear me. This time she will come back to me.

"Little one, it's me." The words barely reach my ears, but I keep going. "You're safe now."

I haven't slept in days and can't remember the last time I ate or drank. My throat dries up as I try to clear it. "Please."

I release a heavy sigh before brushing a strand of hair behind her pointy ear. "I have to go, Ela. I can't delay any longer, but I'll be back. I promise." I deposit a soft kiss on her forehead, then her cheeks, and finally, her lips. "I will always come back to you."

I lift my head as Morthil walks in and shakes his head in defeat. "Her body is perfectly healed, but she is no longer in our realm. Wherever she is, I can't follow. No one can."

Clenching my jaw, I stand.

"It makes no sense, Mor," I say as I pace around the room. "I will summon the best healers of Zetrea once I reach Nyths. We will find a way."

The healer doesn't respond, tilting his head to the side.

"What?" My voice rings loud, disrupting the room's peaceful atmosphere.

"Playing with Death always comes with a price. Her fate is in her own hands, and she has to be the one to come back to us."

A wave crashes against the side of the boat, bringing me back to the realm of the living. We tried everything, and there is no other explanation for her slumber. She doesn't want to return to this life, to me.

"High Lord." A member of the High Guard bows a few feet from me. I relieve him from the formality with a wave of my hand,

and he straightens. "The coast is in view. We should arrive in Zetrea by sunrise."

I send him away with a nod. There is no grieving for me. We can't lower our guard yet.

Someone aided Braern, equipped his fighters, provided the mysterious necklace, and prepared him to take Lóna. Adria was but a taste of what is coming if I can't stop this madness.

Braern corresponded with someone in Zetrea, and its capital makes the perfect hunting ground for me to find out who. My visit to the continent is long overdue, anyway.

Once I've ensured the safety of Lóna, then I will rest. Then, I will grieve the ones we lost. Then, I will bring her back.

<hr />

I glance behind us as our horses gallop on the road to Nyths, leaving clouds of dust in our wake. Ryfa's rooftops glint under the sun in farewell before city structures sink from sight. The dense thicket of dock warehouses and weathered masts dwindle to silhouettes on the uneven horizon until those outlines blur indistinguishably into wild grassland.

The warm breeze does little to ease the heat, and beads of sweat roll down my temples as we cross the verdant fields.

This land hasn't changed in centuries. Roads connect all major cities and plains decorate the central part of Zetrea. Further east, Nyths is surrounded by mountain ranges, protecting its flanks and strengthening its strategic position. Forests occupy the southern region, and great lakes the northern parts, though I have never seen them.

The thunder of hooves in my ears fades away, leaving me to my memories.

I haven't seen the Fae capital since I first came here as a child with my father. As the Lord of the Moon Fae's firstborn, this introduction to Fae society was a necessary formality, though it was more like an invitation to the snake's nest.

Wars broke out not long after, and no Fae in Lóna has set foot in Zetrea since. At least, none on an official delegation.

A visit to the King as High Lord of the unified Fae territories would be the ideal occasion to oust Braern's accomplice, and the missive I sent two days ago from Ryfa will ensure a greeting committee awaiting us in Nyths.

I check the weapon at my side once more, its movement foreign, for my two-bladed sword is no longer on my back. It doesn't allow for much stealth where I'm headed. The rest of the unit is riding around me in formation, their faces stern and focused.

I lift my hand and slow the group's pace to let the horses cool down. We still have another two days' ride to the capital and can't appear to be in a hurry.

Pain flares in my chest again as the bond ignites, ever more intense as the distance with Averion and Elanor increases. The corners of my lips lift into a tight smile.

Love was a mere synonym of suffering and despair for as long as I could recall, until I met her. I'm now holding onto the sharp sting in my heart like a lifeline, a sign she still lives, even if she never comes back to me. I don't know what lies ahead, but the scarred bond reminds me how much I still have to lose.

CHAPTER 2

CALEN

The log burning in the fireplace cracks loudly behind me as I re-read the same line over and over again, not registering a word. Finally giving up, I put the stack of paper down and lean back on my chair to take in the room. Empty leather couches are arranged around a low table and bookshelves line the walls of Azran's office. An ornate gold-leaf frame encircles a vivid oil rendering of Averion's signature white-domed buildings on the wall opposite the mahogany desk.

I release a huff as the irony hits me. This room clashes drastically with its owner. Warm, welcoming, comfortable, and the exact opposite of Az.

The thought brings a smile to my face, a nice reprieve from the constant worry that comes from being responsible for the affairs of the realm in his absence.

"Whatever you are up against, brother, be careful out there," I murmur to the empty room.

A courier arrived with a missive from him several days ago, confirming his arrival in Nyths and intention to visit the royal palace.

A pit opens in my stomach, as all I can do is wait and pray to whoever is listening for his safe return. Ela will kill me if something happens to him. That is, if she ever awakens, and crippling guilt hasn't already driven me to my knees.

I take a sip from the amber drink I've been nursing for the better part of the evening before returning to my correspondence with emissaries from Brimora. Who would have guessed dealing with human royalty could be such a pain?

A chuckle escapes my lips at the pointless question. Frankly, *I* could have guessed that, which is why I've never shown interest in being anything but the General of the Fae armies. But in times like this, there is no staying away from politics. I have to deal with the long line of Lords, Ladies, and emissaries waiting to bring matters to the High Lord of the Fae's attention.

Following Braern's attack on Brimora, the humans stationed their army to guard their northern border and Queen Aanor has proven defiant and on edge, understandably. It's taking great effort and diplomacy to restore communication between our two people. Undoing centuries of barbaric acts and misconceptions will take time. The battle in Adria was months ago, but its scars run deep.

I've just finished drafting a response and begun sorting through what's left for the night when a sharp knock sounds on the door. Clearing my throat, I invite whoever is on the other side to enter.

My mood immediately improves when the redheaded Captain of the High Guard walks in.

Vesta stops at the wooden desk and drops off a report. I barely look at it, too hypnotized by her. The red and gold armor hugs her curves perfectly and makes her emerald eyes pop. This night is taking a turn for the better.

"General."

"How many times do I have to tell you not to—"

"Fine, Cal. Here is the weekly report on the High Guard."

I raise an eyebrow in response.

"Is everything okay?"

"Sorry." She releases a sigh. "There's just a lot going on right now."

I nod patiently, letting her decide if she wants to confide in me.

"The training of our new recruits is going well. Amrynn is still in Morilanthe, cooped up in her palace, her public appearances few and far between."

I'll take that as a no, then.

"So, nothing outstanding?"

She shakes her head and looks towards the door, eager to be dismissed. I'm tempted to let her go, but tormenting her is one of my very few pleasures these days.

"You're doing great, V. I know you didn't plan for these responsibilities, but that's where I need you right now."

She nods.

"Once everything is back to normal, you'll be able to go back to the best depravities Averion has to offer." I wink. "Hell, I would even tag along."

"My true calling," she says, lifting a brow teasingly.

I chuckle, relieved that my lame humorous attempt found its target.

Her face resumes its serious air seconds later.

"Things will go back to normal, right?"

"I've never lied to you. I can't predict the future, but I can promise that I'll do everything in my power to get you your life back. I swear it."

Her eyes light up as a corner of her mouth lifts briefly.

"I miss Ela. I miss my friend."

"She has a history of defying authority and being a pain in my ass, but I miss her too."

"That's Ela, all right. Never one to submit." Her crystal laugh fills the room and air catches in my throat. She laughs so rarely these days, leaving my heart strained as the demons of her past haunt her and I look for ways to bring a smile back to her lips. Though we never talk about it, we have all considered the unsaid. Elanor may never come back to us, and that threat alone has the power to crush a soul and stir painful memories. I'm sure Vesta's late mate, Elis, is among them. "I still don't understand what happened in Adria, or why she won't wake up. It's been months."

I step around the desk and stop a few feet from her.

"Me neither, but she is the reason Az is still roaming this earth. I do not know how, but she kept him alive until I could get to them with Mor." I close my eyes and pinch the bridge of my nose before continuing. "This world has taken a lot from her already."

"It sure has." She gives me a sad smile and takes a few steps towards the door.

Not ready for her to leave yet, I blurt out the first thing that comes to mind.

"I was about to send for some dinner. Do you want to stay and go over the latest reports on the army together? I'm sure there's a thing or two I could teach you." I wiggle my brows. "After all, you're in the presence of the General of the Fae armies of Lóna, as you so mentioned."

I can read the doubt in her eyes, but I stay still, waiting to see what she'll do.

"How generous of you, General. Offering your precious time to a common soldier."

A smile tugs on her lips and my shoulders relax. I motion towards a leather couch with an extravagant and dramatic bow.

CHAPTER 3

ELANOR

Crushed leaves under my boots mute the sound of my steps on wet soil as I progress through the forest, a bow in hand. I scan the grounds just like my father taught me, but find no sign of the deer I'm hunting. I must have missed a turn and lost its trail.

I stop as the cool wind brushes my face. I have no idea how long I've been out there, but my body is strangely relaxed, with not a single bead of sweat rolling down my back.

Branches rustle ahead of me and a massive black wolf emerges from a bush, its white eyes focused on me. The menacing beast advances on me, but I remain still. Fear has no grasp on me here.

The wolf stops with its muzzle inches from my waist and lowers its head against my thighs. My fingers instinctively go to its fur, finding it warm and soft, and my heart sings in response.

"Savage."

His head bops against my legs and both my arms wrap around his neck. A cord vibrates in my core, and it takes me a moment to recognize the wave of emotion blooming inside me.

"I missed you."

I take a deep breath in as I brush Savage's fur, soaking in all the memories trickling back in. From how we met in these woods, our walks in Averion's garden under his watchful gaze, to his last moments he spent shielding me from a blast. My guardian is with me again.

My heart sinks as the dam to my emotions cracks open, revealing a void where a thread of light connecting me to another being used to be. Once vibrant with energy, the sacred filament rests lifeless inside me, its sparkle dulled and its core blackened.

The chirp of birds and buzz of insects stir me from the past, leaving me with the comforting song of nature I've grown accustomed to over the years. The slow decay of time hardly affects the Dark Forest, leaving its grounds untouched, almost as if sacred.

My gaze falls on a bush of wild berries and a chill courses through my body. I can't remember the last time I felt hunger twisting in my stomach, though it's been a dear companion throughout the years I dwelled in these parts of the world. She's always walked with me everywhere I went, but not today.

My brows draw together at the anomaly. I can't place the last time I ate, and yet, I'm feeling perfectly rested and energized.

Another chirp sounds nearby and I scan the forest for its origin, coming up empty. I'm surrounded by mossy trees, full branches and weeds running wild, but no animal lingers near.

A bird responds with a tune, too fast for me to locate it, and I close my eyes.

Focusing on the melodies around me, I count the seconds until a chirp sounds again, followed by a note drowned in the windy hum of branches and buzz of smaller inhabitants of the forest.

One. Two. Three.

Breathing in the forest's scent, my body relaxes as my mind wanders.

Four. Five. Six.

My eyes snap open when I recognize the same melody for the third time.

Once-dulled leaves shine feverishly under the sunlight as branches bow with strange periodicity. The wind brushes my face again, unnaturally warm, and unease curls at the base of my spine.

My feet instinctively dart over knobby roots until I break into a run when the hair rises on my arms.

I storm towards the shack as Savage follows, needing to shake the feeling clawing at the back of my neck. It's probably nothing, I just need to go home.

As the thought crosses my mind, my vision blurs and a ripple echoes in the perfect image of nature around me, turning the trees into wraiths.

"Keep running," I whisper to myself. "Father will know what to do."

Angst stirs in my gut as I push myself further. I focus on putting my foot down, step after step, until the treacherous feeling retreats.

But little by little, doubt creeps back into my heart as blurred images overlay in front of my eyes.

Hints of gold and red armor glint under the sun before evaporating. Crimson irises stare back at me from the shadows before disappearing behind a tree trunk. Phantom-warriors track my steps with menacing gazes.

The shock of each step in my legs recedes to a distant murmur before disappearing completely. My eyes relay each stride I make, yet no impact registers up my nerves as I keep running, weightless.

I stop dead in my tracks, and sensations return to my body. The soles of my boots dig into wet soil, but my breathing remains regular and no ache lingers in the muscles of my thighs.

Savage stills by my side, resting his head against my hip as I glance around. The same trees greet me, the branches bending regularly, letting a soft light in.

My fingers curl in my palm when realization dawns on me. I should have reached our shack already.

My nails dig into the skin where my bow should be, and my blood freezes. My narrowed gaze rakes the landscape, finding no trace of the weapon. Maybe I dropped it during the run.

Dread sinks its claws in deeper as the assumption echoes hollowly in my mind, exposing the lie.

My brows draw closer together and a familiar presence looms in my back, confirming I'm no longer alone.

A hooded silhouette is standing a few feet away from me, their face hidden by dark cloth. But I don't need to step closer to identify its owner.

As I stare into the abyss replacing her face, I remember we've met before, in Adria. And with that thought, I know I'm not in the living world anymore.

A wave of energy hits me, shaking me to my core and undoing the illusion. I left Lóna long ago. My family's shack doesn't really exist here, my father is gone, and so is Savage.

Faces pop into my mind, familiar enough to shake my sense of calm, but not clear enough for me to place them. With only a vague grasp on reality, I realize I've wandered deep into the spirits' realm.

"Am I dead?" My voice breaks the astounding silence around us, each word reverberating in the trees.

"Part of you always has been and always will be," the dark figure says, still as stone. "But that's not what you want to know, dear." Her head tilts to the side. "You can still go back."

Each word lifts a veil over my mind, reminding me of who I truly am—Death's instrument.

My vision clouds and faded images take form in front of me. Scenes of people dancing in a castle meld with the forest background. Onyx and white flowers fill a familiar garden.

Warmth comes over me as I remember walking the streets of Averion and wandering in the palace halls. Beloved faces reform before my mind's eye—Vesta training in the garrison with the twins, Calen's grin widening as he watches, and...

Azran.

His face appears strikingly clear, his flaming-red gaze fixed on some point behind me, and a tidal wave hits me, crashing against a wall tightly built around my heart.

Pain flares in my chest under the assault, but the force recedes as quickly as it appeared, unable to tear down the barrier inside me.

"You would let me go back?" I blink, and the scene changes.

A marshy land, fighting soldiers wearing gold and red armor, their faces coated in blood and ashes, and a storm of fire. I step back, putting my hands up in a pointless attempt to shield myself as the images fade.

"The decision doesn't belong to me."

My gaze lands on Savage by my side and pain twists in my gut.

"What awaits me if I do?"

The words sound foreign on my lips, distant.

Death tilts her faceless head to the side again, and somehow I know her smile widens under the hood.

I blink again, willing the familiar faces and memories to come back, in vain, as I stand alone in the forest.

A storm forms inside me, but it's quickly weathered, and I'm left numb once more, wondering what Death meant, though she left me with one certainty.

A piece of me remains with her. Made from the same mold, I am hers as she is mine, and we are both fated to never feel whole until reunited.

Sitting on the hard ground, I absently caress Savage's warm fur. I'm at a crossroads, my past and future hidden from me.

I can't place it, but something is telling me to go and leave the spirit world. Half of me belongs here, but the other half is stuck in Lóna, anchored in the living world.

My chest tightens at the thought, and another question pops into my mind. Why leave? Why not stay here, where time is suspended and reality is what I make of it? Here I am safe, free of pain, away from the horrors I've had to endure all my life.

Numbness retreats and cedes ground to a sharp sting, polluting the peaceful state of my home. Something is missing, or someone. Azran's face appears in my mind like a confirmation, and even the sense of safety that lived in me here fades away. This doesn't feel like home anymore. Not without him.

I stand and pace the clearing, Savage watching me silently. With each step, the web of illusion retreats, and reality finds me. I remember everything. I remember everyone. I remember the life I left and could go back to.

But I also remember the pain, sacrifices, and suffering.

Why go back when I've already played my part? After all, I fulfilled the prophecy and defeated Braern. I could wait for them to join me here, where I don't have to endure life's ordeals, with Savage by my side.

Maybe I'll stay a little longer, while I consider my options. Maybe I could find my parents here. Maybe I could see them before going back.

⬥

I kick a dried branch out of my way with a huff, the brittle wood splintering satisfyingly under my boot, though it does little to blunt the sharp edge of my restlessness.

I've been pacing the forest every minute of every day, with Savage by my side, coming up empty. All too aware of the illusion around me, I remain powerless. Even if I wanted to, I couldn't leave this place. I'm lost, torn between the memories of those I left behind and the uncertainty of my future.

I don't know how long I've been in the spirit world nor how many times Death found her way to me, but I'm growing really fucking tired of her games.

I'm crossing a clearing when her presence looms behind me.

Looks like I'm due for another visit.

I slowly turn, a rigid smile plastered on my lips.

"You've been wandering here a while," the faceless shape says.

I inhale deeply to bite back a snarky comment. I genuinely don't know whether she hopes I'll stay or go. All I know for certain is I'm losing myself in this realm, any control over my fate gone as I remain here, unable to make a decision.

"What should I do?" I ask as Savage sits by my feet.

"You already know."

I'm tempted to roll my eyes. Each conversation turns more mysterious than the last, with Death unwilling to answer my questions aside from in riddles.

"I've wandered every inch of this place and haven't found a way out," I say, resting my arms on my hips. "I'm walking in circles."

"This realm is yours as much as it is mine. Your eyes wander this place, though you see so little."

"Thank you for the pep talk," I fire back, my words syrupy sweet as I glare at her.

"You're looking for an answer out there, when it lies within your grasp already."

I screw my eyes shut to fight the wave of irritation flooding my mind, and when I reopen them, Death is gone. Of course.

Savage's furry head brushes my leg, stirring me from the contemplation of Death's words. I stare into his white eyes, and like a mirror to my own soul, anger flares inside me.

Death is a cryptic motherfucker.

CHAPTER 4

NYLREN

It's past midnight when I pause at the bottom of the stairway, hidden in the shadows, waiting for the sign.

As always, my shaky hands betray my emotional state, no matter how much I will them to stay still. I've lurked in the darkness for as long as I can remember, trying to disappear in its embrace, but I haven't gotten used to the angst that comes with it.

I wish I could vanish in the shadows forever, or remove the cause of all my suffering, the master I serve and who's granted me nothing but disdain in compensation for the sacrifices I've made.

My heart pounds so loud in my ears it overpowers my senses and I'm ready to jump out of my skin any second as I wait. But the signal doesn't come.

Willing my legs to move, I step out of the shadows and head into the small corridor leading to the servants' quarters, my steps silent. I've made it my life's purpose to become invisible to those who dwell in this place.

I turn a corner and make for the door on the far end of the dim-lit corridor. The wooden panel sits ajar, revealing the small room plunged into darkness.

Hair rises on my arms as I freeze on the landing.

Zavan would never be this careless.

"You won't find him here."

My heart almost gives out at the sound of the deep voice I'd recognize anywhere. It's haunted me far too long.

Turning around, I face my father wearing his night robe and signature smile. Charming and inviting to the untrained eye, but malicious to the bone. The devil personified, the monster I have no choice but to obey, and the one being I can't escape. Yet.

I remain silent, unable to utter a simple word, for I know I won't be able to repress the tremble in my voice. And he hates that above all else.

"There will be no more meddling with servants."

I nod, hoping that will be the end of it.

"I've been too benevolent as a father. I allowed too much when you were an infant, and now look at you. A frail, scared Fae, not strong enough to fight on a battlefield or withstand a conversation."

I clench my jaw and swallow the tears down, a reflex earned by years spent in Father's presence. I haven't cried in decades, but the treacherous tears still come to my eyes every time his disapproval rings, another reflex of my traumatized body.

Gathering my spirits, I ask the question that's burning my lips. "What have you done with him?"

His vicious smile widens. "Me?" He takes a moment to look over his hands and inspect his palms. "Nothing."

I pinch my eyes shut as I imagine blood dripping from Zavan's ravaged face. He was no doubt tortured horribly, cut and whipped until all the nerves in his body lit on fire. I hope madness took him before his body gave out. I hear it can make it more bearable.

He was a good lover. Kind, patient, and funny too. He could be recognized anywhere, with stripes of purple, red, and blue decorating his raven-black hair.

I repress the gag stuck in my throat and remain still. I'd say my heart broke with Father's words, but it was obliterated a long time ago. I barely remember a time when I had one. I'm no more than an empty carcass kept alive for someone else's sick games, no matter how much Zavan tried telling me otherwise. This is just another blow to my body, already beaten to a pulp.

Father's hands might not be red-strained, but the blood of thousands marks them nonetheless. He simply doesn't enjoy doing the dirty work himself anymore. He reserves that for special occasions only, such as my birthday.

"I hate you." The words escape my lips before I can stop myself, and I hold my breath instinctively, waiting for the real beating to commence. This time, I can't help my reaction and screw my eyes closed, bracing myself for the hit.

Laughter fills the air—full, euphoric, gut-wrenching belly laughter.

Opening my eyes, I watch as the Fae responsible for my hateful existence ridicules me, his utter disdain a song in my ears, and a switch flips in my head.

A thought comes to me, the strikingly clear solution to all my problems, and a promise.

One day, I will kill you. One day, I will kill the Fae King of Zetrea.

For the first time, I let him laugh as I picture his headless corpse at my feet, and I'm tempted to laugh too. It's a wonder it took me so long to come to this realization, but I see clearly now. It will be either him or me. I can no longer survive alongside him. Father made sure of it. This is what it will come down to.

This realm will be better without his retched soul governing every living thing with terror, and I will succeed where he failed. I will achieve total control of the land and earn the respect of my subjects. I will find a way to break free.

⸻⸻◆⸻⸻

"Your Majesty."

A messenger bows in front of the throne, his pants and vest covered in dust from the ride across the plains west of Nyths.

Father moves his finger and the rider stands, although he keeps his gaze lowered in the presence of his ruler.

"Speak."

"A delegation from Lóna is on its way to Nyths, your Majesty."

Father straightens his back, wheels turning in his calculating mind.

"Azran, High Lord of the united Fae territories of Lóna, rides with them."

He waves off the messenger, but I remain behind him, waiting.

Father stands gracefully. "So, he has done it. High Lord of the Fae."

He turns towards me, waiting for my acknowledgment. "Boy."

I nod, clenching my jaw ever so slightly at the use of the nickname. I haven't been a boy in centuries. I *never* got to be one. He made sure of it.

"It will be done."

I remember meeting Azran in this very throne room. We were children at the time. We didn't talk much, but at a glance, I saw more than most would have, for I saw the same hatred in his eyes, the same anger towards our genitors.

We share a similar story. Both raised by monsters, robbed of our childhood. The only difference is, his tormentor is dead and he made it out. A rush of anger and jealousy courses through me.

I quietly sneak out of the room and head deeper into the royal halls.

There is something the King wants, and whatever Father wants, he gets. I've always been here to make sure of it.

But this time, Azran carries something I want, too.

The steps of my own plan begin to fall into place as I cross the corridors and make for the dark rooms below the palace.

CHAPTER 5

CALEN

Exhaustion weighs on my shoulders as I sit alone in the dimly lit office. Another long day of administrative tasks, logistics plans, recruitment directives, and supply manifests leaves me drained.

I miss the days Azran and I spent in the field, training men, sparring in the practice ring, or gathering intel.

I rub the ache in my temples, eyes burning from studying maps and reports.

What I wouldn't give for Az to be back, to be surrounded by the grunt of men lifting weights in the yard, or the roar of loud conversations in the refectory. For Ela to be awake, raising chaos and leading Vesta and the twins into a sea of troubles. What I wouldn't give for Az and Ela to be here with all of us. After his past tore them apart, gods know they deserve to find each other in peace.

Alone behind this desk, I only encounter my soldiers' names in neatly inked rosters or requests for provisions, and Vesta's cheerful laugh rarely reaches my ears.

With cold determination, I take up my quill once more and sign another document.

These weeks spent behind Azran's desk are turning me into a perfect bureaucrat and killing me slowly. Were it not for Vesta, I would have lost my mind long ago.

Bracing my elbows on the cluttered desk, head cradled in my hands, I picture Vesta' smile and her voice echoes through my memory, its musical tone backed by iron that matches her fierceness. From the moment I first saw her sparring hand-to-hand as a new recruit, she took my breath away, and she still does.

Things changed since Adria. After we survived the deadly blast, she didn't leave my side and she was there when I needed her the most, taking over the command of the army so I could reach Az and Ela. Even now, she gives me strength, reminding me of the importance of our goal—defeating the remnants of Braern's movement and fighting for peace.

She came back changed; we all did. Facing imminent death does that to a person, a ruthless reminder life can be cut short at any moment.

I try to tame the hope fueling my heart when I catch her staring at me or when her eyes can't hide the desire flooding her body, but something tells me not to give up on her, on us. I can't wish my feelings for her into inexistence and I refuse to even try. I know how amazing we could be together, if only she would see it too.

I straighten, backbone infused anew with iron, and resume my review of various missives.

⊰⊱

The familiar clash of metal raises the hair on my arms in anticipation. There's nothing quite like a sword fight to properly wake me. A thousand times more invigorating than an ice bath, especially when your adversary is a stunning redhead warrior with lethal technique. One wrong move and it's my ear Vesta will cut.

These sparring sessions are a much-needed distraction as weeks blend together and we wait for Azran's next report. I'm making little to no progress with Brimora, and these stolen moments with Vesta are the only highlights of my days.

Azran has always refused to send spies to Zetrea, but I've been toying with the idea for a few days. We could really use eyes and ears there. He's not here to spoil my fun, anyway.

Vesta's sword swings an inch from my face as I step back.

"Careful there, General. Desk work doesn't suit you." Her eyes shine with mischief as I parry and deal a blow at full speed. She counters quickly, twisting her blade free. A smile blooms on her face that I return, set on not letting her win this round. However joyful Vesta may be, she doesn't joke when it comes to training.

Cheers mix with shouts around us as soldiers watch our sparring, encouraging us both.

Her braid flies in the air with each of her moves as she bends and arches her body. My muscles protest when I launch towards her face, but I keep going. She avoids the blow at the last second with a snarl and fire in her eyes.

The soldiers around us observe our dance, but I pay them no heed. Sitting at a desk all day is clearly not the best training. It's going to take all my focus to keep my ears intact, and I love my ears as much as the next Fae.

Our blades lock together, bringing us an inch from each other, and my gaze darts to her mouth. Breaking free, Vesta steps aside before launching another attack that I parry.

I step back and reposition myself, readying for another bout, when Vesta's stare drifts behind me. Shock paints her features as her brows raise, and a grin forms on my face.

"Cheap trick, V. You can do better than that."

Relentless, I wield my sword in an arc aiming at her pretty neck.

My eyes widen when Vesta lowers her sword while mine nears her face.

Pulling my blow at the last second, an inch from her skin, I still.

"What's—" I begin a sentence I don't finish, seeing she's frozen in shock.

Panting, her chest raises rapidly, but her gaze is still fixed behind me.

"General."

I turn to identify the cause of this interruption as Vesta finally stirs from her trance and takes a step forward. A Fae wearing the healers' braid is standing in the entrance of the training center, a ribbon of white silk intertwined in their brown hair.

"It's the Unifier."

My heart stops, and color drains from Vesta's face. As I lower my blade, she steps closer, standing shoulder-to-shoulder with me, tension radiating from our bodies.

"She's awake."

Vesta and I lock eyes for a second before she breaks into a run, not leaving me a chance to say a word.

Following after her, Vesta's boots hit the paved courtyard loudly as I catch up.

We climb the stairs leading to the palace entrance three steps at a time, guards watching us wide-eyed.

"Make way," I command, and they crush themselves to the walls to let us go through.

My heart is beating out of my chest as Vesta accelerates on the last steps.

"Wait up."

She doesn't slow one bit.

"Damn it," I say as I race after her. To hell with appearances.

She pushes the massive double doors open and makes for the marble stairs leading to Ela's room.

CHAPTER 6

ELANOR

I knew what I wanted to do the moment I remembered Azran, though it took me ages to admit it, and even longer to decrypt Death's instructions.

I'd let the fear surrounding the uncertainty of my future trap me in the spirit world, and forgot that I always had control over Death's realm. It is mine too, after all.

My mind made up, I retreat inward, letting the illusion of the Dark Forest fade. Following the thread of power vibrating in my core, I focus on Averion and everyone I left behind. Repeating their names, visualizing the palace and the living world, I walk the path between life and death for what feels like eternity, until sensations return to my body.

My fingers twitch before gripping a cool, silky, smooth fabric—bed sheets.

Fluttering my eyes open, my vision blurs as I try to focus on the tall shape before me. The fog retreats and a grey-eyed Fae comes into view. His face marked by age, a strong jawline and sharp cheekbones give him an awfully serious air.

"Mor."

The name dies on my lips, my throat closing as I attempt to talk, and wrinkles line the corner of his eyes in what I interpret as a smile.

The haze in my mind dissipates as the healer presses two fingers to his lips and murmurs a silent prayer.

"Welcome back," he whispers softly.

My head snaps to other side of the room when the door swings on its hinges, and Mor's shoulder twitch when it crashes against the wall.

No glimpse required; I would recognize that tornado in an instant.

Vesta comes into view, her fiery hair in a braid, cheeks flushed and beads of sweat on her forehead.

"Thank the gods, you're awake." She jumps on me before I can utter a word, crushing me with her armored body, but I return her embrace instantly.

Calen stands next to Mor, panting but smiling proudly.

"Welcome back, Ela."

"You scared the shit out of me, L," Vesta adds, letting go of me to scan my features as I sit up.

Everything is as I left it, undisturbed. The same sheer terracotta curtains decorate the wide glass panels on the walls, and embers burn in the fireplace. Taking a deep breath, I let the smell of fresh linen and smoking logs fill my lungs. I'm home. I made it back to Averion.

I motion towards the bedside table for water, and Vesta jumps on the task before I'm done gesturing. She fills the glass so fast it overflows, giving me an apologetic smile. I would have laughed if my throat wasn't on fire, and settle for a dry chuckle.

Once I've quenched my thirst, I give her a small smile.

"Thank you. It's good to see you all."

Other than my throat, my body feels surprisingly rested. I guess it was only my mind that wandered in Death's territories.

I crane my neck past Mor and Cal, scanning the room through the narrow gap between their shoulders, but it's just the four of us.

"Where is he?"

An excruciating quiet blankets the room as the group exchanges stalled glances. When Calen's brows draw together, my throat closes up and doom settles.

"Where is Az?" I over-articulate each knife-edged word, warning coating my tongue.

I'm ready to stand and go search for him myself by the time Calen finally answers.

"In Zetrea. He had to leave."

My chest hollows as the words ring in the air, trying to permeate the resistance in my mind and the last dredges of hope in my heart.

"No." The choked syllable tumbles out unrestrained. "He should be here."

I shove the covers aside, refusing to remain in this cursed bed any longer. Azran is going to walk through the door any second.

Vesta moves to stop me, the look of pity on her face twisting the knife deeper. Recoiling from her gesture, I scramble back on the mattress, bringing my knees to my heaving chest to shield myself from the heartbreak.

My arms tighten around my legs as I scan the bond inside me, only to find it strained, lit ablaze by Azran's absence. My throat closes up as I attempt to swallow and endure the waves of pain coursing my nerve endings.

Relief wars with renewed longing as reality hits me. He survived Adria and left me. Pieces of my heart detach, turning to dust as the organ is pulled out of my chest inch by inch. I can't see him, touch him, feel his warmth. His memory lingers though he remains out of reach, and every fiber of my being calls to him. There is only absence, stark and life-draining as collapsing stars—annihilating light and warmth, leaving me void.

"He's been gone for weeks, Ela. He tried waiting for you, but we couldn't wake you up." Vesta approaches slowly, taking my hand in hers.

"Weeks?" I ask, swallowing the lump in my throat. "How long have I been here?"

"Adria was over two months ago."

The floral-scented soap Rina is using to bathe me smells heavenly, but the warm water does little to soothe me.

Mor left shortly after Calen and Vesta came to my room and caught me up on everything that's happened since Adria. Braern is dead but his war lives on, and his allies need to be stopped.

I'm trying to wrap my head around it all as Rina runs the wet sponge down my back.

My Fae body healed perfectly, leaving my muscles without soreness and rested, but the lack of training and proper nourishment has weakened me. Nothing that can't be fixed with Rina's cooking and hours in the training center. It's my mind that's the problem.

For me, Adria was days ago, and I remember it all.

I remember the heat wave from when the blast hit me and Savage jumping to protect me, the screams of the dying soldiers, the mushy grounds soaked in blood and ashes beneath my boots, and Braern's empty gaze as his head fell from his shoulders.

I remember the searing pain when Azran's lifeless body laid in my arms, my heart disintegrating before my eyes so shortly after overflowing with love, and the pure madness that came with it, along with Death. The hurt consumed me, overwhelming my soul, pulling me under and devouring every cell in my body. An invisible pit appeared in my chest as our connection imploded, ripping through my body and swallowing me whole.

I remember my bargain with Death, and the spirit realm.

A shiver goes through me as Rina rubs my skin with soap.

"Is the water temperature all right? I could have someone—"

I lift my hand up to stop Rina. "It's fine." I give her a small smile, but she pinches her lips in return, seeing right through me. "I'll finish on my own, Rina. Thank you."

The old Fae lifts an eyebrow but doesn't object. She's always known when to push or let me be.

Once the door of my bedroom closes, my shoulders sag in the bathtub. When they all came in, I saw relief in their gazes but none of the grief my heart harbors, so I put up a brave front. To them, I've been peacefully asleep for weeks, resting my body, preparing to come back. In reality I've been wandering the land of the dead, haunted by illusions mixing with memories, and I left it with no more answers than I arrived with. I'm back in my body, though a foreign feeling lingers. Part of me remains in that realm. And now Az is gone, hunting down Braern's allies and trying to extinguish the flames of war.

I wish I could hide in this room until he comes back, until it feels safe to get out and face the world after what Braern did. My choked laugh fills the air as I stand in the bathtub and grab the plush robe Rina left for me.

Wrapping myself in it, I make for the mirror console. I don't know how I'm going to fool anyone looking like this. I tuck a piece of hair behind my pointy ears and stare back at my reflection. I force a smile to my face, but it doesn't reach my bloodshot eyes.

I turn around and freeze in the bedroom's archway, my gaze surveying the room and landing on the empty spot by the fireplace where Savage used to lay at night. My heart sinks and tears pool in my eyes as I relive it all. This time I don't resist, letting the salted drops roll down my cheeks. He's waiting for me in the spirit world, alone.

I'm sucked into the spiral of death and dark memories and left to debate what hurts most. The soldiers' hateful gaze permanently engraved in my mind when I walked our army camp after the blast had decimated our ranks, the dismembered and burned corpses laying on the battlefield, Azran's lifeless body, or his absence now.

Wiping the tears wetting my cheeks, I dig into the chest at the foot of my bed for clothes.

A pit in my stomach opens as I feel the bond once again, pulsing weakly, each wave more painful than the last, and my anger is born again. I can't hide from the bond anymore, not when I've tasted it, tasted him.

How could he leave me and rob us of our first opportunity to see each other? To Zetrea, of all places. He's so far away he had to cross an ocean to get there, a place I know nothing about.

Another jolt of pain shakes the bond and, just as quickly as it arose, my anger falls. Whatever ache I feel, I know Azran feels it too, and in a fucked-up way, our shared pain comforts me. It is as close to feeling the warmth of his embrace and the safety of his arms wrapped around me as I'll get for now.

"You're going to be all right," I whisper to myself.

Azran is out there, alive, and I know in my soul that he will come back for me. If the past year taught me anything, it's that he always keeps his promises. When Cal sends word, Az will make his way back to Averion. He will raise hell on earth to get back to me, just like he always has.

I repeat the words like a protective chant until they banish the fears shaking my heart.

I've finished dressing when a knock sounds and Vesta's head pops through the opening door.

"There's someone who wants to see you, L."

My heart stops as my brain betrays me, taunting me with the foolish hope that my mate is on the other side of the door. The bond flares again, destroying the illusion as Varan walks in.

My heart sinks and I avert my eyes, unable to find the right words or meet his gaze after our last exchange in Adria. I only remember the venom in Varan's words as his twin laid dying on a cot in the infirmary.

"What's with the silence? Waiting for me to make my grand entrance?" My eyes snap up as Wyn's cheerful voice fills the room.

He takes several steps forward and twirls around, his arms extended to better parade around. Without thinking, I crash into him and pull him in a hug. I tighten my hold around his chest, no doubt crushing a few ribs in the process, and he returns my embrace before clearing his throat.

"It's good to see you too, Ela."

"Stop playing favorites," Vesta says, wiggling her brows at Varan. "I know I didn't get the same hug."

With a small laugh, I let go of Wyn, and my hand goes to the left side of his face, scarred all over. The rosy lines run high on his temples and into his scalp, leaving his blond hair shaved down the middle and still running wild on the other side.

Finally, I meet his gaze. His left pupil is white and veiled, and his glacial blue eye is watching me patiently.

"I'm so sorry, Wyn. I wish I could have done more in Adria."

"Oh, this?" he asks, turning his head to better show me the extent of the damage. "The ladies and gents love the war hero look. And it was about time I give Varan a chance to be the more handsome twin," he adds before shooting his brother a wink.

"Keep telling yourself that." His tattooed brother crosses his arms over his chest, but a smile tugs his lips. Our gaze locks for a second before he looks away.

"You guys haven't changed one bit," I say, resting my hands on my hips.

"If you want my opinion, they've gotten worse." Vesta rolls her eyes. "I've been stuck babysitting for way too long, L."

"Oh, I'm not signing up for that," I say in a huff.

"You two realize we're standing right here, in the same room?"

The twins exchange incredulous looks and Vesta bursts into laughter.

43

CHAPTER 7

AZRAN

Bursting through the door panels with a ferocious roar, I stumble, nearly losing my footing with my bloodied sword in hand.

Barely recovered, I break into a run, though the muscles in my legs protest. With one arm wrapped around my waist to stanch my open wound, I compel one foot in front of the other. Warm liquid pulses under my palm, dripping through my fingers, drenching my shirt and dyeing it crimson.

Echoes of the fight I narrowly escaped fill the halls as my vision blurs from the pain exploding in my head with each step. Growled commands, clashing blades, distorted squelches of weapons finding their marks, and cries of pain reach my ears.

Turning a corner, I bump into a table edge, vaguely aware of something crashing down to the floors. I barely register the scattered debris, my body fueled by adrenaline as I propel myself forward. The flesh around my stab wound burns hot as fire, but I don't dare look or slow down until I reach the end of the hallway.

With a pained groan, I shove yet another door open, the momentum sending me stumbling several steps. Blinding pain flares in my shoulder but I push on.

Muffled clashes of steel fade to a muted clamor as I round the sharp angle of a wall and struggle to determine which way is out. Sweat mixed with blood clouds my vision, burning my eyes as I blink furiously.

Adrift in identical corridors bleeding into one another, I lose all grasp of time or direction as growing frustration floods my veins. My eyes dart around, assessing every option while blistering rage burns in my chest. I stagger on.

My strength is leaving me, slowly draining from my body as I push myself further than I've ever needed to before.

My power is pulsing in my core, though it remains beyond my reach. Each attempt I make to unleash its raw energy yields another burst of pain in my head.

My heart sinks the moment I give up trying, and the ragged breaths I take turn to groans. I try to suck down air to ease the fire burning in my lungs, but only the sharp taste of copper coats my tongue.

Shouts tear through the silence and a pit opens in my stomach, for that can only mean one thing—my soldiers are dead.

They sacrificed their lives to give their High Lord a chance to escape, and I left them behind. Betrayal twists in my gut as my body slows.

Numbness spreads down my thighs, the muscles seizing and rendering them useless. My legs turn traitorous, refusing my mind's commands to keep going as they harden like stone, leaving me at the end of the hallway with no escape in sight.

"Damn you," I bitterly curse whichever God may be listening.

Pressing my shoulder against the door on the left, I find it unyielding, barred from within. I unleash a string of curses under my breath as I'm forced to backtrack the way I came.

With the stomping of boots sounding ominously through the halls, I invoke the last of my strength to keep going, repeating the same words over and over in my head.

I shall rest when I'm dead.

I shall rest when my enemies lay dead at my feet.

I shall rest when Ela is in my arms.

Renewed hope ignites in my soul when my gaze lands on a staircase. Pressing my palm against my waist, I redouble the pressure on the throbbing gash, trying desperately to stanch the steady flow of burgundy seeping between my fingers as I near the landing.

"There," calls a strident voice on my trail, punctuated by quickening steps that break into a run.

I glimpse a horde of attackers swarming the corridor to trap me. My knees wobble dangerously as I lurch onto the stairs. I thrust my arm out to brace against the stone wall, grappling for balance.

"Come on," I grit out between clenched teeth, steeling my nerve and mustering my resolve.

Blood pours from my wound once more, soaking my shirt and the back of my thighs.

"Keep going," I rumble under my breath, the words a battle cry to myself, stoking the embers of my heart.

Squaring my shoulders, I repeat my mantra, using it to fan the flames of my purpose.

I shall rest when I'm dead.

I shall rest when my enemies lay dead at my feet.

I shall rest when Ela is in my arms.

"Stop him!"

A voice rings out on my heels as I stumble frantically down the stairs.

CHAPTER 8

Elanor

I spend the next few days in my room, fueling my body, stretching, and regaining my strength after weeks in bed. I don't have it in me to go to the training center yet. I'm not ready to face the soldiers in the garrison, though Vesta visits me several times.

Nahtar waits patiently for me, set against a wall in the room, its blade shining under the sunlight, and so does my power. I haven't sought it out either. I've spent enough time lost in the realm it comes from, and I'm not eager to taste it again.

I'm still adjusting to the living world, the aftermath of the war, and the secret that is mine to keep—the reason I came back, the reason I find the resolve to get up in the morning and hold my grief at bay.

Although tempted to, I couldn't stay with Death. I don't understand how yet, but as much as I am my mother's daughter, I am hers, and there's still much for me to accomplish here. I thought my destiny was fulfilled with the prophecy and Braern's defeat, but I was wrong, and Azran's mission confirms it.

On the third day, my mate's absence becomes too unbearable as I stare at the same walls for hours with the bond's stabbing ache throbbing in my chest.

Venturing into the corridor, my steps take me to the room adjacent to mine. My hand is on the handle, ready to open it, when I freeze.

As much as I need to feel closer to him, I can't go into his bedroom alone. Too many memories await me. Memories I'm not ready to explore.

I retreat and make for the stairs at the end of the white marble corridor. Climbing several floors, my legs burn with the effort, but I only stop in front of Azran's office. I take a deep breath before entering the room.

I'm immediately assaulted by Azran's smell of pine and citrus, although it's fading.

Embers burn in the fireplace behind his wooden desk. I slowly approach the piece of furniture, walking around the leather couches, until my fingers caress the dark wood. The hair rises on my arm as my mind takes me to a different time. Our bodies devouring each other, a tingle of hate separating us.

Someone clears their throat behind me and I turn, startled. Cal is standing in the doorway.

"I've been taking care of things in his absence."

I nod and step back from the desk. "Of course."

"How are you feeling?"

"Fine."

Cal tilts his head.

"Restless," I add.

"I wish there was more we could do for Az, but right now, we have to wait."

"When did you hear from him last?"

I scan his features and my blood freezes as I detect a hint of worry in his eyes.

"Cal, spare me the reassuring bullshit you give everyone else and tell me the truth."

He lets out a heavy sigh before answering.

"I don't know anything for sure. Last I heard, he got to the capital and intended to pay a visit to the King."

"The King?"

"The Fae King, Airdan." My brows draw together as I wait for him to continue. "Fae are not native to Lóna, as you know. Our motherland is in Zetrea, where the King lives and rules over Fae and humans."

"Why haven't I heard about him before?"

"Relations with Nyths ceased centuries ago, when wars broke out between the Fae factions."

"Why would Azran meet with the King? What does that have to do with luring Braern's allies out?"

"As the ruler of Lóna, his visit to King Airdan is a diplomatic necessity, especially after Braern's defeat and the unification of our people."

"You said Az arrived in Nyths. When was that?"

Cal heads behind the desk and proceeds to tidy up a stack of scattered documents.

"Cal," I let out through gritted teeth, my body rigid with tension.

Seconds stretch before he responds.

"Three weeks ago."

His words crack open the floodgates and I implode, red misting the edges of my vision.

"Three fucking weeks and not a single word since?"

Calen pinches his eyes shut as he weathers my attack.

"I'm going to Zetrea," I blurt out.

"Absolutely not." Calen slams his hands on the desk. "Are you out of your mind?"

"Watch me." I step forward, ready to show him how serious I am. "The real question is, why aren't you already on your way?"

"He ordered me to stay behind and deal with the aftermath of the war. He trusts me to do what's right, and that's exactly what I'm doing."

"And what's right for him? Who knows where he is, and in what state?" I bare my teeth at him, unable to refrain from lashing out. "Why aren't you more eager to protect your High Lord?"

"You have no right questioning my loyalty," Calen thunders, and I pause. "I know who he is to you, Ela. I'm just as worried as you are, but you're not in fighting shape." My mouth opens to argue, but he doesn't give me the chance. "Tell me I'm wrong."

Challenge lingers in his irises, crushing my anger.

I can't. He knows I can't. I haven't touched my blade in months. Defeat stings in the corner of my eyes as my courage wavers.

"He would never forgive me, and neither would I, if something happened to you. Sending you to a place you've never been, out of shape, and barely recovered after escaping death is madness. You have to see it, Ela."

My head drops and I stare at the floor until the tears retreat.

"I was there, Ela. I was the one who got to you and Az on the battlefield. Both of you were hanging onto life by a thread. I'm not playing with fate this time."

I swallow hard as I nod. "Fine."

Calen is right, I'm not ready.

His eyebrows raise slightly, but I give him a small smile instead.

His gaze narrows, revealing he's not entirely buying the act, but I turn around and head out of the office, a plan already forming in my head.

Look at me, learning the time and place for verbal sparring.

"Ela." The General is calling his soldier, but I'm already in the corridor. "Get back here."

His voice rings in the palace halls and a wide smile blooms on my face.

It feels good to be back.

***

When I make it back to my room, I'm ready to answer Nahtar's call. I'm going to regain my strength, and this blade is all I need.

My power reacts instantly when my fingers brush the hilt of the sword. The energy pulses in my core, numbing all emotions, asking me to join the darkness, become one with it, and step into a world I've barely touched before.

My vision clouds and a black veil takes over the room, pulling me to the center of the storm. My body is weightless as I drift towards the dark energy, irrevocably drawn to it, drunk on its power.

My hands lift as heat courses through my fingers and up my arms. I'm losing control, getting closer to the edge, as the energy builds in my palms.

Panic sears through the numbness when my lack of control registers, and I'm transported back to Adria, seconds before the blast decimating our army, alarm prickling at the back of my neck.

A familiar biting pain reverberates down the bond, sharper than I've felt before, and my vision clears as the sting pulls me back from the dark spiral.

Stumbling back, I lower my hands, my chest heaving from the depth of my discovery. An ocean of darkness awaits inside of me, my power transformed, its limits unexplored.

A pit opens in my stomach as I contemplate the immensity of the task that lies ahead of me. I merely toyed with the dark energy in Adria, and I am now stepping into the unknown. Tapping into my power blindly is no longer an option, not with so many people around me.

But I won't let it scare me. Death walks with me and we have a mission to accomplish. If I am to fulfill my purpose, I have no choice but to be ready for what's coming.

"Come on, L," I whisper to myself. "You can do this."

Grabbing hold of Nahtar, its familiar weight in hand, I release just enough power to block off the waves of emotions raging inside my heart and find inner calm.

It's become so natural I don't even think about it, and I begin a series of strikes in the empty space before my bed.

The bond still flares through the numbness, its sting a sharp reminder of Azran's absence as I wield Nahtar. Although thrown off balance at first, I'm getting used to the comforting pain.

I'm coming back to the world of the living. There is purpose and anger in my heart again, fueling me, pushing me to keep going even when my arms tire. The old Ela died in Adria, and the daughter of darkness and Death is reborn.

After hours of dancing with Death, my legs are shaky, so Rina finds me sitting on the floor, panting.

She's carrying a platter full of food, and I couldn't be more grateful.

After eating my fill, I turn to Rina, who is tidying up the room.

"Do you know where I can find Mor?"

The old Fae doesn't stop what she's doing to answer.

"His office is on the same floor as our High Lord's. Two doors down."

CHAPTER 9

Elanor

My knock resounds in the empty corridor as I wait for Mor to open his door.

A muffled voice comes from the other side and I decide to take it as an invitation. I turn the knob and step inside Mor's office.

Parchment and books cover the floor, and every piece of furniture seems to be crumbling under a mass of random objects and scrolls.

I freeze in the doorway, my mouth open as I contemplate the chaos. Wooden shelves filled with more books and trinkets occupy an entire wall, and tables are arranged randomly in the rest of the well-lit room.

The healer clears his throat and I close my mouth shut, repressing a laugh. Mor is standing behind a table, his hands around a book that looks as old as him.

"Can I help you, Elanor?"

I step forward, but my boot hits a small chest lying on the floor, and I give him an awkward smile.

"Sorry," I blurt out. His eyebrow raises in question, and I can't help my next words. "I never pictured your office like this."

This time I can't hold back the wide smile that blooms on my lips.

The corners of Mor's mouth lift briefly. "Everyone has their secrets." Clearing his throat once more, he continues. "I have my own system around here."

I nod, although tempted to argue that no one could reasonably find anything around here.

"Right. I wanted to ask some questions."

Mor gestures towards a stool covered in papers. I make my way there and clear it of its contents, although not without knocking a few things off the tables.

"You knew," I say, once seated. The healer remains silent, forever his enigmatic self. "Before Adria, you told me that we're not all powerless in the face of Death." He nods. "You knew what I am, what I can do."

"I only suspected."

"How? The prophecy?"

"Although you don't remember, we met before, when your parents brought you to me."

My heart stops at the mention of my parents. "What?"

Mor presses two fingers to his lips, and everything falls into place. I've seen this gesture before.

"Ilyana did that too, when I first met her. What does it mean?"

Mor gives me a small smile before answering.

"We're both very old Fae who believe in ancient gods, including Death. She asked me to protect you."

My eyes widen as the missing pieces of my life's puzzle fall into place.

"You cast the spell to hide my Fae heritage when my parents fled?"

Mor nods and air catches in my throat.

"I didn't know for sure until Adria, until you left this realm. That's what happened, right?"

I answer with a nod as I swallow down tears.

"Tell me." Mor's serious tone rings in my ears.

"Death was there. I got stuck in her realm, neither dead nor alive, drifting away." Tears start rolling down my cheeks, but I brush them off with the back of my hand. "I'm lost, Mor."

"You always will be, child. You don't belong entirely in this world, and you never will."

A choked laugh escapes me. "You know how to reassure a girl."

"You may not belong here, but you have a role to play nonetheless. Something evil and powerful stirs in the east. Something Braern was a part of."

"Mor, I'm scared. This power I have, it's dark."

"You should be. Death is powerful beyond measure, and only a fool wouldn't fear her."

The healer steps forward, navigating the chaos on the floor effortlessly, and reaches for my hand.

"The Fae used to believe in all sorts of divinity, and it was said that gods would bear children in the living world in times of need, to help bring balance between evil and good, dark and light."

His words ring truer than any explanations I've come up with, a confirmation of what I long suspected.

"You were sent here with a purpose, daughter of darkness— to wield shadows and flames and restore balance to the world." He presses my hand gently. "You are so much more than the Unifier. Only the gods know what you can really do."

"What if I can't do this alone?"

Mor's eyes light with mischief.

"Who says you're alone?" Pain sears through the bond, and my mate's face appears in my mind. "There's a reason Azran carries a power."

"What do you mean?"

"You both walk this world with the power of beings as old as time."

Part of me still wants to deny it, but I know he speaks true. I felt it back in Adria, then in Death's realm. I always knew we were different, made from the same mold.

"What now, Mor?"

"I think you already know." His eyebrows raise, giving the impression he sees right through me. "Prepare."

I release a heavy sigh, feeling strangely lighter now that this secret is not only my own.

"Thank you," I say as he nods. "For everything."

I stand up, careful not to disrupt Mor's organized mess, and make for the door.

"Never doubt the gods, Ela."

"Well, the gods could have been a little less cryptic," I mumble to myself on the way out. Mor's laughter follows me.

⋯⦿⋯

I stare into the distance, slowly sinking into a leather armchair by the giant windows of the library overlooking Averion. The sun is setting, casting the white buildings in pink tones.

With my muscles sore from days spent training tirelessly and getting back in shape, I'm ready to doze off, an open book on my lap.

I don't remember closing my eyes, but I almost jump out of the chair when the library door creaks open.

Vesta strolls in, her red hair flowing behind her and a wide smile on her face.

"You scared the shit out of me."

"Nice to see you, too." She looks over my shoulders. "Why are you reading about princes of hell and old gods?"

I close the old tome and sit up.

"Just bored and wanted an excuse to doze off," I say casually.

Vesta's crystal laugh fills the air.

"I've got just the thing to stir you from boredom."

I raise an eyebrow, waiting for her to tell me more.

"Let's go. You're coming with me." She snaps her fingers towards the door as I reluctantly leave the warm cocoon of the leather armchair.

"Where are you taking me?" I narrow my eyes at her.

"Tonight, we're celebrating the Unifier and our victory over Braern."

She grabs my hand before I can stop her.

"V. I'm not in the mood for that."

"Nonsense. If we wait for you to be in the mood, we'll never go." I roll my eyes at her words, but she's already pulling me in her wake. "Now, let's get you changed."

CHAPTER 10

ELANOR

Fiddle music and chatter fill the busy tavern as waiters navigate the crowd, unbothered by the warm, stuffy air. A white-haired Fae expertly balances platters filled with drinks of all sorts, and as he nears I recognize Ayas' handsome face.

A blush rises to my cheeks as I remember our last conversation and his advances.

He flashes his brightest smile in my direction, seconds before a drunk patron almost bumps into him and he disappears behind the bar.

Ayas' familiar face does little to calm my nerves, but I follow Vesta to an empty table anyway. She plops down on a chair and orders a round of drinks with a wave.

I scan the crowd around us until Ayas appears with a pitcher and several glasses.

"Here you go. Let me know if you need anything else." His stormy blue eyes scan my face as he cocks a brow teasingly. "Great to see you, Ela."

"Don't get your hopes up, she's taken," Vesta interjects with a wink.

I smile awkwardly, grabbing a glass. "Thanks, Ayas."

The second he's gone, I squint at Vesta, who laughs off my stare and pours us two drinks.

"Cheers, L. To you."

"To us," I answer before clinking my glass with hers.

I press the chilled glass to my lips, allowing the crisp liquid to spill over my tongue, though Vesta merely rocks the tumbler in her palm, watching the amber liquid twirl. Her eyes dart around the room, searching the patrons.

"Looking for someone?" I ask as I put my cup down.

Vesta's gazes narrows with an unspoken threat, but the hint of a smile a moment later renders her stare harmless.

"No."

"Hm. Looks like I missed more than the twins' usual devilries."

Blowing air out of her nose in response, she shrugs off my comment.

"You didn't miss much, it's just... I don't know."

"Yeah?"

"Adria made me... question certain choices I've made."

"Any of these choices have to do with a tall and handsome General?"

She brings her glass to her mouth to hide the grin forming on her lips, just in time for the twins to barge into the bar and crash on the chairs next to us.

I raise an eyebrow at Vesta, but she shakes her head softly and I let it go. She's on her own path with Calen. Hopefully, her fears don't get the best of her.

"What are you drinking, ladies?" Wyn asks, extending a hand towards the pitcher on the table and almost knocking it over.

"Slow down, soldier," Varan swoops in. "You're on a roll tonight."

"Were you bar hopping?" Vesta narrows her eyes at the pair. "Without me?"

Her mouth drops open as her hand flies to her chest dramatically.

I crack a smile and shake off the last bit of tension in my shoulders as the twins burst out laughing.

"Looks like it's a party tonight. And no one invited me?" A wide-shouldered Fae joins the group, one of his hands resting on the back of Vesta's chair.

"Rick," Vesta says in greeting. "Join us. The more the merrier."

The brown-haired Fae grabs a stool and plops himself between us, shining his brightest smile at the redheaded Captain of the High Guard. I only met him briefly before, but looks like he's as obsessed with Vesta as ever. A smile tugs my lips as I observe him flaunting his best attributes.

After another round of drinks, Vesta is fully leaning into Rick's arm, which is still positioned on her chair, laughing at his comments, and I'm not having the worst time either. Until Wyn stands, his drink in hand.

He winks at me, an air of mischief on his face.

"Wyn," I warn, knowing damn well he can't be stopped.

He clears his throat.

"Hear, hear."

Dread fills me as I attempt to tug his sleeve from across the table.

"Sit your ass down," I whisper-shout, but I'm too late.

"Fellow citizens of Averion, join me as I raise my glass to the Unifier, savior of Adria and slayer of Braern."

Warmth floods my face when the words reach my ears, and I tilt my head down, wishing I could disappear and magically travel back to my room.

The scenes in Adria flood my mind, and it's like I'm there again, surrounded by wounded soldiers, rage and shock filling their eyes, their hate and disappointment radiating from their bloodied bodies. Everywhere I turn, I'm met with distrust and shame, and each step adds more weight on my shoulders, more grief.

I pinch my eyes closed, readying myself for the wave of hate, the insults and drinks thrown at me.

The floor trembles as dozens of cheers resound around us and patrons shout in celebration.

My mouth drops open at the Fae surrounding us, smiling proudly and raising their cups. Admiration has replaced the fear and blame I last saw in their eyes.

My gaze widens as Wyn gestures for the crowd to cheer louder with a wide grin stuck on his face. Heat rushes to my cheeks as I try to make myself smaller on my chair, waiting for them to move on to something more interesting.

I nod a few times in the hope it will tame their enthusiasm, but fail miserably. The group takes it as encouragement and their shouts grow louder, sending a rush of warmth up my ears.

Vesta looks at me with pride filling her eyes. I attempt a smile, but it doesn't ring true. Not with Azran away, unable to see this. He was the only one who never looked at me the way they all did, like a monster, like the Fae responsible for the massacre in Adria. If he were here, he would understand that this kind of hurt simply cannot be erased.

It's been a month since anyone has heard from him and I'm slowly losing my mind. Cooped up here with nothing to do but toy with crazy scenarios, I'm a prey to the entire range of emotions known to the Fae. My head is fighting my heart, and I will lose either way.

As each hour passes, the suffering intensifies, and I'm left battling against this roaring feeling churning in my soul. Something is wrong, I can feel it. Everything is telling me to go to him.

My mood soured, I use the distraction of another round of drinks to sneak past Vesta's gaze and make for the door.

I'm almost out of the smelly tavern when someone pulls me by the forearm.

"Ela."

Varan lets go when I pull my arm back. He glances around, the tattooed vine on his neck twisting with his movements.

"I wanted to apologize for what I said to you in Adria." Finally meeting my gaze, he stills completely. "I'm sorry I held you responsible for something you couldn't have stopped. No one could have."

I release a heavy sigh as his words ease the burden I've carried since Adria.

"I would have done the same thing, Varan."

If Wyn hadn't made it, I would never have forgiven myself, so why should he?

"No. Seeing Wyn like that, I... I needed someone to blame. It was misplaced and unfair."

I reach for his hands, pressing them tightly.

"All is forgiven. I'm just glad you're both alright."

"Thank you, Ela." He gives me a small smile. "You've done so much for our people. I won't forget it again."

Retracing my steps, I walk beneath the arch marking the palace's entrance, but I don't head back to my room just yet. Laying in bed alone to stare at the ceiling for hours will do nothing to settle my nerves. Instead, my steps guide me to the balcony beyond the throne room.

I step into the night and stare at the city sleeping down below. Lanterns light the main arteries of Averion as the last inhabitants make their way back to their homes, blissfully unaware of the storm raging inside me.

My hands rest on the cold metal railing made of the four elements of the Fae, symbolizing Azran's dream. Water, Moon, Wood, and Sun united under one banner. A realm where all Fae live in harmony with humans. A stabbing pain goes through the bond, carrying the alarming feeling I've been trying to fight off all day.

For the first time today, I give into the fear.

My heart is beating out of my chest as I imagine the worst. Azran on the brink of death, and me, too far to bring him back this time. I grip the railing harder, until my knuckles whiten, but the cold bite of the metal doesn't help. Instead, my power awakens, calling me, inviting me to numb the fear, the angst, and the dread.

I would answer its call were it not for the steps echoing behind me.

"You're up late, General," I say, swallowing the lump in my throat.

"So are you." Cal stops in front of the railing on my left.

"Vesta and I went to a tavern for a few drinks." A sad smile tugs my lips. "The twins and Rick showed up. That Fae was all over Vesta, it was hilarious."

My attempt to lighten the mood fails completely. Cal clenches his jaw and remains silent, and the pit in my stomach opens once more.

"It was just an illusion, though, because nothing is right, and nothing feels normal. Not without Azran."

"I already told you, Ela. You can't go." He turns towards me, and even the darkness of the night can't hide the worry on his face. "We have to trust him."

I pinch the bridge of my nose.

"The prophecy has been fulfilled, Cal. Braern is gone, I've played my part."

"It's too dangerous."

My mouth opens and closes. I can't tell him. I can't tell him he's not talking to the Fae who believed she was human for twenty-two years, but to a child of Death, nor that the Fae he's known for centuries, his best friend and chosen brother, is much more than a Fae.

"He's my mate. I can't stay here and do nothing." The bond flares as the words leave my mouth, and I put my hand on my chest instinctively. "It's killing me, not knowing where he is."

"You're not ready."

"Try me." My resolve strengthened, I step aside and call upon my shadows, letting him witness but a fraction of what I can do. "Fight me and find out."

The hint of a smile tugs his lips, but he doesn't react so I change strategy.

"What would you do if it was Vesta over there? Alone?" Arching my brows, I continue. "What if you could feel the constant ache from the distance between you pulsing in your chest night and day?"

His features twist in a mask of pain as he sighs, but I don't relent.

"What if your mate—"

"Fine," he lets out. I bite my bottom lip to repress the victorious scream threatening to tear from my throat. "Get ready."

"Thank you," I breathe out, relief flooding my veins.

"I'll have an official letter introducing you as an emissary of Lóna ready by morning."

I nod, barely containing my excitement at the prospect of going after Azran.

"It will offer you passage and hopefully a safe place to look for Az," Cal adds.

I press my palms together, interlacing my fingers and squeezing tight.

"Thank you, Cal. I'll be safe, I promise."

He rolls his eyes at me, clearly not convinced. "You better be."

Turning on my heels, I'm already thinking about my preparations when Calen's voice rings through the cold night air.

"And, Ela?"

"Yes?"

"You're not going alone."

CHAPTER 11

CALEN

After sending Ela to Zetrea a couple of weeks ago, the anxiety coursing my veins has only gotten worse, and I'm in dire need of a break, or a way to drown my fears.

By the time I finish my third pint of ale, I'm inebriated enough to relegate the anxious thoughts that are my usual companions to the back of my mind. Naar is clinking glasses with his squadron and I spot Wyn dancing with a group of Fae, intoxicated and unable to step to the beat of the percussions. The scene draws a smile to my face, and the cold drink in my hand even makes me forget Vesta's absence.

"Cheers, General." Naar approaches, a smile plastered on the face of the usually reserved captain of Averion.

"We've earned this one," I say as I clink my glass to his.

"We sure have."

The captain looks around the room, pausing on each of his soldiers.

"Your mate didn't want to join us tonight, did he?"

Naar's laugh fills the air.

"Come on, you know how much Mor *loves* these gatherings."

As much as I enjoy teasing about the healer and his love for decorum, he's been a true ally and friend throughout the years.

Naar turns towards the door with longing in his eyes, reminding me of what I can never have—someone waiting for me in a place to call home.

"Get out of here, Naar. You've done your fair share of bonding with your squadron." I wave towards the group at the back of the tavern, where Wyn has now taken his shirt off and is singing alongside the band while dancing suggestively for whoever wants to watch.

The captain gives me a small smile before making his way to the door. I consider making a discreet exit myself, but a familiar voice speaks up behind me.

"Don't you dare leave without buying me a drink, General."

A weight lifts off my shoulder as I turn and face Vesta.

I signal for a waiter to bring another round of drinks to my table, and my gaze lands on the redheaded Captain of the High Guard. Stunning as ever, she's wearing an emerald corset and skirt that match her irises nicely.

"What am I good for, if not to buy drinks for gorgeous Fae?"

A flush darkens her cheeks before she regains her composure.

"We're the lucky ones, to have you *grace* us with your presence."

A laugh tears from my throat.

"You've never known how to take a compliment, V."

She sighs dramatically at my comment.

"They're far too boring."

"Because you get so many, I suppose." This time, I force my smile before raising my glass to hers. "Cheers."

"What are you doing here, though, seriously?" Vesta raises an eyebrow before adding, "not that our General needs a reason to join his soldiers in a shitty bar."

My gaze trails across the stuffy room, and I shrug.

"I needed a break too."

She nods and sips from her ale.

"I'm worried," I confess, the words unlocked by her presence. She's the only one I could trust with this burden and who could understand my troubled mind. "The wildest conjectures cloud my judgment, stoking the embers of my fears."

"You know as well as I do that nothing could have stopped Ela from going," she answers as I stare into her green eyes. "I would have done the same thing."

Her voice turns to a whisper, and I nod as she allows me to imagine the impossible.

However hard I've tried to break down the walls she's erected around her heart after the loss of her mate, she's never entertained the possibility of something happening between us. Over the years, she's pushed away anyone wanting more than a few nights with her, but tonight, a sliver of hope lingers in my heart. I want much more than that with her, though I'm not sure I deserve it.

"Come on." She cocks her head towards the back of the room, where a crowd has assembled near the musicians. "Let's dance."

She pulls me by the arm and I follow, too tired to argue, or too inebriated to care. Her flamboyant hair like a beacon in the mass of buzzed Fae, I let her guide me towards an empty corner.

The music is much louder here, and her arms raise above her head sensually as the notes reach her delicate ears.

Enthralled, I move closer to her, slowly rocking to the tune, until we're inches apart. She doesn't step away, and our bodies begin moving together, harmonizing. My hands go to her waist on instinct, but reason makes a comeback and I stop myself.

She looks at me through her painted eyelashes and I lose myself in her gaze. I don't stop her when she grabs my hands and puts them on her waist this time, taking control.

My fingers brush her corset as her hips sway and my breath hitches in my throat. I grip a little tighter, needing to anchor myself after craving her for so long.

Moments later, our bodies are intertwined as we dance in a dark corner, away from prying eyes. Hell, I doubt anyone is sober enough to register what's happening on this side of the bar.

I can't take my eyes of her, needing to engrave this moment in my brain. As I blink, I half-expect to wake up from a dream, but when I open my eyes, she's still here, pressing her body against mine, letting her hands travel my shoulders.

Each touch of her hips against mine sends a rush of heat through my spine, and my heartbeat accelerates.

"Vesta," I growl in her ear as she returns her brightest smile. She will be the death of me.

A commotion followed by cheers sounds behind us, and the energy in the room changes as everyone's attention is drawn to a drunken patron making a heartfelt speech.

When I return my attention to Vesta, her face is inches from mine, her warmth breath a caress on my neck. I lower my gaze and find hers set on my lips. Hypnotized, I watch as her mouth parts, inviting me.

My palms shake as I cradle her face, still scarcely trusting this gift she's granting me.

As soon as my lips touch hers, my body craves all of her. Reason escapes me and every fiber of my soul is consumed by her soft lips.

The music's quick tempo echoes my frantic heart as my soul communicates through hungry lips, relishing in her touch, which I once despaired of knowing outside tortured dreams. I need to sample every inch of her skin. I hunger for her body like a starved man, drunk on her taste.

She meets my kiss eagerly, her palm resting on my chest, opening her mouth, welcoming mine like its true home.

I lose myself on her lips until cheers echo behind us once more.

A Fae bumps into me hard enough to separate us, and I shove him away, my body screaming from the loss. Several people grab hold of the drunk Fae before sitting him down, and when I turn back, Vesta is gone.

⸺⸺◆⸺⸺

The following day, I walk into the garrison around midday for my usual training session with Vesta. She's not here yet, but that's not unusual. Punctuality is rarely her priority.

After acknowledging the soldiers present, I begin warming up. Every now and then, I glance at the door, waiting for the Captain of the High Guard to stroll in, proudly sporting a mean hangover.

I move on to training when it becomes clear she's not coming, and I stop checking the entrance. A pang of disappointment flickers briefly within me before logic reasserts its cool control, my pragmatism rising to dampen the sting.

She made the first move yesterday, approached me, invited me to dance, and I made the second move. I kissed her and she let me, encouraging me to widen the cracks in her armor.

I wield my sword relentlessly across the room, not bothering to hold back my blows. After an hour of this dance, I'm sweating profusely, but my mind is calmer.

When I take a quick break to switch from my long sword and train with two short sabres instead of my long sword, I overhear soldiers chatting in a corner.

"She's a wild one, I'll tell you that." One of the Fae winks at the group gathered around him, eliciting muffled laughs.

"She's certainly not shy," another one adds. "She danced with half the bar last night."

I get closer, my jaw clenched hard as they utter these idiocies. Judgmental fuckers.

"Bars, you mean? I hear she didn't make it back until sunrise," the first soldier counters. "She's a captain I'd like to take orders from, if you know what I mean."

"Me, it's her red hair I'd pull as I—"

A growl tears from my throat, silencing the room as I storm towards them, sabres in hand.

"One more word, and I'll tear those forked tongues from your mouths with my bare hands," I snarl at the unworthy fools whom Vesta would never even glance at. "That is no way to speak about your superior, or anyone for that matter."

Their gazes flee to the ground as they freeze in place. Vesta holds more power over their narrow minds than they have over themselves.

"Return to your posts."

My voice is so loud, it must have been heard throughout the barracks. They scatter like scared animals.

I rarely use threats for those under my command, for there is usually no need. But I'm not above it and I certainly won't have squadrons circulate ignorant bullshit.

We didn't fight for unity and freedom in the Fae realms to reserve it for a select few who deem themselves better than others who live differently. Respect is due to all, or it holds no meaning.

My anger restored tenfold, I storm out of the garrison and into the palace. I lock myself in Azran's office and only emerge hours later once the overwhelming amount of bureaucracy has tamed my rage.

I stop by the kitchen to have dinner sent to my room before making my way to my quarters.

This late at night, the corridors are empty, but when I turn a corner, I stop dead in my tracks. Vesta stands at the other end of the corridor, her gold and red armor hugging her curves, her hair tied in a braid. We lock eyes, and even from a distance, there is no mistaking the look on her face—ready to flee at the smallest hint of danger, yet intrigued.

My stomach twists at her sight, but I don't give her time to say a word. I turn on my heels and take the long way to my rooms. If I push her too far too soon, she will slip through my fingers and I might never get her back.

CHAPTER 12

ELANOR

Another wave of nausea hits me, and my hands go to my stomach as I pinch my eyes shut, waiting for it to pass as I mentally curse Vesta for the hundredth time.

Funny enough, she told me that crossing the Váyan Sea would be quick and easy and that the swaying of the boat would lull me to sleep at night.

I managed to eat a light dinner earlier, mistakenly interpreting this as a sign that my condition was improving, and I'm fully regretting it.

Releasing a breath, I sit up on the cabin's small bed, aggressively eyeing the dark leather tome partially responsible for my state. After borrowing it from Averion's library, I tried reading more on the ship, but it only brought the queasiness back, and it now rests on the floorboards.

It's a collection of ancient tales and myths, and the closest book I've found that speaks of the old gods. I closed it when I couldn't focus on the words anymore, halfway through the part about the origins of magic and dark creatures.

I squeeze my eyes shut once more, taking a deep breath in and out, as waves crash on the other side of the cabin. We've been at sea for two days and three nights and should reach the coast tomorrow. *Fucking finally.*

"Come on, L," I whisper to myself. "Just one more day to go."

I can't wait to get off this stinky boat and feel flat, hard soil beneath my boots.

Sleep has never been a friend of mine, but out here it's become my enemy. Each sway brings another spiral of fear as I wait for us to get pulled underwater.

Milan, the commander of the Fae soldiers escorting me, tells me there's nothing alarming about these waves. But there is nothing normal about a wood structure floating in the middle of an immense body of water.

Seth and Gavriel, two of the guards also accompanying me, outright joke about my discomfort, but I can't bring myself to blame them. The Unifier, sick on a boat. I'd laugh too, were I not constantly on the verge of throwing up.

Saliva floods my mouth and I get up. Needing fresh air, I make for the deck as fast as I can, one hand on the wall, and the other in front of me.

A cold wind brushes my face as I step onto the wet floor-boards barefoot and bend over the rail. I stare at the dark waters as bile surges in my throat, and I can't fight it anymore.

I take a deep breath when I'm done heaving my dinner, my throat on fire. I wipe my mouth with the back of my hand, spitting into the treacherous sea to rid my mouth of the taste.

My watery eyes clear and I grip the wooden rail tightly, taking in the night. Stars decorate the sky, shining bright above us, and a moon crescent hangs above the horizon.

My shoulders relax as I remember who I'm going after. I stay there a moment, picturing Azran's face, and our reunion. My heart swells with hope as I wonder what he'll say or do when he sees me. I've never been huge on sharing my feelings, running away from them has always been more my speed, but I'm ready to face the truth.

A tingle of guilt wakes inside me. He still doesn't know how I feel about him. Hell, I can barely wrap my head around it myself, but he's only ever heard venom leaving my lips.

The bond doesn't flare anymore; the pain in my chest changed. A constant ache lives inside me, like a fire that's been lit and kept ablaze by someone stirring embers.

My stomach drops as I consider the bond once more, and urgency takes me. Tears fill my eyes as I stay there, powerless and alone.

Azran is the only one who truly accepted me as I was. After twenty-two years of living a lie, and being abandoned by everyone I loved, he stayed. Even when I came an inch from killing him, he stayed, ready to die for my revenge, ready to disappear for me to exist. And back in Adria when the bond exploded freely, I felt safe, loved, and like I belonged for the first time. Right before he got taken away from me.

My fingers tighten on the wooden railing as the boat pitches forward and my power flickers with the pain coursing through my body. I let it flow through my chest, hugging me.

Keeping my gaze on the black sea ahead, I focus on the distance as my power unravels, keeping me company, letting me explore my emotions and embrace my anger.

I blink when a light flickers in the night.

It's hard to tell where the sea ends and the sky begins, but I swear I just saw a light.

Squinting my eyes, I search for it again, my power at the ready.

My breath catches in my throat when the light appears again. Dull and almost faded, an animalistic shape takes form in the distance.

I almost lose balance when the next wave crashes on the side of the boat, and I recognize Savage's white eyes.

He can't be here. First of all, because as far as I know he could not fly or walk on water, and second of all, because he died.

The wolf tilts his head, his gaze sparkling, amused.

"Savage," I whisper into the night.

My power echoes in response and his shape gets closer.

A laugh tears from my throat as my wolf's spirit sits on the deck next to me and my hand goes through his fur effortlessly.

Glancing around, I return my hand to the railing to make sure no one sees me losing my mind before checking the web of energy inside me. A new thread of light courses through my veins, connecting me to Death's spirit realm. Dark and decorated with stars, the starlight river peacefully flows through me, and I let myself drown in its comforting warmth.

⁕

A delegation meets us at Nyths' gates and leads us up this labyrinth of a place to the royal palace. The city itself encrusts the mountainsides on different levels.

Milan and I lock eyes for a second as I glance around, feeling exposed without Nahtar. I didn't argue with Calen when he asked for the sword. As much as it pained me to leave it in Averion, it's far too recognizable and would give away my identity at a glimpse.

"Don't trust anyone."

The General's words echo through my mind as we ride into Nyths and slowly climb the city. Greyish stone buildings decorate the paved streets as Fae go about their day, hopping in and out of carriages pulled by horses, undisturbed by our presence.

The higher we go, the fewer humans I notice, although the capital buzzes with activity. Doors open, bells chime as citizens enter and leave shops, and hooves echo on the pavement, muffling the conversations of their passengers.

On the highest level of the city, we come to a halt before immense stone doors. I resist a frown as black-armored guards open the gates to the palace. Carvings of monsters and demons adorn the panels, their teeth-filled mouths agape in silent screams.

It takes me a moment to look away from the horror in front of me, but when I do I clench my jaw. A series of bodies swing from ropes attached to the wall's parapet.

Three humans and a Fae are hanged there, their features forever frozen in a mask of pain. One of the humans has hair painted various colors, though their face is so bruised and swollen I doubt anyone could identify them.

My nausea makes a comeback, for different reasons this time, and my power stirs with my anger. I exhale slowly, trying to keep my composure, as I feel my connection to the spirit realm come alive. Glancing sideways, Savage's shape comes into view briefly, bringing me comfort like he always has.

I glance at Milan, but his gaze is fixed on the doors opening.

On the other side, we ride up another paved street, this one decorated with flowers and trees on each side, contrasting violently with the sight of the gate.

The stone doors close with a bang behind us, the echo reverberating in my bones.

As soon as the palace comes into view, we're greeted by soldiers and a small group of Fae standing before its massive double doors.

The dark, asymmetrical building has innumerable number of arches, stained-glass windows, and narrow bridges connecting different parts of the immense palace. Just like the city it towers over, several levels sport turrets and balconies, no doubt offering a breathtaking view.

Our horses are stopped a good distance away from the entrance and we're invited to dismount. I go first, and Milan and the others follow, taking positions behind me.

My throat dries as I face the welcoming committee by the doors, and the enormity of our task dawns on me. I've never done this before, and gods know diplomacy has never been my strong suit. I'm starting to think that maybe Cal was right about me not being ready.

Thankfully, a dark-haired Fae steps forward.

"Welcome to Nyths, Lady Elanor." With a wave of his hand, an army of human servants descend on our mounts and bags.

His striking green eyes observe me from head to toe and I can't look away. Tall but slender, he wears a leather-collared black ensemble and a brooch on his chest. A gold lily.

Milan clears his throat ever so slightly, stirring me from my state of frozen shock.

"Your Royal Highness." Heat flushes my cheeks as I remember to bow before Prince Nylren. "Thank you for receiving me. It's an honor to be here."

"The pleasure is ours." I look back up and offer a polite smile that he doesn't return. I silently curse myself for not recognizing him sooner, after Cal's thorough lesson on the royal family. "Follow me."

The Prince looks away quickly and turns around.

I send an apologetic glance towards Milan, hoping I didn't massively mess up within our first hour here.

We step inside a hall and my eyes widen. Paintings decorate entire walls, intricate rugs cover the floor, and flowers have been arranged at each corner, infusing their scent through the cold air of the palace. Dark curtains flank the windows, letting daylight shine on the golden molding.

I follow after the Prince as we cross several corridors and enter the most majestic room I've ever seen. The arched ceiling is painted entirely in black spirals and floral art, its corners merging with the walls, making the room seem even bigger than it is.

A crowd of courtesan and Fae nobles stands on either side of the hall, observing our delegation, and I lower my eyes, not daring to linger on the decorations any longer. They all wear colorful attire, much more extravagant than I've ever seen in Averion.

My heart skips a beat as I search for Azran's face in the crowd in vain, my foolish hope crushed instantly.

Our footsteps echo on the obsidian floors leading up to a massive dais covered in forest-green velvet. Nylren walks directly in front of me, blocking the view, and my chest tightens with each passing moment.

After what feels like an eternity, he steps aside.

"Lady Elanor."

The most handsome Fae I've ever seen is standing before me, a crown of gold and emerald decorating his forehead, matching the color of his irises.

His ear-length, raven-black hair reflects the sunlight as he smiles widely, showing off his perfect teeth and sharp jawline.

Prince Nylren goes to stand by his father's side, now a pale copy of the elegant ruler of Zetrea.

"Your Majesty." The ruffle of clothes and leather behind me confirms the whole delegation is kneeling as I bow.

Lifting my head after a decent amount of time, I study King Airdan as he steps down from the dais. His teal shirt has a few buttons open at the collar, revealing a muscular chest.

"You must be exhausted from your travels." He tilts his head to the side, a piece of hair dangling over his captivating eyes.

"I am simply honored to be received in your home, your Majesty."

I lower my gaze, my heart racing as I try my best not to fuck this up.

"What an exciting time, isn't it?" His soft laughter fills the room as he looks around at its occupants. "Lóna and Zetrea, together once more. This ought to be a most joyful occasion, but first, you shall rest."

He claps his hands loudly and servants flood into the throne room, ready to lead the way. Milan's hand moves closer to his sword, startled by the extravagant display, and I barely repress the smile tugging my lips.

"Thank you, your Majesty." I bow once more, eager to leave the formalities behind and get away from the dozens of eyes on us.

CHAPTER 13

ELANOR

The next minutes go in a blur as we follow servants through the palace, and my interest is piqued by something new at every turn. The corridors blend together in an ocean of velvet drapes, luxurious furniture, and artwork. Each corner of the palace is a different shade of dark blue, teal, green, or black, and a full display of its long history.

We go up several stairways, and when we finally stop, I'm completely lost. The human girl showing us to our rooms opens a door, stepping aside to let me in.

"Your bags have already arrived."

A four-poster bed awaits me inside, covered in pillows and sheer curtains. Massive wardrobes line one wall, and two leather chairs face each other below the stained-glass window. The entire room is a variation of obsidian and dark grey, just like the rest of the palace, with layered rugs, gold moldings, and a crystal chandelier bringing soft light to the room.

The washroom adjacent to the bedroom has a clawfoot bathtub and copper accents on the vanity handles. A mirror with a carved wooden frame occupies the entire wall. The room is dimly lit, with only a small window.

After peaking through the door separating the two rooms, I turn and find Milan patiently waiting. I'm completely out of my element. We both are, though he manages to keep a straight face while my mouth is on the floor.

"What the hell is this place?"

Small wrinkles form in the corner of his dark eyes as a smile tugs his lips.

"Are you alright?"

"I'm fine. I don't know what I expected, but this is a *lot*."

"Welcome to the world of Fae politics," he says with a sigh.

"Thank you for coming with me. We're both a long way from home."

He nods. "I won't leave your side. I'll make sure my room is beside yours, and two guards will be stationed outside your door at all times."

My shoulders sag the moment he leaves the room, and I let out a slow breath.

Savage appears in the corner of my eye, his comforting presence giving me the strength to go on. I've survived the most ruthless battles, and this is no different. I will adapt and play the role of the perfect ambassador until I find out where Azran is. Granted, putting on a show has never been my strong suit, but I have no choice.

I don't usually bother with appearances and the games that come with being close to politics, and now, I've been dumped in the middle of them. A snort tears from my throat at the irony.

Well, at least King Airdan seems welcoming. All that's left to see is how far his kindness extends when I start probing and looking for Az. One hour at a time, then.

I snatch the book I brought with me from my bag and hide it under the mattress.

A knock sounds on the door, startling me, and I quickly sit on the bed. The door creaks open and the petite girl I saw earlier slips in, swimming in an oversized cotton dress with a white apron tied around her slender waist. Her shoulders hunch inward, making her appear even smaller, as her wide brown eyes dart around the ornate room nervously. She clasps her hands before her, revealing fingernails ragged from hours of scrubbing.

"My lady, my name is Jaida." She bows quickly. "I'm here to help you unpack your bag and get settled."

She looks as old as me, but the slump in her shoulders and anxious energy radiating from her make the girl seem younger.

"Thank you," I say with a smile.

She points to a gold rope hanging from the ceiling by the entrance. "Should you need anything, you can ring for me at any time."

I nod and she begins putting my clothes away in the wardrobes.

Moments later, another servant walks in carrying a platter of food and refreshment. An older man, given the wrinkles on his marked face. Without a word, he puts everything down on a low table by the window seats and goes to stand in a corner.

I wait several seconds, but he remains perfectly still.

I guess I won't have much alone time, after all.

Unable to resist the delicious aroma in the room, I move to one of the leather chairs facing the table and pick up a slice of bread. Still warm from the oven, the coarse grain crumbs melt on my tongue. I close my eyes and savor the yeasty taste before reaching for a hunk of creamy cheese. The sharp flavor complements the bread perfectly. Juices drips down my chin as I bite into a ripe peach, the sweetness bursting across my palette. I haven't had fresh food in days and this is hitting the spot. With every bite, I feel strength and optimism return to my body.

My appetite vanishes when I uncover a folded note tucked under a plate. My pulse quickens with dread even before reading the message. Could it be from Az? I force a dry, difficult swallow as I open it.

The King is inviting me to join him after lunch. A pit opens in my stomach as guilt seeps in and reminds me I'm not here to enjoy my visit and sample the local food.

I quickly freshen up and change into a black day dress, still unsettled by the absence of Nahtar on my back.

As I'm led downstairs by the old servant, the size of the palace really dawns on me. I need to start memorizing the way and mentally mapping this place.

After an incalculable number of turns and stairs, I return to the immense throne room, although this time it's just me. Allowing myself to study the painted ceiling more thoroughly, I don't hear King Airdan enter.

"What do you think?"

His voice sounds so close to my ears, I almost jump out of my skin as he walks around me.

"Beautiful." I quickly recover and put a polite smile on my face. "Your Majesty."

His eyes twinkle with amusement, making it clear he can see right through my inexperience in these courtly affairs.

"Let me give you a tour of my residence," he declares with a grand, sweeping gesture that encompasses the whole room. Arms outstretched, he waves expansively as if to draw my eye to every ornate detail, from the intricate crown molding to the massive artwork covering the ceiling. "I know it can be intimidating at first, but I want to make sure you feel at home here."

He extends his left arm towards me, and I hesitate for a second before entwining my arm with his. It's not like I could tell the King of Zetrea to keep his hands to himself.

His warm palm covers my hand gently, securing it to his elbow as heat flushes my cheeks.

"After our walk, you'll have to join me for dinner." He motions towards the door with his head, a strand of hair dancing over his eyes as we start walking. "We have much to discuss and discover about each other."

"Of course, your Majesty."

As our steps echo, my heart is beating out of my chest and I hope he can't fucking hear it.

"Grand," King Airdan says.

My eyes are set on a point ahead of me, but I swear I can hear him smile.

"So tell me, how do you find Nyths so far?"

I remark on the splendor of the city, determined to be a good ambassador, and for a time I feel it's going well. Commenting on superficial shit is not usually in my playbook, but I'm a quick learner. As it turns out, it requires little focus or intelligence, and it allows me to map out each turn we make.

Airdan tells me about the palace's history and the colors of his house, representing his family's heritage, showing off his charm in the process. I'm starting to see how he's stayed King for so long. Diplomacy is second nature to him.

As we step onto a balcony, he releases my arm to let me wander and take in the view. The sun and the light breeze softly caress my skin as I study the city below. My eyes dart to the palace defense walls, and a chill runs through my spine.

"I'm sorry you had to ride past that dreadful scene at the gate." Airdan walks up behind me. "This is not a common occurrence, as I don't rejoice in such sights," he adds with a heavy sigh. "I wish we didn't have to resort to such extremes, but the people have to be protected from criminals."

He extends his arm once more, and we resume our visit of the palace grounds. An hour later, we're still wandering the corridors, indulging in polite conversation, though he doesn't mention Azran once, confirming he never made it to the palace.

⸻ ◆ ⸻

When I step into the dining room, I'm incredibly grateful for Rina and her assistance in packing my bag. For once, I feel adequately dressed in the black gown I'm wearing, its padded shoulders encrusted in crystals and long sleeves flowing behind me as I walk.

Lit by several chandeliers hanging from the arched ceiling, a massive table occupies the center of the room, its surface almost entirely covered by plates, cutlery, and candles. Three chairs have been arranged at the end, confirming it will only be me, Airdan, and his son.

Nylren is standing behind a chair, his back straight and arms crossed in front of him, while Airdan steps towards me.

"When I heard we were to receive a delegation from Lóna, I didn't realize they would send their most exquisite and lethal jewel."

The King's eyes glint as they roam over me and I freeze, my heart racing as I try to decipher the look on his face. He can't know about me. There is no way he knows about my powers and what I can do. I've been careful not to let anything slip about who I truly am.

"Your beauty could bring an army to its knees, if you were so inclined. It is a good thing you come in friendship, Elanor, otherwise I might fear for the safety of my heart." His features soften in a smile and my shoulders relax. "Can I call you Elanor?"

"Of course, your Majesty."

My name glides smoothly off his tongue, infused with a delight that sets me on edge. He makes it sounds like it's the most delicious word ever pronounced.

A servant steps out of the shadows and pulls out a chair for me. Airdan sits first, followed by Nylren and me. Once we're all seated, the King claps his hands and a procession of dishes is brought in by servants. Trays laden with meats are presented first, ribs roasted to perfection with crispy fat lining the edges, juicy cuts of steak seasoned with herbs, chicken baked in a creamy mushroom sauce, and slices of pork stuffed with apricots and nuts. Next come baskets of freshly baked bread, still steaming from the ovens, along with crocks of creamy butter. An array of pies and tarts follow, their flaky golden crusts bursting with fillings of meat, cheese, fruit or spiced vegetables.

I do my best to keep my mouth from opening at the sight of the lavish courses and the delicious aromas filling the air.

My plate is filled before I can even lift my fork, but I wait for the King to eat before trying some vegetables.

"Send my best to the High Lord, Elanor."

A piece of carrot almost sticks in my throat when Airdan's words reach my ears. Swallowing with difficulty, I put my fork down before answering.

"I will." A painful ripple echoes down the bond, but I keep a straight face. "Azran wanted me to personally extend you an invitation to Averion so he can show you the best Lóna has to offer."

Guilt floods my veins as the painful reminder of his absence rings in my heart. I should be out there, looking for him, not playing house with a King set on charming me with his words.

"I am most eager to visit your island."

Finding my courage behind a polite smile, I join the dance.

"I hope I'll have the time to explore your beautiful capital." I prick a piece of meat pie with my fork. "I only got a glance on our way here, but I would love to sample everything the city has to offer."

"But of course, my dear. There will be plenty of time for that."

I muster another cultivated smile as I lift the fork to my mouth.

Nylren, seated in front of me, hasn't said a word yet, so I turn to him.

"Your Highness, I wanted to thank you for your welcome earlier today."

Lifting his head from his full plate, the Prince gives me a tight smile and a nod that I return.

"As you can see, I'm the chatty one in the family," Airdan adds with a chuckle. He locks eyes with his son for a mere second, but long enough to reveal his gaze has lost its usual warmth.

A hint of pity flares inside me. I can only imagine what it must have been like growing up in the shadow of Airdan, the charismatic King of all Fae and humans in Zetrea, whose name commands respect and allegiance in all corners of the world.

CHAPTER 14

CALEN

I fall asleep the moment my head touches the pillow after another endless day of meetings with Averion's captains and intendants.

Moonlight is still streaming through the window, bathing my room in soft light, when I open my eyes.

I quickly scan my surroundings, finding everything still and in its place. With my pulse pounding in my ears, I am tempted to fall back asleep, thinking of the mountain of work awaiting me at dawn, but I hold off.

My instinct is rarely wrong.

Faint metallic scraping reaches my ears. It's so subtle at first that I think I imagined it, until my breath catches in my chest when the muted clicks come again, followed by muffled pressure on the door handle. My pulse accelerates, wiping all traces of sleep away.

Someone is on the other side of the door, rattling with its knob.

My alert senses, honed by years of paranoid caution, pick up on the hair-thin sounds of the lock surrendering. The rasp of metal on metal whispers like a shout in the night's stillness.

I ease from bed soundlessly, my hand fisting the handle of the knife underneath my pillow. If the intruder is any good, they'll get in within seconds, so I bunch the covers back in place and stand in the corner.

Working to regulate my heartbeat, I slow my breathing and close my eyes, letting my other senses take over.

A louder click sounds and my eyes snap open.

The slender shape of my visitor enters the room, closing the door with an impressively delicate touch, barely making noise. And as they step towards the bed, I tighten my hold on the blade.

In moments like this, I've learned it's best to strike first and ask questions later. So I do.

Seizing my opponent from behind, I pull them to me with one hand on their mouth while the other goes to their neck, my knife finding their throat.

I freeze when the intruder stills in my arms, my blade ready to plunge into their jugular and redecorate my cream bed sheets. For the first time in my life, I hesitate.

Faced with the complete absence of a survival instinct in my opponent, I delay the inevitable for a split second.

I've never met an assassin unwilling to engage in self-defense. That's not the right line of work to be in, but they should have thought about that before breaking into the room of the General of the Fae armies.

I inhale deeply, ready to dismiss this internal debate when a familiar perfume fills my nose—floral and sweet, with a hint of vanilla.

"What the hell," I blurt out as I release my hold on the intruder's mouth.

"Cal." A feminine voice escapes their throat. "It's me."

My stomach drops and I lower my knife instantly.

"Vesta."

I pull her to my chest with both arms, careful not to cut her as I burrow my face in her hair, breathing in her scent while my brain catches up with the fact that I came so terribly close to taking her life.

Her hand goes to my forearm, gently pressing as she exhales, and we stay there a moment, holding each other.

Letting go of her, I put the knife down and turn her to face me. I catch her widened eyes, the moonlight just enough for me to discern the light tremble of her lips.

"What the hell, V?"

"I'm sorry," she says, her voice breaking.

"No, I'm the one who should be sorry."

Gathering her in my arms, she rests her head on my bare chest as I gently brush her hair and whisper against her head. "You're safe."

I've never regretted sleeping with a knife until now.

She remains silent as her heart pounds against my chest, so I step back and cup her cheek with one hand.

"You pick locks now?" I ask.

She gives me a small smile in return, her hands finding purchase on my ribcage.

"Did you get lost?" I raise an eyebrow, but she merely shakes her head.

Turning her head, she rubs her lips on my palm, softly caressing the skin before depositing a kiss on it.

I still completely and she kisses my palm again, this time with more strength.

"Vesta," I whisper her name when her hands begin tracing my torso, as she moves close enough for me to feel her warm breath on my skin.

Goosebumps erupt on my arms with each touch, and the panic slowly retreats, teasing something else entirely in its wake.

Her tongue darts out of her mouth, tasting my skin before a kiss follows.

"What are you doing?" My voice shakes with tension.

Each touch of her lips is like a punishment, and I'm dying for the next lash of her whip.

"Shhh." She puts her index finger on my mouth. As she presses against my lips, I give up probing for an explanation, set on not stoking the flames of the fears I know lurk beneath her confident exterior. "Let's not overthink this."

She kisses my jaw next and I pinch my eyes closed, praying for the strength to resist tearing at her clothes.

My hands go to her waist as I toy with the idea of pushing her away. I don't trust myself near her. My body begs to relinquish control and surrender to her touch. With restraint the last thing on my mind and forbidden words threatening to spill over my tongue, could I show restraint when I already care so much and she's afraid to? I can't risk exposing the depth of my obsession for her.

Her hand trails down my stomach as if she's heard the prayer and taken it as a challenge. Each subtle caress fuels a tempest in my blood.

I've been to hell and back, survived wars, but this? This is torture of a new kind.

"You're making it really hard for me to do the right thing," I say, staring down at her.

"Then don't."

Her fingers land on the bulge of my undershorts, and she shatters my fragile self-control with a single touch.

"You turn me into a weak, weak man." My grip on her waist tightens. "And you just undid my last restraints."

I close the gap between us, my dreams catching up with reality. Her lips are as soft as I remember, and I'm ready to get lost under her touch.

Her hands make quick work of the last fabric on my body as mine travel hers for the first time, memorizing each curve.

Bunching up her loose shirt in my palms, I tear it open from the back, eliciting a gasp from her throat.

"Tsk, tsk. That won't do, Dove." I kiss under her ear. "I'm going to make you sing, and discover each sound you make until your throat is raw."

Her gaze travels my body, the corner of her lips tugging into a smile in challenge, and she pulls away, depriving me of her touch save for her index on my chest.

She pushes me against the bed until my thighs hit the mattress.

Sitting, I lean on my hands as she removes her torn shirt and wiggles out of her dark pants.

My rock-hard length twitches. She's not wearing undergarnments.

"Was that for me, Dove?" A smile appears on my face. "Bold."

I snatch her waist and position her on top of me, the wetness between her thighs already coating my legs.

I take her lips as she grinds her gorgeous body over mine. She hovers over my erection, teasing, until the determination in her eyes registers.

There's no way I'm letting her do that. Not yet.

"I'm going to savor you, V."

Flipping her around, I lay her down on the mattress and settle between her legs.

Kissing my way down her neck, I take my time, licking and biting every inch of her pearly skin. Her hands grasp my shoulders, holding on for dear life as I grind against her soaked entrance.

Her breathing accelerates as I near her breasts and finally claim their pink summits between my lips.

She pushes her hips forward, seeking me, but I'm not giving in that easily. With her hushed gasps in my ears, I pull back.

Her furrowed brows draw a smile to my face.

"Bastard."

"You've seen nothing yet." My smile widens and I lower myself on the bed, resuming my exploration.

She spreads her legs, guiding me towards her entrance, and I oblige.

The first touch of my tongue on her engorged bud has her arching her back. Moans fill the air as I lap at her dripping pussy like a parched man, my fingers finding her entrance.

The taste of her intoxicating, I lose myself in her folds as I slide a digit inside her.

She exhales slowly, her breathing short. I push in and out of her, ready to make her forget her name, to only remember mine.

Her hands roam the bedsheets, gripping the fabric as moans fill her mouth.

"There you go. Sing for me, Dove."
And she does.

Her thighs tighten around my neck and I gently bite her clit, sending her writhing.

I let her ride the edge for a moment before pulling away.

A growl escapes her throat as I move. I bring my face close to hers, my mouth teasing hers, softly rubbing against her swollen lips, her gritted teeth not far behind.

Her nails trail down my chest, leaving my skin raw, and she pushes me back and straddles me as I sit.

Her thighs lock around my waist, positioning me towards her entrance, and I don't resist.

My mouth crashes on hers as I sink into her warmth, and I don't repress the growl of pleasure tearing through me.

She starts rolling her hips and I watch as my hardened length goes in and out of her slowly. She pulls back, bringing the tip of my dick almost out of her before plunging it back in. Enthralled, I let her set the pace, supporting her back with my arms.

Gods knows I'll never get to heaven in this life, but I now understand what it feels like.

Her smell, her warmth, her sounds. Everything about her is pure bliss.

Vesta extends her arms behind her to lean back as she rides me tirelessly, bringing me to the edge. My fingers find the spot between her legs, circling gently as she nears her release.

Each stroke could be my unraveling, but I hold back, focusing on her and her only.

She lets out a scream as she topples over, her pussy clenching around my length buried deep inside her, and only then do I allow myself to come.

She falls on her back moments later, disconnecting us, and the distance is already too much.

We're both panting, but I can't take my eyes off her. Dawn is near, bringing enough light for me to study her, and I attempt to carve this image in my memory. From her body covered in sweat, her chest rising rapidly as she catches her breath, to her hair cascading around her gorgeous face and her trembling lips. But before I get the chance, she leaves the bed.

I don't dare say a word, too scared to spoil this moment suspended in time as she puts on her torn shirt.

Fully dressed, she makes for the door, and a pit opens in my stomach, widening with each step she takes.

I am utterly lost to her, left to pray this won't be the last I see of her, and royally fucked.

She turns back at the last second and we lock eyes as she scrapes the door with her fingernails.

A week later, I'm behind Azran's desk, attending another meeting after dinner.

As Naar finishes his report on his units' patrols across the territories, reporting no disturbances, the discreet captain leans back against a bookshelf.

I nod regularly as the rest of our army's captains follow suit, sharing updates.

Several heads turn when the office door opens, and my gaze falls on the latecomer. The Captain of the High Guard strolls in, her head held high, confident as ever.

Were it just the two of us, I would scold her for her tardiness and no doubt receive a sarcastic response, but I remain silent and keep my face neutral instead. Were it just the two of us, there are many things I would do, and none involve having an audience.

Vesta plops herself on one of the leather couches and I can't help but devour her with a glance.

I saw so little of her these past few days that I could almost believe I imagined that night, although the memories are too vivid to be a dream. I can still smell and taste her when I close my eyes.

Rearranging the papers on the desk in front of me, I try to concentrate on the reports, but when it's her turn to speak, I can't take my eyes off her. Leading suits her so damn well. She'll never admit it, but she was born for it, although the responsibilities take their toll on her.

Once all captains have spoken, I stand and walk to the front of the desk, leaning on it to take in the room.

"While your High Lord and Ela are away, it is our duty to ensure the safety of the realm. Keep me posted on all developments."

I receive grunts and nods in response, and wave towards the door to release them to their evenings.

"Vesta," I call as she crosses the room.

Her head snaps towards me.

"A word."

Naar exits last, closing the door behind him as Vesta absently brushes the books on the shelves lining the office.

CHAPTER 15

CALEN

"Looking for your next nighttime read?" I ask, and her eyebrows shoot towards her hairline.

"I don't need books to stay busy after sundown," she answers without missing a beat.

I clear my throat and muster a tight smile. I earned that one.

"Is the High Guard ready for the winter solstice celebration?"

The festival is just a few days away, and although the High Lord is usually the one parading through the city, celebrating with its citizens and exchanging well wishes, this year the responsibility falls on me.

"Of course. Patrols have been assigned."

"Come with me."

"Where?"

"To the solstice."

She turns back to study the bookshelf.

"I'll be the one in armor, watching the crowd around you."

I bite back a snarky comment and approach her, putting my hand over hers.

"That's not what I meant." I lower my voice and gaze into her eyes. "Walk alongside me."

"No." She pulls her hand back and increases the distance between us.

"It's just a celebration."

"A celebration where I would *just* be paraded around Averion. A celebration where the Captain of the High Guard would *just* appear to be pining over her superior."

"That's not true." I'm tempted to reach for her hand again, but something stops me. "I know this is not what—"

"You don't think I hear the gossip?" She scoffs. "They can judge me all they want, my life is my own, but I won't jeopardize my career. I won't fuel a new rumor about the General *fucking* his captain."

She spits out the last words with such force that I take a step back. My misguided attempt to connect with her at least earned me clarity on the night we shared.

"Vesta, I would never let that happen."

"I said no."

As her voice raises almost imperceptibly, letting go crosses my mind before revolt follows, and I decide to stand my ground.

"You can push me away all you want, but I'm not giving up." With her silence the only hint that doubt is seeping through her mind, time suspends between us as I look for a way to get through to her. "I know what you've been through. I know the loss and heartbreak you've endured. I know you—"

"If you know me so well, then you should know not to get any ideas about us. I don't do commitment."

She pinches her lips together and the door slams shut behind her seconds later, leaving me to drown in a sea of regret as her soul-piercing words echo in my mind.

Sinking into one of the leather couches, I whisper to the empty room.

"I would never hurt you, Dove."

But the walls don't answer.

I shouldn't have been so insistent, but I guess a treacherous hope had already nested in my heart after our night together.

Vesta will forever be a free spirit, and I'd rather die than attempt to cage her. I won't force her hand anymore. She can have whatever she wants from me, and if it's nothing she seeks, I'll give her that, too.

Laying down on the sofa, I close my eyes for a few hours before burying myself in the mountain of paperwork I still need to get through to avoid thinking.

When my eyes tire again, I get up and help myself to Azran's liquor cabinet. I twirl the amber liquid in the glass while looking out the window into the courtyard.

My trained eyes narrow on a rider approaching the palace gates.

I'm out of the office in seconds, making for the stairs to meet the messenger outside the palace.

I've been waiting weeks for a word from Brimora. Queen Aanor has been reluctant to engage in talks with us and refuses offer after offer.

The missive is either from her or Zetrea. Either way, I cannot spare a second.

The first light of day shines its soft light on the white paving stones of the courtyard as I exit the palace and descend the stairs.

With my attention focused on the rider coming through the gates, I almost don't notice a furtive shape enter the garrison on the other side of the courtyard. I only get a glimpse of the soldier sneaking back to their quarters, but it tells me all I need to know. With long red hair and a short black dress, Vesta disappears behind a door in the blink of an eye.

Clenching my jaw, I return my focus to the horse trotting on the cobblestones. The rider hops off their mount a few feet from me.

"General."

They hand me a missive with a quick bow.

"At ease."

I dismiss the tired Fae with a smile and break the seal on the letter. It's from Brimora.

My eyes dart to the piece of paper and the words traced on it. A grunt tears from my throat by the time I finish reading.

Queen Aanor wants to see Ela. She won't agree to a meet unless the human-turned-Fae attends, and their army will stand their ground until they've confirmed we present no imminent threat.

That's going to prove a tad difficult, given Ela's current situation. I hope to the gods she finds Az and that her big mouth doesn't land us in even bigger troubles.

My mood is souring further by the day as I wait for news and I'm left behind to deal with Braern's aftermath.

***

Averion's streets buzz with activity for the solstice.

I usually enjoy this day, but this year feels different. We still haven't received word from Ela, although she's been in Nyths for almost two weeks. I've been in shit positions far too many times to not recognize the feeling forming in my heart.

I put up a brave front nonetheless, smiling, greeting, and engaging with our citizens like I always have.

Vesta is never far behind me, silent and focused on scanning our surroundings.

The cold afternoon doesn't deter anyone and the crowded streets overflow with merchants, musicians, and flowers. The aroma of sweets and pastries coats the air as I go from stall to stall, shaking hands and complimenting the sellers on their products.

The celebration goes well into the night with gift exchanges and dancing, two traditions of this solstice. And when the night falls, the city lights up and the fun begins. Lanterns and candles adorn each doorstep and window, with some inhabitants even putting up light garlands between buildings.

Cheers erupt all around us at intervals as offerings are made to bring luck for the coming year.

Families smile back at me, blissfully ignorant to the menacing storm brewing across seas and to our southern borders. Each wave takes a chunk out of my heart. Each smile is a reminder of what I don't have and that the only family I've ever known is far away, in danger.

I used to torture myself wondering why I couldn't have what everyone else does. A partner. Someone to share my life with. Someone to love and be loved by.

Before losing my family in the unifying wars, the only thing I was ever praised for as a child was my fighting skills. For a time I believed that if I became the best at it, my parents would finally see me. But they never did, and I ended up finding Az, betraying them, and earning a lethal skill set in the process. My parents passed and never rescinded their banishment. The day I gained a brother, they lost a son.

I don't regret doing what I did, but some actions simply have soul-altering consequences. I now understand why I can never walk the path of life with someone by my side. The blood coating my hands can never be washed, and I can never be worthy of the love I used to seek.

It's well after midnight when I make it back to the palace, exhausted and numb from the buzz of the city. I dismiss my guards and head straight to my room, ready to crash on my bed and forget the weight that's dragging me down. I slip under the covers naked, too tired to bother with a shirt.

I don't remember falling asleep, but I wake a couple of hours later in the darkness. My eyes beg to close again, stinging and in pain from what little sleep I managed to get.

I turn in bed, laying on my side to try and steal a couple more hours of rest. I feel myself falling when a scratch on my door startles me.

Fingernails are slowly rasping on the door, intentionally.

My palm closes around my knife before letting go.

Someone is adeptly and quietly working to gain entry, their stealthy movements barely discernible.

Vesta's shape comes into view moments later as she closes the door behind her.

"Good evening, Dove."

She freezes, probably letting her eyes adjust as I sit on the bed, the covers already pushed back.

She walks up to me until she stands between my legs, her skin almost touching mine.

"All my other *friends* call me V."

My hands shoot up, finding purchase around her waist and ass, locking her in.

"All your other friends will be six feet under if you mention them again, Dove."

A growl forms in my throat and her crystal laugh fills the room in response.

CHAPTER 16

Elanor

With Nylren as my guide once more, the garden is unusually silent, our footsteps on the graveled path the only disturbance.

The palace grounds have an eerie stillness to them, devoid of birdsong or wildlife of any kind. Twisted, spiky vines and thickets of thorns dominate the landscape, covering every inch not occupied by the stone trail. It's less a garden and more of a maze of hostile vegetation, arranged in dense barricades with narrow passages. Shadows cling to the overgrown corners and even the flowers bloom in threatening strangling clusters rather than cheery beds. Unease grows with each step I take, and I find myself longing for Averion's joyful gardens.

When King Airdan announced he would be busy over the next few days, I thought I would finally get the chance to investigate the city. My excitement quickly dimmed as I realized he wouldn't leave his guest alone, assigning his son to accompany me instead.

As each hour passes, angst floods every bone in my body. I'm nowhere closer to finding Azran. I'm kept busy with useless walks within the palace walls, introductions to nobles, fancy dinners, and pointless displays of artwork.

I've got to admit that Nylren's reserve makes for a surprisingly comfortable companion. Less diplomacy and decorum are needed with him, since he doesn't talk much.

At least Milan doesn't leave my side. He follows me everywhere, always a few steps behind me through this joke of a mission turned golden cage.

We discussed sending him or one of his men into Nyths, but opted against it. They would be spotted in an instant and there is no legitimate official reason I could use to explain that away, but I'm not giving up.

I spent the last few days looking for a way to get information, and as it turns out, I have one. I'm looking at it right now.

Cold air whips my face as I study Nylren. His gaze is fixed on the horizon. Eye contact is not really his thing, and he spends most of our time together looking at his shiny black boots. He must have memorized each detail of the shoes by now, from the way the leather folds with his steps to the silver buckle around his ankles.

There's something about him. I got a glimpse at his relationship with his father over dinner, and let's just say that their dynamic is weird at best. The only father-child relationship I've ever witnessed was mine, and ours was never that distant.

Airdan always appears put together, confident, and charming, but Nylren's different. I just need to figure out if he can be trusted enough for me to attempt something. I need to play a more subtle game than the one I'm used to. Hell, subtlety has never been my thing, but I can learn, right?

Straight up asking him for help is out of the question, but maybe he could be useful some other way. I can't afford to sit still any longer. Staying put, surrounded by frivolities and sterile conversation, is killing me.

I'm restless, my power unstable, and even my connection to the spirit world and Savage is not enough to keep me hopeful.

Nylren clears his throat before pointing to a small turret ahead.

"The armory and training grounds are over there. Do you dabble with the sword?"

"Yes." The word leaves my mouth with more enthusiasm than anticipated, so I quickly add, "sometimes."

I calm my racing heart, reminding myself I can't go around parading my fighting skills.

"We should go." Nylren nods towards the palace. "It'll give you something more exciting to do."

We exchange one of our rare moments of eye contact, and the tiniest smile tugs his lips. I guess I'm not doing the best job at pretending that I'm entertained.

**

I plop down on the edge of my bed as I soon as I make it back to my room, Milan right behind me. Holding back my strikes with Nylren has proven even more testing for my sanity. It does nothing to ease the tension in my body, far from it.

"At this rate, it is going to take me weeks to gain Nylren's trust."

"Do you really think he can help?" Milan's dark eyebrows shoot up on his forehead.

"What other option do I have?" I raise my hands in defeat. "I can't walk into the royal chambers demanding a battalion of soldiers to start searching for Azran."

"Don't you think it's weird that the High Lord got to Nyths with a delegation but never made it to the palace?" Milan asks quietly.

My mouth opens and closes again as I consider his words. Tilting my head, I study his face. Milan can be stoic, but if there's one thing I've learned, he doesn't speak idly. And Calen wouldn't have assigned him to my guard if he didn't trust him.

"You think—"

He shakes his head and silences me with a wave of his hand before pointing to his own eyes and ears.

My brows draw together at his implication.

I can't say the idea's never crossed my mind, but I dismissed it early on, as I couldn't make sense of the King's potential motivation in this mess. Maybe I dismissed him too quickly, though.

Could he be tangled in this shit? What would he gain? And if not him, could someone else here know something?

I smooth the skirt of my violet dress and sit up straight.

"You may go, Milan. I will retire for the night."

His brow furrows at my sudden change of tone, but I nod reassuringly.

Once alone, I prepare for bed, and by the time Jaida enters to help me, I'm already under the covers.

"My Lady, is there anything else you'll be needing tonight?"

I repress a yawn, covering my mouth with my hand. "No, thank you. I will rest, now."

After Jaida closes the door behind her, I pull out the book I brought with me to Nyths from under the mattress and flip through its pages.

I've read it from front to back, but it's gotten me nowhere. Just like Mor said, gods used to walk this earth ages ago, taking carnal form and toying with the forces of good and evil. Death was among them, reaping the souls of those whose time had come, and keeping a watchful eye over the balance of the world.

The gods no longer dwell among us, taking their names with them as they departed, and leaving only the phantoms of their purposes in old texts. Death, Nature, War, Love, Fertility, and Justice.

In places, the pages are so worn the letters have blurred, making them impossible to decipher. I don't know what made them leave, or why Death inhabits me, but I'm determined to find out. Did we provoke their wrath or expel them? Was the world a better or worse place without them in it?

Part of me refuses to entertain the idea the gods were a menace, for that would confirm my worst fear—evil stirs inside me, threatening those I love.

Settling back into the pillows behind me, I call on my power and retreat inwards, seeking peace and calm. The dark energy instantly floods my body and mind, taming the fear and angst, although never truly able to hide the still-strained bond.

I live in a constant state of hurt, my heart set on fire, never truly numb even with my power set free, but it's the best I've got. A part of me never wants the pain to go away, not until I've found Az and told him what I need to tell him. In a fucked-up way, I'm still connected to him, and I'll take this over his complete absence or the excruciating hurt I tasted when he laid in my arms, his blood decorating the grass around us.

Hours later when sleeps threatens to take me, I resist, searching for the pain, exploring the most horrifying memories I have to keep me up, to keep me focused and alert.

When I'm sure the whole palace is asleep, I toss my covers aside.

I'm up in seconds, already dressed. I eye my boots in the corner of the room but opt for leaving without. Although the palace is covered in rugs, I can't risk the sound of my soles hitting the floor.

I open the door just enough to glance around the corridor. The movement attracts the attention of Gavriel and Seth, standing guard in front of my room.

With my finger pressed against my mouth before a word leaves theirs, I step into the hall. I sign for them to stay put and close the door behind me. Both pairs of eyes shoot daggers, but I don't care. We all know they can't make a scene and wake Milan. I give them a knowing look before sneaking away, assured of their cooperation.

My heart pounds in my chest like a drum, the rhythmic thud echoing in the silence of the deserted halls. I turn a corner and call on my power, cloaking myself in shadows. The halls are eerily silent except for the sizzling oil of the torches.

In the dimly lit corridors, elongated and distorted shadows dance along the walls, cast by flickering torchlight behind sculptures and art pieces, turning the place into a haunted castle with monstrous figures lurking in the corners of my vision.

The darkness of my power envelops me, clinging to my every move as I press myself against the cool, rough surface of the corridor.

As I move cautiously, the distant creaks of the ancient palace settling into the night accompany me. Fear tinges the edges of my consciousness, making every creak and flicker an ominous sign of potential discovery.

I haven't forgotten the last time I tried sneaking around in a palace, and every instinct in me screams to go back to my room.

The last time didn't exactly go well, only it was in Averion, a place I've learned to call home.

With each passing moment, the tension heightens and keeps my senses on high alert, but thankfully the useless walks around the palace have at least helped me memorize the layout.

My pulse stops sounding so loudly in my ears as I manage to get a grip and find my way through the empty hallways, my target in mind.

I enter a spiral stairway, pausing on the landing to listen for footsteps. The steps have been left bare, with no rugs to muffle sounds, which could play both in my favor and disadvantage. I've mapped out the way to the royal chambers a thousand times in my head, and this is the trickiest part. If I encounter someone in the stairwell, I'll be royally fucked. The hiding spots are almost nonexistent.

I listen carefully for sounds of another soul wandering the corridors but come up empty.

I begin climbing the stairs, holding my breath as I count the steps and landings I come across. The royal wing is two floors up.

With a hand against the cold stones, I let my steps guide me until footsteps echo from above. I freeze.

Sending a rush of power to crush the wave of fear forming in my heart, I consider my options. By my count, I'm closer to the upper floor than the lower one, but if the night stroller is closer to me than I think, I could run right into them if I keep going.

With no time to further weigh my options, I climb steps two at a time, careful not to make a sound, silently thanking my past self for deciding to go barefoot and praying to whichever gods decided to put me on this earth.

The footsteps are getting closer and a shape appears on the stone walls of the tower I'm climbing. My blood freezes. I have mere seconds before I'm discovered.

I crush myself against the far wall, gathering my shadows and calling on the darkness around me to make me hers and shield me. If they're carrying a torch, I'm done for.

My hands search the stone behind me as the shadow stretches, confirming the passerby has light, until my fingers find purchase in an opening. I step aside and discover an arrow slit in the wall, the opening so narrow I didn't notice it on the way up.

The gods may be looking out for me after all.

Squishing myself into the tiny opening, I clear the steps, darkness still wrapped around me, just in time for a hooded figure to round the bend. I press myself against the cold stone wall, the rough texture digging into my back as I melt into the shadows.

The figure hurries downstairs, the hood casting a deep shadow over their face, rendering their features indistinguishable. A solitary torch clutched in their gloved hand illuminates the immediate vicinity, sending dancing tendrils of light across the stone steps. The flickering flames cast a warm, golden glow that briefly reveals the metal buckle on the figure's boots.

The hooded figure's cape billows behind them, a dark cascade that conceals any hint of their identity. The only sound that betrays their presence is the soft shuffle of boots against the cold stone, echoing through the narrow passageway.

I release a breath when they're too far to hear, and quickly make my way out of this damned spiral stairway.

I crouch against a wooden chest in the hallway, giving myself a few seconds to regulate my breathing.

I've been to fucking hell and back, quite literally. I can do this.

Azran's face appears in my mind, and I keep going, set on finding out what goes on behind closed doors here.

I make it to the royal wing, but freeze on the stairs' landing. Light is streaming from a doorway a few steps away. The King and Prince's chambers are further down, and I'm not sure what lies behind this door.

Looking both ways, I get closer as muffled voices reach my ears. I repress a grunt of frustration when I realize I can't make out the words, but don't dare lean my head against the wood.

A laugh resounds, chilling me to my bones, high-pitched, unrestrained, and *familiar*.

The hair rises on my arms as I listen attentively for another hint.

I step away abruptly when steps approach, warning that someone is coming to the door. I dive behind an unidentifiable piece of furniture.

I wait for the door to open, but it never does, keeping its occupants and their secrets frustratingly out of reach. The footsteps retreat. Letting out a slow breath, I make for the spiral stairway once more and head back to my room as fast as I can.

I can't recall how many times my heart almost stopped in the last hour. I'm done for the night. I learned my lesson in Averion and won't take unnecessary risks out here.

I don't know who I'm dealing with but I'm not about to find out by getting caught wandering the castle in the middle of the night. I doubt my charm would be enough to fend off inquiries.

CHAPTER 17

ELANOR

There is no mistaking the look Milan shoots me when I exit my room the next morning in Jaida's tow.

Being constantly accompanied by an escort has its perks when it comes to avoiding a scolding from my protector after my nightly escapade.

I don't even make eye contact with him. There's nothing Milan could say that I haven't already told myself.

It was dangerous, but worth it.

Granted, my heart almost gave out about a hundred times, but I learned that secrets are definitely being kept in this place. I couldn't identify the owner of the laugh or the mysterious hooded figure, but not getting caught is still a win in my book. It's at least given me the confidence, or illusion, that I can do this.

I spend the morning browsing through pointless books in one of the palace libraries, the King and Nylren busy tending to other business.

I'm also left alone for lunch, although always under the supervision of Jaida. Once I finish eating, I push my chair back just as the doors open and a servant enters.

"Prince Nylren will meet you in the training center, Lady Elanor."

"Very well." Onto the next steps of my plan, then.

Milan still hasn't said a word to me, silently brooding a few steps behind me as we walk the palace.

When we enter the training center, Nylren is already there.

"Your Highness."

He turns as I step inside, greeting me with a small smile. Dark purple circles his bloodshot eyes today, revealing his exhaustion, although he tries hiding it with a polite upturn of his lips. Suffering seems etched in every line of his haggard face.

"I hope your day was pleasant so far, Elanor."

The door closes behind me and I turn back, confirming Jaida is gone, leaving me alone with Nylren and Milan. The guard goes to stand in a corner by the entrance of the plain room. With large windows, the only decoration on the stone walls, this is by far the least ostentatious room in the palace.

"Very. How was yours, your Highness?"

"Monotonous." He motions towards the weapons rack. "Governing can be like that."

I follow after him, eyeing one of the long swords on the table and extending my hand to grab it.

"I would recommend the short sword, Elanor. It might be better suited for your stature."

I freeze mid-air, considering the rest of the weapons placed before me.

"Of course." I grip a small blade instead, biting back a retort. "Thank you."

I make eye contact with Milan as I turn around and find a twinkle of amusement in the guard's gaze.

I spend the next hour training next to Nylren, listening to his recommendations with a smile. My power remains locked away and I hold back my blows, carefully playing my part in this game of pretense.

Nylren trains with knives, aiming at a target on the wall. His grip on the blades a little loose, he misses most hits, but I keep my mouth shut.

I go through basic routines, slower than I normally would, barely breaking a sweat but pretending to be out of breath every now and then.

"Does Azran encourage all Fae to wield swords in Lóna?" Nylren's voice fills the air as one of his knives hits the target.

My heartbeat quickens and I clear my throat as I lower my blade.

"The High Lord doesn't discourage it."

The Prince goes to pick up his blades and I give him a small smile.

"I met him, you know? Azran." My blood freezes and I stretch my shoulder blades to cover my reaction. "We were both children at the time."

I chuckle lightly, trying my best to hide the shock of hearing my mate's name on his lips.

"I had no idea, your Highness."

"Different times."

He shrugs off his words with a tight smile, leaving me wondering.

Little by little, Nylren is opening up, confirming I shouldn't dismiss the possibility of working with him. As the days go by, I'm starting to see a softer, more approachable side to the Prince.

"To be honest, I don't usually train as much, though I appreciate you making time to join me," I say, to keep the conversation going.

"I know how dull the palace life can be while my father is otherwise occupied."

"And I appreciate that, your Highness."

"You don't have to call me that when it's just us." He looks around. "Nylren is fine."

Taking this as a sign of trust, I decide to see how far this progress can get me. Maybe I'll be able to steal a few hours alone.

"Sounds good, Nylren." I stretch out my arm, faking the fatigue and strain in my muscles. "Do you mind if we call it a day and I go get cleaned up?"

"Of course." He puts down his knives and calls for a servant to accompany Milan and me back to my room.

As we walk through the palace, I go over different scenarios in my head. If I'm quick enough, I can make my way out of the palace and into the city.

If anyone comes looking for me, I can feign ignorance saying there was an opening in my day. King Airdan told me there would be time to explore Nyths, after all.

I almost slam my door in Milan's face when I get back, eager to bathe quickly and seize the opportunity.

I open the faucet and remove my clothes while I wait for the water to fill, leaving them bunched up on the floor.

Once there's enough water for me to get in, I sink into the warm bath, allowing myself a few minutes to relax before grabbing the soap. A floral scent fills the air as I rub my body clean and rinse.

I stand in the tub, ready to get out, and look for a towel. Shit. I left it in the bedroom.

I hop out of the bath and go to the vanity where a small hand towel awaits. I pat my face dry and squeeze the excess water out of my hair with it, letting water drip on the dark floors. That will do for now.

I quickly brush my hair in front of the condensation-covered mirror, keeping my reflection hidden, but I put down the brush when hair rises on my arm.

Goosebumps erupt all over my body as a cold wind blows through the room, sending the sheer curtains rustling, and my vision darkens. My power responds immediately, and my connection to the spirit world awakens.

A window slams shut and I startle, my concentration lost.

I take in the room and chuckle, relaxing my shoulders to shake away the paranoia.

In the mirror, the steam from the bath is evaporating little by little, and my reflection comes into focus. Something stirs in the corner of the reflective glass and I grab the towel to wipe the rest of the fog.

A cry dies on my lips when my mouth is covered by the hand of an intruder, and I drop the towel on the floor.

His other arm finds purchase around my waist, securing my arms in place. His muscles tighten against my resistance until I freeze in his embrace.

Tears fill my widened eyes as long hair brushes my naked shoulders. Seconds later, he removes his hand from my mouth and lets it fall to my neck.

My mate's crimson eyes are staring back at me in the mirror, his face bruised and cut.

I sag against Azran's chest, needing to feel his body and smell his scent to confirm I'm not dreaming.

His chin slowly rests on my head as he lets out a heavy sigh, his fiery gaze locked with mine, and the bond explodes in my chest.

The constant ache is relegated to a distant memory, all traces of doubt and hurt erased. My heart swells and tears roll down my cheeks as shock makes room for relief and ethereal harmony. He's here, he found me, just like he always promised.

I lower his hand to my chest, needing his touch more than anything I've ever longed for in this life.

"Why did you come here?" His tense voice is barely more than a whisper in my ears, yet I've never craved the sound of it more.

My trembling hands go to his, tightening his hold around my body.

"I was looking for you." My voice breaks, unable to hide the storm of emotion flooding me. "No one's heard from you in weeks. What happened?"

"I'll explain later." His crazed eyes scan the room. "We have to go."

I try to hold his forearms, but he pulls away and motions towards the wardrobe for me to get dressed.

His name dies on my lips when I meet his gaze, redder and angrier than I remember.

Dried blood covers his torn clothes and his left thigh sports a mean gash, still oozing fluid. I'm about to argue when the look in his eyes registers.

The closest state I've ever seen him in was back in Adria, when the two of us were fighting against a horde of rebels, but this is different. He looks panicked, demented almost.

Az scans the room like a caged animal, so I hurry to the bedroom and put on a shirt. He follows after me, his leg dragging slightly.

Digging inside the wardrobe for a pair of pants, my fingers stub against a ridge inside the massive piece of furniture. I almost miss it the first time, but there is no mistaking the lever I just found. I grab the edge of it and pull, revealing a small door and passageway, wide enough for an adult.

"Is it how you—"

"Shh." His eyes widen and I pull my arm out of the closet.

A sharp rasp sounds at the door, and before I can even turn, Az is a blur, vanishing into the closet.

My pulse roars as the handle rattles and slowly twists to reveal King Airdan, frozen in the doorway.

Heat floods my cheeks as I scramble to snatch a robe and cover myself.

"My apologies for the intrusion, Elanor." The King doesn't bother averting his gaze and shines his brightest smile at me instead. "I've cleared my schedule for the evening in hopes you will forgive my failings as a host."

He takes a step closer as I clutch my robe tightly.

"Join me for dinner," Airdan offers, his invitation phrased like a request, though his tone brooks no argument.

My mind races, picturing Az hiding just feet away. One wrong move and I will expose our ruse and endanger us both.

"I... of course, Your Majesty." I lower my eyes demurely, hoping Airdan can't hear my heart slamming inside my chest. A predator's patience radiates from him as he observes me, seconds ticking by like an eternity.

"Meet me in the dinning room when you're ready."

His eyes wander on my neck and legs before he looks away and makes for the door.

I'm ready to release the breath I've been holding when he turns back.

"I'm looking forward to an evening together."

"Me too, your Majesty," I say as I lower my head in deference.

I barely hear the door close with the blood pulsing in my ears.

My heart sinks when I turn around and find Azran emerging from the secret passageway. His hate-filled eyes land on the door before meeting mine. But it's not Azran standing before me, a shadow of him maybe, the enraged monster.

"I can't go," I whisper, though we both already know it. My absence would raise alarms in seconds.

A storm rages within the bond as dark waves wash over it. The tender male I found in Averion is long gone. The warlord who never abandoned me, too. He's been replaced by a beast, rage bleeding from every pore.

"I'll meet you here tonight." The words rasp between his barely parted lips. His chest heaves like he's been sprinting, limbs coiled with dangerous energy. He looks out of breath and out of his mind.

"Wait—"

I reach for him instinctively, but he's already vanishing down the secret passage.

CHAPTER 18

ELANOR

My hands shake as I put on the first dress I find and twist my hair in a simple bun. I finish buttoning the front of the dress with shaky fingers and sit on the edge of the bed.

Tears well in my eyes as my hands slide loosely into my lap. What the fuck is going on? Azran is here, alive, although his mind seems to be holding on by a thread. His horror-stricken features forever engraved in my head, I can't shake the panic swelling in my heart.

How could I have not noticed the secret passageway earlier? It was right under my nose all this time. A gateway to Az and gods know what else. Has he uncovered Braern's allies and gotten tangled up with them?

He barely looked at me. I wince as I remember the darkness running through the bond. Maybe he changed his mind after Adria. Maybe he...

I stand, stopping myself from going there. One thing at a time. First, I need to get this dinner over with so I can get the fuck out of here and bring Az back to Averion. Cal and Vesta will know what to do.

I scrawl a vague excuse about urgent business in Averion on a scrap of parchment and leave it prominently on the bed. As soon as dinner ends, I am fleeing this gilded prison. Mending political ties can wait, getting to Azran can't.

My skin crawls, recalling the King's unwanted advances since my arrival. Some are likely calculated maneuvers, probing for advantage in future negotiations, but the undisguised hunger in his gaze tells me that's not all there is to it.

If playing to Airdan's attraction gains me freedom tonight, I can't dismiss the option. It's merely another weapon in my arsenal. The thought twists my gut, but I'm desperate. I need this plan to work without a hitch.

A vibration in my power directs my attention to a corner of the room, and warmth washes over me. The wolfish shape of my faithful companion takes form. He's always here when I need him most.

"I miss you, Savage," I whisper. "I could really use you here."

His white eyes twinkle as he wags his tail happily, rekindling a sliver of hope in my heart. Everything will be fine. After dinner, I'll see Azran again and he'll explain everything. We'll slay our enemies and go home together. He was probably unsettled because he didn't expect me to come here and I know he doesn't want anything to happen to me. I momentarily let my fears get to my head, that's all.

Once we've destroyed the last of Braern's poison, we'll have eternity together.

The thought brings a smile to my face and courage to my heart. I found him. The strain in the bond is gone and the darkness will finally retreat for good in my life. I'm ready to leave it all behind and embrace happiness. I *fucking* deserve it.

Smoothing my dress with one last fortifying breath, I steel myself to face the King again.

<hr>

An hour later, servants clear our main courses to make way for dessert and a guard walks into the dining room to murmur in the King's ear.

I force myself to breath evenly and keep my eyes on the Prince sitting across from me rather than let my imagination run wild.

True to form, Nylren hasn't said much and barely meets my gaze even as our plates are whisked away unfinished.

At his father's sharp nod, Nylren rises and steps out of the room while the guard takes position behind the King. The sudden move raises the hairs on my neck, but I maintain a neutral mask.

"May I say that Nyths suits you well, Elanor?" The King brushes his hand through his dark hair, letting it fall over his emerald eyes.

"You are beaming, tonight. Any particular reason? Did you best my son at swords?"

"I owe it to you, your Majesty." I chuckle the compliment off. "You've gone out of your way and spared no effort to make sure I enjoy my time here." His green eyes sparkle in response, clearly enjoying the praise. "Thank you, your Majesty."

"You're most welcome." He grabs his cup of wine and sips on it slowly, not breaking eye contact with me. "Anything for you, Elanor."

Airdan's pupils cloud with ever-growing desire as servants return to place ornate dessert displays between us.

I take a small helping of a fruit pie sitting in front of me to escape his intense gaze. I can play the flustered lady a little longer if it'll earn me his clemency when he finds out I'm gone. Plus, I don't want to appear in a rush and raise alarms.

The door to the room creaks open once more and Nylren takes a seat back at the table, his expression unreadable. His hands disappear under the table to his lap and unease settles in.

I politely engage in conversation with Airdan as best as I can until desserts are removed too.

My heart races when Airdan clears his throat and leans back, signaling he's finished. Fucking finally. A few more minutes and I'll be with Az, just a few more minutes.

"Thank you for another lovely meal, your Majesty."

"But of course, my dear." He waves both of his hands in the air. "You have a lovely night."

Seizing my opportunity, I stand and bow gracefully before making for the closed doors, knowing that Milan is waiting in the corridor. I haven't had the opportunity to tell him about Azran yet, but I'm sure he'll be just as eager as me to leave Nyths.

I stare at the wooden panels as my steps resonate on the floor, my heart beating out of my chest. Freedom is within reach and I'm ready to leave politics behind. It never suited me.

I slow as I wait for the royal guards to open the doors until I eventually come to a halt. The soldiers don't budge an inch, still as stone while they stare at some point behind me.

I clear my throat awkwardly, unsure if I should formally ask for the doors to be opened or wait a moment longer. Neither Fae acknowledges my presence.

"You really think I'm going to let you go like that, Elanor?"

My stomach sinks as I turn around to face the King and his son.

"What do you mean?" I swallow the knot in my throat. "Your Majesty."

"You think I'd let an exquisite, murderous creature like you escape my grasp?" All trace of charm has left his viridian irises and his face has turned cold. "You don't think I have eyes and ears in my own home? Or in Lóna, for that matter?"

My mouth drops open and my hand instinctively goes to my back, missing Nahtar more than ever because there is no mistaking the threat in Airdan's tone.

"Seize her," Airdan commands.

I call out to Milan at the same time and spin to face the approaching guards. Retreating until my thighs hit the long table, I call on my power and my vision darkens.

Muffled shouts and steel clashing on steel sound behind the door, confirming Milan heard me.

When the first guard lunges at me, I hit him with lethal energy. I don't watch as his body goes limp against the wall and focus on my second opponent instead, letting obsidian smoke swirl around my hands. I'm not holding back anymore.

The wooden door gives way beneath Milan's weight, shards flying as his body tumbles across the threshold and crashes to the floor.

My eyes widen at the blood pooling beneath his chest and his lifeless stare. More soldiers take position in the doorway.

Rage floods my veins and my hand shoots out towards them, hoping to open a passage. Dark ribbons leave my fingertips before evaporating into thin air, the energy sucked out of my body as a metal collar locks around my neck. Pain drills through my head as fire extinguishes within me instantly. My power is replaced with acid burning through my nerve endings, paralyzing me as the spirit realm retreats before disappearing in an internal blast that shakes me to my core.

I turn, wide-eyed, and find Nylren stepping away from me, his harsh gaze meeting mine without reserve as Airdan's maniacal laugh fills the room.

"We know all about you, Unifier."

"You can't do this," I say through gritted teeth, pain still radiating through my entire body.

"Watch me," Airdan answers.

My arms get twisted behind my back and shackled, straining the muscles in my shoulders. A growl tears through my throat as I try to fight back, but each movement sends needles into my brain and I can't see clearly anymore.

"It's a shame, really. I thought I was beginning to win you over." Airdan walks around the table to face me while his guard tightens his hold on me. "But you only came here to spy for your High Lord."

The King's fingers go to my chin, caressing it gently. "Or should I say, your mate?"

I manage to free my head from his touch as madness flirts with me at his mention of Azran.

"Where is he?" I bark back.

"Sorry, I interrupted your little reunion earlier." Airdan's laugh fills the room once more, a dark and sinister sound. "I hope it was worth it, because that's the last you'll ever see of him."

A cry escapes my lips as I thrash in my bonds, my head exploding with each attempt. Liquid drips down my nose and into my mouth, leaving a coppery taste on my tongue, but I don't care.

Rage blinds me, mixing with the pain as my skin is set on fire, the blood in my veins turning poisonous and burning everything in its path. I think I dislocate my shoulder in the process, but I can't really tell. Everything hurts so bad it doesn't make a difference.

"Save your energy, Elanor." A devilish smile forms on Airdan's handsome face. "You're going to need it."

Agony blazes through every nerve, but my own suffering hardly registers. All I can see behind my clenched eyelids is Azran's face. He's in danger, maybe already dead, and I'm powerless to save him.

The collar and shackles sap my strength as effectively as the pain. I strain against them desperately, letting the metal bite at my skin as I rack my brain for a way out. I can't lose Azran again, not when we got so close to leaving this place.

The bond is obscured by torment, but I cling to the hope he's still alive. I would know if he was dead, I would know.

I repeat it like a mantra, using the words to focus past the blinding agony. Azran's alive. I'm alive.

I resist with everything I've got until blood fills my mouth, its metallic taste lingering on my tongue, and the world goes dark.

PART II

THE GHOST OF NYTHS

"This is my game now."

CHAPTER 19

Nylren

Father sits back in his chair, putting both feet up on the empty dinner table. I haven't moved since the guards took Elanor's body away, merely replaying the scene in my head, relishing in the surprise on her face when I put the collar around her neck.

She never suspected she'd walked into the devil's lair and my own personal hell. Although Father's charm is legendary, she would have never joined him willingly. And now, I will find a way to use her capture to my advantage.

I shall do as Father wishes so he never suspects my darkest desires. He seeks to break her, turn her into one of his weapons, and I will oblige his every command. While he loses himself in his obsession over her, I will spin my own web, setting pieces on the board, in the shadows. Father will be so enthralled by her potential, he will fail to see the growing threat.

"You did good, Nylren. I'm proud of you."

Air is sucked out of my lungs by the words leaving my father's poisonous throat, and a hint of guilt flares in my cold heart. If only he knew what I have in store for us.

"Your mother would be, too," Father adds.

I still perfectly and meet his gaze as he mentions her. He so rarely speaks of her that I'm left on edge, waiting for more.

It's not love I feel for her, but mere curiosity. The desire to understand the monster sitting in front of me, and find another way to gain power over him. Love, I feel for no one, not even myself.

I have no recollection of her. All I've ever known is what her absence created—an endless pit of hate and madness in Father's heart.

The humans had no idea what they would unleash when they killed Airdan's mate eons ago, days after my birth. They sealed their fate, condemning themselves to an eternity of servitude and death under my father's rule.

It's been his mission ever since. Cruel at heart, rather than doom them to extinction, he's vowed to force them all to their knees.

Nothing enrages him more than seeing these frail beings dividing us and driving us to kill each other over them.

"Come. Sit." Father motions towards my chair.

Still in shock from the words of praise, it takes me a moment to put my body in motion. I cautiously take place next to my father as my brain grapples with reality, unable to reconcile the horrors he's put me through with this outburst of appreciation.

The relaxed Fae in front of me clashes with the mental images carved in my head. My face turns to his, but my vision blurs as memories flash in my mind's eye. The sleepless nights spent suffering, unable to find a comfortable position, my body too damaged to bear even a shirt, each gust of wind setting my slashed skin, still oozing blood, on fire. The constant belittling and humiliation. The shell of a person I've had to become to survive. The things I've had to do.

"How did you find out?" He claps his hands with excitement and the visions disappear.

I clear my throat before answering.

"Her eyes."

His smile widens, encouraging me to tell him more.

"They would twitch at the mention of Azran. And I found her sneaking around the palace last night, hiding in the staircase leading to your chambers, although she had no idea she got caught."

"Wonderful." My father brushes his hands through his hair, a force of habit. "That was observant of you."

I keep the rest of the explanation of my discovery to myself. He doesn't need to know the entire truth. In fact, he can never know the entire truth.

It is my best-kept secret and one I will take to my grave, for it holds the one thing I can never share with a living soul. Were someone to find out, they would hold the key to controlling me, absolute power over me.

Were someone to know my worst fears, they would own me.

Fear, in my case, for there is only one.

A mate.

I will never let myself live and breath for another, trapped and at their complete mercy, and gift my father leverage on a silver platter.

I chose my partners cautiously throughout the years, knowing they would all end up dead, hung, or tortured to death. Zavan had recently joined the long list of my ghost lovers.

I researched fated mates for decades, reading every text ever written on the matter. When research wasn't enough anymore, I started abducting couples, holding them in a warehouse in Nyths to study and torture.

I studied their reactions to the presence, pain, or death of their partners. I even pretended to free some, watching as they embraced each other, noting how their scent changed when together, their essence merging, only to catch them again. I whispered their mates' names as they laid strapped to a table, watched their pupils dilate.

That's how I learned about Elanor and Azran.

"You sold her out the second you found out." Father's words stir me from my daydream. "Ruthless like your father."

And I would do it again in a heartbeat. It was nothing personal. She actually tried befriending me, the foolish girl. She doesn't know that there is no room for kindness in this world.

I learned that lesson early on. My father has never let me forget it, which is why I cannot let his poisonous words get to me and threaten my plan.

Although, I must admit that hearing these words from his mouth doesn't leave me indifferent. I didn't realize a part of me still yearns to hear them. Elanor is not the only foolish one, after all.

"I learned from the best." I incline my head slightly, measuring my next words. "I'm curious, Father. How do the collars work?"

He looks away to study his ring-decorated hands.

"That's the thing about immortality, isn't it? After a while, the years blend together, boredom seeps in, and the only way we can keep ourselves entertained is to scheme and wage wars. We flirt with the prospect of our deaths." He raises an eyebrow, daring me to question him. "But no one sees the bigger picture. There is no one alive who remembers how long I've walked this earth. I've made sure of it. No one to remember what I've seen and found."

He pulls out a small notebook from a pocket in his velvet jacket and waves it around. The cover is so damaged, it's a wonder it hasn't disintegrated yet.

"Magic used to be everywhere until we became overconfident and excessively ambitious. Some tried rivaling with gods and the gods took back their gifts. But they were too soft in their punishment, for they left us with one thing."

"Healing magic," I answer bluntly.

"Precisely." He opens the small book, taking a moment to browse through it. "All magic is interconnected, you see? I figured out a way to tap into it and reconnect with the lost forms of power. Nothing is out of reach for me, now."

"And Braern helped you test it."

Father slaps the notebook shut and a rictus forms on his lips.

"Braern was a fool, but a useful one. He was never going to live. He was far too treacherous to keep around, but he served his purpose."

I nod several times, letting him revel in his genius as his fingers go to his neckline, disappearing beneath his dark shirt and revealing the glimmer of a gold chain.

My pulse pounds in my ears as I glimpse the pendant concealed around his neck. Hair rises on my forearms, which I keep hidden under the table, and a theory forms in my mind.

"This is what we've been waiting for, Nylren."

Father removes his feet from the table, straightening his stance, and the pendant disappears.

"Azran and Elanor can yield powers that, once harnessed, will make me invincible. Then, we will set the humans in their rightful places, at my feet or in the ground."

CHAPTER 20

ELANOR

Needles shooting through my skull confirm I'm still alive and bring with them a cruel reminder of my failure.

I've wandered long enough in Death's realm to remember pain has no grasp there, and that I've not been granted immunity to the horrors of the living world. An angel of Death, condemned to suffer the worst humanity has to offer.

"Welcome back, Elanor."

A distant voice rings in my ears as I try to hold on to the darkness, willing my consciousness to escape this place.

Cold seeps through my bones and humidity sticks to the clothes on my back. I have no idea where I am. All I know is I don't want to be here and I shouldn't have let my guard down.

Water drips on the floor, each drop a stab in my head that relegates the sweet reprieve of nothingness further and further away.

Cold metal touches my chin, forcing its way between my lips. Liquid pours over my mouth and down my throat. Instinct kicks in as I choke and spit the foreign drink out, spilling it all over me. It freezes me to the bone and sets my throat on fire.

A violent cough shakes me, pulling on the strained muscles in my arms, which are tied to the chair.

I've never had to imagine what being skinned alive would feel like, but if I were to venture a guess, I'd say it would feel like that. Each nerve ending in my body lights on fire, from the tip of my head to my ankles secured to the chair legs with tight rope.

I blink several times, willing my eyes to open. The room I'm in is dark and empty except for a silhouette in front of me.

Pain flares behind my eyes, neck, and arms as Nylren's face comes into view. My eyes pause on the traitor for a moment before I try turning to see behind me.

I manage a few inches before the pain stops me.

"Azran," I croak, trying to keep panic at bay.

"How's your head?"

Asshole. If only my head was the issue. My entire body is shot up with pain. Each thump of my heart brings a new wave of impossible hurt, like acid pumping through my veins, boiling, sharp.

"Where is he?" I grit out behind clenched teeth.

"You're asking the wrong question." Nylren approaches with the cup, and this time I pinch my lips closed. "You should be focusing on what's going to get you out of these restraints."

I can't see straight; his image is going in and out of focus.

"What do you want?"

"I want to learn about you and your *abilities*." Nylren gets closer, his face inches from mine as he lowers his voice to a whisper. "I've only ever wanted to help, Elanor."

"Is that why you put this collar around my neck?" I bark back, and ache radiates behind my eyes.

Were my mouth not dry, I'd spit in his face so he'd drop the act. A distorted snarl is the best I manage.

"I suggest you cooperate, Elanor." His brows furrow as he steps away. "You will merely put yourself through endless suffering if you don't, and we'll get what we want either way." Pain retreats long enough to let fear seep in. "Trust me. You don't want to discover the many ways my father has to bend someone to his will."

I look away as searing pain courses my body and my power slowly suffocates, buried so deeply I can barely feel it.

"Don't be stubborn, Elanor. Please."

I clench my jaw hard enough to dispel the tears pooling in my eyes and face him again.

"Go to hell." Our gazes lock. "You do realize playing Daddy's errand boy will never earn you what you seek so dearly?" Shock paints his features, and that view alone makes each word worth the pain. "I guess I'm not the only stubborn one."

A choked laugh tears from my throat and a new wave of acid burns through me.

"You don't know what you're talking about."

"I know this much." I suppress the nausea welling up in my chest with a wince before making eye contact again. "You will be rotting in the ground before the day you feel your father's love."

I'm scanning his face for a reaction, but his cold mask returns.

"You've made your choice, then."

I stare at him with defiance, my chin up and head held high as he walks out of the room, holding my breath.

The first tear rolls down my cheek as the metal door slams and my head drops to my chest. Sobs follow not long after as I try to catch my breath, but come up short of a way to keep the pain at bay.

My gaze fixes on the stone floor, watching as tears pool on my lap, my head pulsing horribly with each moment that passes. I pray for the abyss to claim me again.

⬥

The door closing on its hinges startles me awake, but the King doesn't grant me a look. He walks past me as I remain still, refusing to glimpse behind me and show fear.

"Given that our attempt at friendship has not proved useful, I will spare us both a repeat performance and get to the enjoyable part."

Metal clings as he moves around objects of various sorts.

When he finally comes into view, he still doesn't look at me, completely absorbed by what's in his hands. Leather straps hang from his palm, each strip decorated by a small carved bone at the end, and he caresses them like a lover.

His tender gaze turns devilish when he takes me in, and the gravity of my situation finally dawns on me. I'm the animal and he's the master, a sick one who's going to take his time and play with me.

I swallow the lump in my throat and focus on his gestures as he moves towards me excruciatingly slowly. The bastard takes his sweet time, building anticipation.

"You know what to do when you've had enough."

Amusement twinkles in his crazed eyes as he circles me, and in that moment I swear to not utter a single word in this room. As Nylren so nicely pointed out, I'm nothing if not stubborn. They're about to learn the true meaning of the word.

I clench my jaw and try retreating inside my head, seeking the familiar place of comfort amidst the pain, knowing it's about to get a thousand times worse. But numbness evades me, the constant drilling in my skull keeping me present and hyper-aware of each nerve ending in my body.

I will endure this. I have to. I've known pain before and this will be no different. This sick fuck loves seeing me like this, and I won't give him the satisfaction of hearing me scream. Over my literal dead body.

A smile tears from his lips, my only signal before the whip falls on my chest.

Tears immediately prickle as fire erupts all over my skin, but I hold back a cry.

Looking down, strips of my dress fall on my lap, red lines decorating my bare skin.

"Stings, doesn't it?" His emerald gaze turns dead cold as I release a short breath, trying to see through watery eyes.

I manage to hold back my screams for the first twenty lashes, until my blood redecorates the floors, until I see stars, until the pain takes over my entire nervous system, until I can't anymore and cries fill the room. I lose count after that, the spiked leather strips robbing me of my last bit of pride.

I thought I had known torture before, not realizing mine had been mental and self-inflicted—a non-negligible difference.

Airdan leaves me hanging on by a thread, waiting for darkness to take me and fulfill the only promise I know holds true in this life, but it doesn't come.

I stop counting the days not long after his first visit, the state of my blue dress the only indication of how much time has passed.

Shreds of bloody fabric hang loosely around my waist and shoulders, my skin laid bare underneath. I would have imagined the temperature of the room to be the last of my worries, but the cold in my bones might be the cruelest form of torture. My body is on fire, acid running through my veins, but I'm freezing to my core, the burn in my wounds intensifying with each breeze that makes its way through the cracks in the door.

My state worsens when I'm on the brink of falling into the shadows. Shaken by trembles, I can't control my body anymore, and each shudder heightens the pain until exhaustion finally takes me, or madness. I can't tell them apart anymore.

With a song of fire and ice inside my head, a poisonous magic pulses in my heart, keeping my power at bay, torturing me when I'm awake.

My joints swell to the point where I can't feel my wrists and shoulders. I can't tell if I've lost my limbs or if it's my brain trying to protect me from further pain. I can't tell if the jolts of pain are phantom when feeling returns to my arms in waves.

My captors have found a way to slow my healing. I figured as much when the ache didn't dull after their first three visits. Sick bastards. The fancy dinners and strolls through the park are long gone.

CHAPTER 21

CALEN

I swallow the amber liquid in one burning gulp. The subtle notes of oak and spice turn to acid on my tongue as I glare at the ominously teetering piles of correspondence, but not even liquor can numb the dread in my heart. Grabbing the first scroll, the words blur as I read reports of violent clashes on our border with Brimora.

Bile sears the back of my throat as the list of the dead and dying imprints on my eyes. Four wounded in our ranks and a dozen humans killed.

I sweep my arm violently across the desk's surface and parchments scatter in an explosion of chaos, glass shattering against the floor, ink bleeding into abstract figures on the pages.

"Damn you, Az."

The curse tears from my throat as I attempt to calm my racing heart.

"You may have doomed us all, this time."

Were it not for his absence, we wouldn't be in this mess. He always has to put his ass on the line for heroic missions, which inevitably leaves me to clean up the mess. He has to be the one to save everyone, and I'm left struggling to prevent our realm from descending into civil war.

What happens if Azran and Ela are dead, their bodies rotting on a dark street in Nyths? How do I save Lóna?

Rumors are already circulating around their disappearance. Neither have been seen in the city for months, and our people's trust is disintegrating before my eyes.

Units are reporting deserters and none of our messengers have returned from Morilanthe. Amrynn is out there doing gods know what and it reeks of deception. She will do anything to position herself in the widening power void.

Without Azran's vision to unite us, how long can allegiances born from sacrifice and bloodshed withstand before dissolving entirely? If this goes on much longer, the territories will descend into madness and make the unifying wars pale by comparison.

Doubt festers like poison in my heart as I contemplate the possibility that the reward for our years of struggle might vanish in an instant.

My shoulders sag under the invisible weight of my responsibilities and I bend to gather the papers at my feet. Stacking the missives and reports in a pile, I rearrange the desk as best I can.

A small piece of parchment crushed under my boot catches my eye. Flattering the missive as best I can, my gaze traces Vesta's word. Looks like I'll be seeing her tonight.

I let out a heavy sigh. She's the only one keeping me sane, although she's another reminder of all I fear. How can I protect her from what's coming? I can't shield against all threats, not when they're coming from all sides.

A knock warns me before Barus steps in. The intendants' eyes dart to the mess on the floor before his mouth opens.

"Anything I can help you with, General?"

"No, I'm fine." Seeing Barus stand still, I motion towards the scattered paperwork before sitting back in my chair. "I'll take care of it."

The map carved on the surface of the desk draws my attention until Barus clears his throat.

"You may go. I'll call for you if I need anything."

Barus takes a step back hesitantly, his brows furrowed together, but I don't repeat myself. He knows better than to question a direct order.

Returning to the map, I find myself contemplating unthinkable options as my fingers brush over Zetrea's territory. Our world oscillates precariously atop this elaborate house of cards only Azran could maintain, and we're in dire need of strong allies. One decisive gust and everything collapses. Who do I turn to without Azran?

Confronted with the prospect of his indefinite absence, an impossible choice presents itself. I've never met the King of the Fae, but he's by far the oldest and most cunning there is. He's probably older than Mor, and gods know the knowledge and power he holds. Our best chance might lie in an alliance with Airdan.

Bile rises in my throat once more as I consider our options. Do nothing and watch anarchy devour society from within, or dare an alliance.

A plan forms in my mind, a last resort to save the Fae and prevent the realm from descending into chaos. I fist my palm, my decision made. The Fae need a strong and visible leader, not one stuck behind a desk all day.

"Barus," I command as the intendant freezes in the doorway.

"Yes, General."

"I need you to set up a town hall for all citizens in two days' time and a council with Averion's captains tomorrow."

"General?" Barus' eyes widen.

"Times are changing. Set it up." I muster my sharpest tone and let the General in me take over, leaving no room for debate.

"Very well."

Barus retreats with a quick nod, and as soon as the door closes behind him, I dig through the stack of documents in front of me.

I find a blank parchment and a quill and get to drafting until my hand hurts.

Rummaging in the carved desk, I retrieve the official seal and envelopes. Breaking the wax stick with more force than necessary, I hold it to the fire's eager flames before letting molten red beads drip on the four envelops, sealing them.

Tharrion's missive will raise his arched brows, but he was ever the pragmatist. Irann will no doubt require leverage to assure the cooperation of the Wood Fae. Keryth should be receptive to my words. Only Amrynn's response fills me with dread, for she has the most to gain from our disarray. Hopefully the promise of shared rule here will distract her restless ambition, if only temporarily.

Four letters, four hopes for salvaging unity amongst our factions.

Revulsion curdles my stomach, but I force my stiff legs back to the liquor cabinet and swallow another searing mouthful. Liquid courage, or at least numbness, before undertaking the last distasteful task of this awful night.

I draft another short missive that I tuck into the pocket of my trousers. This one doesn't require a seal, for it's going to an old friend, only a single letter to decorate the back of the envelope.

"M.

Dark times await come dawn."

———◆———

When Vesta strolls into my bedroom, I'm ready to surrender every fiber of my being to her touch to escape the dread tightening its hold on my heart.

Worry mingles in her emerald eyes as she sheds her dress, but I pull her close, our bodies the only truth that matters now. Determined to scrub anguished choices from my mind, I let myself drown in this stolen moment until we're both spent.

I sag against the headboard as she pants, her body laying across the bed at an angle. Her chest glimmers, flushed peaks still tight from moments before. As I admire her body, guilt stirs in my gut. Stuck in my own despair, I'd relegated my adoration for her to an afterthought.

"Stay the night," I offer.

Vesta hops off the bed as soon as the words leave my mouth. She grabs her short dress, lying on the floor, and slips it on effortlessly with her back turned to me.

"What's wrong?" I ask, longing for her to unburden her fears and voice every doubt festering inside her so I could banish them for good.

"Dove?" I murmur, craving the gift of her trust.

"Stop calling me that." Her sharp tone rings in the air. "I'm not a bird whose fate is to be caged for a man's pleasure."

I repress a frustrated growl and sit on the edge of my bed, still naked.

"Do you know why I call you that?"

She lets out a huff and turns to face me.

"Because you'd rather have me trapped here with you than free out there. No matter the consequences. No matter if it kills me."

I'm on her in seconds, madness shaking my heart.

"No." I grab her by the throat, tightly enough to silence her but not enough to cut her access to air. I reign in my anger as I wait for her to meet my stare. When she does, challenge lingers in her irises, along with a hint of lust.

"Because doves symbolize freedom, and I've always understood and respected that about you." My thumb brushes against her throat before I release her. That she believes me capable of harming her hurts more than any blade could.

"If being with me feels like a prison, leave," I say. "I don't want that either."

I'm about to step back when her gaze falls on my mouth.

Her hands go to the thin straps on her collarbones and slide them over her shoulders. Her delicate fingers land on my wrist and she pulls me against her.

Warmth radiates from our bodies so close together, and my pulse quickens.

She reaches for a kiss on the tip of her toes, eagerness guiding her tongue as she claims my mouth. My arms wrap around her waist, letting her take the lead.

She pushes me until my back hits the wall, sending a rush of heat through my middle. Her hand grabs mine and guides it towards her throat.

I tighten my hold on her neck and a moan escapes her lips as one of her legs slowly rubs against my thigh.

"Make me sing," she whispers against my mouth, her warm breath caressing on my face.

As she relinquishes control for the first time, I vow to never make her regret it. If it is pain she seeks, I will oblige, merely making her wish she had offered sooner.

I lift her off the ground and press her body against the wall as her legs cross behind my back.

Grinding against her, I devour her neck, licking and biting until her moans fill the air. Her wetness coats my hips as my cock slides against her entrance, circling and taunting.

Her fingers dig into flesh as she grips my shoulders tightly, and her hold threatens to send me over the edge. I am ready to repent for my sins at her altar.

I return my focus to her mouth and position myself at her entrance, still teasing her tense bud of nerves with the tip of my length.

I hold her up with one arm while the other goes back to her neck, gently caressing her skin, feeling her pulse beneath my fingers.

A gasp leaves her mouth when I can't hold back anymore and plunge inside her. I tighten my hold on her throat.

She's dripping with wetness as our bodies collide, each thrust reverberating loudly in the room. Her eyes roll back as I move in and out of her.

She chases her release and I cling to each ecstatic cry—heavenly notes to my ears.

"See how well you take me?" I whisper against her mouth.

I release my hold long enough for her to suck in another breath before I dive back inside her and claim her lips again.

Her release nears as her pussy clenches around my cock and she shatters in my arms.

Vesta loosens her hold on my shoulder and I slowly let her down, my hands on her back to steady her.

I'm readying myself for her to pull away, but she sags against my chest and deposits the softest kiss on my skin instead. I instinctively hold my breath, willing this moment to last a lifetime.

I consider repeating my offer for her to stay, or even for me to have food brought up, but I opt against it. I've pushed her enough for one night.

A newfound trust has bloomed between us tonight, and I will sacrifice all to defend it. Joy swells in my heart as I watch her dress and tie her red hair in a low bun.

"Good night, Dove."

A smile tugs on her swollen lips as she opens the door.

CHAPTER 22

CALEN

After I end the meeting with Averion's captains the following day, Vesta stays behind.

She stands when the door closes, resting her hands on her hips. I cock a brow, waiting to see what she has in store for us.

Slowly approaching, she stops inches from the desk before slamming her hands on its surface.

"Have you lost your mind?" I straighten in my chair as her voice fills the air. "This plan is madness."

"You know as well as I do, there's nothing more we can do for Az and Ela," I answer in a calm tone, refusing to fuel the fire burning in her gaze.

"After all these years defending him, that's how you want to handle this?"

I pinch the bridge of my nose, taming my own emotions before I answer.

"If there was another way, I would go to the ends of the earth to find it, but we're out of options." I clench my jaw. "If we want to save Lóna, we have to do this."

"You've truly lost your mind."

"This was his dream, not mine." I tap my index on the desk. "That's all it ever was, a dream, and now it's gone. Just like they're gone."

As hard as it is to admit, it's the truth.

"So your loyalty really doesn't mean anything."

A growl tears from my throat. "Careful now."

"This is wrong and it will never work." She squints at me before crossing her arms. "I don't want any part in it."

"It's too bad I'm the General and you're not," I snap at her. "My decision is final. We leave within a fortnight."

"So, now you care about rank," she huffs.

Her eyes still carry fire, but my words have hit their mark.

I release a heavy sigh when her shoulders sag and I stand to reach for her hand. She has to understand why I'm doing this.

Vesta snatches her fingers away, brows furrowed and lips pinched, breaking my heart without uttering a single word. Whatever progress we made in the last weeks disappears in the blink of an eye.

"Dove." I soften my tone, hoping it will be enough for her to stay. I don't know if what we have means anything to her, but I can't lose her too.

"Don't," she snarls.

"Out with it." I motion for her to speak with a wave of my hand as irritation blooms in my heart. "I'm doing my best to keep everyone alive, including you. So, what would you have me do?"

She retreats as I round the desk to get closer.

"How am I to behave with you? Because I can't tell anymore."

A frown appears on her forehead before she shakes her head. "Not everything is about us. Why do you have to complicate everything? You're the one who wants more out of this."

"Is that so wrong?"

"Unlike you, I don't need to tie myself down." She chuckles at the words. "I never want the bond again, you hear me? I'd rather go off to war than feel that thing inside me again. To Zetrea it is."

All I've ever wanted was to feel worthy and deserving of true love, her love, to belong and be unconditionally loved in a bond, but I have my answer now.

When my mouth opens, then closes, her features soften.

"I can't do this, Cal. I can't go down that path again."

"What? The bond?"

"Not everything is about the freaking bond. Enough about that." She rolls her eyes at me. "Why do you seek it? It's a curse."

I take this other slap to the face, one more hint and confirmation of my unworthiness. I've felt it my whole life, but I've heard enough.

"Very well. I won't waste your time anymore." I walk to the door and fling it open, not daring to make eye contact. "We both have work to do."

"Great." She walks past me before pausing, her nose wrinkled. "I'm sure you'll have plenty of options for a rebound."

I slam the wood panel within an inch of her face. "That's unfair."

Finally facing her, I let her see the hurt in my eyes.

"Not once did I dangle your nightly escapades in the city in front of your face or ask for exclusivity to your body, and now you throw this in my face, as if it's a likely scenario." My heart tightens as I struggle to keep my voice calm and collected. "I'm not the one finding my bed untouched in the morning."

I regret the words the moment they leave my mouth, but it's too late.

"You know nothing." Vesta pushes me aside with her full strength and swings the door open.

She's halfway across the corridor when she stops abruptly and looks back at me with tears in her eyes. "For the record, I haven't been with anyone else since that night."

⚬

I inspect my reflection in the mirror once more, stopping on the red details in my gold armor. A different kind of battle awaits me today, one with the citizens of Averion.

I haven't spoken with Vesta since yesterday, though I find her waiting by the palace doors, ready to escort me with the High Guard.

As I mount my horse, I glance at her, but she avoids my gaze. Once ready, we ride through the archway delimiting the palace walls and head into Averion.

The closer we get to the city center, the more people we encounter, all headed in the same direction. Most stores are closed, their owners probably at the central plaza. I straighten my spine as we travel the rest of the way, stoically ignoring the gawkers and hushed speculation trailing our passage.

With the hooves of our mounts beating the paving stones, I focus on getting through the next hour. The immensity of my task dawns on me when the High Guard begins clearing a path through the crowd amassed in the plaza.

The whole city has assembled in front of the makeshift platform erected in its center to hear me speak.

We stop our mounts behind the dais draped in crimson and gold fabric, and I wait for Vesta and her unit to spread around the stage before stepping up.

I tower over the assembled masses, holding their nervous chatter in check with a piercing stare. Ripples of silence spread until even the farthest citizens stands in mute attention.

"Citizens of Averion," my voice booms, used to bellowing over battlefield chaos. "It grieves me to confirm rumors about our Lord and Unifier's demise."

Murmurs churn through the crowd at the blunt admission, but I slam my gauntlet against the podium, the sharp crack restoring order. "They abandoned obligations to us all. But I will not abandon our people or this nation, now under my leadership against the growing threat of our enemies."

I sweep my gaze side to side, meeting random sets of eyes to drive the words deeper. "Despair solves nothing. As your new ruler, I vow to defend what we built here with every resource I have." They need confidence now, not sympathy or platitudes. Those can come later, once stability returns.

"The army remains stationed at our borders, and increased patrols will scour the city day and night to safeguard these walls." I pause for greater effect. "Your safety and our unity remains my singular priority."

My final promise rings out over the silent masses, denying further dissent. Time suspends, accompanied with deafening silence, until a lone angry retort knifes towards me from somewhere center-crowd.

"Usurper!"

My blood freezes as the insult echoes between the buildings surrounding the plaza, and it's not long before others repeat it.

"Traitor!"

Soldiers look hesitantly in my direction for instructions, but I signal them to stand down with a wave of my hand. This reaction is to be expected. I became one of them by betraying my own blood, and they all know it. As much as I've tried, I've never been able to truly shake this reputation.

I defied my clan and family to join Azran and worked towards unity just as hard as he did, but people conveniently omit that part.

Hostility fills the air, and the cheerfulness of the Winter Solstice that was mere weeks ago is long gone. Approval has left the faces of Averion's citizens, replaced with fear.

An object hurtles out of the crowd towards me. I twist sharply but Vesta moves quicker, deflecting it with her sword, and tension explodes into chaos.

Cries erupt on all sides as citizens scramble over one another, desperate for a shot at me or an escape. Through the din I glimpse Vesta's features as she scans the crowd, muscles tense, ready for further attacks. Her vivid eyes slice sideways, pinning me briefly. Simmering behind her duty-bound facade lurks fury and accusation. That glance wordlessly conveys her disappointment.

"Guards." I square my shoulders. "Return order to the city. Make sure everyone gets home safely."

The familiar commands help anchor my own whirling doubts.

I step down from the dais moments later, reaching for the reigns of my horse. Vesta follows suit and we ride back to the palace. Once within its safe walls, I order a curfew.

This city needs a grip of steel to prevent further dissent in our ranks. Within the first hour, I've already earned a new nickname, but I refuse to go down in history as only that.

The moment I lock myself in Azran's office, I vow to do whatever it takes to succeed. All that's left now is identify who to bring in on this, for the next steps of the plan requires absolute trust.

CHAPTER 23

ELANOR

A breeze pulls my broken body into its frozen embrace once more as my awareness surfaces.

Footsteps echo around me, but I don't open my eyes. As always, I cling to the mental haze as long as possible. Airdan or Nylren can rot in hell for all I care.

A snarl tears from my throat when my shoulders are pulled back, the muscles protesting the aggression.

"Shh." Hot air is blown against my neck.

The fucking nerve of these entitled bastards. Now they want me silent?

I stir in my bonds, slowly coming to my senses as a retort forms on my tongue.

"What the—"

The insult never leaves my lips.

My visitor rattles the restraints on my wrists, each movement chafing atrociously against my reddened skin.

My eyes snap open when the shackles unlatch and my arms fall idly against me. My breath hitches in my throat as I try to calm my racing heart. This is not real. It can't be.

The room is as I left it, dark, bare, and freezing. My dried blood still coats the ground.

"Elanor."

Another whisper fills the air.

My eyes widen as a tall figure steps out of the shadows to face me. Before I can process what's happening, Azran kneels before me to undo the ropes tying me to the chair.

The remainder of my strength leaves me as I collapse onto him. He catches me before I hit the ground, my head resting on his chest. Needles drill into my brain as his strong arms hold me tightly.

Warmth returns to my body at his contact and my hands respond as I grip his shirt, needing to make sure he's there with me. Water fills my eyes as I choke on my sobs, burying my face in his neck and holding onto him like my life depends on it.

Strands of his hair brush my cheek as he pulls back. "We have to go."

I can hardly discern his features in the shadows, only his eyes darting around the room. Tears roll down my face as relief floods my body. He's getting me out of this hell.

I stand on wobbly legs as he helps me up, holding me by the arm. He motions towards the door with a sign of his head, but I pull him back and point at my collar.

A chuckle escapes his throat as he turns to face me, and my brows furrow. I need out of this collar if we're to make it out of here alive. I need my power and strength back.

I stare at him as he meets my gaze for the first time. A smile is plastered on his handsome face, though it doesn't reach his eyes. His eyes. They're different.

Calm and calculating, their usual fiery gleam is absent. I find no trace of fury in them.

His hand shoots towards me and closes around the collar, and fear floods my system.

"Az—"

Laughter fills the room before his name leaves my lips and his face distorts in a sick rictus.

He's completely lost his mind. The High Lord is gone, his mind obliterated. That's the only explanation.

My hands go to his as I try to undo his death grip around my neck, in vain. He only tightens his hold and brings his face an inch from mine, forcing me to stare into his eyes. His warm breath caresses my skin and I stand there, frozen in horror, as his irises change color, from crimson red to emerald green.

With his terrifying giggle in my ears, his face transforms until it's replaced by an all too familiar one.

My body doesn't belong to me anymore. I can't move or escape Airdan's grip as he laughs in my face like a lunatic.

My eyelids refuse to close and all I can do is watch the King of Zetrea mock me, shredding the illusion with a snap of his fingers.

I'm back in the chair I never really left, and my heart breaks into a million pieces.

"You make it so easy." Airdan manages a few words between bursts of laughter. "Beautiful. Truly marvelous."

Tears roll down my cheeks of their own accord as the dream shatters and so does my body. Pain flares in my nerve endings, taking over once more. It felt so real.

"This might be my best work yet."

My lips part as my mind explodes. Each second of lucidity I've managed to steal, I spent racking my brain for a way out, searching for a crack in the magical net cast around my power.

Physical pain I can endure. I can build tolerance. I can lose myself in it, become a shell of myself, and survive until an opportunity presents itself. That's what I was holding onto. Faith in my resilience and ability to endure any horrible thing life throws at me. Just like I've always done.

But this?

My resolve shatters. He can take my body, scar it, burn it to shreds, but not my mind.

A hole opens up before me and swallows me whole. He's going to take everything. My mind, body, and soul. Incoherent thoughts twirl in my head, mixing with images of Azran and Death, drowning out Airdan's voice. His mouth is still moving, but I can't make out the words.

None of it matters. A fire is raging in my soul, destroying everything in its path, tearing me apart from the inside out.

My heart pounds in my ears as I topple over the edge of sanity.

Screams reach my ears and it takes me a moment to realize they're coming from my mouth. Airdan looks at me with pride in his eyes and I thrash in my bonds. Pain flares in my shoulder but I barely feel it.

Pure rage is filling me. I will kill him or die trying. Nothing else matters anymore. He tainted the one safe space I had left with his sick magic. My own mind.

And he came after Azran.

Amusement twinkles in the corner of Airdan's emerald eyes and my vision blurs, filling with dark spots.

A liquid drips from my fingers, confirming the shackles are digging into my wrists, drawing blood, and I release a shattering scream.

I pour all my rage and madness into it, willing my power to break free of its restraints with everything I've got. I scream until darkness fills my vision, until I can't see Airdan anymore, until an image flashes in my mind.

A willow tree overlooking a flowerbed.

The cry dies on my lips, leaving my throat raw, and my heart stops. The picture overlays the dark cell, taking over my mind.

A garden of onyx and ivory flowers, their petals blowing in the wind, coming alive under the caress of the sun. With that image, my mind crosses an ocean.

I'm back in Averion, walking the palace grounds, Savage on my heels.

I hold on to the memories, ragged breaths escaping my lungs as I try to focus on that mental image.

Little by little, madness retreats.

Memories flash before my eyes, bringing me back from the edge as sensation returns to my body in waves of pain.

I can't remember what the sun feels like on my face, nor the grass under my boots. But I can picture the willow tree in the palace gardens and the strong Fae waiting for me there.

Airdan hasn't stolen everything from me yet. I still have one thing. A reason to hold on.

The hope that Azran is still alive.

Airdan walks in, his usual charming smile adorning his lips, a glass vial in hand.

At first, I debated who was worse, the King or the Prince, but now I know. Airdan's spirit is fucked beyond measure, the mind games, deceit, and false charm his most prized skill set.

Each of his visits carries unbearable suspense. I never know which side of him I get to see until it's too late. Until he's knee-deep in my blood or my mind. The crazy motherfucker is obsessed with inflicting the most pain my body can sustain and enchanting his way into my head.

His son is more methodical, impersonal, cold. Although torture could be considered the tool of mad men, he doesn't get sick and twisted enjoyment out of the task.

"Elanor." Airdan walks past me. "A pleasure to see you, as always."

He takes his sweet time digging into the stack of torture devices displayed behind me. It's part of his routine to give my mind time to run wild picturing the cruelest instruments, trying to guess which weapon he will select, which technique will inflict pain next, his words or his hands.

Airdan steps in front of me with an assortment of knives in hand. Ah, there we go. We're getting into knife play today.

I keep my snarky comment to myself, holding onto my promise not to utter a word in front of him. He's taken enough from me.

"Let's switch things up today, shall we, Unifier?"

Silence is my only response, and his eye twitches in annoyance.

I cock a brow in challenge, waiting for his next move.

The cold breeze subsides and a semblance of warmth returns to my body as I ready myself to endure the pain to come. Comfort is an illusion here. It doesn't exist, and I know not to hold on to its false promise, even for mere seconds.

My stomach drops when the poison retreats and my blood stops boiling. I've gotten so used to it, I forgot what it's like not to feel its constant ache. I almost don't believe, at first.

I'm convinced it's another one of his ruses until the acid dissolves in my veins, leaving only a dull throb, and my power awakens. My eyes widen as I feel the dark energy coursing through my system, eagerly reclaiming its rightful place. With it, a familiar numbness takes over. My eyes roll back as I taste the shadow world again, flirting beneath my skin, begging to get out and show him what we can do together.

"Show me." Airdan's voice trembles with excitement, barely containing himself.

The corner of my lips curve into a smirk as I tame the energy, locking it down inside me.

Over my dead body, *asshole*.

The first blow lands on my chest, slicing through rosy skin barely mended from his last visit. I welcome the sharp sting of the blade with a hiss, blowing air out of my nose.

"I said show me."

I clench my jaw, set on not showing him shit, and earn new cuts in the process. I smile when blood splashes on his pristine white shirt. Erasing the smug look on his face is worth all the pain in the world.

I fucking hate how he looks at me, like he owns me, like I belong to him.

"So, you want to play games." He pulls out a small knife from his set and rests the tip on my bare leg. The cold surprises me, and goosebumps erupt all over my skin.

Airdan slowly drags the blade over my thigh, almost caressing me with it.

My breath hitches in my throat when a piece of my skin peels off with the knife, revealing the bloodied flesh underneath. I stare at my leg, not feeling a thing until the pain flares and explodes.

I tremble, my hands closed in fists and my knuckles whitening as I repress a scream.

My power responds instantly, jumping to the surface, begging me to release it and fight back. A rush of energy fills my head, but I don't let it show. I won't play his game. Instead, I infuse the tiniest sliver of power to numb the pain and push it away.

Airdan and I lock eyes as he slides the small blade beneath my index finger nail next. Oh, this is going to hurt like a motherfucker.

As promised, he rips off several of my nails, leaving my hands dripping blood, but I don't utter a word. Misery is part of me now. Pain is my new normal. I can't remember what it feels like to not suffer every second of every day. Part of me thinks I never will, but it's fine. It means I'm learning to survive with it.

"Tell me, Elanor." He wipes his hands on his dark pants. "What did you see in Azran?" A growl forms in my throat at the mention of my mate. "Why you picked a Fae who fails to match your true worth and potential is beyond me. Help me understand why you would settle for someone utterly beneath you."

My power thrashes inside me. I can barely contain it.

"He's merely a puppy trying to take on wolves. A harmless and insignificant being."

The last thread that was holding me back snaps, and my vision darkens. Dark energy leaps from my chest before I can call it back. The shards of shadows go right through him before disappearing.

Panting, I screw my eyes closed to try and rein in the fury fueling my power.

"Beautiful." My eyes snap open as Airdan licks his lips and extends a hand to caress my face. I bare my teeth with a snarl, but he pulls away before I get the chance to bite his finger off. "My murderous creature."

I stare back into his eyes and my blood freezes. A knot forms in my stomach as shame and disgust fight for the front row seat. My power shuts down instantly, retreating to the hidden corners of my soul, hiding from his lewd gaze.

My chest caves in as cold sweat trickles down my back. He wins this round, and I'm left grappling with what's left of myself, feeling soiled and tainted. But Airdan, his emerald eyes shine with lust.

CHAPTER 24

ELANOR

My captors make sure to keep me alive. I suspect the thick and smelly mixture they make me choke on every day has something to do with it.

I'm covered in scars, and dried blood coats my hair and body. My head is under constant assault from the collar and the bond is drowned in pain. I can't tell if it's there anymore. I can't tell if Azran is alive or not.

Each awakening leaves me yearning for oblivion. Each session pushes the limits of my body and mind. My power flickers several times, my shadows escaping me unwillingly. And each time, Airdan gobbles them up like a madman, reveling in them, taking notes, and sometimes bringing his son back into the room with us to show him. I'm no more than an exotic monster to them.

As much as I dread my captors' visits, I've also started looking forward to them, for I know their end at least brings back the darkness.

The only comfort I find lies in my silence. With my screams their only gifts, I still haven't said a word. They know nothing of the true depth of my power or my heritage. They know nothing of the Death curse I carry. That, and the gardens flooding my mind when I can't take it anymore and insanity threatens to take over.

My gaze fixes on the bloodied ground as my mind takes me someplace where I can forget about it all. I'm picturing the dark forest when laughter stirs me from the daydream. My eyes dart around the room to identify its source.

I know every inch of this cell by heart. I've had weeks to memorize the shape of each stone, carve the smell of the stale, cold, and lifeless air in my brain, and bathe in its stillness.

Everything is perfectly quiet until I hear the chuckle again. Chills run down my spine as I recognize the same laugh I heard in the palace but couldn't place. Airdan's mysterious guest is here. That, or I'm losing my mind for good.

No. This is real.

I push back the pain to try and make out the words being exchanged outside my cell. But the poison is too strong and the blood pumping in my ears too loud.

My whole body tenses when the metal door swings on its hinges, and my heart drops in my stomach.

Amrynn saunters into the room, her blond hair perfectly combed and falling in waves to her naked shoulders. She lifts the hem of her strapless dress to avoid the pools of blood at her feet as she takes position in front of me, a cold smile on her face.

An imperceptible gleam in her silver eyes is the only indication she recognizes me and is at least slightly shocked by my state, or maybe simply repulsed.

I glimpse the shape of Nylren as he closes the door behind her.

The moment it's just the two of us, I release the venom pooling on my tongue. My promise doesn't extend to Amrynn.

"You treacherous bitch."

That sick laugh of hers fills the room again as she tucks a piece of her perfect hair behind her pointy ear.

"I'm doing what is best for my people. Something you know nothing about," Amrynn snarls back at me. "You would understand, had you dwelled in this world as long as I have."

"You're a stranger to selflessness. You have no idea what it even means," I taunt.

"Shouldn't you be trying to gain my favor to get out of this place instead of spewing hateful words?" A devilish smile crosses her red lips.

"Spare me your bullshit." I roll my eyes at her words. "You don't give a damn about anyone but yourself. You can maybe fool them, but you're not fooling me."

"If you gave in, King Airdan would forgive you." She waves around the room, her nose wrinkling at its pitiful state, or mine. "You don't have to die like this."

"Save your pretend pity and snake tongue."

She shrugs and starts studying her painted nails. "Very well, then."

She turns on her heels, gathering her skirts in her hands. She's halfway across the room when I realize this might be my one and only chance. I have to know.

"Why betray him?" My voice is merely a whisper, but she pauses to face me. "I understand you owe me nothing, but your own blood?"

"Azran had it coming." Her disdain is almost palpable.

"Have you seen him?"

She cocks a brow but doesn't respond.

"Is he here?" My voice trembles as I ask the questions burning my lips.

There is no mistaking the superior air on her face. The bitch wants to see me beg. I bet she would undo my restraints herself just to see me crawl at her feet.

"Tell me." I fist my palms and close my eyes long enough to gather the courage to crush what's left of my ego. "Please."

Her victorious smile is the last thing I see before she turns and leaves the room.

My enraged screams fill the halls until my throat is raw, and I'm sure they'll accompany her into her nightmares.

Another name.

Another name has been added to my list.

The list of people who will die slowly when I get out of here.

⸺◆⸺

My eyes flutter open, finding my cell as I left it. Bare. Cold.

I pull on the shackles as I attempt to stretch my arms and relieve the pain in my shoulders. I know it's useless, but I can't resolve not to do it. It's part of my routine. It's all the fight left in me and I won't let it go. I won't abandon myself even when the rest of the world has.

My skin is chafed raw from the metal and I breathe out as the pain trickles through the rest of my body.

I pull once more, and warmth floods the muscles in my arms. My eyes roll back as the shortest relief rushes through me and I manage to move my shoulders. I forgot what my body could do when not bound to a chair.

A faint moan escapes my lips and I freeze. I've never had that much slack on my restraints.

Ever so slowly, I pull again and a link loosens.

I crane my neck to examine the handcuffs, unsuccessfully, and I brace myself, trying to tame the hope blooming in my heart. Has my straining damaged the restraints enough for me to slip out of them?

I gather my hands close together and pull as hard as I can in opposite directions.

The chain clangs heavily on the ground as one of my wrists breaks free of the restraints.

In complete disbelief, I roll my shoulders and rub my hands together to instill warmth and diffuse the pain.

I wait for Nylren or Airdan to storm through the door and tie me back down, but everything is perfectly still and silent. With no time to think, I reach for the rope between my feet and undo it as fast as I can with my chipped nails and scarred fingers.

The chain hangs from my left wrist, still attached to the handcuff around it. I grab it to prevent its noise from alerting nearby guards as I make for the door on trembling legs.

I'm out of breath when I reach the door, but don't stop. The sadistic assholes never lock it. They don't think I could ever get out of here. Let me prove you wrong, motherfuckers.

I step into a corridor dimly lit by torches and my hands go to my eyes. I haven't seen light since they locked me up, let alone daylight. I have no idea whether it's night or day.

The narrow hallway leads me to a spiral stairway. Leaning in the doorway, I brace myself for the climb.

I make it to the top with my lungs on fire and my head ready to explode, but I push on.

This might be my only chance.

I walk onto a plush rug and the soft fabric hugs my toes, bringing some warmth back to the frozen bits. The silence around me is so loud it's like I'm screaming my thoughts.

Moonlight streams through massive windows, illuminating the corridor in soft light. I know these halls. The royal quarters are just ahead.

I freeze when I catch movement to my left. A mirror.

I wince as my reflection greets me. My cheeks are hollow, my eyes sunk into their sockets with dark purple underneath, not to mention the dried blood and cuts all over my face and chest. I barely recognize myself.

I tear my gaze away from the sordid observation and keep going until I find the staircase leading to my old room and the kitchens.

Steps echo down the hall and I dive into the stairway, hiding away in its shadows. A guard walks past me before turning a corner and disappearing.

I'm about to descend the first step when my knees buckle. I find purchase on the stone wall and steady myself as a string of curses fills my mind.

My gaze darts to the other end of the corridor, where Airdan and Nylren's rooms are, and my right hand goes to the collar around my neck.

Each rasping inhale fuels the inferno raging in my lungs. My muscles are atrophied from lack of movement, most of my wounds are still oozing blood, and each step feels like it could be my last.

I'm so fucking tired. I don't know if I have it in me to make it out of here. In fact, I don't think I will.

But if any fiber of my ravaged body and soul remains intact, it is my wrath and drive for revenge. I don't need my power to send Airdan to his doom.

Death. Give me the strength to see this through.

I pray silently to the old gods who put me on this wretched path and my purpose becomes clear as day. I was sent here to end his miserable life and save the rest of the world from his poisonous mind. I was sent to avenge the dead, to avenge Azran.

I grit my teeth as I make for his room, a hand on the wall to guide me.

All my thoughts quiet down as I turn the knob of his bedroom door and slip inside.

Complete darkness greets me, and it takes my eyes a moment to adjust to the layout of the room. A massive four-poster bed sits against the far wall. A shape takes form on top of it.

Airdan's chest rises and falls peacefully as I get closer and look for a weapon. I'll choke him to death if I have to, but I'll take all the help I can get.

My gaze lands on a letter opener resting on stacks of papers on the desk to my right.

The handcuff chain rattles as I seize the makeshift weapon and I freeze, waiting for Airdan to stir. I'm ready to pounce on him, but he doesn't move, his breathing regular.

I'm towering over him on the edge of the bed when another predicament dawns on me. I can't reach him without stepping onto this massive mattress. Fucking hell. Can nothing ever be easy? Once I step onto the bed, I'll have mere seconds before he wakes up.

Taking a deep breath, I leap on the mattress, my knees sinking into the soft cushion on either side of his body, the letter opener tightly gripped.

I let go of the chain in my left hand and aim the weapon at his throat.

Airdan's eyes snap open, and I know something's awfully wrong when I find no trace of sleep in his emerald irises.

His hands grip my thighs, securing me on top of him.

"Foolish girl." A smile blooms on his face. "Go on. Show me what you can do."

Alarm bells ring in my head, telling me to get away, but his hands roam my legs, making their way around the shreds of my dress.

My mouth opens but no words come out, like my voice has been stolen, and so has my free will. I'm frozen in place as he caresses my skin.

My eyes widen when his hand nears my waist. I scream for him to get away from me, but the room is utterly silent except for his accelerating breathing.

"You know you want to." His gaze lingers on my chest.

My hands do not respond. I'm still gripping the letter opener, hovering an inch from his neck. An inch too far.

His fingers brush my bare waist through the torn fabric, and a wretched need blossoms within me at the touch, a silent scream stuck in my throat and wetness rolling down my cheeks.

I jump out of my skin when the cries reach my ears.

I'm on the chair in my cell, my hands and feet tied as I left them. Sobs shake me as my head falls to my chest, the illusion broken.

None of it was real, and yet I can't shake the revulsion and angst. Airdan's magic shatters my soul, chipping at it little by little, taking my will and strength, breaking me.

Since my father died, I've always been a force to be reckoned with. I never allowed anything to get in my way. I had one certainty; I would go to the ends of the earth to avenge the dead, save the people I care about, and fulfill my purpose. I've always been strong, brave, lethal even. But now, I hardly recognize myself.

I don't react when soldiers barge inside the room. I can't tell what's real anymore. I can't see through the tears and the tremors shaking my body. I barely feel their hands on me as they lift me to my feet and carry me from the room.

My feet drag on the stone as I'm pulled forward. My survival instinct makes a brief appearance, urging me to open my eyes, look around, figure out what's happening. But I don't care anymore.

My body hits a cold and hard surface, and I lay there. I don't even move when the shackles around my hands and the neck collar are removed. Another trick, I'm sure.

CHAPTER 25

CALEN

Cold air sweeps through the palace halls and the corridors lose their usual warmth. This place feels dead, lifeless, like a battlefield without the corpses but the same astounding silence.

Servants, usually full of cheer, now hurry down corridors, trying to disappear in the shadows. Even Averion's usual hustle and bustle has quieted. I close my eyes, willing my ears to remember the joy of this place and the laughter of its inhabitants.

I get to the courtyard as the sun sinks into the horizon, the moon a small crescent high in the sky. There's no time for me to enjoy the view. There's no time for me to enjoy anything these days, nor rest. There's too much to do and too much to figure out.

I quicken the pace and enter the garrison to check on our units. The clashing of swords greets me, confirming that several soldiers are still training.

I remember a time when swords were reserved for displays of strength and agility. Artistry in its purest form, hypnotizing and grandiose, but as beautiful as the art of wielding swords may be, we've long lost it. Only the remnants of the wars remain in the exercise, forever ingrained in our souls and bodies. Another reminder of why I have to do this.

Fiery strands of hair catch my eye where Vesta is talking with Wyn and Varan. I hold back the smile tugging my lips at the sight. The years have done nothing to tame their wild spirits, and those damn twins are always stirring up trouble.

My almost smile turns into a frown as I observe their exchange more closely. Vesta puts a hand on their shoulders as they nod, and my heart breaks a little more. We've barely spoken since my address to the citizens of Averion and she's doing a great job avoiding me.

Wyn's eyes dart to me and the conversation quiets down. Keeping a straight face, I go around the room, assessing stances and giving encouraging nods. Now more than ever, my presence here is key.

A change in leadership is never easy, especially when it lies on a bed of rumors.

"General."

A messenger clears their throat behind me as they hand me a piece of paper.

"Thank you," I say, dismissing them with a wave of my hand.

It's a message from the Sun Fae of Kalar.

My eyes scan the content of the missive before tucking it inside my leather vest.

Tharrion just agreed to the plan.

I storm out and make for my office. Everyone steps out of my way, but I catch their startled gazes.

⋅•◦•⋅

Hours later, my eyes snap open, irritation winning over exhaustion and getting the better of me. Another sleepless night it is.

I stare at the ceiling a while longer, tortured by memories of Vesta's mouth all over my body and her cold gaze. I royally fucked this up, but there's no time for me to dwell on it.

Tossing the covers to the side, I dress quickly and leave my room.

As I wander the palace, my steps lead me to the courtyard for fresh air and the barracks, as usual. I've always had a penchant for self-destruction.

I quietly make my way through the building, my gaze fixed on a door at the end of the corridor. A door I irrevocably find open, an empty room waiting beyond, with a cold bed inside.

I usually keep walking, but tonight I can't force my legs to go on and I step inside Vesta's room. She's the most solar Fae I know, yet her quarters carry no warmth. There's barely anything here, and no personal effects except for a small wooden sculpture on the bedside table. A leaf, the only reminder of her past and dead mate.

Whispers stir me from the trance and I head back out. Guided by the murmurs, I pause by the garrison's entrance.

Wyn and Varan are huddled together by a pillar, the faint light of the wall torches highlighting their features.

"I can't believe they would do this, run away like that."

Wyn's voice carries an undeniable hint of anger.

"That's enough, Wyn," his twin answers.

"Either that, or they're both dead."

"Enough," Varan says sharply. "You heard Vesta. We don't have a choice."

Wyn bares his teeth. "Forever the level-headed one, brother."

"And you're forever the careless fool."

"This is not a joke to me. I didn't destroy my face for this, you hear me?"

Varan's hand goes to his brother's shoulder, pressing tightly. "No one but Braern is responsible for this."

Wyn mumbles something in return, but doesn't argue.

"What would you have me do?" Varan continues.

"Follow orders," I say, stepping into the light. The twins straighten, casting their eyes to the ground. "Our goal remains unchanged. Unite and protect the Fae."

Wyn opens his mouth, but his brother elbows him in the ribs.

"Yes, General," Varan answers for the both of them.

I nod in response before walking away.

Why can't they understand I'm doing what's best for all of us? Have I ever let them down in the past?

I rack my brain for a better way, though I know there are none. I've spent hours going over everything I know and don't, leaving no stones left unturned, trying to avoid the inevitable. But it's time I dance with the devil.

They all look at me like I'm the enemy, like I chose any of this, when the choice was robbed from me the moment Azran left. My soldiers used to look up to me, admire me; now they fear my steps. Az often hinted at the toll leadership takes on a soul, but only now does that isolation register in my bones. Damn him and his wretched politics. To hell with it all.

I have to leave and make sure Lóna is protected. I didn't spend the better part of my life spilling my people's blood for it all to be taken away from me. Not now. Not ever. Few memories remain untainted by the horrors of war, and I refuse to believe the years I spent fighting for this land have been for nothing. I won't let them. Someone has to make the hard call, and if no one else will do it, then it will be me.

CHAPTER 26

AZRAN

Twenty-seven.

I've spent twenty-seven days rotting away in this cell since my re-capture.

With only spoiled chunks of bread the guards throw through the bars of my cage to keep count, the last of my sanity holds by a thread, but I am no longer alone.

I roll over with a grunt, crushing my broken ribs under my own weight in the process.

Pain explodes in my chest as I swallow a scream and stare at the ceiling of my cell until the yellow dots disappear from the corner of my eyes.

I never thought seeing stars would bring me such comfort. It's the only familiar and least alarming thing here. And the dots do add a decorative touch to the bland walls. Being trapped in this hellhole gets boring pretty quickly. Cal would hate it. A grin tugs my split lips as I picture him in the opposite corner of my cell, but the flickers of light return and my brother's face vanishes from the grime-covered stone.

It is when shadows viciously eclipse my vision that dread latches itself around my pounding heart, for it is a good indicator of when I'm about to lose consciousness—one of the first lessons my genitor taught me, when I was barely four.

I've got to hand it to him, his teachings have proven useful in the past months. Were it not for him, my wasted body would be naught but bone and memory beneath the cold earth by now.

Gratitude for the years of torture inflicted in my youth floods my scarred mind, revealing how deep Airdan's claws have sunk into my broken spirit. Maybe Nylren had it worse than me, after all.

A hoarse laugh escapes my dry throat, lighting it on fire and transforming into a cough.

I spit out the blood before I choke on it and wipe my mouth with the back of my hand.

Ragged breathing in the cell next to mine draws my attention and I turn my head in its direction.

With no light in the dungeons, not even the glimmer of a torch, I can't make out if the stranger is human or Fae through the metal bars.

Pain is still ringing in my head and coursing my body, so I wait a while longer before attempting to move. I've got nothing but time in here. Another chuckle tears through me, rapidly turning into a bark.

Most days, my resolve dangles from the same thread as my sanity. Others, madness comes along for a ride. Today I'm not certain which will win.

I finally find the strength to prop myself up on my elbow and sit up. I drag myself over to the bars of my cell, one of my legs limp behind me, my knee bent at a weird angle.

I forgot about Airdan's twisted sense of humor. My cellmate shall wait a little longer.

I stare at my leg, assessing the damage and probing with my fingers. I need to twist the knee cap back in place. Better that, than for it to heal this way.

I let out a shaky breath and brace myself for the pain. This is merely another round of caring for my destroyed body, and another lesson I owe to my father. The mean bastard certainly taught me a lot.

I stifle the laugh forming in my throat, for the agonized cackles promise only sharper pangs, and I have no interest in putting myself through another grueling round of pointless suffering.

I clench my jaw as I grab hold of my thigh and shin with both hands. Without thinking, I snap the bones back in place with a savage roar.

Fire travels my leg and vertebrae and I breathe through each wave until the pain settles to a more bearable level.

When I'm recovered enough, I focus on the shape on the other side of the bars. I can't make out their face, but my stomach drops at the sight of the small female body splayed across the stone.

A pointy ear sticks out of the mass of brown hair on their head, and my blood freezes.

"Can you hear me?" My voice trembles as I call out to her.

Her breath remains irregular and ragged, but she's too far for me to assess the damage to her body.

Tears trail down my dirt-smudged cheeks, flowing free as I fall perfectly still. Recognition ignites every cell in my body as the truth shatters all flimsy barricades erected around this sealed-off corner of my soul. The bond stopped flaring the moment I set eyes on her.

"Ela." The whisper barely leaves my lips before my voice breaks.

My mate lies crushed before me—her shattered body haunting evidence of the torment inflicted on her by my fault.

Reaching through the metal bars of my cell, I extend both arms with enough force to rip my shoulders from their moorings—anything to close the few impossible inches separating us.

My blood turns to acid as my fingers grasp at air and she remains but a breath away from me.

I roar hoarse pleas into the echoing dungeon and call her name again and again, in vain.

What have they done to her?

I'd convinced myself she made it out, but the iron force of her will met its match in Airdan. And she paid the ultimate price for gambling her freedom against my condemned soul.

The knowledge of my culpability shreds the last of my sanity, for her presence here is my doing.

<hr />

I draw blood scratching my nails on the stone of Ela's cell, helplessly looking for a way to save her.

"Ela."

My scream drowns under the sound of footsteps. Boots hit the ground, but my gaze remains on her body.

"Ela."

The door to my cell opens and guards pull me off the ground. With a snarl, I push them away, rage gnawing at my soul. I won't be separated from her, not again.

"Let's go," one of them barks.

A pair of soldiers grab me. I topple over the edge when I can't hear her breathing over their shouts. Unleashing my power, I thrash in their arms uselessly, and what's left of my strength leaves me in seconds.

They're all protected against me, and I'm no more than a Fae whose body has been broken too many times.

"Ela."

My screams fills the dark halls of the dungeons as I spit curses and threats. They may mutilate me beyond salvation, but breath by breath I will crawl over bloodied stone and scale hellfire ramparts to reclaim her soul.

I only stop when no sound comes out anymore, my throat so dried I can barely suck in breath.

"I see you found my gift."

Airdan's cold voice fills the air as guards strap me to the metal chair in our usual torture room. The same instruments line the walls, most covered in dark crimson.

I attempt a snarl, unable to repress my fury, but only choke on it.

Airdan snaps his fingers and a guard walks in with a pitcher of water they throw in my face.

"Get a grip, Azran. I need you lucid today." He snaps his fingers again, and a funnel is stuck down my throat. "Let's talk, shall we?"

I gargle and choke on water poured too rapidly down my throat until the funnel is removed.

"So, how do you find her?"

I'm still catching my breath when my head snaps to the side from the force of Airdan's slap. Strands of my hair dangle weakly in front of my face as I see stars.

"You realize this is all on you? Had you not tried to take me on, Elanor would be safe and sound, enjoying Nyths, and... other things."

He shoots me a wink, and this time a growl tears from my lips.

"Keep her fucking name out of your mouth," I breathe through my ravaged throat.

"We both know she would be better off with me." Airdan leans against a wall, his arms crossed over his chest. "I think she started realizing that, too."

"You could never be worthy of her." I eye him up and down, baring my teeth. "Were your crimes avenged and your body dragged across all Zetrea until your bones turn to ashes, you would never be enough."

"Her cheeks used to redden at my words before your ridiculous attempt at contacting her." Airdan's fingers go to his mouth to rub his lips slowly. "But now, we're back on track. If only you knew the things I tease her with in her dreams. I just love the feigned innocence in her eyes."

"I will kill you and destroy everything you've built. Then, I will let humans tear your body to pieces and bathe in your blood."

Airdan's laugh fills the air. "As if you could. Who is not enough, now, Azran?"

I suck in a breath, trying to push back the memory of Ela's body in a cell.

"Why?" A smile blooms on Airdan's face as my question echoes in the cold room. "Haven't you taken enough?"

"Oh, this little rendezvous? It's merely for my amusement. You know ruling can get tedious at times. You, I keep for when I need something to take the edge off."

My power holds no secret to him anymore. I couldn't fight it very long; the bloodlust has always been too strong. I've been its servant ever since it claimed me.

"Let us get started, shall we?"

Airdan selects a pair of scissors, and my brows furrow. That's an unusual pick, even for him.

"We're going to play a game. I'll tell you what I plan on doing to our dear Ela and you tell me if you think she'll like it."

I stretch my neck, trying to ease the tension forming between my shoulder blades.

"And what happens if I don't want to play?"

He snaps the scissors in the air twice.

"First, I will let her do whatever she wants to me. Cut, slice, and hurt me as much as it pleases her until she learns to trust me." Airdan grabs a handful of my hair and lifts my head. "I like a little pain, and I know she does, too. She will be on her knees begging me to take her before long. What do you think?"

He lets go to stare me down, revealing nothing but evil in his emerald eyes.

"Hm, nothing?"

I hear the snap of the scissors before I realize what he's doing.

A long strand of my hair falls to the ground, joining the dirt and dried blood. I pinch my eyes shut as a piece of my soul goes with it. It's just hair. It will grow again, no matter what it means to me.

"What about that lovely mouth of hers? I bet she knows how to make good use of it, doesn't she?"

Memories flash in my mind, now tainted by his snake tongue.

Scissors snap again. And again.

Alarm seizes my pounding heart as the wounds of the battered boy I once was tear open anew. I was robbed of my free will before, but my spirit endured. I will cling by bloodied fingernails to this nightmare's edge until I stand atop the smoking pyre of Airdan's legacy—his glassy, lifeless eyes reflecting the ravaged ruin in my wake.

"Or should I take her ass?"

A bestial rumble tears from my chest, the sound of primal fury straining against its mortal cage of bone and flesh.

"Oh. I've hit a nerve, it seems." Airdan's retched laugh sounds behind me. "Yes, I'll claim that round ass of hers next."

With each second passing, weight lifts from my head, like a year taken off my life. And sure enough, I feel like I'm back in Morilanthe.

Each of Airdan's taunts eat at me, waking my rage, destroying every bit of me left.

Cold runs down my cheek in a single tear, the only one I'll allow to mourn my strength, my fight, my path, and my hair.

This stops here.

Ela needs me. Insanity is no longer an option, and neither is giving up. As long as my lungs hold a breath, I will hold on for her.

I'm thrown back in my cage hours later, feeling like a stranger in my own body and mind, robbed of my identity and courage.

"Az."

Everything else disappears the moment Ela's voice rings through the cold air.

I crawl to her, scraping my knees and palm on the rough stone until my arms can reach through the bars of my cell.

She's still lying on the ground, same as I left her.

"Ela." I extend my fingers towards her, but she barely lifts her head and her eyes remain hidden under her hair. "I'm here."

Fire shoots through my shoulders as I attempt to touch her, comfort her.

"I'm so tired, Az."

Her once vibrant voice emerges mangled, unrecognizable, each labored rasp carving fresh wounds across my heart. Were it not for the bond flaring inside me, I wouldn't believe my own eyes. Her shaky legs are an inch from the tip of my fingers, my absolution so close, yet so far as her broken body clings stubbornly to life.

"I know, little one."

My voice breaks as my heart shatters for her. I'm lying there, powerless, while her fire goes out. I would not wish this torment on my worst enemy.

The distant, dank chill enveloping our cells seeps deeper into my soul with that realization as her parched lips move gently, shaping words too garbled for me to decipher.

I failed. I couldn't save her or protect her, and now we'll endure this hell until Airdan gets what he wants or tires of us. It might as well be until the end of time.

CHAPTER 27

NYLREN

Footsteps echo in the throne room as the dark-skinned Fae approaches. Handsome, were it not for the gold and red armor on his torso.

Royal guards block his escort at the entrance, but he doesn't slow down, his gaze set on the throne upon which my father rests.

Once within hearing distance, he bows.

"My King."

His sultry voice reaches my ears although his lips remain hidden under his braided head.

"Calen."

The Fae bows once more as Father greets him.

Morbid fascination roots me in place, unable to wrench my gaze away. This thirst to know, to understand the tableau before me, overpowers revulsion.

The General of Lóna's armies and Azran's right hand has come to Zetrea. The Sun Fae who betrayed his own blood, and whose exploits as a military strategist have traveled across seas.

Calen inclines his head towards me, but not before making eye contact, letting me gaze into the infinite pools of his treacherously beautiful azure irises.

A glimmer of green catches my eye where a silk ribbon clings to his biceps, and Father's eyebrow shoots up when he notices it.

Time suspends its course as tension crystalizes around us, but Calen doesn't move an inch, holding his head high and keeping his stance wide.

"I come of my own free will." Calen's focus goes back to my father. "Azran knows nothing of my presence here. In fact, he hasn't been seen in months." Hostility is almost palpable, and my hand inches towards the faithful blade tucked in my sleeve. "I've taken over Lóna and come with an offer."

"You bring terrible news. What dire times for your island home." Father's tone is warm and welcoming, although his eyes tell another story.

"Such ill tidings," Calen says as a smile appears on his face. An interesting choice on his part, but not quite convincing enough to fool me.

"What is this offer you speak of?"

"I come to pledge my allegiance to you, King Airdan. As General of Lóna's armies, I know how to recognize power and opportunity."

Treachery does run in his blood.

"What would I gain, if I were to accept this?" An amused smile appears on Father's face as he waits for the General to answer.

I'm surprised he's willing to see where this goes.

"Lóna. Control over its territory, armies, and citizens."

Father motions for Calen to keep going with a sign of his hand.

"Ryrza harbors traitors to the crown, and it would be my pleasure to rid you of those vermin."

I squint my eyes at his mention of Ryrza. What else does he know of our dealings with rebels down south?

Keeping my mouth shut, I glance at my father as he repositions himself on the throne. A whistle escapes his lips.

"And what do you stand to gain?"

"Revenge." The word tears from Calen's throat instantly. "After spending decades fighting for a Fae who's never acknowledged my influence, he elevated humans to the same rank as some of our brothers in arms." His eyes flash with uncontained bitterness, and saliva forms at the corner of his mouth. "I left my own blood for Azran, and it was all for nothing."

"What tells me you won't do the same to me?" Father remains perfectly collected before Calen's display of emotion.

"Nothing." The General tilts his head in challenge. "Only your belief in the depth of my rage. I'm a vindictive motherfucker when I want to be."

The King's laugh sounds in the hall.

"That, I can believe."

A twinkle of pride shines in Father's eyes and I dig my nails into my palm. He cannot be buying this act.

"Maybe it is time I step in to guarantee safety to our people across the earth." Father and I lock eyes for a moment before his gaze returns to Calen. "Our people deserve to live united and at peace, wouldn't you say?"

"My thoughts exactly." Calen nods.

"I assume you came here with a plan, General. What do you propose?"

"Grant me passage to Zetrea with my most elite warriors. Let me bring Lóna's finest fighters to you, your Highness, and I will fulfill my vow of allegiance."

I tense and step forward, but Calen's voice fills the air once more.

"I will be the sword in your hand, finishing what you started here before we move on to Brimora. The humans won't stand a chance."

After an interminable silence, Father stands and makes for the door behind the throne.

"Come."

He's always had a flare for the dramatic.

Guards carrying torches flank Calen as Father enters the dungeons with me in tow.

With my jaw clenched tight, I go over all possible scenarios of this masquerade as uncertainty claws my insides. Something is not adding up in Calen's plan. I must find a way to warn Father without bruising that inflexible pride of his.

When Father slows, I manage to lock eyes with him. He pins me with a cutting glare before I utter a single syllable. I snap my lips shut, his threat implicit, and humiliation scalds my skin at the silent dismissal.

I've learned to interpret each look or minuscule gesture Father makes, and there is no doubting this one. He's willing to test how far Calen's treachery goes. Time will tell soon enough if my instincts prove reliable or merely paranoid.

I scrutinize the General, my fingers never far from the dagger in my sleeve, ready to jump at the slightest hint of danger.

When we step into the dark corridor where our prisoners are held, Father nods to a guard. The tall Fae goes to the cells with his torch and clangs his sword against the bars.

The prisoners stir, covering their eyes with one hand while reaching for each other through the bars.

I can't help the smile tearing from my lips when Azran manages to grab his mate's hand. The two of them are complete and utter fools. This little plan of theirs will never succeed.

I step aside to let Calen take in the scene and watch him as a hawk might a rabbit stirring in tall grass, tracking each nuance that might betray his intentions.

Apart from a slight flare of his nostrils, his features remain perfectly neutral. He doesn't reveal a hint of emotion as he considers the state of his High Lord.

I've got to hand it to him. If he's faking it, he's putting on a perfect act. A Fae after my own dark heart.

My smile expands when shock paints Azran's face and his lips distort into a feral rictus. His swollen and bruised eyes widen when Calen steps into the faint light of the torches secured to the walls.

"Vagabonds wander far from home these days. Just as you said, ill tidings indeed." Father's dark voice rings through the air and the corners of Calen's lips lift.

My posture stiffens as an inkling of trust blooms in my cold, dead heart. I could use an ally here. Dare I even say it? I could use a friend. I've always longed for the kind of unwavering support others were granted. Not love or devotion, but strength for a common purpose.

Who's being a fool, now? I crush this hope in a heartbeat. There is no room for him here.

"What happens to them matters not to me." Calen's voice has darkened significantly, his tone so low it's almost a growl. "As far as I'm concerned, the High Lord is dead."

The deepest snarl shakes the ground, reverberating against the metal of the cage, unsettling the air.

"These vagabonds are nothing more than caged beasts."

The General's voice is the last one Azran and Ela hear before we make our way out.

CHAPTER 28

NYLREN

When we step back into the well-lit and heavily-decorated corridors of the royal palace, Father pauses.

"Join me for dinner, General," Father says, his words more command than request.

"The honor would be mine, your Majesty."

I barely restrain the urge to roll my eyes at the transparent posturing unfolding before me. Clearly, Calen has mastered the dance between rulers and subjects, understanding when to duck and weave or simply mirror steps.

Moment later, they stride in tandem into one of the dining rooms as I trail behind, my knuckles whitening in my closed fist.

Servants scurry ahead of us to shake out tapestries, polish silver, and arrange chalices in a well-rehearsed ritual. Not one dares meet their sovereign's eye, focusing only on preparations.

The restrained dance between cautious allies and proud ruler continues on as the general matches Father's intricate steps fluidly and takes a seat.

Our trio now assembled around the polished table, an orchestra of servants presents dish after elaborate dish, roasted pheasant garnished with currants, venison pie dripping juices that scent the air with game and cloves, and various arrangements of winter vegetables.

Father eyes the spread, visibly weighing satisfaction. His mood is known to shift based on quality of the meal or accuracy of the preparations. Even Calen cannot restrain his admiration, his eyes darting between my father and the table befitting the highest nobility.

Silverware whispers over fine porcelain as Father slices into the pheasant, savoring a mouthful dramatically before nodding approval, and servants remaining in the room exhale in discreet relief.

"You must have fascinating stories, General, from years commanding armies," Father remarks before sampling the venison.

Calen dabs his lips, buying a moment's thought before answering.

"Too many to recount them all, and I'm sure far too boring for your table, your Majesty." The General stabs at a piece of meat with his fork. "I must say, Averion pales in comparison to Nyths. The work you've done here is impressive."

"I will have to visit soon," Father answers.

"Of course, your Majesty. Once we're done with the vermin in Ryrza and Brimora, your realm will extend as far as the eye can see."

"Right to business, I see?"

"I am a pragmatic, your Majesty."

"Very well, then. What of the leaders of the Fae factions in Lóna?"

"I've been assured of their cooperation. They understand that uniting under your banner will bring nothing but success and riches."

"We'll discuss commercial routes and tax treaties in due time."

"Of course, your Majesty."

I spend the rest of the meal scrutinizing every word from Calen's mouth, every change in his facial expression, what he chooses to eat, until the main courses are removed.

"When will you depart?" Father asks as cakes and pies are set before us.

"By morning, with your permission. I'm eager to serve you and prove my loyalty."

"Hm." Father finishes chewing.

"I've always been a man of action over words." Calen shoots me a wink, but I remain perfectly stoic.

"We would expect nothing else from the traitor of Lóna," I retort.

"One of many names I've been called." Calen shrugs my comment off.

My lips remain sealed for the rest of the course. Finally, servants walk in to remove desserts and Calen clears his throat.

"Your Majesty, with your permission, I would like to make a brief stop by the dungeons before I go." Father tilts his head, the only sign of his surprise. "I want to look that joke of a High Lord in the eyes one last time."

A calculating smile appears on Father's face, and I bite back the words forming on my tongue.

"But of course. Guards, escort him."

Father always loved playing games, but I'm afraid this time he won't win.

Calen stands and bows deeply before the King.

"Your Majesty."

Turning to me, he inclines his head.

"Your Highness."

Calen leaves the room, leaving me alone with my tormentor, a million questions burning my lips.

Father is still cleaning his plate, savoring a piece of orange cake as I wait patiently.

"Out with it."

His harsh tone pierces me through the bone and I open my mouth.

"I do not trust him."

"Nor do I, but wouldn't life be dull without these games?"

"I'm merely trying to—"

"Do you think me an imbecile, boy?" I wince as Father cuts me off. "Do you think all this could have been achieved without risk?"

"Of course not, Father."

I lower my head, letting humiliation wash over me until my resolve strengthens. He's making a mistake, a mistake I wouldn't make were I the one ruling Zetrea.

"Whatever the outcome, I will win. If Calen is lying, after serving me his strongest warriors on a silver platter for me to crush them, he will offer the perfect opportunity to bring our forces across seas. If not, he shall do my dirty work for me. Either way, Lóna is mine."

I glance towards him, only to find him staring at the empty space next to him.

⸻◆⸻

My footfalls vanish into the woven depths of the rugs adorning the floors of the palace as I make my way to my chambers.

Mere feet from my room, my head snaps to the side at the faintest click echoing from somewhere down the corridor, the sound no louder than the latch of a door lock falling back in its place.

I pause, straining to catch another whisper of movement in the ample silence enrobing the palace halls.

Curiosity stirs in my gut and I enter my bedroom, making no effort to muffle the sound of the door closing behind me.

In a few steps, I reach the tapestry lining the wall next to the intricate glass panel offering a high view of the courtyard. Lifting its corners, I slip through the hidden passageway behind it without a sound.

I steal into musty darkness, letting the heavy draperies fall back into place. Cool drafts swirl up from winding corridors as I vanish in shadow and sneak through narrow pathways built inside the walls themselves.

My fingertips trace along lichen-slicked stone until the faint outline of steep stairs takes shape in the gloom. Even in complete darkness, I know these corridors like the back of my hand. For years, this forgotten stairwell has granted me discreet access to all levels of the palace, including the servant's quarters.

I push on, becoming one with the walls and shadows, a phantom visitor of the palace.

Dust fills my throat despite my countless prowls through these passages, but I focus on the stone beneath my palm.

Pressing deep inside this overlooked labyrinth, I pause when my hand finds the latch of a concealed wooden door.

I settle vigilantly into this spy nest that likely whispered a thousand secrets to others before me, and my fingers trail on the panel until I find what I seek.

Calming my racing heart with a deep breath, I bring my face an inch from the door and peek through the hole in the panel.

Perhaps tonight, this place will reveal one more secret, if fortune blesses this incursion.

My vision adjusts once I blink away the dust twirling in the stale air of the narrow passage and I still when a silhouette comes into view on the other side.

Our guest is walking to a double bed weighed down by a multitude of pillows, each a different hue of emerald and obsidian. Amrynn's long blond hair cascades over her shoulders as she undoes the intricate hairdo at the back of her head and strips away her crimson dress.

Goosebumps flare over her arms as the silky fabric of a night robe caresses her skin, and her head snaps to the corner of the room I'm lurking behind.

Blood pumps loudly in my ears, but I remain frozen in place, not daring to breath or blink. A framed landscape painting covers the wall and the hole in its canvas is undetectable to a Fae's eyes, but I'm in no habit of tempting fate.

Amrynn's grey eyes dart around the room like a snake searching for a rodent to sink its fangs into for what feels like eternity before her shoulders relax.

Lifting the hem of her dress, now pooled on the floor, she pulls a thin blade from the fabric and tucks it beneath her pillow.

Even when Amrynn has fallen asleep, a hand gripping the knife beneath her head and her chest rising regularly, I remain behind the peephole a while longer.

The threads of the future remain tangled, but if there's one thing I know, it's that the Lady of the Moon Fae has loyalty for no one but herself. Her allegiance means nothing, and I don't plan on letting anyone get the better of me.

So, I watch as Amrynn's regular breathing fills the room.

I watch as dust settles around me, and I become the ghost of Nyths until my vision blurs and dark spots form in the corner of my eyes.

I watch as the scene before me transforms and a body takes shape at my feet. With lifeless viridian eyes and a mouth similar to mine, crimson pools beneath the corpse, the thick liquid spilling over the hardwood floors, permeating each crack in the boards, tracing a path towards me until the warm blood reaches my feet.

With Father's cooling body mere feet away, my fingers fold into my palms, gripping metal. When I uncurl my fingers, a gold medallion sits in my palm.

My burning eyes blink away the vision and a grin forms on my face. The key to my freedom is within reach.

It's well past midnight when I retreat to my chamber, a thousand scenarios running wild in my mind.

Father's games could cost us everything, but I will not be another chess piece on his board or Amrynn's. This is my game now.

CHAPTER 29

AZRAN

Ela's hold loosens under my palm and her rage radiates through the bond as darkness threatens.

I tighten my grip instantly, digging my nails into her hand to keep her still.

Her eyes snap to mine and I shake my head almost imperceptibly as the torches are extinguished.

Calen's words echo in my mind, but I remain focused on Ela to keep her rage at bay as the King leaves with his son and newfound ally, my brother. His name is forever tarnished, tainted, and rendered meaningless.

Alone once more, Ela's fury explodes down the bond, relegating my heartbreak to a distant memory.

"Fucking bastard."

I pull her to me through the bars, trying to keep her calm by brushing my fingers along her palm. There is no point in overexerting herself. She's barely able to crawl as it is.

She snaps, pulling her arm free. "How can you do and say nothing?" Her whole body shakes with rage as the words leave her cracked lips. "Your own family betrays you and you don't lift a finger?"

A snarl tears from my throat as her words pierce my heart like arrows, their poison seeping into my veins. Her eyes shine in response, relieved to find the monster inside me fighting to be unleashed.

I screw my eyes closed, willing my mind to stay in control.

"We need a plan, Ela," I whisper through gritted teeth.

"You heard him. We're out of time." She bares her teeth at me. "If it were anyone else, you'd be trying to snap these bars in two. You've lost your edge."

Acid runs through my veins once more and I can barely contain the bloodlust rushing through me. Her words have always hurt the most.

"When we're out of here, he'll get what's coming to him." I grip the bars separating our cells until my knuckles whiten. "I swear it."

Her hands wrap over my fingers as Ela brings her face an inch from mine.

"Fuck your empty promises."

———◦———

We spend the next hour in eerie silence, Ela keeping her distance from my cell and leaving her words echoing in my head. Her ragged breaths reach my ears but I can't make out her face in the darkness, only the mass of her body curled on the stones.

I instinctively reach for her through my cage when footsteps sound. The dungeon door creaks open, but she doesn't move.

The faint light of a torch fills the dark space, revealing Calen. Wincing at the aggression, a growl tears from my throat.

"Enjoy the rest of your miserable life in here, *brother*."

Blinded by the light, I can barely make out his features, but that doesn't stop me from crashing against the cell bars with a roar.

"You piece of—"

The guard's baton collides with my face.

"Shut your mouth, dog."

Calen's laughter sings in the air as pain flares in my cheek and blood drips from my nose into my mouth.

By the time I can open my eyes again, he's gone.

Glancing towards Ela's cell, I wait for another poisonous attack to leave her mouth, but she pulls herself to her knees instead, her fingers digging into the stone.

"If we're going to die here, I won't go without a fight."

Her whisper is charged with simmering rage, twisting her voice into a darker one I barely recognize.

"Ela. Don't." I reach for her ankle, but my fingers only grasp at the stale air.

"Save your energy," I snap.

Her dark laugh resounds, confirming she's not herself anymore. In fact, she never has been, here. Maybe madness finally took her like it threatened to take me. She hasn't undergone what I have in this life. Maybe her mind didn't make it out of Airdan's torture chamber.

She's been going in and out of consciousness for days, barely able to utter a coherent sentence, and Calen's visits might have just tipped her over the edge.

I follow her from my cell as she grips the metal door of her cage.

"Ela."

Her head tilts back, her long hair falling over her scar-covered back. My eyes dart around the room in search for something to stop her as my rage awakens with hers, mixing with panic. Her pain erupts down the bond before she retreats into her darkness.

I'm losing her. She's inches away and yet slipping through my fingers.

"Ela." I clench my teeth, trying to keep my voice from trembling. "Listen to me."

She doesn't move, her hands still locked onto the metal railing. Energy emanates from her, dark spirals twirling in and out of her weak body.

Unintelligible whispers fill the air, and it takes me a moment to identify the source as Ela.

I call her name, over and over, in the hopes I will bring her back from the edge before she overexerts herself and dies in front of my eyes.

"I can't lose you, Ela. Stop this."

She feels dead through the bond. Life has left her soul, leaving only darkness and death.

The whispering of her name turns to shouting when her body starts shaking uncontrollably, but she doesn't relent.

I've never hated her stubbornness more than I do in this moment. It will be her doom and mine, for I can't live in a world she's not part of. I won't.

"Ela!"

Footsteps echo down the corridor and guards rush in, alarmed by the sound of my screams.

Relief takes me when the two soldiers walk in, their hands on their swords. They'll be able to stop her. They have to.

They light the torches again, providing enough light for me to gaze upon the love of my life burning herself out. Ela's eyes are rolled back in their sockets, her body shaken by tremors.

"Help her." I grip the bars until my finger protest the pain, but I don't let go. "Please."

"I told you to shut your mouth." The one with rings up his nose barks at me, aiming the tip of his sword at my face.

I'm about to snarl back when a hissing sound stops me. Faint light is streaming from Ela's palms.

"What is she doing?" Pierced-nose advances on Ela's cage.

"She can't do anything. These walls are warded against her," the other answers, although he unsheathes his sword, too.

The metal bars turn orange under Ela's touch, and my eyes widen.

"Over here, bastards. It's me you want." I slam on the metal in an attempt to divert their attention.

Their gazes dart towards me as the bars of Ela's cell sizzle and melt under her fingers. A moment later, she launches at the guards with a growl.

Her hands land on their throats, burning through the flesh and boiling their blood. Their screams are swallowed by fire and their souls leave their body as they collapse to the floor in a symphony of awful gargles.

I remain frozen in place, hypnotized by the fire dancing in Ela's palms as she turns to me, her eyes dark raging globes in the night.

She moves before I do, quickly working through the bars of my cell.

When a molten pile of lava pools on the ground in front of me, she storms through the corridor.

Energy rushes through my blood like acid as I pull myself up and stumble from the cage, following her.

Still unsettled, I do my best to catch up, trying to keep my breathing regular and my stance steady.

I crash against a stone wall, barely able to stay upright as her shadow disappears behind a corner.

I'm losing her, but calling out her name is out of the question. We can't risk more guards heading down here.

I instill strength in my legs, pouring every last bit of power I have left into them as I blink rapidly.

I catch up with her in a stairway and lunge at her, pushing her against the wall and forcing her to stop.

"Follow me," I command.

Her dark eyes scan my face and her head tilts as the words register.

"No more fighting," I say. "We're getting out of here as fast as we can."

She's about to argue, but I silence her with a stare. Neither of us knows how long she can go on like this, and I'm certainly running on fumes.

I make my way up, glancing behind me every now and then to make sure she's keeping up.

Shouts assault my ears the moment we hit the ground floor. We freeze long enough to exchange a glance and I break into a run, making for the kitchens.

Her footsteps hit the ground not far behind and that's all I can focus on. She's still running. She's still breathing.

"Bring them to me. Dead or alive."

Airdan's raged-filled voice tones in the air, like it's coming from all around us. I scan the corridor ahead and keep running.

"If I can't have you, then no one will, Elanor."

His voice echoes at full force as my eyes dart frantically. Whatever devilish magic he's uncovered throughout his wretched existence is following us, entrapping us within the walls of his home.

We turn a corner and run into a small squadron.

Darkness instantly flares down the bond and fire flows on my right. The first two guards burn alive before they can release a breath, and my fist lands on a third, crushing a skull.

Ela is unleashed, burning through limbs and flesh while I hammer down my fists and smash noses and windpipes.

Moments later, I barge into the kitchens with adrenaline pulsing through my veins.

Servants scream as they flee before us and we make for the back door.

I hit the door shoulder first, smashing through the wooden panel.

The cold night air brushes my face and Ela runs past me into the streets of the capital.

———◦———

My lungs are on fire, I'm seeing stars, and my legs are threatening to collapse under my weight.

I have no idea how long we've been running. It feels like hours. All I know is, we're heading to the lower levels of Nyths and they're still chasing us. Airdan will not relent, the whole city is waking up, and torches brighten our trail as doors swing open behind us.

Boots hit the paved ground, haunting our steps, and echoing at every corner.

Ela's power has vanished from the bond and she's fallen behind me. With each second, her ragged breath grows louder.

I stumble down a narrow street, exhaling loudly through my nose. Hope is slowly leaving me, and the same disillusion is taking Ela's heart.

A faint light catches the corner of my eye down the alley.

With no time to second-guess myself, I crush myself against the wall and squeeze into a narrow passageway. Leaning against the wall, I grab Ela by the waist and pull her after me.

She collapses in my arms, struggling to suck in breath.

I scan the back alley we're in for an exit or a hideout, but come up empty. Footsteps are closing in around us.

"Ela." She lifts her head, revealing her crazed eyes circled in deep purple. "Your shadows."

I hate myself for asking this of her after she's given this attempt her all.

She screws her eyes shut, not hesitating for a second, and darkness floods the bond.

I pull her tightly to me, holding her up against me, willing every bit of strength left in my body to hers.

The footsteps slow to a halt.

Scanning the other end of the street, my eyes widen at the sight of guards whose heads are turned towards us.

I hold my breath, keeping as still as I can. If Airdan's wards are as powerful as he says, there's nowhere we can hide, and his soldiers can see right through the shadows.

I count the seconds, waiting for them to draw their swords and storm the street, until finally a reprieve comes.

"Keep moving." A bearded Fae points in another direction. "Let's go."

Relief floods my veins as Ela rests her head on my chest.

My stomach drops when I can't feel her heartbeat. Shaking her in my arms, I'm about to call her name when she looks up.

Darkness recedes and her hazel eyes meet mine. Her face bears the marks of her stay at the palace, and I can't look any longer.

"We need to move," I whisper.

Dragging her behind me, I move down the narrow passage, making for the other end.

I glimpse beyond the corner, only to find the street crawling with guards carrying torches. Backing away, I lean against the building, racking my brain for a way out of this madness.

Hair rises on my arm when Ela's weight on my back disappears, and I turn.

Ela's gone. She was here seconds ago, right behind me.

A gust of warm wind blows against my back as a pair of arms wraps around my middle and pulls.

CHAPTER 30

AZRAN

I shove blindly, aiming for the mass behind me.

My blow finds its target as a body hits the ground, and I whirl around, searching for my assailant. I'm surrounded by four walls and a Fae with both hands in the air in surrender, but there is no sign of my mate.

In what appears to be a small kitchen, faint light streams from a candle on a wooden table, just enough to reveal the busted lip on my aggressor's tanned face and her dark brown eyes.

A shape emerges from the back of the room seconds later and Ela's gaze pierces the darkness.

I'm about to lunge towards her when another familiar shape steps into the light and I keep still. Draped in red velvet sleeves, Vesta's arm is wrapped around my mate's throat, holding her in place.

"What is—"

"Az."

My blood freezes as Calen steps out of the shadows and positions himself next to the Fae I don't recognize.

"Let her go, or I swear on everything you hold dear, I will kill you all." I bare my teeth at him and get in a fighting stance. "You have three seconds."

The room falls to complete silence as my eyes dart between them. Three. Vesta's breathing accelerates when she meets my eyes. Two. Calen's head turns to Ela. One. Oh, he's dying first.

Seeing red, I launch towards Calen.

"Az."

I hold my blow at the last second when my mate's faint voice reaches my ears, and my gaze snaps to hers.

Vesta's hold loosens around her neck just as Calen steps forward.

"Brother." A snarl tears from my throat, but it's not enough to silence him. "We don't have much time. We came to help. It was the only way for me to get past Airdan's suspicions," he says in a rush. "Az, come on. You know me better than that."

Sweat trickles down his temple and a vein bulges on the side of his neck as he searches for the right words. He reaches a hand out to me.

"I don't know what I know anymore, *brother*," I spit out.

"I gave you the signal when I came back down to your cells, Az." Calen's arm falls slack to his sides, defeated.

"What signal?" My rage is overwhelming. I'm holding on by a thread. My body might be on the brink of exhaustion and death, but as long as a drop of blood remains in my veins, I will fight to protect Ela, even if it's the last thing I do.

"Just like we did back in Morilanthe." He raises his hand, showing four fingers and his thumb tucked in his palm.

I squint at him.

"After months of torture in the dark, you thought I could see this shit?"

Calen stares at me in confusion before his chuckle fills the air. The chuckle turns into full-blown belly laugh, a smile tugs on Vesta's lips, and even Ela's shoulders relax.

"I told you it would never work." Vesta points her finger at Cal.

I stare at the lot of them in complete disbelief until Ela's snarl tears through the laughter. Her eyes fix on the dark-skinned Fae who'd moved an inch closer to me.

Cal steps between them, raising both hands. "Everyone, calm down."

Vesta releases Ela, who stands aside, at equal distance from her friend and me.

Calen waves towards the Fae. "This is Rensyl. She's with us."

Rensyl steps back, keeping her hands visible.

"You can call me Ren." She inclines her shaved head slightly. "High Lord."

"Az, if you give me a moment, I'll explain everything." Calen motions towards the chairs around the table, but I don't move. "Milan left messages in the palace kitchen every other day, notes

Ren would pick up. When he didn't check in, we knew something was wrong."

Ela's gaze darkens and her sadness travels down the bond. None of the soldiers who came to Zetrea with Ela or me will ever return to Lóna.

I feel an irrepressible urge to extend my hand to her, kiss the hurt away and banish all remnants of what happened in those cells from her memory. If only I had that kind of power.

Calen's voice stirs me from wishful thinking.

"Ren was placed in Nyths decades ago, and I reached out to her when Ela went looking for you."

"After I explicitly told you not to place anyone in Zetrea," I say, crossing my arms over my chest.

"You're welcome." He shoots me a wink, but I don't react. "It didn't take me long to realize Airdan was the mastermind we were after. Unlimited resources, ancient knowledge, power, and motive—he has it all. He undoubtedly placed spies in Lóna and has been watching our every move, which is why we couldn't walk into Nyths without a solid story."

Cal rests his hands on the back of the chair in front of him, his knuckles whitening under the strength of his grip.

"Seeing you and Ela in that cell and having to pretend like I didn't want to tear out their throats was the hardest thing I've ever had to do."

Calen's broad shoulders slump under some invisible weight, azure eyes glassy with self-recrimination.

"You have to believe me," he rasps, his voice cracking. He looks at Ela. "I'm sorry I couldn't get to you sooner."

Ela nods before turning to Vesta and extending her arms.

Her friend crashes into her embrace, returning the hug tightly as the tension defuses.

"I was worried sick, L," Vesta whispers, a sob shaking her voice.

Cal and I lock eyes as he gives me a quick nod. My inclination to kill him on the spot has lessened, but I'm not ready to admit it just yet.

Ela breaks her embrace with Vesta long enough to utter a few words.

"There's something else you should all know." She steps back to face the group. "Amrynn was here. She came to visit me."

"What happened?" A deep frown appears on Calen's forehead, his eyes holding the same wariness mine did when she told me.

"She asked me to join Airdan's side."

Cal's growl fills the room the moment the words leave Ela's lips.

"That viper."

Amidst the chaos of the last distressing hours, it's good to see that some things remain unchanged. His profound hate for my cousin hasn't wavered.

"She's dug her own grave," I add, bitterness coating my tongue.

My eyebrows draw together when Ela's presence fades down the bond, and the rest of the world disappears as I try to make eye contact with her.

We lock eyes as she sways on her legs, right before they give out.

"What about—"

Vesta's question is cut short as I lunge forward with my mate's name carved on my lips.

I'm with her in a heartbeat, catching her before her body hits the floor.

My blood freezes as I gather her limp body in my arms, her pulse so slow I can barely feel it.

"Are we safe here?" I ask sharply, trying to keep panic at bay.

"Yes, High Lord," Ren answers without skipping a beat.

Shaken from her torpor, Vesta is with me in seconds while Ren makes for a kitchen cabinet to grab healing ointments.

The red-haired captain extends her arms towards my mate and I pull back instinctively.

"I've got her," she says with a calm voice, but I don't release my hold on Ela's unconscious body until she cocks her head in Cal's direction. "There is still much for you to discuss, but she needs rest."

The urge to protect Ela tears through me, the energy inside me thrashing and calling for Vesta's spilled blood, for there is no right or wrong when I'm in its grasp. There's only survival, and adversaries standing between me and my mate.

When Vesta's worried gaze meets mine, I find the love we share for Ela in her eyes.

I call my power back as Vesta releases a short breath, and ever so slowly, I let go of Ela.

CHAPTER 31

CALEN

Azran stands in front of the bedroom door where Vesta is watching over Ela, close enough to hear the slightest flutter in the sheets or her heartbeat. The remainder of his self-control is probably being used to not kick the door in.

He meets my stare, and the crimson retreats in his irises before his eyes scan the kitchen meticulously.

One of his eyebrows shoots up when he realizes it's just the two of us.

"Stealthy, right?" I say. His jaw is still clenched tight, but a twinkle of admiration shines in his eyes. "One of Ren's many talents."

I wave towards the table and the refreshments that have been placed on top of it before letting out a sigh when he doesn't move.

"You're holding on by a thread. Please, sit down." My words have no effect on him so I add, "she's in good hands."

After an interminable silence, his mouth parts.

"I can't—she still needs me. If I stop now, I won't get back up."

The shaking in his fingers does nothing to ease my concern, but I keep my voice steady and calm.

"You're not alone anymore. She will be fine, and so will you."

The internal debate raging inside him is painted all over his torn face.

"You're no use to her dead. I promise you are both safe. It's over, Az."

He finally takes a step towards the table, reaching for a glass of water he downs in one go before resting his hands on the wooden surface for support.

His shirt is torn apart, revealing a multitude of new scars. The only visible part of the trauma, for I'm sure Airdan didn't stop there.

He lifts his head to meet my gaze, letting me see the hurt and shame shaking his heart. The sight takes me back to the day we met. He had the same look in his eyes, carried the same hurt. I had hoped never to see him like this again—destroyed, an empty shell, like a pale copy of his true self.

Like he can read my mind, he gives me a small smile, and I swallow the lump forming in my throat. *What have they done to you, brother?*

"I can't stay much longer if I don't want to compromise my position with Airdan."

"Does he trust you?"

"No, but he's a gambler. He's curious to see how this plays out," I add. "How did you guys get out?"

"Ela."

My brows draw together in confusion.

"She lost her mind after you came back down, or so I thought, until she started melting the bars of our cells. She can wield fire without Nahtar." Az turns his hands over to stare at his palms. "She's so much more powerful than I thought. I underestimated her. We all did."

"Remind me never to piss her off," I say with a chuckle, still trying to wrap my head around what he's suggesting.

Azran's smile widens and this time it meets his eyes as he opens his arms. I release my first full breath since we all stepped into the safe house and pull him in a strong embrace.

"I'm sorry it took us so long to figure it out." His shirt is soaked in a mix of sweat and blood, but I don't care. I only tighten my hold on him, gripping his body with full force.

A gasp tears from his throat and his body tenses before I realize, a second too late, I'm hurting him.

"Shit, sorry."

He steps back with a cough, reaching for the table again to steady himself before sagging on a chair heavily, exhaustion finally taking over. His features transform in a mask of pain, and he repositions himself.

"Never pull something like that ever again, Cal. I came an inch from killing you tonight."

I take the chair in front of him. "We need a better signal, that's for sure."

The smile tugging on Azran's lips disappears as his gaze darts to the bedroom door, straining to catch any faint sound coming from the other side. A second later, his shoulders relax.

"So, what's next?" He refills and empties his glass with one chug.

"A boat awaits us in Ryfa. We rendezvous there. Take a day to rest, let the madness of your escape die down, and leave. Ren knows this city like the back of her hand and will help you."

Az winces as he leans back on his chair.

"I wish we could all leave now, but there is no way I can sneak you past the patrols with us. I need to maintain my cover as long as I can."

My brother shakes his head in disbelief at the cockiness of my plan.

"Assuming we make it out of here, then what?"

"We gather the armies and prepare for his attack. He will come after us all the second he finds out. When he does, we will raise hell on earth, together." I extend my arm towards him and he catches it, squeezing my forearm tightly. "Airdan needs to be stopped."

"He will be." A devilish smile blooms on his torn face. "I made him a promise, and you know I never break my promises."

We both nod, exchanging a knowing look. From this point on, just like we agreed when we met, only death will stop us.

"Just stay alive long enough for us to make it back to Lóna together, asshole."

"And don't get double crossed, prick," he says.

Letting go of my arm, Azran finally caves and starts picking at the food, each slow bite eliciting a wince.

His eyes dart to the bedroom every now and then as he chews on dried meat and cheese.

After a few minutes, he catches me observing him.

"What?"

"What about Amrynn?" I ask.

"You heard me." He tears a piece of bread from its loaf. "There is a tombstone in Morilanthe with her name on it. She's spent too many years playing games, and she got caught."

He goes back to his meal, but pushes his plate aside after another small bite, his stomach probably unable to sustain more food after being starved for months.

"We need to leave." We can both hear Ela's regular breathing from across the room, and I would bet my right hand that Vesta is standing behind the door, eavesdropping on our every word. "I'll go get Vesta."

Az leans back on his chair and nods, barely able to keep his head up.

"And you need to rest," I add.

He responds with an unintelligible grunt, but doesn't move from the chair.

I freeze when I'm halfway across the room, a smile tugging at my lips.

"Nice haircut, by the way."

His eyes snap to mine, the hurt in it quickly replaced by gratitude.

"Needed the change."

"It fits the new you." I shoot him a wink, for I can only imagine how soul crushing it must have been for him.

He tilts his head to the side in question, letting me see the irregular length of the strands above his ears.

I nod towards Ela's room. "You deserve this."

He gives me a skeptical look, one of his eyebrows raised.

"You do," I continue. "Get it inside your thick head."

An unconvincing nod is the best I get out of him. At least they're out of those damn cells and together. He'll have to figure out the rest on his own.

I turn towards the bedroom.

"Vesta."

She steps out a second later. Her piercing green eyes barely pause on me, but that brief glance is enough to take my breath away.

"Ela will be fine; she just needs to rest." Her voice has recovered some of its usual cheer. "It's good to see you in one piece, High Lord."

Azran gives her a small smile in thanks, and we make for the door. There is much for us to do, but first, we need to make it out of this city crawling with soldiers.

My hand on the door handle, I wait to make sure no sound is coming from the alley it opens to. Satisfied, I turn the knob with a glance back at Az.

"If you plan on staying up all night to guard the safe house, check the cupboard." I nod to the one on the far right of the kitchen wall. "Brought you a little something."

CHAPTER 32

CALEN

"Follow my lead," I whisper as Vesta and I step onto a major artery of Nyths.

A group of soldiers turns the corner, heading straight towards us.

Vesta's breath quickens when I stomp towards them. The tallest of the lot notices, and his dark eyes narrow.

When we're within hearing distance, the two Fae flanking him lower a hand to the weapons on their belts.

The woman's neck is blacked out under an unidentifiable tattoo, making it look like her head rests directly on her wide shoulders. I eye the design, trying to make out what it could be. Crows and chains, maybe, though part of it could be the head of a snake. Her crooked nose and yellowed teeth add a particularly welcoming touch to the look.

Upon closer inspection, her counterpart doesn't offer much solace. With long, thin hair falling on either side of his wrinkled face, hallowed cheeks, and sunken lifeless eyes, he is as cheerful as a graveyard. He's frankly repulsive, but that doesn't stop him from studying Vesta greedily.

I bare my teeth when the walking corpse of a solider has the audacity to let his gaze wander her neckline.

"Soldiers." I muster as much condescension as I can. "What is the meaning of all this agitation?"

I wrinkle my nose slightly as I eye them up and down.

"We're making our rounds," the tall Fae explains.

I don't respond immediately, letting an uncomfortable silence settle.

"My Lord," he adds hesitantly.

"Quite a boisterous endeavor, wouldn't you say?" I turn to Vesta as I roll my eyes. "A disturbance to guests attempting to enjoy the capital of our great King."

"Indeed, this is ridiculous." She gathers her skirts with a huff. "Far less enjoyable than I would have imagined. Let's go."

"Of course, dear."

She grabs my forearm and we stroll in the direction of the palace without another word to the soldiers.

Once we've walked past several groups of soldiers unbothered, Vesta's shoulders relax.

"Dear?" She's the first to break our silence, her lips pinched tightly.

"Would you have preferred 'my lady?'"

She doesn't respond, but her steps accelerate slightly.

"'Dove,' maybe?"

Sweet victory coats my tongue when her breath hitches in her throat. I know I shouldn't revel in this pettiness, but she fakes her indifference so well, sometimes I wonder if she even remembers our nights together.

The massive stone wall surrounding the palace appears at the end of the main street. Its hideous doors stand wide open to let units in and out of the grounds. The agitation might finally prove useful to us by helping us walk in unnoticed.

Everyone is so busy following orders and looking for Az and Ela that no one questions our late return.

I let out a breath in relief when the palace door is in sight, and Vesta's hold on my arm loosens, ready to discard it the moment we step inside.

The castle's entrance is only a few steps away when the massive door swings on its hinges.

A familiar dark-haired prince greets us with a cold smile, stopping on the doorstep of his home and blocking the way.

"Your Highness." I keep my features neutral as I greet him with a polite nod. The ruffles of Vesta's dress confirm she bows beside me.

"Isn't it cold for a night stroll, General?" His gaze travels to Vesta's forearms, covered in goosebumps.

"We were hoping to discover some of the many distractions Nyths has to offer."

"Tonight, of all nights." He looks around the courtyard, taking in the mass of soldiers swarming the grounds.

I tilt my head to follow his glance. "What's happening?"

"Why the sudden interest in our affairs?"

"I'm merely striving to show my worth as an ally. We can help."

"As far as I'm concerned, your loyalty remains to be proven."

"I thought that putting the lives of Lóna on the line for our King would warrant at least a sliver of trust on your part."

"Trust is earned."

"Indeed," I respond, not missing a beat.

"You left our side awfully quickly earlier today. I wonder what for."

We lock eyes as his question rings in the air, unanswered.

"I don't appreciate whatever it is you're insinuating," I say with a growl.

"Were you not caught wandering Nyths after dark, I wouldn't need to insinuate anything."

I remain silent and look around the courtyard, keeping my heart rate steady. Soldiers are being dispatched, their orders barked loudly, although the suspects are never named.

"Who are you looking for?" I ask, cocking a brow.

"No one you should trouble yourself with."

"Considering what I'm about to do, this sounds like something I definitely should trouble myself with."

A cold smile forms on my lips while his remain pinched. He holds impressive control over his emotions, but tonight his anger betrays him. I seize the opportunity.

"This wouldn't have anything to do with our late High Lord, would it?"

Nylren's eyes flicker at my words. "We have everything under control."

"Like hell you do," I spit out.

I turn to Vesta, whose gaze is fixed on Nylren, panic inhabiting her irises.

My head snaps back towards the prince when his snarl reaches my ears.

"Do you really wish to begin our alliance by insulting King Airdan in his own home? By all means, I'll lead the way to his chambers so you can try that to his face."

He bares his teeth at me, offering the most overt display of emotions I've ever seen from him.

Vesta's hand closes around my arm, and I take a deep breath before meeting Nylren's gaze again.

Appeased by the show we're putting on, his cold mask is back on.

"You focus on keeping your promises, and we'll keep ours," he adds.

"We're on our way to do exactly that."

Nylren nods before stepping aside to let us in.

"Give my best to your father. We'll send word as soon as we reach Lóna."

⸺◆⸺

The first break of day on the horizon doesn't bring calm to Nyths. Soldiers patrol the capital with renewed vigor. Hooves hit the paved street as units gallop from one point to the other, barking orders and knocking on doors. Citizens are stirred from sleep regardless of their status and pulled out of their homes to allow guards to search the buildings.

I keep my focus on the city gates ahead, Vesta and our escort in tow on their mounts.

We're forced to a halt when half a dozen soldiers block our path.

"Hold up." A burly Fae with several insignias on his jacket steps in front of my horse. "Step down your mounts. No one is to leave Nyths without permission from the King."

I stare him down, but he doesn't break eye contact.

"Who do you think you're talking to, guard? It sure as hell can't be me."

I bare my teeth at him when his hand lowers to the axe on his side.

"I'm talking to you, pretty boy."

A dark chuckle tears from my throat as I shake my head, silently assessing our options.

"Either you get down, or we make you." A blond soldier behind the captain steps closer, a mean rictus on her face.

I'm off the horse and face to face with the captain in the blink of an eye, the tip of my knife an inch from his veiny throat. His eyes widen almost imperceptibly, but my gaze lands on the soldier behind him.

"Come near me, soldier, and it will be the last thing you do."

She has the intelligence to freeze and appear slightly alarmed.

"What is your name, soldier?" I return my focus to their captain.

"Lhoris, my lord." His throat bobs again my blade as he gulps down his saliva.

"I hope I see you upon my return to Nyths, Lhoris." The knife digs into his skin just enough to draw a drop of blood. "I'll be sure to mention our interaction to King Airdan over dinner."

I'm back on my horse in seconds, digging my heels into its sides.

"Open the gates."

Lhoris barks orders, and we're out of this wretched city a heartbeat later.

CHAPTER 33

ELANOR

The usual cold seeping through my bones, freezing the tips of my fingers and toes, has been replaced by a comforting warmth. The strain in my shoulders has gone, and so did the pain in my middle.

This feels wrong, terribly wrong.

It takes me a moment to recognize the feeling swelling in my chest. Fear.

I wiggle my toes, confirming I can move them just fine, and feel every tingle. My heart beats rapidly as sensations return to my body.

The mattress hugs my body, supporting my weight, and the sheets caress my skin as if made of a thousand feathers.

Stretching my arms, no longer imprisoned in chains, my hands go to my chest as I slowly emerge from slumber.

My eyes snap open when my fingers reach bare skin on my neck. The collar is gone.

My chest rises rapidly as I scan the windowless room and memories trickle back in. There's barely enough light streaming through the door, but it's enough to confirm I'm no longer in my cell.

It wasn't a dream. This time, I got out.

Vesta is here with Calen—and another Fae, although I can't remember her name.

A subtle headache forms behind my eyes as I replay last night in my head.

Rensyl. Yes, she helped us.

Tears well up in my eyes as I realize I'm safe and this wasn't another of Airdan's tricks.

I can't bring myself to leave the bed just yet, so I count the seconds in my head, needing to make sure this is not another illusion.

Twelve. Thirteen. Fourteen.

A shudder shakes my body and I screw my eyes shut. Airdan's illusions all felt so real.

Twenty-six. Twenty-seven. Twenty-eight.

Although, not quite as real as this. I bunch up the sheets in my palm, feeling their softness. I'm safe. Forty.

Forty-one. Forty-two.

Another three hundred and forty-two seconds pass before I notice the tug inside me. The bond is there, pulsing regularly, unrestrained. Its echo carries safety and reassurance, although it's also mixed with a different kind of fear.

I let out a heavy breath, steadying myself as curiosity overpowers the angst in my heart. I get up, my legs still a little wobbly, and make for the door. I've managed in far more dire states, and if memory serves, I'm not going far.

As soon as I open the kitchen door, my hands go to my eyes. Natural light streams from a round skylight in the middle of the room, its brightness blinding me.

I blink furiously, willing my eyes to adjust faster, and when they do, my breath hitches in my throat.

Sunrays hit the side of Azran's face. He's passed out on a chair, his head resting on his arms, crossed on the table. His back rises and falls with each ragged breath, but he's here, alive.

His presence alone makes the space shrink on itself. A small oven stands against the wall opposite the entrance, wood cabinets framing its sides. The walls are bare except for a small bookcase in the corner next to an aged leather armchair. The skylight as the only source of light in the room makes for the perfect safe house, rendering it completely undetectable to the outside world. The only visible exit is the front door, smaller than most doors and designed to fade into the wall. That, and another door next to the bedroom's. A washroom, I presume.

A used rug whose pattern has long been worn out by boots adorns the wooden floors. Apart from that, it looks like no one ever took the time to decorate this place. It's been stripped to the bare minimum. No avalanche of embroidered pillows on the bed or the armchair, no pop of color, and an overall complete absence of style. I love it.

A piece of paper on the counter catches my eye. Careful not to wake Azran up, I tiptoe around him and grab the note.

*"The **Myra**. Dock two.*
Cal
**ointments and bandages are in the cupboard"*

I swallow the lump in my throat as I put the note down. My mouth is so dry, I almost choke.

Turning around, I bump into a chair, stubbing my knee on its backrest with a grunt. I repress the curse forming on my lips as my eyes snap to Azran's limp body, still sleeping.

I let out a breath and rub my leg vigorously before making my way to the other side of the table, noticing the pitcher of water and the food.

I freeze a few feet away from Azran, my purpose long forgotten by the bond exploding in my chest. How will I ever get used to this? To him, so close to me?

My heart strains like the organ can't contain my feelings. Back in the dungeons, after I was thrown in the cell next to his, I was barely lucid except for the one thought looping in my head; the regret and hope that he knew what I never told him.

The bond pulses so strongly I worry it will wake him up. I can barely stay upright under its force as it screams to be let out, just as I want to scream it to the world. It's not a desire anymore, but a primal need to touch him, hold him, and be held. I need his touch like I need air. I need to feel his gaze all over me and find the same necessity in his hazel eyes.

Tears well in my eyes once more as the hope of a life alongside him is born, however fleeting.

Resolve steadies my mind as I make for the bedroom. I've fought for just about everything I've ever had in this life. Why stop now?

I find a blanket in the small chest at the foot of the bed, the only other piece of furniture in this room, and head back into the kitchen.

After placing the blanket over his shoulders, I plop down opposite from him and help myself to several glasses of water, unable to refrain from drinking too much.

Nausea strikes moments later as water fills my empty stomach, but I stay there, watching over him, making sure his breathing remains regular as memories overlay reality. I'm back in the cage, my hands burning through the metal as Azran screams my name over and over. I taste the blood on my tongue, feel the heat under my fingers, and get lost in the rage shaking me to my core as Death answers my calls.

I'm still not sure how I managed to summon her, I only know she was listening, willing to show me how to destroy the world and grant me incredible power.

I used to be scared of the darkness within me, but Airdan rid me of that fear. It's a part of me, granted by Death herself, the origin and the end, my bearer.

I've never felt more powerful, and yet a new fear is born, or rather an old fear rekindled and reinforced through the bond. What if he's changed his mind? I can't shake the look of pure madness I saw in his eyes back at the castle, and the way he wouldn't meet my gaze once we escaped. What if he leaves?

The old demons are back, ready to jump at the opportunity to instill more doubt in my heart, but I won't let them. Not this time. I've wasted too much time already.

A rush of pride courses through me, relegating the fear to a corner of my mind. He wouldn't abandon me. Not after standing up for me the way he did in front of Cal. I saw it in his eyes. He was ready to kill his only family to save me.

He is my family now.

Azran stirs in his sleep and I jump to my feet.

I kneel by his side as his crimson eyes flutter open.

My lips part, but no sounds comes out.

He winces in pain as he lifts his head to rest his back on the chair. Only then does his gaze meet mine for a mere second, and what I see in it crushes the hope just born. The heartbreak in his eyes is almost palpable as he avoids my gaze.

A crack appears in my mental resolve as I stand and fill a glass with water. I bring it to his lips with trembling hands, unable to settle the panic in my heart.

Only his pain erases my own. He's in a much worse state than I ever was. His head bobs weakly to his chest as he tries to pull himself up, bracing a hand on the table.

"Wait."

My voice doesn't feel like mine when I reach for him to help him stand.

He doesn't respond so I wrap my arm around his chest and help him to the bedroom without another word. It's a miracle we make it without tumbling to the floor. He sits on the mattress with a hiss and I let him go.

I'm about to step back when his chest leans forward dangerously, and I catch him before he collapses.

Ever so gently, I remove his torn shirt from his back and lean him back on the bed before tucking him in as best I can, my movements slow and weak.

I don't get another glimpse at the hazel lingering in his eyes, as he keeps them closed the entire time, but once I'm sure he can't fall off the bed, I retreat to the kitchen.

"No."

His croak barely reaches my ears, but I freeze. His eyes are still closed, his suffering painted across his torn face.

Does he want me to stay or leave? I'm about to ask when his breathing deepens. I guess I won't know until he wakes up. If he wakes up.

I silence the treacherous voice in my head and, with the last of my strength, go to the kitchen and swing open the first cupboard I see. I find the ointments on the first try.

"Yes!" A cry tears from my throat as I snatch the small vials and jars. Thank Death for labels.

Back in the bedroom, I do my best with the limited instructions that were left. I pour several drops of a dark liquid in his mouth and place a greyish salve on the deepest cuts on his chest.

When there's nothing else I can do for Azran without waking him to turn him over, I use some of the salve on my own wounds.

I return to the kitchen, trembling from exhaustion and worry. Although my body didn't break under his weight, my heart shattered in a million pieces.

Pulling a chair out, I plop down at the table and force myself to eat. I know my body needs fuel, although my heart is not in it.

By the time I'm done chewing on bread and cheese, my balm-covered cuts are radiating a soft heat.

I stare at the ointments for several minutes before mustering the strength to rise, the vials in hand. I open the cabinet in front of me, having forgotten which ones the medicine came from, and almost drop the small containers when my eyes land on Nahtar, propped against the back of the cabinet next to Azran's two-bladed sword.

I blink several times and my mouth drops open. Putting the vials on the counter, I reach for my weapon, and relief floods me the second my fingers find its familiar hilt.

My power responds instantly and a dark fire runs down the blade. I close my eyes, allowing myself to savor this moment, the strength in my grip, and the energy flowing through me. With Nahtar in hand, my connection to the spirit world awakens, and it's like my father is with me again. I can feel his strength and picture his bearded face smiling upon me, even after everything that's happened.

Whatever energy Nahtar instilled in me vanishes the moment I let go of the blade. Pain in my joints and chest return, and so does the exhaustion.

My eyes dart around the kitchen, debating returning to the bedroom or sleeping in the armchair.

I give it about two seconds before I make for the bedroom. I didn't sleep on soiled ground and wet stone for weeks to refuse a warm bed, with my mate in it.

CHAPTER 34

ELANOR

Complete darkness obscures the bedroom when my consciousness surfaces in the middle of the night. My eyes half-open, I can barely discern Azran's shape beside me, his chest rising and falling an inch from my face.

Too exhausted to second-guess myself, I nestle against him to steal a couple more hours of sleep.

I wake up alone. With last night a distant dream, I stare at the ceiling. Everything feels unreal. We made it out of the dark cells and now have a plan to leave this place for good.

Faint noise streams from the kitchen, confirming Azran is up. I still can't believe he's out there, and that we're in the same place, sharing a roof even for just a moment before we have to run again.

Clutching my arms to my chest, I let out a heavy breath. I know I need to face him. Part of me wants to stop caring and just jump into his arms, whether he'll have me or not. But the other part of me, the reasonable one, crushes the idea. Funny, that my cautiousness would choose today of all days to reveal itself.

A small smile blooms on my face as a familiar warmth washes over me. Savage is sat across from me, his furry head tilted to the side.

He was the bravest companion in life, and still is in Death.

In his presence, my own courage surfaces.

I toss the covers aside and get up. My body is still heavy and sore, but I'm feeling better. A quick scan of my legs confirms the salve has healed most of my recent wounds, and the red around my wrists is almost gone.

My gaze stops on the torn dress hanging from my body by a thread. I ought to make a great impression, wearing that rag. Gods, I miss Rina. I miss being home.

I try readjusting the fabric to cover some of my scars, but soon give up. What I need is a proper bath, only there is no conveniently filled tub in the bedroom, not even a bucket of water.

I run my fingers through my tangled hair as best as I can and take a deep breath.

I open the door and Azran freezes, an empty plate in hand.

He looks so different, and yet the same. He's wearing a clean shirt buttoned halfway up, revealing his torn chest. Bruises decorate his handsome face and strong jaw, now shaved clean. The short hair highlights his sharp features, and his eyes carry no trace of crimson.

"You're up," he says, slowly putting the plate down.

I nod, my heart beating wildly. I missed him so damn much, I feel like I'm going to explode. Hope swells in my core when he meets my gaze. Everything is telling me to run to him and forget about the rest of the world, so I take a step forward, but he looks away.

I stop dead in my tracks, his rejection a stab in my heart. He barely looked at me, but I guess that split second was enough for him to make up his mind.

I can't do this. I can't be in the same room, this close to him but with this abyss separating us. I don't understand his reaction, only that the bond is raging through me. I need to talk to him, touch him, but he's keeping his distance. Turns out, yesterday was definitely not an invite for me to share a bed with him.

I glance around the small kitchen, my gaze landing on the one door I haven't opened yet, next to the bedroom.

Words lodge in my throat and I step towards the closed door, praying to Death it's unlocked.

I close the distance in a few steps and the knob turns under my fingers. I sag against the door the second it closes.

A tear rolls down my cheek, but I swallow my sobs. I refuse to let him hear me ugly cry after I so valiantly ran away.

Damn it. I should have said something, anything, like ask him what his problem is. What the fuck is wrong with me? Why do I feel like this?

My heart pounds in my ears as I try to blink away the tears clouding my vision.

The clink of dishes from the other side startles me. I push off from the door and quickly wipe the rest of my tears with the back of my hand.

The cold tiled floors under my bare feet grounding me, I realize I may not have made such a terrible decision by coming here. Like the rest of the safe house, the washroom is minimally equipped. A large wash basin, bucket of water, and chest occupy one corner, and a small vanity with a sink and mirror the other.

I could use a bath. If not a fucking *thank you*, I've at least earned that.

My resolve weakens slightly when I realize the water in the bucket is cold. Maybe not a bath, then, but a good wash.

Cold was putting it nicely. The water is downright freezing. Each splash numbs my muscles, and with them, my feelings. For that, I'm grateful.

I watch as the dried blood and grime washes away. I eye the small bottle of soap set on the ground and, after careful deliberation, dump half its contents over my head. I rub my scalp until my entire head is scrubbed clean and dump another bucket of icy water to rinse.

When I'm done, I snatch a towel out of the vanity and dry myself as quickly as I can. I dig into the chest and dress in a clean linen shirt and pants.

My teeth stop chattering after I pat dry my hair with the towel and tame it with a comb sitting by the sink.

I finally pause to face my reflection in the mirror. I don't look that bad, all things considered. Hues of purple and yellow cover my face and arms, but the cuts are healing nicely. I drag my fingers along the red scars circling my chest, souvenirs from a lifetime ago. The memory of the darkclaws doesn't elicit terror anymore. I've seen and gone through too much since.

A sad smile tugs my lips as the wraiths of another time haunt me, bringing me back to the moment I first met Azran.

I've come too far to give up now. I'm going to face him, whether he's ready or not, and I'm going to tell him everything. I need him to know everything.

I pause in front of the door, trying to figure out where to begin. My stomach is in knots by the time I put my hand on the handle.

I release a deep breath as I prepare myself to pour my heart out and face my biggest fear. I murmur a silent prayer for Death to grant me her unwavering support. I'm going to need all of it.

When I can't wait any longer, I pull the door open.

My chest tightens when the warmth of the room greets me.

Azran is waiting before the threshold, his arm frozen mid-air in a fist and heat radiating from his chest just inches from my face.

My blood freezes as an impossible need rushes through the bond.

Gathering what's left of my courage, I slowly lift my head to face him. Gods, I forgot how tall he is.

We lock eyes and my breath hitches in my throat when he doesn't look away.

Tears rolls down my cheeks as he meets my gaze, letting me see that his hazel eyes scream with the same longing.

I crash into him, burying my face into his shirt and hugging his waist so tightly my hands hurt.

An eternity passes before he wraps his arms around my shoulders and rests his chin on my head.

Thump.

His lungs expand with each deep breath.

Thump.

His pounding heart echoes in my head, screaming its existence and strength. And in this moment, I know. I know that each heartbeat sings for me, and that my entire world rests on that sound.

Thump.

It's strength contrasts so strongly with the memory of its devastating absence it's almost painful. The ghost of my heart shattering to pieces forever haunting me, I know that dread will accompany me to my grave.

Never again. I will never go through that again. I swear it. I won't live in a world he is not a part of.

I inhale deeply. I could drown in his scent of pine and citrus, and it wouldn't stanch my need for him.

"I've missed you, little one."

He tightens his hold and my heart explodes, unable to contain our bond.

His voice is like a caress in my ears, silencing the fears and replacing them with blind trust. I only hug him tighter, unable to utter a word without choking on sobs.

I never thought I'd hear these words, no matter how many times I dreamed of seeing him again.

He's here.

I'm home.

CHAPTER 35

AZRAN

Ela's arms, tightly secured around my middle, press on my broken ribs, but I'm simply content caressing her damp hair, reveling in her touch.

She hasn't uttered a single word, but what else is left for her to say? She said enough in the dungeons. Her damning words have not left me, nor has her accusatory tone. I don't blame her, only myself. Only the truth has the power to scar me, and she spoke no lies then.

I pull back when the temperature of her body finally registers. Her arms are frozen and her skin is covered in goosebumps.

"Are you cold?" I reach for her face to wipe the tears drying on her reddened cheeks.

She shakes her head and, when I let go of her, her brows furrow together. A sliver of hurt travels her irises as she pinches her lips in annoyance before her features harden.

Recognizing that look, I know I have mere seconds before the first jab rolls off her tongue.

"I failed you," I blurt out.

Her mouth opens and closes as she swallows whatever she was about to say.

"What—"

"You said it yourself, back in the cages." I meet her gaze, letting her see the guilt I'm drowning in. "Alone, I could manage the torture, but when they dragged you into this hell with me, I lost it. My *edge*. I couldn't see a way out and I couldn't risk you getting hurt any further until *you* found a way."

"I didn't mean any of it. I was just—"

"You said enough." I cut her off sharply. "And you were right."

"No." Ela reaches for my hand, but I pull back.

"Ela. You had to save me from the grip of death not once, but twice, because I was too blind to see."

"That just makes us even." I cock a brow, not expecting her retort. "*You* came every time I needed you. I simply returned the favor." Her confidence wavers slightly. "I couldn't stay in Averion, alone and wondering what happened to you."

"I'm sorry I left you." I screw my eyes shut. "It was the hardest thing I've ever done. I was by your side every hour of every day, fearing for your life and your soul, wondering if you would wake up. If only I had waited a little longer, I could have saved us both this torment."

"I never blamed you, Az." Ela steps closer to me. "For any of it."

She won't admit it. She's refusing to see the truth, but I'll make her.

"Airdan got me the second I stepped into the palace. I had given up by the time you arrived, but sensing your presence within his grasp drove me to the brink of madness. I broke out of my cell. Only, I failed you again, miserably, exposing you and getting us both caught." I straighten my back and lock eyes with her. "I couldn't protect you. I couldn't keep my promise."

"Stop talking like that. What is wrong with you?" Her anger radiates down the bond, teasing mine. "You're holding yourself to standards I never set."

Her widened eyes scan my face, trying to make sense of it all.

I bare my teeth at her in a snarl, releasing my power and letting her feel the unstable beast beneath the surface. She needs to see me for who I am.

Whatever quality she saw in me was nothing but an act. I ran from the horrors of my childhood and suppressed my own emotions behind a steel wall. I became controlling and calculating so as to never feel again, until she came into my life and changed everything. And I ended up right back in a cell, weak and powerless. All of this was for nothing. I failed again. I couldn't free myself or her, the one person I would give my life for in a heartbeat.

Ela's rage pulses down the bond, although she's doing a good job keeping it in check. I don't think I've ever seen her show this much restraint, certainly not with me.

"I almost lost you," I whisper.

"I'm right here," she answers, guiding my palm to her heart and laying it flat against her heart. "Right here."

Her heartbeat flutters beneath my fingers, but it's her broken body sprawled over the stones of her cage I see, and I pull my hand away.

"Airdan told me everything he did to you, just to have the pleasure of seeing me break. When your body was brought before my eyes, bloody and torn apart, all I could do was stare as you laid unconscious on the floor, his words echoing in my mind."

Tears return to Ela's beautiful eyes, but I keep going.

"Then I betrayed you again. I tried stopping you. I didn't believe in you. I was too scared to lose you."

"Enough." She shoves me until I hit the table behind me, her voice trembling with rage.

I lean down, bringing my face inches from hers, and her breath hitches in her throat. Ever so slowly, my fingers go to the scars on her arms, caressing each cut and bruise.

"Why can't you see these are my doing? This is all on me."

"And I'd take each of them again in a heartbeat, if it meant finding my way back to you."

Her mouth is moving, but I don't hear the words. Nothing she could say would save me from this crushing guilt.

"You've faced more horrors in this life than most, and yet you can't recognize when a monster stands before you."

"But you're *my* monster."

Her voice breaks and her words find their target, shattering and healing my heart at once.

I'd stopped hoping for her love, and yet here I have it. I know the courage it must have taken her to utter this simple word to me, *hers*, making her acknowledgment and absolution my most prized valuables.

My resolve shatters when she leans in to deposit a kiss on my mouth with trembling lips.

"You know nothing of what I've done, little one. Why would you want something that's broken?"

"There's beauty in broken things. You taught me that, just like you taught me I was worth fighting for."

On her tip toes, she rests her forehead on mine, inhaling deeply before continuing.

"Why won't you extend the same grace to yourself? Why can't you see what I see?"

"Because no one ever did, until now." I relax under her touch, letting go of some of the shame I've been holding onto. "I'm so sorry. Please, forgive me."

"Under one condition," she taunts, her voice no more than a whisper.

"Anything."

"Let me in," she says as her warm breath caresses my face. "We fucking deserve this."

Her voice falters, hazel eyes glazing until wetness pools in mine too.

A smile tugs my lips and I nod before dropping a kiss on hers. She swallows my hesitancy in a heartbeat, pressing her mouth to mine.

Tears roll on her face, wetting mine, and my hands go to her waist to pull her closer still. Wrapping my arms tightly around her frame, my lips crash against hers once more.

I leave a trail of kisses down her cheeks, rediscovering her face until her tears are no more. Each brush of my mouth against her skin tastes like salvation, each chuckle tearing from her throat is like absolution for every tortured hour apart. I've missed her so damn much. I've missed her like warm sunlight after endless winter nights.

"Say it," I whisper against her skin.

She doesn't answer right away, so I hover over her ear, letting my breath tease her.

"Say it," I repeat, need fueling my voice.

The corner of her mouth lifts into a knowing smile.

"You're mine," she says. I close my eyes, willing time to suspend as her words tear through the last of my resistance, eclipsing the shame and disintegrating the shackles of guilt on my wrists. "And I am yours."

A wall I didn't realize stood between us crumbles and the bond takes form in my mind. Strings of light intertwine, connecting us as she accepts the bond for the first time, as she accepts me as her mate. An unbreakable link, stronger than steel, everlasting, shines between us in symbol of our commitment to each other.

When I open my eyes again, I know she feels this change too, its reciprocity and intensity. Our connection is so strikingly clear, it's all I can see as the room around us disappears.

"Kiss me again," Ela says against my mouth, her eagerness palpable. "Kiss me until I can't feel my lips anymore."

I close the distance between us.

A rush of heat travels down my middle when her tongue meets mine. My hands shake with the need to feel her shatter under me, while hers travel my chest.

It takes my entire resolve to tear myself from her touch, but I do.

She lifts her head, pure hunger filling her gaze, her chest rising rapidly.

"We need to go. Ren will be back any minute."

She grunts before pulling back.

"Eat something." I glance towards the kitchen skylight as its light dims. "Nightfall is close."

She nods before reluctantly seating herself at the table and picking at the food in front her. I sag against a kitchen cabinet, still trying to tame the need in my core.

"Az," Ela breathes, the single syllable laden with aching want.

"I'll never get tired of hearing you say my name like that," I whisper.

Turning around, she reveals the fire burning in her gaze, filled with pure animalistic need.

"And I'll never get tired of you looking at me like that."

A grin crosses my face as memories of her body beneath mine flood my mind. Her eyes travel my body from a distance.

"Enjoying the view?" I ask.

She straightens in her chair before flashing me a devilish smile.

"Very much."

A chuckle tears from my throat as I move closer.

Cupping her face, I run my thumb over her cheek and lips until her eyes veil with angst and a pit opens in my stomach.

"What is it?"

"Don't ever push me away like that again, or you'll find out the true meaning of rage."

My heart expands tenfold to find more room for my love for her, as if it could be contained by flesh and blood, and the corners of my mouth lift into a wide smile.

Pulling out the chair next to her to sit down, my mouth opens, but the promise never leaves my tongue.

Her eyes widen, meeting mine, when scratches against the door reach my ears.

I glance to the side as she stands as quietly as possible and blows out the candle on the table.

Seconds later, she meets me by the cupboard where I've already snatched my two bladed-sword. She grips Nahtar and her irises darken instantly.

The room is plunged into utter silence and darkness as we take position on either side of the door.

Ela gathers her shadows and I hold my breath, waiting for the door to open.

A silhouette slides through the opening before it closes again and Ela raises her sword a little higher.

A glint of emerald shines under the moon rays streaming from the skylight, and my blade twists.

"It's me."

The voice pierces the bloodlust and I freeze.

"Were you followed?" I ask, lowering my blade as Ren walks in wearing Airdan's colors.

"No. I have our way out." She points to the armor on her chest. "And news."

"Sit." I motion towards the table, but Ren shakes her head.

"We don't have much time."

I nod to her, both in acknowledgement and thanks.

"Reward is being offered in exchange for information about you. Anyone found wandering after dark is tortured into confessing imaginary crimes and hanged by dawn. Soldiers are conducting raids and terrorizing the city."

"These people have nothing to do with us." Ela's anger echoes through the bond as she turns to me. "We have to do something."

I shake my head before addressing Rensyl again.

"Thank you. The risks you're taking do not go unnoticed."

"High Lord." She bows and eyes the weapons still in our hands. "We need to go."

I cock my head towards her armor.

"This is how we're getting out of here?"

A devilish grin forms on her face.

"Follow me."

CHAPTER 36

AZRAN

Ren glides soundlessly ahead, one with the shadows as we trail tight on her heels, senses straining at every cross street.

Everything is perfectly quiet, and I barely notice when Ela's shadows gather around us.

Lit on either side by hovering lanterns, the cobblestone streets lead us away from Nyths' center. We're moving slow, careful, so as not to disturb the silent night with our steps.

The pale light of the moon glints off the windows and dark buildings, giving them an ethereal shimmer as we sneak past them. As expected, the city is free of passerby, its perfect stillness reeking of fear and angst.

We turn into a wider artery and my pulse quickens.

Tension radiates from Ela, like ripples in the dark, as she freezes, before I turn my head a second later.

A patrol is walking towards us, their swords clinking against their armor.

The shadows thicken as Ela grabs my forearm and Ren slowly pulls us back to the street we just left. The patrol's boots thunder against the ground as they get closer.

Ela presses her back against the alley wall, melting into its inky shadow, and I position myself next to her, closest to danger, a hand still gripping my weapon. Steadying my breathing, we become as still and flat as the stones on our backs, and I let her darkness embrace me like a cloak, its solid mass obscuring our forms.

The patrol pauses at the intersection and I cease motion entirely, willing myself invisible. My limbs freeze, my chest barely expanding with breath. We wait, shapes devoid of detail in the night's camouflage, as the group of soldiers scan the alley.

Ela's power flares when the seconds turn to minutes.

"Wait," I whisper down the bond.

My muscles scream for release, but I remain a statue, letting the blackness render me a part of the wall itself.

The soldier closest to us shakes their head after an interminable wait, and the patrol heads back into the main artery, passing the pool of darkness shrouding us.

Only once the footsteps have faded into the distance do we finally peel ourselves from the wall.

Ren slows our pace as we approach the end of another block, craning her neck to peer past the building.

Sweat trickles down my back and my entire body tenses when Ren takes the side street. She leads us to a back alley running behind a building.

With no lanterns to light the area, Ela drops her shadows. It takes a second for my vision to adjust.

The alley opens to a small courtyard, a single door leading inside a building closed shut.

A stable huddles against the side of the structure, darkness laying beyond its corner.

The hair rises on my arms and a low growl tears from my throat as I scan the dead-end Ren led us to.

"Over there." Ren points to the stable, leading us to a stack of hay in a manger.

Digging inside with both hands, she pulls out armor plaques adorned with emerald stripes.

"Nice," Ela lets out as she grabs the pieces Ren hands her.

We leave the alley moments later, dressed as Airdan's soldiers, ready to push on until Ren's raised fist freezes us mid-step.

With military precision, she sinks against the street wall, head canted to catch the faintest disturbance. We hold in place, suspended breaths and hammering pulses the only betrayal of our anxiety. When no alert comes, she signs us to move forward.

The labyrinth of streets weaves endlessly, but Ren selects each turn with assurance, steering us clear of wider arteries where we would easily be spotted.

Every few strides Ren halts, ears tuned to soldiers' boots thudding on paving stones, until we're off again.

As we turn a corner, the outer defense wall of the city appears at the end of the street.

"Ren," I whisper, cocking my head in that direction.

She shakes her head slightly.

"Two dozen soldiers guard that door. We make for the western exit."

I grip my weapon a little tighter and follow her, Ela in my tow.

After an eternity wandering Nyths' streets and avoiding patrols, salvation beckons in the form of bolted city doors set into massive walls. Our freedom awaits mere feet away, only between us and escape stands a squad of guards.

We move into fuller torchlight, our borrowed uniforms granting us fragile anonymity.

The four guards straighten their stances, and their hands near the weapons at their belts as we approach.

"Shift change," Ren says steadily as the enemy scrutinizes us.

"Where's your fourth?" a tall Fae asks, stepping forward.

One soldier's gaze is fixed on me, scanning my body until his eyes dart to my shoulders.

When the sharp-eyed sentry notes the distinctive weapon sheathed on my back, dawning recognition widens his gaze. No other blades match mines anywhere across the territories.

I flick a split-second glance to Ren and Ela.

We charge as one, and chaos erupts. Ren's knife embeds in the gap of one guard's armor as my two-blade sword makes an arc and digs into another soldier's chest. Ela lunges at the third guard, cutting through his abdomen. I twist to silence the remaining soldier, too late.

Screams leave his throat before my blade sinks in it, alerting the city to our presence.

As his body hits the ground, Ela and I take position against the door while Ren wrestles with stiff locking bars.

"It's stuck," she says, straining under the effort.

"Fuck."

Ela's curse sounds as a dozen soldiers fill the street, their captain leading the charge on horseback.

They're onto us seconds later, and decades of lethal training kick in.

Two opponents fall when I swing my weapon, willing my body to hold on despite the pain flaring in my chest and arms. The rest of them leap forward to meet our attack with startled shouts.

Sparks spray off ringing blades parried inches from vulnerable points. Next to me, Ren and Ela trade vicious blows with the other troops, slowly forcing us back against the door step by step.

"Kill them," the captain orders before jumping off his horse to join the fight.

Risking a backward glance, I glimpse Ela slamming elbow strikes into her opponent before slipping a dagger smoothly under his ribs.

Too many of them are left. It won't be long until we're overwhelmed.

A uniform sneaks past Ren, taking position behind her.

"Ren."

My warning comes too late, and the soldier's blade lands in her neck. Her body hits the ground, revealing the hatred etched on her killer's snarling face. With a burst of energy, I smash through his guard and pierce his emerald armor with the tip of my blade, dropping him gurgling with twin gashes across his chest.

I turn on my heels just in time to catch a glimpse of a soldier plunging a dagger viciously between their captain's ribs. Before their leader's body pitches forward, the traitor's sword slashes the throat of the soldier beside them.

Ela and I stagger back, colliding hard with the door as warm blood sprays across our faces. Shock freezes our reflexes for critical seconds as we gape at the carnage this foot soldier unleashes on their own comrades.

With lethal efficiency, the blood-drenched soldier executes the remaining escorts, whose bewildered hesitation leaves them defenseless against the whirlwind now in their midst. When four corpses lay cooling at the traitor's feet, the killing stops, all enemies slain.

Chest heaving, the soldier slowly turns to face us as Ela and I huddle, ready to attack.

The soldier tears away their helmet, revealing a tumble of golden hair and piercing grey eyes that punch the air from my chest more violently than any sword could.

"Looks like I got here just in time," Amrynn purrs, flicking carmine drops from her gauntlet with nonchalance.

Ela and I exchange a glance, still on alert as we grapple for coherent thought.

"What are you doing here?" Ela snarls.

"What does it look like? Saving you," she says, her eyes scrutinizing our bodies. "Looks like we got the same idea, cousin."

"How did you find us?" I retort, distrust coursing through my veins.

"Easy." She huffs. "After slipping my guard, I killed a soldier snoozing on his post and waited in an alley by the outer defense wall. They all underestimate me when I bat my eyelashes, seeing the Lady of the Moon Fae before the warrior, conveniently forgetting I've waged wars alongside you for decades."

I squint my eyes at her, waiting for the full story.

"When I heard the clashes of swords, I knew you two couldn't be far, so I joined the patrol. They didn't even notice, in their eagerness to reach the gates."

Amrynn reaches for the reigns of the fallen captain's horse and hands them to me.

I hesitate for another second until she puts them in my palm and closes my fingers around them.

I cock my head, motioning for Ela to get behind me, and Amrynn reaches for the metal bar on the door, yanking at it until the mechanism gives way.

The door creaks open, barely wide enough to slip through in single file, and Amrynn turns to us, a smirk on her lips.

"I have not lost all loyalty to our home, however hard you may find that to believe."

She answers the question burning my tongue as she steps aside to let us through. Shouts echo from the depth of Nyths. We have mere minutes before we're found again.

"Go," Amrynn adds.

Ela and I lock eyes before I hand her the reigns. Hesitation glazes over her irises, but she nods and guides the horse through the door.

"What about you?" I ask Amrynn.

"Don't worry about me, Az." She reaches for her soiled helmet and puts it back on. "I'll be fine."

It's no longer the Lady of Moon Fae I'm looking at, but my cousin, and for the first time I believe her. With that look, I recognize the little girl trapped in Morilanthe with me, at the mercy of cruel parents.

With a sharp nod, I disappear through the opened gates.

Ela is already mounted on the horse. She extends a hand to me, and I pull myself over the saddle behind her.

"Thank you," Ela blurts out as she glances back at Amrynn, watching us from the doorstep.

With no time to waste, I nod to her, and my heels squeeze the sides of our mount. I can't linger on Amrynn's fate when ours is still uncertain.

I don't hear the gate closing above the gallop of the horse as we break free and ride into the night's shadows.

For good or ill, our secret is out, and the hunt will only quicken from here.

CHAPTER 37

AZRAN

We drive our mount relentlessly through the night, with no glance spared for the shadowed city fast disappearing past the horizon.

We have to put as much distance as we can between Airdan and us before we can even consider stopping. Only then will I let my abused body's agony catch up with us.

Ela bends low over the neck of the stallion as the jolts from hard riding exacerbate our sore bodies, but we keep going, determination blazing bright in our hearts.

Ryfa awaits at the end of a two days' ride west, but it will probably take us closer to three since we'll have to lay low during the day. Airdan will no doubt send units after us the moment he finds out that we escaped his grasp, and night will provide better cover to avoid detection. We can only hope Amrynn buys us a little more time and finds a way to save herself.

As our horse thunders through the moonlit plains, the tall grass ripples like ocean waves as far as the eye travels, except for the occasional trees interrupting the flat expanse. The rolling grassland around us gives the illusion of freedom and possibilities of a life together, almost within our grasp.

Gradually, the achromatic canvas turns cobalt with the first hopeful rays of dawn creeping tentatively over the distant horizon. As we crest a hill, the emerging sun caps each grass stalk in gold, transforming the prairie into a glittering sea of riches. Rosy hues appear across the cloud-streaked sky until the fiery orb breaches fully over the plains, bathing the grass ripples red and orange.

With daylight, I finally slow our horse, its sides heaving and head drooping in exhaustion. We slide stiffly to the ground and I turn slow circles.

The horse's labored breathing interrupts my reverie, its endurance tested to extremes by the night crossing. My own lingering injuries pulse hotly now that we've stopped. We all need rest before we can continue this desperate run from Airdan.

I scan the horizon, the sea of grass offering little cover from sharp-eyed pursuers, until a small copse of trees a quarter-mile away catches my eyes.

Ela follows my gaze and nods, weariness bowing her small frame as well.

We lead the stumbling horse towards the distant oaks, and when we reach their cover, Ela slides down against a broad trunk while I tie the horse a few feet away.

She undoes the straps of her blood-soaked armor before tossing it behind a bush.

"How are you feeling, little one?"

"Like I've been run over by a horde of darkclaws."

"You know darkclaws are solitary beasts. They don't travel in packs."

My heart tightens when her chuckle reaches my ears.

Digging into the saddle bags, I find water and some meager provisions.

"Thank the gods," Ela blurts out when I extend the waterskin in her direction.

I let her drink her fill before helping myself and reserving some for our mount.

"I can't believe we made it out," Ela says, sagging against her tree. "Were it not for Amrynn... Do you think she's still alive?"

"I hope so. She's more resourceful than most," I answer. "Get some rest, I'll keep watch."

She resists for a solid ten seconds before her eyelids lose that fight.

I scout the area briefly while keeping an eye on her. I take position a few feet away, my weapon in hand. We're at a disadvantage. Airdan's soldiers know these hills better than we do, and in daylight we'd be way too exposed to travel.

I grip my two-bladed sword a little tighter and retreat to the shadowy cover of the trees when riders appear on the horizon, too far to detect us.

When the danger passes, I make quick work of some of the rations in the captain's bags and leave a portion out for Ela. For now, her chest rises and falls regularly, and I'm left to my thoughts.

I had little faith in Cal's plan, but maybe it wasn't so crazy after all. We've always set out for the impossible and somehow come through. I'll make sure the next few days are no different. We're getting on that boat to Lóna.

My gaze inevitably returns to Ela as my heart calls to her, and regret opens a pit in my stomach. There's so much she doesn't know about me and so much I want to share with her still.

I make several rounds throughout the morning to keep an eye on our surroundings, which helps me stay alert despite the exhaustion weighing down my every step.

Ela stirs around midday, a little less pale than before. Her eyes flutter open, revealing that resolve I've grown to love more than anything else in this world.

"Hello, little one," I greet through the bond as she stands.

"Your turn." She points to the spot she just left by the tree trunk. "I'll keep watch."

A smile tugs my lips, matching the one blooming on her beautiful face as she approaches me, scanning my features.

I meet her in a couple of steps and she stops me, her hands going to my chest, gripping the fabric of my shirt and pulling me close. Her lips meet mine softly, her touch gentle and intentional, taking my breath away.

I revel in this side of her I rarely got to see until now. Her protective walls have vanished and she's showing me her tender side I always longed for.

"Black and white," I say as she pulls away.

"What?" She cocks an eyebrow.

"My favorite colors."

She eyes me sideways, but her sparking eyes betray her piqued curiosity.

"I want you to know everything about me. I want us to have more to ourselves than scars and horrifying memories."

"I want that too."

She motions for me to continue with a wave of her hand.

"White was my mother's favorite color."

Her eyes widen at my words. "The gardens in Averion. They're for her?"

I nod, suddenly finding this exercise a little less comfortable.

"Do you remember the necklace I gave you?"

"It was hers?" she asks with a wince.

I nod with a chuckle. I didn't get to watch her throw it out of a window, but I'm sure she remembers that day well.

"I'm so sorry, Az. I had no idea."

"You had every right." I give her a small smile before straightening my back. "I know what it feels like to grow up without a mother, so I know what I took from you."

My heart pounds in my ears and panic twists my gut as I wait for her to say something.

"I know nothing will bring her back, but I swear on my life that if I could I would, Ela. I am so terribly sorry."

Her eyes lose their playful glimmer, but I don't utter another word, letting her silence eat at me.

I'm walking the edge of a precipice, waiting for her to push me, because I will let her. I'm hers to do whatever she wants with.

She steps away, hands forming fists, and I keep my gaze on her face, refusing to look away as she releases her hate on me. If hitting me is what she needs, I won't stop her.

It's not forgiveness I seek. I know I'm not deserving of it. I merely hope she finds a way to live with herself in my presence. If being around her causes her any further harm, I will rid this earth of my curse.

Warmth finds my cheeks, but instead of a slap, her hands cup my face.

"I believe you."

She deposits a soft kiss on my lips moments later, and relief floods my veins. Before I can utter a word, she snuggles against my chest and wraps her arms around my back. My heart is on the verge of imploding.

I gather her in my arms, unable to wrap my head around the possibility of a life together she's just offered me.

"Tell me about your mother."

Her voice barely rises above a whisper, but it carries no hurt and the bond echoes in confirmation.

"She died giving birth to me." My head rests on hers. "All I know of her, I've learned from stolen glimpses of her room when my father forgot to lock it."

"I'm sorry, I had no idea," she says, her hand rubbing my back in circles.

"I lost both parents that day. My father resented my existence from the moment I took my first breath, and he spent the rest of his life making sure I knew it." Her hand freezes in place but I continue, ready to bare myself before her. "I spent weeks in dark caves under the Moon Palace, shackled, bloodied, in my own filth, licking the paving stones for drops of water. All to make me stronger, he would say, but it was merely retribution for killing my own mother."

"How old were—"

"It started when I could walk," I answer bluntly.

A gasp tears from her throat.

"It's all right, little one. I survived."

"Would no one help you?"

"No one would dare challenge the Lord of Morilanthe." I exhale slowly. "A group of older Fae cornered me one day and pushed me off a tower. I laid on the ground, my body broken, barely breathing, too badly hurt to call for help but not badly enough to die, until finally a servant found me. My father did nothing. After that, I learned to fend for myself."

"How did you not burn the place to the ground?" Ela asks, her voice trembling with furor.

"As long as my father lived, there was nothing I could do, so I left for war as soon as I could wield a sword. And after he died, I didn't see the point anymore. I had found purpose and the world was rid of him."

"What about Amrynn?"

A sad smile tugs my lips.

"She saw me that day, at the foot of the tower. Shame and guilt filled her eyes when she walked away, refusing to meet my gaze." A growl reverberates against my chest as Ela voices her disapproval. "My uncle was a cruel man. She dealt with her share of horrors."

"She went through the same shit as you, and instead of sticking together, she turned a blind eye?"

"Betrayal was the only way she found to survive. Never trust, never rely on anyone, never settle down. She has loyalty for no one but herself, or so I thought."

Ela's rage erupts through the bond, teasing my own.

"I learned that love was painful and hate was a consequence for my shortcomings."

Tears pool in her darkening eyes as her anger fuels her power.

"I cannot wait to show you how wrong they were."

"You already have, little one."

My words smother her rage instantly and her lips find mine, sending the awful memories into oblivion. Each kiss fills the cracks in my soul and with each of her touches, hope returns.

"Thank you for telling me," she whispers against my mouth.

"What else would you like to know? Ask, and I will tell you."

"Nothing." She deposits a quick peck on my lips and releases me. "Get some rest."

Sleep takes me the moment my head hits the bed of grass until Ela wakes me up at nightfall.

We get back on the horse and ride through the night, eluding patrols scouting the area. We're forced to pause several times and find cover, but by dawn we've made good progress.

We stop at the top of a hill behind large bushes and I take first watch as Ela falls into a deep slumber. Our Fae bodies heal with each hour that passes, but there is no repairing the invisible damage we both suffered.

CHAPTER 38

NYLREN

I stare at the wall until the stones blur and the corners of my vision darken.

Pain explodes in my head when the slap lands, setting the side of my face on fire.

Bright spots replace the haze before my eyes, and another zap of pain follows, like Father somehow managed to pin needles under my skull.

The silence in the dark room is astounding, Father's groans the only disturbance when he hammers another blow to my face.

Kyren. Yalath. Corym.

Another hit and a coppery taste soaks my mouth.

Haryk. Yesren. Ailas.

I keep my eyes open, but I can barely see. The small firepit to my left does nothing to clear my vision as blood and sweat coat it.

Zavan.

I list their names over and over again like a prayer. Forcing myself to remember each of them while my father takes his rage out on me, just like he did on them, is my own twisted way of honoring them in death. They remind me why I have to stay strong, why I can never let Father see the depth of my despair.

Each strike fuels my resolve until I reach a familiar numbness. A chuckle escapes me when my mind shuts down, distancing itself from the pain in my body. In this out-of-body experience, my mind is sheltered with the remainder of my sanity.

"What's so funny, boy?" Father snaps, reaching for an instrument other than his own hands. Something made of steel, if I had to guess based on the sound.

My head bobs, weakly resting on my bare chest as I try to suck in a breath. Bits of my skin are missing, carved out by my father's hand.

No. No. Lift your head.

I muster the strength I have left to tilt my head to the side and spare myself contemplating the horrors wreaked on my body. Reality has a nasty habit of sneaking back in when I'm faced with it.

"How could you let them escape Nyths?" Father's voice fills the air once more, his tone colder than ever.

I stopped trying to answer and reason with him long ago when I'm on this side of the conversation, strapped to the chair.

The leather belt over my stomach is merely to stop my body from toppling over, not to restrain me. He knows I gave up fighting ages ago. He only went harder when I tried, which turned out to be a very efficient way to sink obedience into a child's head. Father is nothing if not thorough.

Father's steps echo around me as he wanders the dark room with blood dripping from his fingers.

The pile of bodies we found by the western gate sentenced me to this hell. A traitor walks our ranks, but I won't find them until I'm out of this room, and Father is done looking for answers I don't have.

"What do you know?" His hand returns to my face in seconds, his fingers tightening around my cheeks, crushing my broken jaw. "They must have received help. Who could have betrayed me?"

Drool mixed with blood escapes my lips, eliciting a sneer on his face.

"You're always there, lurking in my shadows." A thousand blades sink into my mouth as his fingers dig into my cheeks. "Tell me what your little spies are up to."

My gaze widens as I try to decipher the look in my father's eyes, but I remain silent.

Releasing his hold on me, he slaps me again.

"I know everything that goes on in this city. I know you better than you know yourself." He lowers his face near mine, letting me smell the poison mixed with alcohol he drinks every night. He says it's to build his tolerance, but it's a wonder Death hasn't claimed him yet, with his insides rotting a little more each day.

"From your most secret dreams to what you whisper in the night when you think no one is watching."

A pit opens in my stomach as he plays on my worst fear.

My body never belonged to me, but my mind is my only possession and Father cannot have it.

Letting out quick, shallow breaths, I focus on regulating my heartbeat, pushing away the pain and meeting his gaze. Time to put on my best show yet.

Kyren. Yalath. Corym.

I repeat the names religiously, keeping the panic at bay as I wait for his next words to crush what's left of my soul.

Haryk.

Father turns away violently with an exasperated huff.

I keep my breathing as steady as I can, willing my consciousness to retreat to the corner of my mind where it can escape, even if for a few seconds only.

Flames dance on Father's face as he stares into the hearth, his features frozen in a neutral mask.

The fire crackles, sending embers flying, and his eyes widen.

"Sanev."

I freeze as he whispers the name.

"Dear, I have tried my best, but I failed you."

He lowers his head as his hands caress the air, outlining the shape of a face.

"I know." He nods vigorously, grabbing the shoulders of Mother's wraith.

He is in another world, absorbed in the contemplation of flames, his mind split between this world and the next. If I had known Azran and Elanor's escape would allow me to see Father descend into insanity, I might have freed them myself.

The bitterness that was flowering within me gives way to a sliver of hope. As much as I hate that he gets to escape this wretched place in mind and see Mother, this is the confirmation I've been waiting for. He is not invincible.

A new realm of questions assaults me. Can he still tell reality from illusion? What sparks these episodes? How can I use this in my favor? I've always kept Mother's name out of my mouth for fear of triggering his wrath, but what if I've been wrong this whole time?

A growl tears through his throat when his head snaps towards me, and my blood freezes. Tenderness has left his gaze, letting his rage take over.

The glance we share tells me he's well aware of what he's just revealed.

Fury twists his features and I can't look away, not even when the tip of a hot metal rod digs into my shoulder.

Blood sizzles under the ember-reddened instrument and air flees my lungs.

Time suspends while my brain catches up with reality, everything in the room perfectly still.

My scream shatters the respite when Father twists the metal rod, tearing through muscles and flesh.

"You're going to pay for this. You're going to pay for it all."

My father's rictus widens, the muscles on his arm tensing from the pressure he's applying.

Maybe freeing the traitors wouldn't have been worth it after all.

After working another hour on my destroyed body, Father's shoulder sag.

"Guards," he barks.

Soldiers enter seconds later, ready to serve their sovereign.

"Alert Ryfa and get me the Commander of the Emerald Legions."

"Yes, your Majesty."

The soldier is about to turn back on their heels when Father opens his mouth again.

"And get Amrynn down here."

Curiosity soars through the pain at the Lady of the Moon Fae's mention. I'll seize any opportunity to see into her endgame I can get, and this encounter ought to be most interesting.

I keep my gaze on the bloodied ground until Amrynn's heels echo down the corridor and she enters the room.

A gasp tears from her throat as she lays her pale eyes on my wrecked body.

"That will be but a fraction of what I do to you if you fail me."

Father's voice remains steady as the threat leaves his lips and Amrynn nods in confirmation.

Her unblinking gaze remains fixed on mine, letting me contemplate the pools of treachery shining in her irises. Not even her perfectly cultivated air of shock and elegant dress could mask the deceit lurking in those grey eyes.

This honey-voiced viper has clearly adopted cunning artifice, though her next stroke hides elusively for now.

"Come. There is something we must discuss."

Father motions towards the door without a backward glance.

Tension melts from my body as their footsteps fade, shadows embracing me once more.

CHAPTER 39

ELANOR

Azran is laying sideways next to me on the grass, his head resting on his folded arm, when I blink my eyes open.

"How did you sleep?"

"Good," I lie as I nestle my face against his chest, soaking up the warmth of his body.

I rest my cheek on his collarbone, breathing in his familiar, comforting scent.

"Ela."

His vocal chords vibrate as he whispers my name. Unable to resist, I tuck my head into the curve of his neck and brush my lips against his skin. Being near him is its own reward, but I have to face the reality of what's to come.

"The nightmares. They've changed," I let out.

"Tell me," he says, stroking my hair. "What do you see?"

"Fire and a dark figure in its midst." I close my eyes, trying to remember and escape at the same time. "A horned warrior with a weapon at his side, staring at me."

"I see the fire too." I lift my head to face him and grow still, waiting to hear more. "Your nightmares. What were they like before? What did you see?"

I swallow the lump in my throat and prop myself on my elbows.

"I saw Adria, a battlefield full of charred bodies, fire climbing to the sky, and ashes everywhere."

I manage to keep my voice steady, but it's pointless. My grief and guilt scream down the bond.

His hand goes to my cheek, gently rubbing with his thumb.

"You did everything you could, Ela. Never forget that."

"There was another nightmare."

I stare back into his hazel eyes and find no trace of judgment. Part of me knows he would go to the ends of the earth for me, he's proven it countless times, but somehow, I can't entirely believe that anyone, let alone him, would drop everything in the blink of an eye for me.

A blissful rush courses down the bond, almost in response, and I close my eyes for just a moment, letting myself indulge in his undying love.

"Another battlefield, torn bodies at my feet, blood dripping from the two swords in my hands, and a voice. Someone is calling for me, but I can never turn around to find out who."

"Cal. It was Cal."

"How can you—"

"It was my dream. We share more than our lives, little one."

"How?"

He brushes over my sternum and near my heart, hinting at the bond between us.

"Our power comes at a price. Through nightmares, it shows us our worst selves, what we can do, what we did, and what has happened or may happen." He taps my skin gently. "And this, connects us, lets us gaze into each other's souls." My mouth drops open slightly at his words. "At least, that's my best working theory."

His chuckle fills the air. A sound I so rarely heard before that he is now gifting me, but that I can barely receive. I can't get the horned warrior out of my head.

My heart sinks. If I saw Adria's future, then it means he is real and he's out there waiting for me.

My mood instantly sours. There is no escaping this chaos. No matter what I do, what madness I escape, another hell awaits. But this time it's different because I have something to lose.

Goosebumps erupt all over my skin and Az tightens his hold on me.

"What do you think it means?" I ask.

"Which part?"

"The horned warrior and the fire."

"I don't know. What does your power tell you? What does it feel like when you're there?" The crimson returns to his irises as he scans my face for a hint, his fear mirroring mine. "Death?"

"No. I mean, yes, but it's different. I feel Death everywhere, always, especially in my dreams, but there's something else. Something more intentional."

I take a deep breath and everything clicks.

"It feels like war, brutality, and bloodlust," I say. "It feels like you."

He nods cautiously as he stands, his face a perfect mask, his fears mastered while mine take over. Darkness flares inside me and I jump to my feet as my power begs for release and calls for revenge.

"How can you be so calm?" I ask, staring at my palms. "How do you keep the raging beast at bay?"

"He's right here, always lurking beneath the surface," Azran answers, his eyes blazing with intensity. "I've had more time to train and learn to hide it, that's all. And right now, there's nothing we can do. We need to stay focused."

Comforting heat radiates from my hands, calling me to battle, calling for the flames of Hell. A halo of light circles my palms, turning the skin orange, revealing the bones and veins underneath.

"There are more ways than one to seek revenge," Azran says as his hand covers mine, pressing gently. "After spending a lifetime suffering from the blind rage of others, I learned there is only one response."

I slowly release the hold on my power, letting darkness retreat and his features soften.

"Promises," he adds.

"Promises?" I squint in response.

"That's the only way I found to remain sane while powerless. Oaths to your future self." His fingers intertwine with mine and all traces of anger leave me. "I promised myself many things growing up."

I tilt my head, eagerly waiting for more.

"Never to let anyone touch me, belittle me, hurt me the way my father did. Never open my heart to anyone. Never cut my hair."

He lets go of my hand to run his through his short hair.

"Why?" I blurt out, unable to tame the pain flaring in my heart as his irises glisten with hurt.

When he meets my gaze again, his eyes are cloudy, lost in some distant memory.

"My father forbade me to grow my hair," he explains. "One year, I refused to cut it, so he shaved my head himself with a sharp razor, discovering yet another way to inflict pain and humiliate me." One corner of his lips lifts into a half-smile. "Cuts on the scalp take a long time to heal. Another way for him to control me."

Though no tears roll down his face, his hazel eyes well with anguish that overflows with each slow blink and I stand there, listening with trembling hands, afraid to reach for him and see him break.

"The moment I left Morilanthe, I started growing my hair out. I swore to never cut it, and I kept that promise as long as I could."

As the words reach my ears, I picture it. Az as a child, longing for love and safety, only to have it forever held out of reach by a wretched being.

Azran's eyes scan my face for a sign, pleading for relief and comfort, and I step forward to embrace him.

His arms wrap around my waist as he pulls me close and I bury my face against his chest.

"However ridiculous this may sound, it was the only way I found to regain control over my life at the time. Every time I looked in a mirror, I saw who I had become, how strong this made me, and I swore never to let anyone take that away from me."

His grip on my back tightens and I let out a shaky breath.

"It's not ridiculous." Tears pool in my eyes, threatening to spill. "I had no idea, Az. When I met you, I thought you were some entitled Fae, and I treated you terribly. I'm sorry."

He pulls back, and I manage to keep the tears at bay long enough to blink them away.

"I deserved it."

"You never did." I shake my head as the words leave my mouth. "Thank you for letting me see this side of you."

He offers me his brightest smile in response, one that reaches his hazel eyes and creates dimples in his cheeks.

"We're both on a path, little one. We've both known darkness."

I nod as I cup his cheeks, stroking the skin curving above his smile.

"No one will ever know the violence it took for you to be this gentle, but I do."

Azran tilts his head, pressing into my hand.

"I know."

<hr>

The sun is setting when Az and I eat the last rations of dried meat and prepare to ride out. We're packed in seconds, only carrying our weapons with us.

"We should be in Ryfa by dawn," he says, as he mounts the horse and extends his arm towards me.

My hand goes to his and I take position between his legs. With his strong chest against my back instilling warmth in my body, I lean back as he guides us away.

"Let's hope Calen is still waiting for us," I whisper.

"He will be."

The horse breaks into a trot, and with the last light of day, we disappear into the night.

CHAPTER 40

ELANOR

The cacophony of Ryfa's bustling port fills our ears as we creep towards it under moonlight. Leaving the exhausted horse to graze the plains, we cover the remaining miles on foot to avoid unwanted attention.

We pass sleeping farms and storefronts, alert for threats but focused on advancing steadily seaward. My body screams for rest, each hard-won step intensifying the struggle. Beside me, Azran fares little better, face gaunt and ash-pale in the occasional pool of torch glow as we cross the dark avenues. But neither of us dare utter a single complaint as we move through the streets with stubborn will coursing through our veins.

We keep our heads down until we reach the waterfront, crammed with salt-weathered warehouses and taverns reeking of brine, sweat, and stale spirits.

Calling upon my shadows, Az and I stick to the dark corners and head towards the docks.

A few drunken snores echo from shadowed alcoves as we get to the creaking piers. The gentle lap of inky waves against barnacle-crusted poles fills the air. Our target is within reach.

The *Myra* floats on the other side of the dock, pitching slightly with the waves, its cabin sunken in darkness.

I pause behind wooden crates, still a good distance from the pontoon where it anchored, and Azran at my back.

He goes around me, ready to cross into the open where my shadows will offer little protection, but I yank him back.

"Soldiers," I whisper down the bond.

I cock my head towards the buildings surrounding the docks as shapes emerge from their shadows and he crouches to the ground, seeking cover behind the crates.

"Calen," he says.

"They need to be warned," I add.

I peek behind the boxes, assessing the rest of our surroundings. Stacks of ropes, barrels and various crates line the docks and pontoons.

My eyes catch on a discarded bottle tucked against a crate, just visible in flickering torchlight. About a finger's worth of amber liquid still sloshes inside, not near enough to identify by scent from this distance.

"What's the chance this crate is filled with bottles?"

I glance towards Azran as his gaze sharpens, a grin spreading slow as my unspoken suggestion takes root.

Calling on my powers, I let warmth spread through the palm of my hand and aim at the crate.

It goes up in flames and a small blast detonates seconds later, scattering wood and glass across the docks. That ought to do the trick.

I duck behind the wooden box as shouts ring out and swords are drawn.

"Ready?" Az asks, his hand tightly gripped around his two-bladed sword.

Mine goes to Nahtar and I nod sharply.

We break cover, sprinting towards the soldiers fighting our own on the pontoon, but more flood out of the buildings surrounding the docks, encircling us.

I spot Calen, already engaged in a fight alongside Vesta, but Az and I are forced to fight back-to-back against the soldiers coming at us from all sides. Half of them go to the pontoon while the rest turn to face us, cutting us off from the boat.

Nahtar sinks into my first attacker as Azran's blades sing behind me. Smoke fills my lungs, but my only focus is on the next attack and parry.

My sword finds flesh again, tearing through a soldier on my right. I deflect a hissing cut and leap sideways to hammer down another blow. My arms protest each arc but I push through.

Blood splatters on my beige shirt when the tip of a blade finds my shoulder, and my power answers. Blocking off everything around me, my eyes narrow on the one responsible.

The massive Fae grins at me, perfectly unaware of the hell I'm about to unleash. Obsidian ribbons leave my fingers, seizing him by the throat and muffling his gargles as acid burns through his skin.

His body hits the ground as Azran cuts another attacker in half, splitting his torso from his legs, but more are coming.

"They were waiting for us," I snarl.

Azran's crazed eyes meet mine for an instant before he moves on to his next target, and I do the same.

I push back a soldier and parry another blow coming at my face, forcing me to retreat until my back hits Azran's.

The group of Fae is cornering us and freedom seems further and further away.

"On my signal, duck," I command through the bond.

"Ela."

I dismiss his worried tone and call on the tenebrous energy, letting it swallow me whole. My vision darkens until the world transforms in hues of grey and black. My eyes roll as Death takes over, fueling me with her wrath.

Drunk on power, dark ribbons erupt from me, destroying any soldier that engages me.

I glance at Azran as a grin forms on my face.

"Now."

Extending both hands, fire pours from my fingers and sword, burning blindly. The acrid smell of smoke mixes with burning flesh as I dance with Death, and screams echo in the cold night air.

Turning around, I let the dark flames spread through the docks, licking at the crates and engulfing terrified soldiers in their blaze.

When the screams die, so do the flames.

Azran is on me instantly, holding me up as I sag against his chest.

The echoes of a distant fight reach us and Azran turns his head. Soldiers are still fighting on the pontoon.

"I'm fine. Go," I say as I regain my feet, Nahtar still in hand.

After scanning me quickly, Azran makes for the end of the dock, leaving a pile of bodies behind him.

I eye the burning corpses at my feet, still on high alert although my legs threaten to give out from under me. Once reassured no more soldiers will emerge from the warehouses behind us, I make for the pontoon.

By the time I reach it, the battle is over.

I scramble over the rail with Azran's help, slumping beside him as my quivering limbs betray me. We lock eyes as triumph blazes in his irises.

We made it. Against all odds, we fucking made it.

Vesta shouts commands for the boat to sail. Our soldiers are bloodied, but the crew spreads out to unfurl the sails and crank the anchor, obeying her orders without pause.

I prop myself against the mast, straining to calm my ragged breaths as the ship lurches into motion.

Calen finishes wiping his blade clean on his sleeve before gripping Az's shoulder. They thump each other's backs, their fingers grabbing anything they can find purchase on.

"That was one hell of a risky plan," Az lets out, still out of breath.

"Never doubted you for a second, brother." Cal shoots him a wink as he lets go and turns to me.

"Impressive, what you did out there." He motions towards the back of the ship. "Cabin's this way. You've both earned the rest."

"Thank you," I answer as Azran reaches for my hand.

I let him lead the way, too exhausted and stunned to do anything else.

As the cabin door opens, I glance back at the docks and city fading behind us, encircled in smoke. When I meet Azran's gaze again, my heart swells near to bursting. His eyes are no longer haunted by Airdan's ghost, but blazing with his newly liberated spirit.

In that wordless look burns our future. Come what may, we will face it hand in hand.

⬥

A sickening lurch in my stomach yanks me from restless dreams, the blooming queasiness impossible to ignore as I wake in the middle of the night to the ship pitching at sea.

Azran sleeps soundly next to me, and although tempted to stay by his side, I lift the covers and silently ease out of bed.

Another wave of nausea hits me as I stand and slip into the corridor, dimly-lit with a few lanterns. With both hands on the walls to keep me steady, I make my way towards the deck.

I jump back when a door swings towards my nose, narrowly avoiding a painful collision.

"Damn it—"

"Sorry, L." Vesta's cheerful face pops out from behind the door panel. "I didn't hear you."

I wave off her apology, grateful the door didn't hit my face, and she squints at me.

"You look like shit."

"That's because I feel like shit."

My hand goes to my mouth as soon as the words leave my tongue, and queasiness flares. My stomach twists, threatening to expel last night's dinner, and I swallow the acidic lump in my throat.

A chuckle escapes Vesta's lips before she grabs my arm to guide me to the back of the ship.

"Come with me."

We enter a galley where the light of a lantern reveals a small table, wooden cabinets, and no doubt my face turning greener with each wave that rocks the ship.

Vesta digs through several cabinets before handing me a small vial.

"This should help you sleep, and hopefully settle your stomach for a while."

I eye it suspiciously before downing its contents in one gulp.

Vesta's head cocks to the side and a grin tugs at her lips.

"Don't you dare make fun of me."

"Oh, come on." Loose strands of red hair swings before her eyes shining with mischief. Her grin widens. "The mighty Unifier has sea sickness. I can't wait to tell Wyn and Varan."

"You're not gonna say a word. I swear I'll kill you."

I step forward before freezing in place, another wave of nausea forming in my throat.

"Not in that state, you won't," Vesta answers as her laughter fills the air.

I join her seconds later until my hands go to my stomach and I pinch my lips shut to repress a gag.

"Let's get you back to bed."

⸻◆⸻

I'm alone in bed when I wake several hours later. Light streams through the closed door, confirming Vesta's potion alleviated the nausea, at least temporarily.

I indulge for a moment in the feather pillow and mattress bringing relief to my spent muscles and weary bones, which for months have known only cold stone.

Rolling over, I exhale fully, a foreign peace settling my soul for the first time in ages. I am warm, whole, and my throat is free of thirst.

Even my stomach is giving me a break, but there's no telling how long the reprieve will last, so I get up to find Azran.

Still wearing my blood-soaked shirt and pants, and with only a small wash basin and towel at my disposal, I clean my face as best I can before digging into the wooden box beside it. A proper bath will have to wait.

A smile tugs my lips when my eyes land on a mirror, a pair of scissors, a comb, and a razor. I leave everything on the bed, which takes up most of the room, and head onto the deck.

Azran stands at the bow of the ship, his muscular frame casually draped along the railing as he gazes into the distance. His neck and bare arms soak up the sun's warmth and a wayward breeze teases loose blond strands of his hair.

He turns around as I try sneaking up behind him, sensing my presence. A grin plays on his lips.

"Hi."

"Come with me," I say, grabbing his hand and leading him back to the bed we shared last night.

"Sit."

He glances at my instruments still laid on the covers, but obeys, a twinkle of amusement shining in his eyes.

He lowers his head, giving me permission as I take position between his legs, and I get to work.

I grab at longer strands of hair on top of his head, brushing through with the comb before pinching a piece between my fingers and cutting it. For a moment, nothing breaks our silence except for the crisp, clean snip of the blades as I even out the top of his hair.

I climb on the bed behind him to look at the back of his head and keep going, opening and closing the scissors as chunks of hair fall.

Azran's words loop in my head, details of his childhood, and the look in his eyes I just can't erase. His breathing is regular, but mine quickens as I picture the horrors he's gone through.

When I grip the razor, I can't help the tears from pooling in my eyes as grief washes over me, for not knowing, for only finding out now. Azran tenses almost imperceptibly under my touch and I pause until his shoulders relax.

I make quick work of shaving the hair at the back of his neck and above his ears.

I brush through his hair with my fingers to check the length, my emotions running wild though I try to silence them. Revenge calls to me, pushing me to scream my rage at the world down the bond.

This world keeps tearing us to pieces, taking aim and crushing us at every turn, and maybe Death sent me here to destroy it all.

"All done," I say with a trembling voice. I hop off the bed to face him and inspect my work.

Azran pulls me to him and I sit on his lap, legs spread apart, scissors, comb, and razor still in hand.

"Don't cry for me, little one. Save your tears for our happiest days, which are still to come."

I rest my forehead on his and brush my lips over his mouth. His arms wrap around me and he closes the distance between us. His kiss is demanding, filling me with desire and sucking the air out of my lungs.

Azran catches my lip between his teeth, a growl tearing through his throat and lighting my core on fire. His hand travels my back before settling under my thighs.

A squeal escapes me when he lifts me, securing my body against his. The instruments clatter to the floor, but Azran is already laying me on the bed.

He removes his shirt, letting me admire the muscles on his chest and the V emerging from the waistband of his pants.

His eyes smolder with a new intensity, revealing the depth of his desire, and I need that look carved into my memory.

"Why are you still dressed?" His voice is filled with need as he crawls to me.

"You do it so much better than I ever could," I reply with a grin.

Moments later, I'm naked on the blankets, his warm body pressing against mine.

He lowers himself but I stop him, my hands around his face bringing him back to me.

"I need you right here." I press my lips against his before pushing his chest so he'll flip over.

Bracing my hands on either side of his head, I straddle him. A groan escapes his lips when I grind against his hard length and his hands land on my thighs, securing me in place.

I drag my fingers along his cheekbone and sharp jawline. He kisses my fingers when I brush them over his lips, the small gesture leaving me breathless.

My heart is pounding in my chest, ready to shatter my ribs like it can't be contained. And neither can my love for him. The words sit on my tongue, straining to be free, to cry out my devotion as I drown in this overwhelming feeling.

"I'm sorry it took me so long," I blurt out, my fingers frozen inches from his face. "To see you. See us."

"Little one, you could have taken eternity and I would have waited."

The unsaid words burn my tongue, threatening to pour over until I decide to jump off the ledge.

"I love you."

The words spill out in a rush, lifting an immense weight off my chest as I stand on the edge of a cliff. I've never said it to anyone, not like that. I thought I never would. Love was never in the cards for me, until now.

Azran closes his eyes and I hit the ground. Those three words hang in the air like a vow, leaving me vulnerable and exposed to his silence. Floodgates to fear open before me, a fear I cannot contain.

In the second it takes me to utter these three words, I step onto a battlefield with no armor.

My instincts scream for me to run, to protect myself, but I fight back.

I've run away from him, before, and he stayed, enduring the rejection. I'm done running.

I reach for his face, gently brushing his cheek.

"Show me your eyes," I say, my voice barely more than a whisper.

Please. Show me your eyes as mine scream my despair, my hope.

I've never needed to hear his voice more than I do now. They say eyes are windows into the soul, and I need to gaze into his like my life depends on it.

CHAPTER 41

AZRAN

The rest of my life disintegrates, its horrors long forgotten, for there's only her. No one has ever said those words to me, not a single soul. My mother never could, and my father chose not to. But the only person I truly care to hear them from is her, my mate, the one I was destined for and the only soul I would sacrifice everything for.

My eyes snap open when her distress resonates down the bond.

Her face hovers over mine, her hair cascading around my ears. A slight tremble crosses her lips.

"I love you," I whisper back, my voice shaking with emotion.

My chest tightens as her unsteady fingers caress my face. I should have said that ages ago. That she would even consider I didn't reciprocate her feelings hadn't crossed my mind. I was trying not to scare her off again, when I should have told her over and over, any chance I got.

I deposit a kiss on her swollen lips as her relief floods the bond.

"I love you," I repeat.

I move on to her reddened cheek, and the corners of her lips lift into a smile.

"I love you."

I grab her hand and bring it to my lips as tears well in her beautiful eyes.

"I love you."

I can't stop the words from leaving my mouth, and her widening smile does little to slow me down. After keeping the words so tightly bound for months, they tear through my throat in an attempt to catch up on lost time.

A pressing need takes hold of me, the need to say it to her over and over again so she'll never forget. These words have to be etched into my heart and hers.

"I love you," I say, as I kiss a path from her collarbone to her neck.

"Good," she lowers herself to whisper in my ear before claiming my mouth as hers.

Her tongue teases mine and I tighten my grip on her thighs.

She chuckles against my mouth, grinding against me, her arousal dripping all over my erection.

A groan dies in my throat as her soaked pussy teases me.

"I need you," I let out.

Each caress of her body sets a fire ablaze inside me.

"Please," I whisper as she pushes against my chest for support and hovers over me.

She undoes the last of my restraint and I'm ready to beg.

A growl coils past my lips as she impales herself on me.

Ever so slowly, she begins moving on top of me, leaving me bare before letting me fill her up again, and I can't look away.

The hair framing her face bounces with her movements. And as she leans closer, strands whisper across her reddened cheeks.

I claim her mouth to dull her moans, grunting against her lips as my body tenses under her touch.

Pushing on my chest to sit up, her nails dig into my skin until my ribs catch fire, but none of it matters. I'm touch-starved and she's the only remedy.

One of my hands goes to the tense bud of nerves between her thighs, rubbing as she grinds on me, while the other goes to her beautiful face.

I trace her cheek with my fingers, brushing her parted lips as she rides me slowly.

Her tongue wets the tips of my fingers until she claims them in her warm mouth. Biting back a growl, I keep caressing the apex of her thighs. She rolls her hips, pulling me deeper inside her.

Her breathing accelerates each time I sink into her, and she takes my fingers deeper in her throat.

Arching her back, her mouth parts and I withdraw my hand to cover her lips as a muffled moan escapes her throat.

Her inner walls clench around me until she nears her edge and topples over. I find my release inside of her while she collapses on top of me.

I brush over her hair. We're both left panting. With Ela curled up in my arms, our bodies a tangle of limbs, the pieces of my soul reassemble. Torn apart by life, but finding peace in each other, I'm hers as she is mine—Death and her monster.

Eternity lays at our feet, and for the first time, I allow myself to indulge in its promise. I can picture it; I can picture us together in Averion. Ela storming through my office to pull me away from my duties, me feigning indignation and letting her. Ela doing as she pleases in our realm, wreaking havoc wherever she goes, with me in tow, unable to refuse her demands.

I can't help smiling, until fear sinks its teeth inside my heart and the image of hellfire takes over my mind. I screw my eyes shut as dark flames rage around us, threatening to tear us apart.

"Don't leave me," I say as the nightmarish visions take root in my soul. I tighten my hold on Ela's body.

She tenses under my hands before tilting her head up.

"They would have to rip my dead body from your arms."

Only when she voices the fear shaking both our hearts, only when we finally face it together, do I find comfort in a simple realization.

"Do you think my love for you so frail that something as elemental as Death could keep me from you?"

Her smile stretches from ear to ear, lighting her flushed face with joy.

I'm still lying in bed fifteen minutes later while Ela leaves to get us food, her words echoing in my mind.

The rest of the world goes on, with no idea how much has changed in the span of a few seconds. My life was black and white until she brought the color to it, and there's no going back.

"Until Death do us part, and even then," I whisper to the empty cabin.

⋯⋯◆⋯⋯

Forty minutes later, I head out of the room in search of Ela, who hasn't returned.

Stepping into the narrow corridor, I bump into Calen and Vesta. Cal crushes himself to the wall to let me pass as Vesta's eyes dart away from his face so she can stare at the floor boards.

I stifle a smile until they're behind me. A lot has changed in my absence, and not all for the worse.

A few doors down, dishes clatter in the galley, followed by a series of profanities.

I lean against the doorway and find Ela trying to save the meal she just made as the ship rocks with the waves.

"Fucking hell."

Despite my best efforts, a burst of laughter sneaks past my lips when Ela adds a variation, having dropped another utensil.

She spins around, her brows furrowed, and rests a hand on her hip. She eyes me with a serious air before her features soften into a smile.

"You should do that more," she says.

I cock a brow in response, unsure what she means.

"Laugh," she adds.

I shrug off her comment. "Being myself has never been something I could often indulge."

"Then you should try it."

"Try what?" I ask, amused.

"Swearing."

I shake my head.

"That's not for me."

"Why the hell not? You're the High Lord, after all. You can do whatever you want."

"No." I quell my emerging grin, since she doesn't need more encouragement. "I'll help you."

As I offer, she extends a hand, but I stop dead in my tracks when her face changes color.

"Damn it," she lets out, swallowing with difficulty.

"What is it?"

"I forgot to tell you. I don't do well on boats."

She runs out of the galley, a hand over her mouth, and I can't contain my laughter any longer.

After everything she's been through, I would think sea sickness would grant her mercy, but she spends the last days of our trip back to Lóna bent overboard, proving me wrong.

I stay by her side the whole time, holding her hair despite her colorful protests, and trying to find something that will settle her stomach.

When we finally reach the shores of Sun Fae territory, she's the first off of the ship and onto a horse, eager to leave the boat's constant pitching behind.

"I'm never setting foot on one of those monstrosities ever again," she huffs, tapping her horse's side with her heels.

PART III

THE SCALES OF JUSTICE

"Fuck this world that's always wanted us dead."

CHAPTER 42

CALEN

My horse breaks into a trot on the familiar trail leading to Averion. Azran rides by my side.

The city's white domes shine like jewels under the sunlight, but as much as the view usually brings me comfort, today my heart sinks with it.

I've gotten used to returning to Averion victorious and acclaimed, ready to leave war behind. But today another war awaits us, possibly the most crucial one we've ever had to wage.

Hooves beat on the ground as the rest of the column follows, eager to enter the city.

I glance behind me, locking eyes with Vesta. Her gaze carries the same doubt my heart does. Does it extend to her decision about us? Probably not. She's made that clear, and yet, a sliver of hope simmers inside me.

We pass Averion's gates an hour later, and guilt twists in my gut.

Our convoy moves cautiously through the streets, all senses heightened as doors creak open and stall owners lay out goods in the gentle dawn light. Every hoofbeat echoes sharply in the narrow avenues, and I tighten my grip on the horse's reins at the uneasy quiet pressing in around us.

As more citizens start their days, their eyes peer from windows and mouths open at Azran's unmistakable silhouette.

Voices swell like a breaking wave as sleepy curiosity explodes into elation and clamor, disrupting the eerie morning calm. Shutters fly open fully as the residents lean out, yelling joyously to neighbors.

The streets fill rapidly with a growing press of bodies hurrying along our flanks, like fish swarming to a crust of bread. Excited cheers ring out amidst myriad shouts and sobbing prayers of thanks.

"The High Lord and Unifier have come."

"Azran has returned."

Stoic as ever, Azran's gaze remains locked on the palace archway looming ever closer. I can't bring myself to meet the eyes of the passerby, although for very different reasons.

I dismount when we ride past the garrison and make for the massive stairs leading to the palace doors in Azran's tow, Vesta and Ela not far behind.

Barus is waiting for us in the entrance. His eyes widen when Azran steps inside before he dips into a deep bow.

"High Lord."

"Barus," Az offers. "Arrange a meeting with Averion's captains. My office. One hour."

"Of course, my Lord. It's good to have you back."

Meeting my gaze, Barus inclines his head before scurrying away.

After Az and Ela exchange a lingering glance, she makes for the stairway without a word.

Vesta clears her throat and Ela pauses, an awkward smile on her face.

"Sorry. I'm going to stop by my room to change and freshen up. Wanna come?"

"You do need a bath, L." Vesta chuckles as she follows Ela and calls over her shoulder. "We'll meet you in the office."

When it's just the two of us, Az raises his eyebrow at me.

"What?" I ask.

He cocks his head in the direction Ela and Vesta just went.

"No funny retort or comment? I wonder if the Captain of the High Guard has something to do with our General's sudden shift in personality."

"Your time in Zetrea has damaged more brain cells than I thought, Az."

"Hm." He chuckles. "I'll go clean up, too. See you in an hour."

I grunt in agreement and turn towards to the barracks.

"Cal." Azran stops me, grabbing me by the arm. "You did what you had to do."

My shoulder sags under the weight of my crushing guilt. I hated every second of my reign of terror, although it was a necessary step.

"I never wanted to take your place, Az."

"I know. You were always more of a soldier than a politician."

"Az, I'm so—"

"You have nothing to apologize for," Az says, cutting me off. "The months you spent handling the realm's affairs was punishment enough. Don't beat yourself up."

He slaps my shoulder gently as I nod, hoping his words will sink into my brain.

⸻◆⸻

An hour later, Azran is standing before his ornate desk, clad in a dark silk shirt embroidered with a red and gold insignia, the rich fabric hugging strong shoulders. His short hair shines as he surveys the assembled captains with calm authority.

Ela stands at his right, changed into practical leathers, her sword never far from reach, and I'm on his left. Eren and Lana occupy one of the leather couches, inclined eagerly forward. Vesta leans back against the bookshelf as Elion and Yhen take posts by the door, their heads bent together whispering and their eyes flickering between Azran and I, a million questions burning their lips.

When the door closes behind Naar, who takes position on a leather couch, Az nods in my direction, letting me kick off the meeting.

"Thank you all for coming," I begin. After spending days racking my brain for the best way to navigate this conversation, I cut to the chase. "After Adria, we launched a covert operation in Zetrea to identify Braern's allies. Everything I did in the recent months was to maintain our cover across seas."

The announcement rings out, sending shockwaves through the room. Surprise registers on every face, leaving our captains wide eyed, their jaws dropped and foreheads furrowed. Hushed whispers swirl as they discreetly exchange sideways glances.

"Today we return victorious, in great part thanks to Calen's sacrifices," Azran adds, leaving out details about his or Ela's capture, as agreed.

A heavy silence falls for one suspended moment before excited speculation breaks out in a rush of interrogation.

"Why the secrecy?" Yhen's voice tones above the chaos, and voices quiet down.

"Our enemy has ears and eyes everywhere, including in this very city," I answer.

A barrage of questions explodes from every corner of the room as voices overlap into a din. Queries about the identity of our foe are the only ones I can decipher.

"Airdan."

The room descends into deafening silence as Azran utters the bastard's name.

"The King of Zetrea aided Braern and is set on destroying all who oppose his ideology. He seeks to crush all humans under his rule and take over Lóna." Straightening his back, he continues. "Airdan is no doubt preparing his offensive as we speak, if his vanguard hasn't left already, and we will meet him head on."

"Damn," Elion lets out, voicing I'm sure what everyone else is thinking.

"What of Averion's citizens and the army? The troops' morale is hanging by a thread," Naar says.

"Our people will be informed, and Calen and I will address the army together."

Everyone nods their approval until Azran steps forward.

"Calen acted from necessity, but shadows serve us no longer. If your trust in me yet stands, I will lead the fight against this snake in our home."

Tension fills the air as Azran's crimson gaze falls on each person in the room. No accusations etch his sharp features, only resolve.

In answer, one by one the captains lower their heads, fists crossing hearts in salute. Hard-won respect shines in every eye, conveying their allegiance.

"Very well." Az's voice rings solemnly in the air and he steps back to lean against his desk.

"Eren," I call out, and the purple-haired captain straightens his back. "Keryth's fleet will play a crucial role in this battle. If his forces can't hold off Airdan's army, Daenia will turn into a death-trap. We will need your expertise."

"Of course, General," the Water Fae says as he stands to face the room. "A massive network of canals and bridges circles Daenia's islands. Under Lord Keryth's rule, the city transformed into a thriving center of trade and culture, from the bustling eastern docks to the merchant and arts quarters."

I nod regularly as Eren talks about his home, and the other captains memorize every word that leaves his mouth.

"Daenia boasts marble fountains tall as three Fae amidst bustling markets, sculptures dotting winding boulevards, and towers brushing clouds. The city crawls with civilians, and its decadence makes for a treacherous battleground."

Eren steps closer to Az and I, pointing to the desk behind us. "May I?"

Az accepts with a quick nod.

Reaching for a quill and parchment, Eren hastily scribbles a rough sketch before lifting the piece of paper for all to see.

"Several major arteries lead to the center of Daenia and its plaza, Endya. Almost a city within Daenia itself, Endya is surrounded by a high wall, a large canal, and four main entrances. Wide platforms of various heights rest on the outskirts of the plaza, with stairs leading to each level. A cluster of tall constructions within a labyrinth of streets rests in its center." Eren pauses to catch his breath. "If the city is overrun, Endya is the last place we want to find ourselves."

The atmosphere shifts palpably and tension fills the space as the Water Fae steps back. I dismiss him with a nod.

"Prepare your units," I command. Everyone lifts their heads a little higher, ready to obey. "Barus, you know what to do. As soon as we're ready, we march to defend our western shores."

Lana stands, and her eagerness sets everyone in motion.

The room empties in seconds, new determination shining in the captains' eyes.

"Welcome back, General," Naar says as he exits behind me.

Most captains descend the stairway, but I keep walking down the corridor, another target in mind.

Vesta's hand grips my shoulder.

"Cal, wait up." Her emerald eyes scan my face as we wait for the others to clear the floor. "How are you holding up?"

"I'm fine," I lie.

Acid churns in my stomach at the memory of this masquerade of a coup I had to organize. Rumors about my true allegiance will never fully die, and I'll forever be known as the Usurper of Averion.

"You don't look fine. You haven't said a word since we set foot in Lóna."

"I said I'm fine." Bile surges in my throat as the harsh words leave my mouth, and she crosses her arms over her chest, her brows furrowing.

"I need you in Daenia. Keryth has to be warned." I look away, unable to hold her stare. "Take the rest of the day if you need, but leave by sunrise."

"So, this is how it's going to be? You're sending me away?" she snarls back, her emerald eyes like daggers in my chest.

"I'm asking you to help me because I trust you."

"And what are *you* going to do?"

"Can I count on you?" I counter, not bothering to answer her question.

"Of course," she says with a huff.

All traces of her cheerful self are long gone, erased by my hand. A price everyone who gets close to me pays. Others have paid more dearly, and never made it back home.

I cock my head towards the stairway and she steps back, a small line creasing her forehead. Her mouth opens slightly as she stands there, frozen in place, and for a moment, the General retreats, leaving room to the Fae carrying far too great a burden on his shoulders.

She has no idea how much I hate pushing her away and pretending that it's not getting to me. Someone had to make the hard decisions in Azran's absence. My sole purpose was to prevent further deaths, even if I can never erase the blood already on my hands.

Truth is, if I could send anyone else, I would. If I could stay by her side to salvage what we had, I would, but she's the only one I trust with the fate of Lóna.

Her features soften and her lips thin before she retreats to the stairs.

I wish I could tell her. I wish she could see inside my head. I wish for many things to be different.

"Be safe," I blurt out. That's the best I can offer, right now.

She freezes on the landing as the words ring in the air.

"Always. And Cal?"

"Yes?"

"I'm sorry I doubted you when we left for Zetrea."

It's past midnight when I step into the courtyard after helping Azran draft missives all day. Messengers have been dispatched across the Fae territories and Brimora, but all we can do is hope we won't be too late to stop Airdan.

A threat is on our doorstep, and Queen Aanor is as much in Airdan's aim as we are. It's only a matter of time before his focus turns to her, and without us, her kingdom will fall. Airdan will erase Brimora off the map the second he gets the chance, and our defeat will mean just that.

Our relations with Brimora, flimsy as they may be, could determine the victor of this war.

The cold night air greets me, gently brushing my face and relegating these worries to the back of my head.

My steps slow when I near the garrison. Vesta is probably there, packing a bag of fresh clothes and getting ready to leave. I almost come to a halt as the idea of paying her a visit crosses my mind.

Her apology still rings in my ears, leaving me wondering if we could pick up where we left off.

I could go to her, tell her how hard this is for me, how much I hate it, and that the only thing I dream about is her.

I turn my head and make for the gates. Another Fae at her beck and call, waiting to tie her down, is the last thing she needs, I'm sure. And although that's not what I want for us, I don't know the words to convince her of that.

I shake my head and push on, keeping my pace steady.

Moments later, I step onto a paved street in the heart of Averion. A wooden sign hangs above a door, a tree painted on it.

The door slams open as two patrons step into the night. Soft light streams from the doorway, just enough to reveal the wide smiles on their faces as they hold each other to stay upright. The pair mumbles unintelligible words before their laughter fills the air.

A gust of warmth hits me when I step inside, along with a sea of indistinct voices. Fae and humans are drinking and dancing together to the music of a band playing in the corner. Drinks are being passed around, splashing as patrons try to avoid bumping each other.

My shoulders relax instantly at the merriness of the Tree of Life.

I make my way to the counter by the stairs where a burly man waits.

"General." He greets me with a nod. "It is an honor to host you. Same room as last time?"

"That would be great, Kyrt."

A smile appears on his bearded face at the use of his name.

I deposit a few silver coins on the counter and turn as the inn keeper looks for the key. Resting my elbows on the counter, my gaze goes from customer to customer, soaking up the cheer of this place. Most are completely inebriated already, spilling drinks on their best attire. A colorful lot. It's a miracle we don't have to handle more brawls and disturbances in Averion.

An odd sensation prickles on the back of my neck and I lock eyes with a dark-haired Fae sitting in the back. A suggestive grin tugs their red-painted lips before their eyes dart back to the Fae sitting across from them. Tanned, with their hair braided to their scalp, the Fae openly undresses me with their green eyes. My admirers intertwine their hands together, but neither breaks eye contact, letting me consider their proposition.

I turn when Kyrt clears his throat behind me.

"Your room is ready, General."

"Thank you, Kyrt."

Accepting the key, I take the side door leading to the rooms. I don't spare another glance behind me, but a thought lingers in my head—a promise to myself. If I make it back from the battle that awaits us, I will go out and let go of my worries occasionally. It won't wash away the sins, but I sure as hell deserve a night off if I'm not dead by the end of the month.

Once inside the room, I check the windows, making sure they're closed before pulling the dark velvet curtains over them. A small fire burns in the hearth, its warmth and soft light giving the space a cozy touch. The plush rug and canopied bed add to the room's welcoming air.

I remove my red and gold vest before my gaze drops to my embroidered shirt and pleated pants. I strip to my undershorts quickly, letting the clothes pool on the floor beside my boots. These won't be needed tonight.

I catch my reflection in a mirror leaned against the wall, and a smile tugs my lips.

If Azran were here, he'd tell me that nobody likes a self-absorbed prick and to put some pants on.

I reach into the chest at the foot of the bed with a chuckle and put on the dark linen ensemble I find.

After strapping my boots back on, I cover my shoulders with the dirt-strained cape lying at the bottom of the chest.

Moments later, I sneak out the back door of the Tree of Life.

Pulling the hood over my face, I step onto the paved streets of Averion. The cape does a surprisingly good job at protecting me from the wind as I slip past the few Fae wandering the city.

A door opens onto the street, its light catching me by surprise, and I turn my head the other way at the last second.

Careful not to step too heavily on the paving stones, I check behind me after turning a corner. This time, I keep my head down when I walk past windows and passageways lit by torches.

My heart pounds in my chest as I sneak into a dark alleyway. Its only door is easily missed if you don't know what you're looking for. Most passerby walk past it without ever realizing it's there.

I check my surroundings before knocking on it using a specific sequence.

An eternity later, the door opens, revealing nothing but pitch black inside.

"You're late."

CHAPTER 43

CALEN

"You've always had a way with words, old friend," I answer, scanning the darkness.

The scrape of a match sounds before a candle is lit, revealing Mor's wrinkled face. He's standing beside a desk covered in papers and jars, ink spilled on various spots. Tidy as ever.

"You might need to work on your delivery, though. It could use a more welcoming touch," I add.

"Calen."

"Morthil."

The healer's features are frozen in his usual serious air, lips pinched and a small frown creasing his forehead.

"So you have succeeded."

"I wouldn't put it quite that way, but Azran and Ela are back, yes." I move closer as he steps behind the desk and takes a seat. "Is it ready?"

Mor pulls a set of vials from the desk drawer, some darker than others.

"These are for the water supply." He pushes one with clearer contents forward. "These are for your trusted circle."

The healer twirls a dark vial, revealing a thick liquid that leaves traces on the glass with each swirl.

"Why do I have to drink the one that looks like that? Couldn't you add a little something to make it more appealing?"

"Quit being a child."

I roll my eyes at his words. I bet the old bastard did it on purpose.

"Are we sure this is going to work?"

"I am no cheap magic wielder," Mor answers, his nostrils flaring with irritation.

"I know, but a lot rests on this."

"You will feel a warm tingle in your hands in the presence of a traitor, for as long as this is in their systems." He points to the clear vial.

"Have you tested it?"

Mor tilts his head, challenging me to say the name burning my lips. As much as I hate asking this, we all have our weaknesses.

"Naar. Have you tested it?"

"How dare you?" He stands abruptly, sending his chair crashing to the floor. His hand goes to his belt, where various satchels hang.

Tension fills the room as we stare each other down. As masterful as Mor's healing magic is, he no doubt knows how to inflict pain.

Gods know how long he's roamed this earth and what the true depth of his powers is.

"You know I can't leave any stones unturned." I bite back a snarl and take a deep breath instead. "But if you say it works, I trust you."

Mor's shoulder relax, and just like that, the tension retreats as he rearranges the contents of his desk, finding some sort of order in the mess.

He reaches for the vials and hands them to me.

"It works."

I cock a brow in question and he nods back.

A small smile tugs my lips and his features soften. He actually tested it on his mate. The stern bastard never stops surprising me, though his social skills could use some work.

I spend the next few days checking on our troops and meeting with Azran and Naar to weed out traitors in our midst.

Desertion persists in eroding our ranks, and several supply wagons have been sabotaged while others never made it to Averion, confirming that Airdan's influence in Lóna extends further than we thought. If left unchecked, his reach holds the potential to cripple our efforts.

Azran and I have waged more wars across all Fae territories than I can recall, and maintaining tactical advantage relies on safeguarding our military intelligence against further leaks. We must prevent Airdan from gaining further access to our plans before our chances of victory turn to dust.

"How many?" I ask as I take the scroll from Naar's hand.

"Seven." The red-haired captain stands back from Azran's desk. "No one from the palace, but all close enough to gain access now and then."

Seven spies identified in Averion alone. Betrayal twists in my gut as I read the list of the Fae now imprisoned in cells beneath us and hand the parchment to Az.

"Thank you." I let out a forceful breath before meeting Naar's gaze.

He deposits the empty vial on the desk with a nod. "What now?"

I dig in my pocket and swap the vial with a fresh one, smirking.

Az and I exchange a knowing look before I answer.

"Now, promotions are in order."

I walk them out and close the door behind me.

With the sound of my steps as sole companion, I make my way to the courtyard.

Wyn and Varan wait for me by the door, as requested in the missive I sent earlier. They salute when I stop a few feet away.

"At ease."

"General," Varan greets me as he relaxes his stance.

"Given recent events, squadron assignments have changed."

The twins exchange a worried look before Varan steps forward.

"What are our new orders, General?"

"You've both been appointed captains, effective immediately."

I repress a grin as Wyn's eyes widen, the rosy lines of the scars on his left side stretching with the movement.

"Thank you, General. It's an honor."

Varan's tone is unusually quivering, but that's as far as he'll show his surprise. Unlike his brother, whose mouth appears to be frozen open.

Varan clears his throat and his twin comes to life.

"That's amazing." Wyn looks at his brother with stars in his eyes until Varan squints at him.

"It's an honor, General," Wyn adds with reddened cheeks.

"You both deserve it," I say, resting my hands on their shoulders. "Follow me."

They scurry along behind me as I head for the garrison, a grin stuck on my face. Sharing good news is one of the best parts of the job.

The smile doesn't linger long, given that their excitement is about to go down a notch. They've been vetted and need to be kept in the loop for what's coming.

We pass the training center moments later, and the twins slow as I turn into a side corridor.

"Are we not headed to the training center, General?" Wyn asks, his excitement barely contained. Looks like I picked well. Two units are waiting for them there, ready to meet their new captains.

"You are, but we're making a stop first," I say, turning the knob of a door.

We enter the Captains' Quarters and I invite them to take seats.

They comply in silence, their eyes darting around the neatly decorated room. A colorful rug adorns the floor and chairs have been arranged all around the table.

"What you're about to hear cannot leave this room." I stare them down, trying to convey the importance of this conversation. "Is that clear?"

They both nod vigorously, and Varan straightens his back.

"As you know, Airdan is sailing to Lóna after the High Lord and Elanor's covert mission in Zetrea."

Wyn's throat bobs as he swallows the lump in his throat and Varan stills perfectly.

"But traitors walk amongst our ranks." I circle the table and sit in front of them as their mouths drop open. "Until we've identified all of them, you're to report any suspicious behavior in your units."

Varan's eyes dart between his brother and me, trying to comprehend what I'm suggesting. Wyn sags against the backrest of his chair. His face is two shades redder and I'm not sure he remembers to suck air in.

"What the—"

"Wyn," Varan growls, forever trying to keep his twin out of trouble.

"Your reactions are to be expected."

As soon as the words leave my mouth, Wyn's hands fly as he gestures wildly.

"I knew it."

"What are you talking about?" Varan cuts him off with a shake of his head.

"I knew there had to be a good reason behind all the secrecy." Wyn points at his brother with a chuckle. "Although, *you* had no idea."

"You had no clue either, stop bragging."

A victorious smile spreads on Wyn's face while Varan's brows furrow together.

I let them bicker for a moment before interrupting.

"All right." They both stop mid-sentence before settling back in their seats, and I can't help the corners of my mouth lifting into a smile.

"Only a select few have been brought into confidence. Everyone else will be kept in the dark."

Their features harden and lines appear on their foreheads.

"We can't risk someone slipping up, but troop morale needs to be maintained. Can I count on you both?"

"Of course."

"Always, General."

I nod sharply. "The army is almost ready. We move out in the coming days."

The atmosphere darkens instantly and silence falls over the tension-filled room, reality dawning on the new captains. Wyn reaches for Varan's hand to squeeze it tightly, and his brother releases a heavy breath.

"I'm sorry for appointing you to your new stations in these conditions. We're living through dire times, but I know we can make it through. I believe in both of you." I pause, letting each word sink in. "Now, since it would no doubt prove impossible for you to keep this secret from each other, you're being briefed together, but this doesn't leave this room. Understood?" A devilish grin forms on Wyn's face, and his brother elbows him in the ribs. "You will not discuss this with anyone. Those in the know have received the same instructions."

"Of course, General," Varan answers solemnly.

"Not a word," I add, and Wyn nods. "This is our best chance at saving Lóna."

"You have our word, General." Wyn's voice fills the air, carrying his resolve and determination.

"Good. Now, go meet your units."

Their cheers erupt as I leave the room and make for my bedroom, carrying a new fire as I climb the palace steps. I'm regaining the trust of my men with each day that passes.

CHAPTER 44

Elanor

A steady burn spreads through my thighs as I stretch, a silent confirmation of my poor condition.

We left Nyths four weeks ago, but my reflexes are still slowed by my weakened muscles.

I need my strength back if I'm to stand a chance against Airdan, so I hold the pose until my muscles feel like they're going to snap.

Standing, I embrace the sting lingering in my body as my muscles awaken.

Nearby, Azran rolls his shoulders and warms up in silence, his breathing perfectly regular. I can't help but stare as his shirt collar falls open with his movements, revealing his chiseled chest.

Following his address to the army, Az has spent all his time in the palace, working alongside Cal and our captains to prepare for Airdan's attack. We barely get any alone time, unless our training sessions count. We both need to get back into shape and quickly. War won't wait much longer.

A magnetic pull radiates from Nahtar, still in its sheath against the wall of the training center next to Azran's weapon. My sword whispers my name, seeking me out, and like an itch under my skin, I'm dying to answer its call.

Closing the distance in a few steps, I reach for Nahtar.

A breeze warns me and I turn swiftly, my hand tightly wrapped around the hilt of my sword.

Azran's blade comes straight at me and I parry before it crashes into my nose.

My eyes narrow and I bite back a snarky comment. Azran's lordly behavior is back, his posture rigid and expression clouded.

"All right. Let's fucking do this," I say as I take position in front of him, an idea forming.

Azran nods, still not uttering a single word. He waits for me to launch an attack.

If the High Lord is back, then he's in for a lesson too.

Staying perfectly still, I wait for the first sign of his impatience. When his eye twitches and the line between his brows deepens, a smile stretches across my mouth.

"Come on, say it." I tilt my head in encouragement. "Give it a try."

A wave of exasperation washes over his face and his fingers drum on the handle of his two-bladed sword. I scan the bond for confirmation, but I am only met with calm and a hint of amusement.

"It's not that hard. Seven letters."

I mouth the curse word silently, exaggerating the two syllables, and he chuckles in response, letting go of the irritated facade.

"Come on, Ela." Azran waves his weapon. "Make your move."

"Not until you say it. I need a little encouragement."

"Since when have you needed encouragement to fight?" Azran asks, his pointed stare conveying his skepticism.

"Since I've decided we're not leaving Averion until I hear you swear."

He sighs and begins pacing around me.

Swinging Nahtar around, I follow his steps, moving with him as he becomes the predator and I the prey. His hesitation seeps down the bond, telling me he won't go for it, but I won't relent.

The words reach my ears a split second before I dive out of reach, one of his blades missing my head by an inch.

"Let's fucking do this."

A snicker escapes my lips as I turn and raise Nahtar. Pride flares in my heart when he wiggles his brows to taunt me, crimson decorating the corners of his irises. I love this side of him.

The swords screech against each other in a violent clash, my parry stopping Azran's swing cold. He shoves me, forcing me off balance as he sweeps his weapon towards my knees.

I lunge to the side to put some distance between us, but Azran doesn't give me respite. Coming down with an overhead strike, I barely deflect in time, the impact reverberating through my elbows. I'd forgotten how strong he is.

A grin appears on his handsome face and rage fills my lungs instantly, daring me to let out a growl and unleash my power.

Resisting, I focus on moving faster. I can defeat him without the lethal energy.

The years of training slowly return to me, the memory in my muscles strengthening my defense until I move onto offence. Aiming at his side, I shift my balance and strike at his shoulder.

A victorious snarl tears from my lips when the tip of my blade finds its target, drawing blood.

Half an hour later, I'm sweating profusely as we meet each other fiercely.

My legs are trembling and a stitch is flaring in my side, but neither of us will yield. I can't even put into words how much I love that about him. He never underestimates me, never tries to make it easier for me, forever my equal in this life.

Another of his strikes hits my back and I stumble forward, almost dropping Nahtar. I recover at the last second, spinning with a growl in my throat.

Azran lowers his weapon, a bead of sweat trickling down his neck.

I cock a brow in question and he nods before sagging heavily against a wall. We're both heaving, and neither of us have it in us to utter the words to conclude our training session.

"Fuck," I let out, out of breath. My lungs are on fire.

I let go of Nahtar and sit on the floor, too exhausted to stand.

"Your elbow." I lift my head to face Azran, waiting for him to explain. "You drop it. It weakens your blow."

I nod, taking his advice. It would be reckless not to.

Azran reaches for the waterskin he brought and hands it to me, his two-bladed sword still in his other hand.

"Does it have a name?" I ask, before taking a sip of water and handing it back.

He follows my gaze before answering.

"Dagrassaeb."

"That's a mouthful."

A twinkle of amusement shines in his hazel eyes.

"What does it mean?"

"Deathbringer."

"Fitting," I say with a dark chuckle, a lump forming in my throat.

Just like that, the fears that had retreated to a deep corner of my mind flood my system again, bringing doubt with them.

"What is it?" he asks, putting Dagrassaeb and the waterskin down.

Damn bond. There's no hiding anything from him anymore, but I can't tell him what I recently started to suspect. It would break his spirit like it's starting to shatter mine.

Ever since Adria, I've grown closer to Death, though I can't explain how.

It started as a ripple in my power, like a drop in the sea tainting the water. My power is changing. I'm becoming stronger, and as I do, Death's call is getting louder. She's calling me to her, calling me home.

The spirit world feels but an inch from my grasp. Savage's soul is an almost constant presence in my mind as Death's hold on me deepens.

I think I'm running out of time.

"How will we defeat Airdan?" I blurt out, needing to say something, anything, to escape the thoughts storming in my head. "His wards against our powers are strong."

Azran's shoulder sag.

"We will find a way."

"We don't know how much power he's managed to harness from either of us."

"You're right, we don't."

"I'm scared," I whisper, only able to offer a partial truth.

Azran extends his arm towards me and I put my hand in his.

"Me too," he says as he pulls me to him.

I wrap my arm around his middle, and his hand strokes my back.

"I've never seen you scared."

"I was never afraid to step into battle before. I've got too much to lose, now, and too much to look forward to."

I nod as tears well in my eyes. Vesta's warning against the bond comes back to me. Only now do I fully understand what she meant. Being in Azran's arms is the most at peace I've ever felt, and yet I've never felt more at war with myself or the world.

Azran pulls me closer, wrapping his other arm around me and holding me tight.

"So, we're going to find a way, just like we did with Braern."

"Damn right," I say.

"Braern used a medallion to wield power. Airdan, the collars. These artifacts anchor magic. We just have to find Airdan's and destroy it."

A sliver of hope forms in my heart but I crush it instantly, having learned never to trust its dangerous attraction. Still his words reverberate, kindling forbidden sparks against my will.

"I have big plans for you and I," Azran whispers against my forehead before depositing a soft kiss. "Does that frighten you?"

"No," I say at once, my voice hard and determined. "I want you. I want us."

I lock my own dreams in an iron chest deep in my heart. I want to live. I want to see another sunrise, and another, and another until I can paint the rising sun with my eyes closed. And I want to do it all with him at my side.

"When this is over, I will take you to the most beautiful places on this earth." His voice breaks, but he doesn't stop. "I want to see the look on your face when you gaze upon frozen lakes, falling stars, and colors exploding in the sky." I press my lips together as salty tears roll down my face. "I will bring you to where it all began, on the highest Blue Mountain peak where fate brought us together."

He brushes his finger against my back as I nod weakly, clinging silently to this living vision he paints in tender strokes.

"Will you take me to Morilanthe?" I ask. "I want to see where you grew up."

"That, too."

His eyes sparkle like a thousand stars, filled with his promises and dreams for us. I don't have the heart to tear it all down.

"I need you to know," I whispered against his lips, "I am darkness and light, and every piece of me belongs to you."

<hr>

Sleep evades me, and I find myself wandering the palace halls. War is calling, its threat looming over our heads. With each day that passes, the knot in my chest tightens.

I roam the corridors of my home aimlessly, heels indenting plush runners before meeting unyielding marble at regular intervals. My eyes glaze over ornate frames and canvases as flickering torchlight plays vainly across the paint.

My steps lead me to the library and I peer past the entrance as memories flash before my eyes, memories from another time. This room witnessed the first threads of my life's unraveling and its tomes held the secrets of my childhood, revealing how my father used to walk these halls too, alongside my mother. My throat tightens. When water fills the corner of my eyes, I screw them shut.

Turning on my heels, I resume my stroll through the palace, memorizing the feel of each step, the smell of burning candles, and the quiet of the night.

Before long, tears roll down my cheeks unchecked. I've been running away from myself for so long, staying focused on what awaits me, that I never really took the time to appreciate what I've been granted. A life of heartbreak and truth, of sorrow and bliss, of vulnerability and strength. I no longer live a lie, cloaked in my own rage, constantly alert, fighting the world and myself.

I tighten Azran's shirt around me as I step onto one of the balconies overlooking Averion. A cool breeze greets me, leaving the salty trails on my cheeks burning and sending strands of hair flying around my face.

"Thank you," I whisper to the night.

The stone shocks the sole of my feet with each step, its sharp bite keeping my dark thoughts at bay, grounding me.

"Thank you for guiding me home," I rasp as my voice breaks. "Thank you for letting me experience a love I never thought I deserved."

Fresh tears reach my trembling lips as I take a deep breath, letting crisp air fill my lungs, though it does little to alleviate the pain in my chest.

My power flickers inside me, slowly flooding my veins until darkness swallows the fear and the bite of the wind is relegated to a distant memory.

I allow myself to drown in darkness until I'm one in Death, until my vision blurs, until the world disappears and the only sensation left in my body is my heart pulsing in my ears, and revenge twisting in my gut.

Souls will soon be called back to my realm. In their thousands, I will collect the lives of those whose time has come.

Warmth returns to my body as fire spreads to my fingertips, and I release the hold on my power to enter the palace.

Retracing my steps back to Azran's room, our room, I slip inside without a sound.

I find Azran where I left him, his body tangled in the bedsheets, his breathing regular.

Moonlight streams through the glass panels behind the bed, highlighting his relaxed features. My heart expands in my chest, striving to escape its carnal envelope and burst. I never knew a love like ours was possible; unconditional, boundless, and absolute. The kind of love only gods could grant.

After undressing, I ease slowly onto the mattress, tucking my elbow beneath my head before nestling against Azran's warm body. With the touch of his skin, the rest of the world disappears, and I find safety.

I slip my hand around his waist to caress his side, slowly dragging my fingers across his body. Leaning my head against his rising chest, I drag my nose along his neck, depositing soft kisses against his warm skin and breathing in the scent of home.

His arm wraps around me, pulling me closer.

"Leaving me for another already, little one?"

His sleepy voice murmurs down the bond, piercing through the anguish lingering in my heart, and a smile tugs my lips.

"Exploring my options," I answer before grabbing the skin of his neck between my teeth and biting gently.

A low growl vibrates in his throat, so I add, *"I'll always come back for you."*

His eyes flutter open as his hand goes to the side of my face to tilt my head up.

"And I, for you."

His lips find mine, pressing against my mouth, sealing our vows.

CHAPTER 45

AZRAN

A brisk wind caresses my head as I descend the palace steps, my short hair offering little protection against the elements.

The High Guard is assembling in the courtyard. The full moon lights the stones in hues of grey, and torches reflect on their gold and red armor.

With Dagrassaeb secure on my back, I pause on the last step and let my gaze travel the faces of the soldiers ready to march to war.

Averion's captains stand before their units, their back straight as Calen walks among them, his braids tied at the back of his head and his helmet in hand.

I scan the fighters mounted on horses, and determination settles in their clenched jaws as I lock eyes with them. I force myself to carve each face into memory, instilling as much strength as I can in my gaze. My brothers and sisters in arms will march by my side once more, and they won't all make it back.

Whipping gusts lash the courtyard in invisible torrents, funneled by the surrounding buildings into brisk, biting flurries.

My heart sinks with impending doom on the eve of battle. I've long lost count of the many fights I survived, but bloodshed still awaits us all. Before long, a sea of corpses will cover this land we all fought so hard for.

Soldiers' faces lift in my direction, but it's not me they're looking at.

With Ela's presence looming behind my back, I half-turn towards the top of the stairs, and my breath hitches in my throat.

A hooded silhouette emerges from the palace doors, towering over us with her dark cape flowing around.

As Ela walks down the steps, Death walks with her, and the daughter of darkness is reborn tonight.

Wind swirls in unpredictable currents, rustling over the paving stones before intensifying into angry squalls.

Ela's cape opens, revealing carved symbols of midnight and alabaster on her armor. Obsidian plates rimmed with ivory scrollwork cover her torso, turning her into a harrowing vision promising only hell.

Death has joined our earthly place at long last, to reap a harvest of mortal souls.

I extend a hand when Ela reaches the bottom steps, and she accepts.

Scanning the darkness beneath her hood, my gaze meets hers as torches reflect in her stormy eyes.

"Ready?" I ask down the bond, and she answers with a nod.

With her hand in mine, I face the warriors as the rhythm of iron-shod hooves on stone rings out, echoing from the high-walled courtyard.

"Tonight we march for Daenia and our eastern shores."

My voice booms powerfully over the assembled ranks, effortlessly projecting to the farthest edges of the courtyard.

"Tonight we march for freedom, and in defense of our people."

Snorting breaths blast from flared nostrils as the mounts shift restlessly beneath armor-clad riders.

"Tonight we march towards death or victory."

Tension ripples through the High Guard as my words fill the air and our mounts are brought forward.

We lead our forces through the arch and into Averion moments later.

⸺◆⸺

The ground trembles beneath thousands of hooves as we're joined by Irann's forces on the borders of Averion's plains.

Across the hilly terrain, our battalions advance like great armored beasts, the sun glinting off iron plate and spears shifting in perfect unity. Squadrons of mud-spattered foot soldiers march in lockstep, their cadence punctuated by the calls of horses.

My power roars inside me, calling for the blood of our enemies and the crumbling of this world under the flames of war. Ela's presence strengthens my resolve, though I can barely feel her down the bond with her powers obstructing our connection.

We ride tirelessly through the first light of day and don't relent until we reach Daenia's shores at the end of the following day.

Calen brings the army to a halt as we lay eyes on the sea channels circling the islands around Daenia. The rivers sparkle like jewels under the sun, now low in the reddening sky.

Saltwater canals divide the Water Fae islands like a glimmering blue net, with narrow bridges connecting the scattered archipelago.

Before long, the barren field transforms into a sprawl of tents and fires as battalions hastily throw up shelters against the fading light.

Calen dispatches scouts to the bridges and throughout the camp to keep watch for enemies as Ela and I walk to the High Lord's pavilion.

Soldiers trudge between orderly rows of billowing canvas, some clustering together while squires lead lathered warhorses to makeshift paddocks. Veterans sit watchfully around fires, their thousand-yard stares still seeing the remembered dead.

Heads turn as we weave between warriors, and murmurs follow our steps.

Ela's steps slow when a Wood Fae soldier stands up, his gaze fixed on her. His armor glints under the late afternoon sun.

I draw closer to my mate, ready to step in at the slightest hint of a threat.

"Glory to the Unifier."

Pride swells in my heart when more soldiers rise to echo their comrade's call.

"Unifier."

Several bow their heads as they utter the word like a prayer. Sanctity fills the air and the hair rises on my arms when the procession continues, following us until we reach the pavilion at the center of camp.

Lifting the flaps with one hand, I let Ela go in first.

Removing her hood with a quick tug, Ela unsheathes Nahtar from her back and puts it down with trembling hands.

"Rest while you can." I point to the bed in a corner. "We don't know how much time we have before battle."

"I'm fine."

Her low voice is barely more than a whisper, so I catch her by the arm.

Meeting my gaze, she reveals her darkened irises. Her lifeless eyes confirm she's keeping her fears at bay with her power.

"Please."

Dismissing my request, she makes for the small display of food arranged by camp aids earlier. The flaps of the pavilion lift.

"High Lord," Irann greets me as she lowers her crowned forehead. "Unifier."

Ela lowers the cup she just filled, returning a quick nod.

"Irann," I invite her in as Calen follows, his captains in tow.

They take position around the tent, waiting to give their reports.

"Have we heard from Tharrion yet?" Irann jumps in.

"He's positioned by Daenia's southern border, keeping watch on the shores," I answer.

"Any word from Brimora?" she continues, and I shake my head.

"Nothing yet."

Eerie silence falls over the tent until Calen steps in.

"Reports."

The captains come to life.

"The last of the army has reached camp. Horses are being cared for and food distributed as we speak."

"We're ready to march on Daenia on your orders, High Lord."

Nodding in agreement, I lock eyes with Calen.

"We'll wait for the Captain of the High Guard to return before leaving."

His shoulder relax almost imperceptibly at Vesta's mention.

After the last update, the captains trickle out of the pavilion and I cock a brow at Cal, who hasn't moved.

"What?" A grin forms on his face.

"Get out of here."

"Right." His smile widens as his eyes dart between Ela and I, but he leaves.

Extending both arms towards her, Ela sags against me, the invisible bond pulsing between us as she releases her power.

So ends our respite. War awaits and the semblance of safety we tasted in Averion shatters. A crack in my heart forms as reality dawns on me, and fear's unfamiliar hold takes me, leaving me equally terrified of its intensity and grateful for its presence. This dread only shows how much my life has transformed with the light Ela brought to it.

Her love flares in my chest as she squeezes me tightly, and I know mine for her shines just as bright down the bond. With this simple gesture, resolve joins fear.

Tomorrow I will walk alongside Death, her power entwining with mine, ready to destroy anything in our path.

I pull back to cup her cheek gently.

"I've never cared much for divinity, but you made me a believer," I whisper against her lips. "Let this be the hour when we dance with each other, in war and bloodshed."

My power flickers at the thought, ready to be unleashed and render me invincible.

"This is merely another path we must take to reach what lies beyond destruction, a life together with you forever."

We lock eyes, her darkened irises meeting the crimson in mine, and exchange silent vows.

"Let us show the world what Death and her monster can do," she adds.

She closes the distance and her lips crash against mine. I hold her head as my tongue meets her, eagerly exploring her mouth and setting the bond on fire.

A choked moan tears from her throat as our kiss leaves me breathless.

A hint of warmth flares in my fingers, and I tear myself from her embrace.

I stare down at my open palms, calloused skin streaked with thin scars and weathered from decades of wielding swords. Slowly, I curl my fingers in, pressing down into the lined flesh as heat spreads over my skin and wrists.

CHAPTER 46

NYLREN

Blinding ruby rays crest the roofs of Daenia, and the Váyan sea shimmers as the sun sets, leaving just enough light to reveal the white flag flapping in the wind atop of our mast.

With Zetrea's fleet at my back, I stand in Father's shadow on the deck of our ship, still pitching in the waves. With each dip of the boat, the muscles in my legs strain, flaring with pain. I repress a wince.

Father glances at the white fabric flowing in the sky, and a grin tugs his lips.

Daenia's soldiers have amassed on their docks, ready to launch their vessels at the slightest hint of our attack. Our peaceful disguise is holding them off for now, but there is no telling how long this semblance of truce will hold. I suppose it will last as long as the King allows it.

Father's intense gaze sweeps the horizon as Dran steps forward. "Launch the watercraft."

The commander of Zetrea's army barks orders and soldiers come alive.

A small vessel descends to the water moments later, and the scarred face general steps onto the rope ladder.

He disappears behind the wooden railing, his massive axe sheathed at his back.

"Bring out our guest." Father snaps his fingers and the cabin door swings open.

Amrynn emerges from darkness, the skirt of her azure dress perfectly pleated, although her arms are tied behind her back.

With another snap of the King's fingers, she's freed of her bonds and a soldier digs his blade in her back to push her towards the railing.

Her eyes glaze over me, as if I am made of air, to stare down my father. His grin widens.

A snarls tears from Amrynn's throat, but she keeps walking.

Feisty, but not to the point of having a death wish, she descends the rope ladder.

Several guards join her, and another two watercrafts join their expedition.

A brisk wind carries the splashing of oars until the roaring waves swallow that, too. I'm left to contemplate the white flags flowing in the breeze as the group rows forward.

"She will serve her purpose after all," Father whispers to himself.

I bring the spyglass to my left eye as we wait for what feels like an eternity before the vessels reach Daenia.

Docking on a pontoon, Amrynn and Dran touch land before the rest of our soldiers join them, still carrying our white flags.

One of our men waves his flag pole in the air twice as enemies crowd the pontoon.

I flinch when Father's laughter rings out.

"Send these fools into the abyss of the sea they love so much."

I'm thrown off balance as an astounding blast echoes from the hull of our ship.

The spyglass breaks in my fall, cutting my hand.

Blood drips from my fingers, and shards of glass dig into my palm as I grip the railing to stand.

Father doesn't spare me a glance, his eyes narrowed on the coastline.

I peer overboard in time to see more metal balls leave our hull in a thunderous explosion.

Blasts sound around us as the entire fleet opens fire on the city, and the docks descend into chaos with Father's ruse revealed.

"Burn this city and kill all who resist."

Father's voice booms in my ears, his power increasing its volume tenfold.

Oars descend into the water and our ship leaps forward moments later, the wind having picked up in our sails.

I can't make out what's happening clearly without the spyglass, but the sight before me demands no interpretation.

The wind carries the echoes of the fight on the dock as projectiles tear holes through warehouses, sending stone flying.

The ship's deck shakes with each volley and the wood creaks with the force of the blasts.

Several boats of Daenia's fleet attempt to slow our progress, meeting us on the dark waters.

Metal balls fly everywhere and one hits the mast of an enemy frigate, splintering the wood. Another follows, damaging the hull.

A crash to our left tells us when two ships collide. Before long, enemies board the deck, swords drawn. Our soldiers engage them fearlessly.

The sea heaves in violent tumult beneath our warring galleons, hulls rocking amid explosions of cannon fire as infuriated commands ring out from each vessel's deck.

⚬

With Daenia's fleet sunken into the bay, the army unleashes fire on the city the moment we dock. Explosions fill the smoky air as our units swarm the quarters behind the harbor, setting the night sky ablaze.

Commander Dran leads the charge, his death squadron killing all in its path as they flood the streets filled with civilians evacuating.

Father and I remain with the King's Guard at the back of the offensive, our steps following the destruction to the heart of the city.

The grey paving stones are repainted crimson and covered in dust. Mounds of smoking debris litter streets now exposed to open sky, where towers once scraped clouds.

My boots splash in puddles of brown water as we pass a majestic fountain now laying in ruins. Below, the canal runs choked with rubble, its surface glinting obscenely from slick traces of gore.

Collapsed parapets and bridges transform elegant avenues into clotted arteries, brick avalanches leaving bodies crushed in their wake.

The ground shakes beneath our steps as more blasts detonate in the distance, soon followed by screams.

My gaze lingers on exposed rooms, household tableaux frozen mid-scene, as we pass a side street. Shattered stained-glass windows hang by a thread onto walls blown open to reveal entire lives destroyed in the blink of an eye.

A glint catches my eye, and I freeze. A toddler is hiding in the shadows, squeezing the hand of his older sister and holding a small, dust-covered wooden boat.

My head snaps back to the main street when Father's voice rumbles in my ears.

"What is it, boy?"

Keeping my breathing steady, I force myself to continue without glancing at the alley.

"Merely contemplating the depth of your power, Father."

He wrinkles his nose at my comment, eyeing me in disgust, but my gaze goes to his neckline where the key to my freedom awaits.

Today, Daenia burns, and so do the flames of hope and treachery.

"Forward," he commands, and our column resumes its advance.

Father's wrath knows no bounds. He won't stop until Daenia's beauty is nothing but a memory. By morning, this place will have been razed to the ground, its sculptures, historical landmarks, and mosaic tiles reduced to rubble as Father turns the once-azure canals blood red. And by morning, I will no longer be the ghost of Nyths walking in my father's shadows.

CHAPTER 47

CALEN

My gaze turns to the east as I scan the horizon in hopes of spotting a rider across the bridges, copper hair glinting like embers with flickering shades of auburn, but come up empty.

Standing a few feet from the High Lord's pavilion, I close my eyes as the rays of the dying sun hit my face and take a deep breath.

Warmth tingles at the tips of my fingers. My eyes snap open to scan the soldiers moving around me.

"Cal."

Footsteps tell me of Azran's approach, Ela not far behind. Our gazes fuse in tacit accord, propelling us into motion.

A knot forms in my stomach and I repress the urge to fist my hands. We've come too far to be betrayed now.

I make eye contact with the soldiers I pass and the tingle in my hand intensifies, its warmth spreading to my knuckles.

My hand moves imperceptibly closer to my sabre, only I'm surrounded by our own soldiers, all wearing armor, some even helmets, and I have no idea who I'm looking for.

I scan their faces, following the intensifying warmth spreading to my palm and reorienting my steps as smoothly as possible to avoid drawing attention. I've always walked the ranks of the army, but this time it's different, because I haven't regained the trust of all of these Fae.

When the heat in my hand becomes almost unbearable, I check my palms to make sure there's no sign of magic. Nothing can reveal I'm onto the traitor in our ranks.

I come to a halt between two rows of soldiers. Some are sitting, talking in low voices, while others stand, their tense faces betraying fear.

Spotting Naar's squadron a short distance away, I lock eyes with the red-haired captain, and he disappears in the mass of soldiers when I don't return his nod.

I return my focus to Az and the soldiers around me, hair rising on my arm. My head snaps to a group on my right. It happens so quickly, I almost don't notice the Fae's cerulean gaze aimed at me like daggers. The next second, her blond head escapes into the sea of soldiers.

"Az," I whisper as I stride past him. I don't need to turn to know he's following, taking a wider path to cut off the traitor with Ela. It's the blue-eyed Fae. I know it in my blood.

Come on, think like a traitor. You've done it before.

She's not running yet. If she were, she would leave a trail as the army split in her path. Running will remain her last resort, for it will identify her immediately. Her best bet is to walk out.

The warmth in my hand is dying down, so I pick up the pace.

The army is no more agitated than before, but I've never been more on edge. We can't let this traitor escape this close to battle and risk shattering our soldiers' resolve.

"Make way," I say as I hop over a soldier laying down and cut through a group of Fae to head east.

The traitor knows she's been found, so she can only head in one direction. Daenia. Her only chance is to make for the Water Fae city and hide until she can join Airdan's forces.

When the edge of the army is in sight and I still see no sign of the blue-eyed Fae, I break into a run, the heat in my palm returning tenfold.

Agitation stirs ahead, and it's like the army closes around me as soldiers stand and shouts fill the air. The mass of fighters presses around me, gathering to our eastern flank.

"Make way." My voice booms, but it's soon outmatched by the commotion erupting ahead.

Metal clangs and my blood freezes. There is no mistaking that sound. I can summon it every time I close my eyes.

"Make way," I repeat, pushing soldiers aside and surging towards the fight.

A flash of red hair appears in the mass of bodies, and I crane my neck to see. Naar is engaging a soldier, sword drawn. He spins to defend himself, and the blond-haired traitor comes into view between a pair of soldiers in front of me.

I push them aside.

"Move. Move. Move."

When I make it to the edge, soldiers are frozen in place around me, unsure which fighter to side with.

A growl tears from Naar's throat as the traitor's blade slices through his thigh, and he falls back. I jump forward, unsheathing my sword.

"Seize her," I order as I lunge for her, but she's already breaking into a run, freed of her last obstacle.

A group of soldiers follow and screams fill the air.

I don't spare a glance for Naar, still on the ground.

The traitor climbs a small hill and I struggle to close the distance. A snarl leaves my lips as I strain to run faster.

She disappears over the hill and my stomach drops. Seconds later, I reach the other side, blinded by the setting sun ready to disappear on the horizon. My hand flies to my eyes to block the light reflecting in the river and I stop dead in my tracks.

A Fae is standing on the bridge with their back turned, their long braid flowing in the wind. A white silk ribbon intertwines with their dark hair.

Mor, a short blade in hand, crimson dripping from the tip, towers over a body at his feet.

My pulse quickens as relief floods my body. I lower my sword.

Thank gods for this old bastard.

Mor meets my gaze as I take position beside him.

"Naar."

His eyes widen as the name leaves my lips, and I nod towards the army behind us. He takes off at a run, and I turn to face the soldiers gathering around me.

The mass of soldiers splits as Az emerges, his widened eyes fixed on the horizon. Lifting his arm, he points behind me.

"Cal."

Purple and grey decorate the bruised sky as the last fiery sliver of sun vanishes below the sea's dark rim, plunging the world in shadows except for a single light.

Flickering flames leap towards the darkened sky, a false dawn cresting the bleak horizon in hues of orange fury as a seething inferno devours the edge of the world, and Daenia.

With urgency in every fiber of my body, I call my men to arms and bark orders until soldiers run back to camp to warn the rest of the army.

I'm about to turn back when a flash of red catches my eye. A rider is crossing the bridge, the hooves of their horse hammering the ground.

Vesta jumps off her mount the second she reaches the other side before running to us.

"Airdan is attacking on two fronts," she lets out between pants.

I reach for her as she stumbles.

"Half of his fleet anchored in Daenia—the rest made for Lóna's southern shores and Ecya."

"He's going to try to encircle Daenia and trap us," Azran's voice booms in the air.

"Tharrion won't have enough men to push him back," I say, doom seeping through my body.

"We need to send forces south," Azran agrees.

Vesta eyes dart between the two of us.

"I'll go," I offer. Vesta's mouth opens, ready to protest, but I silence her with a glare. "If our defenses fall in Ecya, Lóna and Brimora will be at Airdan's fingertips. With the Váyan Sea and the Eidune Range in his back, he'll storm Kalar and march on what's left of us."

Azran responds with a sharp nod as I turn to him and extend a hand. He grips my forearm tightly.

"Give them hell, brother. We'll hold off Airdan in Daenia."

Az leaves to gather the army, and Vesta faces me. Her fist hits my chest before I can utter a single word, and pain flares in my ribs as she readies herself for another assault.

"Why do you always have to sacrifice yourself for us?"

Vesta tries to land another hit, but I catch her fist mid-air. Alarm stains the verdant pools of her irises, and I pull her into an embrace.

"I'll be fine, Dove." I infuse quiet steel into each syllable, hoping to quell the tempest in her eyes.

Her body relaxes in my arms as I rest my head atop hers.

"I'm sorry for everything. These past months have been unbelievably difficult, and you were the only light in the dark."

She pushes back, features twisting in outrage.

"You don't get to say goodbye like this."

I raise a hand to cradle her delicate cheek.

"You won't be rid of me so easily, Dove."

"I'm sorry I got scared." Her voice breaks as she kisses my palm. "I don't want to lose you."

"You won't," I counter. "I'll join you in Daenia as soon as I can."

She nods before stepping back.

"I am a tough bastard to kill."

I shoot her a wink, but the smile she offers doesn't reach her emerald eyes.

With trembling breaths, I tear my hand from her face, the warmth of her touch making the cold road ahead cut all the sharper.

Turning away, I force my legs to obey as the weight of unspoken words crushes me.

With each agonizing step I take, regret eats at me, but I don't turn back. If I do, I don't know if I'll have the strength to walk away from her again.

Strong fingers encircle my forearm, anchoring me in place with pressure and silent pleading.

Vesta yanks my arm, pulling me to her as her mouth crashes on mine.

With quaking breaths, I commit the curved shape of her lips to memory in a kiss that echoes vows still unspoken between us.

"You come back to me, you hear me?" she whispers against my lips.

"I promise."

CHAPTER 48

AZRAN

With labyrinthine canals dividing isles and narrow sloping bridges our only passage between isolated plots of land, it takes us crucial hours to reach the battlefield.

The cavalry crashes through the last shallow river separating us from Daenia in a spray of silver droplets, their thunderous pace never slowing as they power through mud and water alike.

We reach the western edges of the city with the first rays of sun and storm through the open main gate.

My heart pounds in my chest as I guide our column down an avenue. Citizens fleeing Daenia fill the paved streets, some carrying bundles on their backs and children in their trembling arms. Their faces light up when their gaze falls on us, though no warmth lingers in my heart. My people need me. They have suffered enough, and I won't let Airdan's madness destroy what I've spent centuries fighting for.

Ela's rage stokes mine and I spur the sides of my horse, focusing my wrath on the coming battle.

Smoke rises above the elegant buildings lining the street, confirming the battle is still raging. Airdan progressed deeper into the city through the night.

Power floods my veins, instilling strength to my body and mind as bloodlust calls.

Airdan's debts will be paid in blood. I will avenge every stolen soul with red-handed fury until his crushed body feeds the worms. His screams will echo into eternity as his line ends by my hand.

Hooves strike the paving stones as we near the center, greeted by more horror-torn faces and destruction.

We cross paths with bloodied soldiers running through side streets, and a chill courses my spine. The city is on the brink of collapse, and so is Ker's army.

Leading our troops across an elegant bridge, the distant song of steel and slaughter sets my soul alight with hunger. The promise of havoc beckons, kindling my bones with the purpose I was forged to fulfill.

As Ela and I lock eyes, her gaze betrays the same fierce anticipation I feel curling down my spine. Her irises cloud with darkness, mirroring my own with their gnawing thirst for violence. I glimpse our twinned reflections—warriors bonded by oaths sworn in venom to a revenge long in the making.

"I'll stay by your side," she says down the bond, her voice drained of all warmth.

"This madness ends today," I answer. *"With you and I."*

"Airdan won't see another sunrise."

Though Ela's chilling oath resonates through me, it is the merciless tongue of Death herself I hear.

I spur my horse and raise Dagrassaeb high above my head when Daenia's battalions appear in the forum at the end of the street.

"To me," I bellow when we reach the mass of soldiers fighting and my two-bladed sword sings, slicing through flesh and bone.

Blood splashes my armor, and I dig my heels into my mount's sides to push forward.

"To the High Lord!"

Shouts echo my call and I scan the chaos to find the commander.

Impaling a fighter before making an arc with my sword, I jump from my horse and join the soldiers already on the ground.

"To me," I thunder, in an attempt to bring back order to our ranks.

I hammer my sword down an enemy's neck and spin to parry an attack. Vesta joins the fight with the High Guard, Eren's units not far behind.

Before long, my roars fill the air as I deal blow after blow, letting my wrath rain down on our opponents. My blade twists in a soldier's middle and I redecorate the street with his bowels.

Ela engages two soldiers at once, parrying and shielding their attacks before returning fatal strikes.

A Fae emerges from the bloodshed, limping, her short purple hair standing out amidst the madness. Crimson covers her chest plate and a nasty wound mars her thigh.

"Lieutenant Safrin, High Lord." Her eyes dart around for signs of danger. "Airdan's forces caught us by surprise on the docks. We've been pushed back to the Merchants' Quarters."

"Where is Lord Keryth?" I ask, slaying another fighter.

Safrin lunges to the side, escaping death by an inch before spinning and slamming her sword into her attacker.

When the Fae lies dead at her feet, she meets my gaze before shaking her head in defeat.

"Last I heard, he took several units to Endya."

My heart sinks at the mention of Daenia's central plaza. Resting in a perfect circle in the heart of the city with four access points, it was designed to bewilder and enthrall. While a prowess of architectural feats, the tall buildings offer little cover and no strategic advantage.

However breathtaking Endya may be, it remains undefendable without an army. Ker knows this better than anyone.

"What madness led him there?"

"Reports claim the Lady of the Water Fae was there when Airdan attacked, but we haven't been able to reach them."

I screw my eyes shut and let out a growl.

In an attempt to save the Fae he loves, Keryth trapped himself and sealed all of our fates.

Shouts echo ahead and the forum floods with soldiers wearing the emerald color of Airdan's house.

"Vesta," I call, and the Captain of the High Guard reaches me seconds later.

"Split up and go around. We make for the central plaza."

With a nod, she calls several units back before leading them through a side street. I jump back into the raging battle, with Ela right behind me.

Bloodlust sings in my veins as I seek my next target and crimson splatters the grey stones.

Cries of fury rise around me as soldiers lunge forward, only to be slain by Dagrassaeb.

My blades cleave through armor, flesh, bone. Two soldiers fall, their mouths open in wordless screams. A fetid smell mingles with spilled entrails as I wrench my sword free to parry a hatchet.

I drive my weapon through the next attacker, splitting them from collar to sternum. Fluids jet from the screaming gash and I push on, ignoring their attempts to stanch the lethal wound.

Lungs heaving in the stinking air, my very soul cries out for more slaughter.

Once the forum is cleared, we go from bottleneck to bottleneck in narrow streets as Airdan's explosive powder blasts around us, wreaking havoc through the city.

My boot lands in a gore-slick puddle and blood splashes when I strike another enemy in a debris-filled avenue. Bodies litter the canals around us as collapsed roofs rest on fallen walls.

Ela stays by my side, slicing through any approaching threat. Our bond floods with darkness and wrath as Death and her monster fight in deadly harmony.

I lunge forward, digging my blade into a Fae's side and cutting the throat of another in one move. No more ruse. No more political games. No more dancing around devils who call themselves King.

Eren's growls meet mine, though sheer madness and grief shine in his eyes at the sight of his bloodied homeland.

He attacks another soldier, recklessly exposing his right side. Closing the distance in a jump, I land at his back and deflect a blow coming at him.

He spins, but my blade is already sunk deep in the emerald armor of the enemy.

"Focus, Captain," I say through gritted teeth.

Eren's mouth falls agape, eyes sweeping frantically across the dreadful sight, lingering on the dead civilians sprawled across the cobblestones, before he manages a faint nod.

Deflecting a cut aimed for my ribs, Dagrassaeb digs into a soldier's neck, claiming yet another life.

Averion's captain is still frozen in place, his lips parted in an anguished gasp as his wide eyes track the streets where innocents lie slaughtered.

"*Ela*," I call down the bond.

Her name conveys my command more deeply than language could, and we pivot as one. She moves to cover our rear while I turn to face the Water Fae.

"Eren."

His youthful eyes clash with my battle-hardened ones in a look I've seen far too many times on a battlefield. No mortal mind was built to withstand the permanent imprint of these horrors.

"We will avenge every last one of them." My hand lands on the back of his neck. "Our people need you."

Snapping out of his petrified daze, Eren tips his chin.

"Airdan needs to be stopped."

The captain clenches his jaw and I nod back.

"Can I count on you?"

"Yes, High Lord."

Letting go of him, I dive back into the butchery, my faithful mantra echoing in my mind.

I shall rest when I'm dead.

I shall rest when my enemies lay dead at my feet.

I shall rest when Ela is in my arms.

CHAPTER 49

CALEN

Fear shakes my heart as we follow the sea channel south of Daenia to Ecya. Airdan must have docked right at the border of the Water Fae territory, on the strip of land connecting him to the rest of our territories.

An inferno burns to our left as we ride tirelessly towards the coast, a permanent reminder of the hell where Vesta and Az are headed.

I bring the army to a halt behind me with the first light of day. I gaze upon the mass of soldiers in front of us. Airdan's ships tower in the distance, their masts flying his emerald flag, and Daenia's islands jut from the water on our left.

I bring my horse around as soldiers tighten their hold on their reigns and weapons, their captains at the front of the line.

"Wyn. Varan. Take the northern side."

Riding up our column, I give orders.

"Lana and Elion, circle to the south."

Silence settles as hundreds of soldiers await my next words, angst twisting in their guts like it twists in mine.

"Brothers and sisters," I roar. "I call on you to defend Lóna with your lives and fulfill the oaths you have taken."

Shouts echo my words, diffusing the fear and tension in our bones, as I raise my sword to the sky and swing it towards the battlefield.

Averion's cavalry launches forward as I lead the infantry. Our squadrons spread across the blood-soaked plains, crashing against enemy spears as we join forces with the Sun Fae in heart of the battle. Tharrion's soldiers open a passage as fresh troops reinforce their defense.

My blade swings at the emerald helmets I ride by, splintering shields and cracking skulls, my fighters in tow.

I jump off my mount in the heart of the battle, my eyes glazing over the corpses lying on the muddied grass. Hammering a blow, my sword locks with one of Airdan's men. With a roar, I kick his leg at full force. Bones crack as his knee snaps, and he goes down with a scream. Plunging my blade into his chest, the cry dies on his lips.

Metal tearing through flesh reaches my ears as Death sinks its claws into my senses and the General takes over. Locking down my emotions, I turn to my next target and lunge.

My opponent slain, I pause to reassess the terrain. My eyes dart to a body crushed under soldiers' boots. His face is torn in a silent scream, his lifeless eyes mirroring the sky, and his chest is caved in, the yellow and blue of his armor drowning in crimson.

My jaw slackens before my head snaps towards hints of Brimora's colors in the sea of bodies. Queen Aanor sent some of her soldiers, and most of them lie dead at my feet.

It would take three of the strongest human fighters to take down a single Fae, and Airdan's best fighters came here.

"Calen," a strong voice thunders over the chaos, and I search for its bearer.

A soldier extracts himself from the mass of bodies, his helmet reflecting the sunlight. He sports a mean cut to the chest.

"Tharrion."

We clasp hands briefly.

"Queen Aanor?" I ask, panting.

"She sent five hundred soldiers. This is what's left of them." He looks around, his eyes falling on the destroyed corpses at our feet.

I nod sharply as I swallow the lump in my throat.

"I bring a thousand fighters with me."

"We could use the help," Tharrion says, pointing to the east. "Their ships are still docked a mile away. We're trying to push them back to the shore."

A grin crosses my face. "Let's show them what Sun Fae are made of."

His beard parts to reveal a devilish smile before he turns.

"Push them back. To the sea!" Tharrion's voice booms in the air as he jumps back into the fight. I follow, my training and instinct taking over.

Blood splashes as I dig my blade into a body and parry another attack. I feint to the left before raising my sword and dealing a deadly blow to the Fae's chest.

Elbowing another attacker, I spin and slay the burly Fae standing before me.

I lock away any thought of Vesta as my blade sinks into flesh. She's somewhere in Daenia's labyrinth of streets and canals, but the thought only floods my veins with panic.

Grunts sound all around me as I force myself to breath in and out with each strike to keep my muscles from tiring too quickly.

Sweat drips down my forehead profusely and my braids are coming undone from the bun at the back of my head, swinging into my vision. Salt stings my eyes as the drops roll down my temples, and I blink furiously as I hammer down my sword.

The rest of the world disappears as I'm left to face a horde of enemies fighting with all they've got, my men around me.

Ferocity guides each of my blows as I calculate each parry and attack, but we're not progressing fast enough. Urgency twists in my gut as Daenia burns in the distance.

A reprieve comes around mid-day as cries tear from the enemies' throats.

Smoke billows on the horizon, and tension ripples through our ranks.

"Airdan's fleet. It's destroyed."

Shouts rise all around me and my head snaps to the shore.

"Look."

"Airdan's fleet."

I push aside the men in front of me to get a clearer view and stop dead in my tracks.

Mats are crashing down on decks as boats sink into the bay before another fleet of frigates, a fleet flying Brimora's colors.

A cry of victory flares in my throat as I raise my sabre high, knowing the tide is about to turn.

We push through the emerald army with renewed fervor as their spirits dampen with the loss of their ships. Cornered between a mass of raging Fae and the sea, their confusion plays to our advantage.

I slay another invader before Tharrion pulls me back.

His chest wound still oozes blood, and his face is pale.

"We'll secure our shores and finish these bastards off."

"Tharrion, you're in no shape to fight. We'll stay," I counter.

"No." He shakes his head, panting. "Daenia needs you."

Turning, I spot two of his fighters. "You two. Keep your Lord safe. Do not leave his side, you hear me?"

They give me a quick nod before one of them answers.

"Yes, General."

Tharrion huffs, and I lock eyes with him.

"Stay alive. We'll need you when this is over."

"Go, Cal. We've got this."

With a nod, I leave Tharrion and call my fighters back.

"To me," I shout at the top of my lungs.

As more soldiers rally around me, I spot several of our captains.

"Varan. Lana. Pull back."

With wide gestures of my arm, I retreat until a Fae stumbles forward, the reigns of my horse in hand.

"Thank you, soldier."

With a sharp nod, I mount, gaining a better vantage point.

My eyes dart to one of my captains, knee deep in bodies, his arms soaked in blood and a rictus on his torn face.

"Wyn," I call out.

His head snaps up, revealing crazed eyes. Varan reaches his twin and yanks him back to let Tharrion's men take his place.

Moments later, the cavalry is back on horses and riding out of the battlefield. Soldiers too incapacitated to ride are left behind. Others share a horse, theirs lost to the butchery.

My heart sinks as I glance back at my homeland and the dead bodies scattered across the Sun Fae plains.

Each stride of my horse radiates down to my bones, and determination settles in my heart as Daenia's islands appear in the distance.

CHAPTER 50

CALEN

The acrid scent of sulfur hangs heavy in the air, biting at the back of my throat with each breath. The harsh, choking smell permeates my surroundings and mixes with the metallic tang of blood while the suffocating heat of Daenia's afternoon sun clings to my body.

The battle rages on, but all I can focus on is that bitter smell and dread's mantle enshrouding the battlefield. Urgency floods my veins as my sole focus becomes survival.

We're making our way towards the heart of the city, but each step is harder than the last. We arrived spent, only to find obstacle after obstacle as destroyed bridges prevented us from crossing canals. Daenia makes for the most impractical battle-field, with its narrow passageways, arches around every corner, and civilians running through the streets to escape the massacre.

I hammer my sword down on a soldier's neck while fending off another attack with my shorter blade. The street can't fit more than five soldiers at a time, so I make my way to the front of the line to make a dent in their defense.

Screams and cries fill my ears, but I've known too many battlefields to let them get to me anymore.

Block. Slice. Counter. Lunge. Another body falls at my feet.

Any chance I get, I scan the mass of soldiers around us, searching for the rest of our army and Azran.

A growl tears from my throat when a soldier's blade cuts my forearm. Spinning, I plunge my short blade through his chin. A pair of soldiers wearing emerald take position in front of me, their uniforms already tinted crimson.

Lunging at me together, they force me back a step to parry. I lose balance as I hit another soldier in my back, and clench my teeth in anticipation.

A blade digs through my thigh as I recover from the tumble, raising my weapon too late.

A soldier jumps in front of me, engaging the pair, and I don't need to look twice to know their lives just got cut short.

Bright light shines on my left, and I'm thrown to the ground again by a deafening explosion.

My ears are ringing and dark smoke twirls all around me, filling my lungs and throat.

Movement appears in the corner of my eyes and the ringing quietens, giving way to piercing screams and blades clashing.

I roll over with a groan, having landed on my injured leg, and scrape the ground near me for my weapon.

My greatest failure resurrected; Airdan has again deployed his explosive powder. That sadist destined for the fiery pits of hell corrupts the rules of war.

I climb to my knees to search through the dust. I have mere seconds before the smoke clears and soldiers rain down on us once more. My fingers find purchase on something hard, and I grip on instinct.

I let go a moment later with a scream, my palm scorched by heated metal. A gust of wind hits my face, carrying the scent of death and clearing the smoke.

Emerald armor emerges from the darkness as soldiers step towards me, and I catch a glimpse of my sword a few feet away.

Sounds return in full force, shouts and orders barked as more soldiers regain their feet.

Without thinking, I lunge towards my sword, relying on my injured leg to hold as I reach for my weapon. A blade misses my neck by an inch as I leap to my feet, sword in hand, ready to impale the next bastard crazy enough to take me on. The hilt digs into my injured palm, but letting go again is not an option.

A form dives into the group of enemies and Airdan's soldiers start falling to the ground, one after another. Fiery red locks tumble in unrestrained strands as a fighter swings their blade.

Moments later, Vesta stands alone among the bodies, blood coating her hair and face. A fatal beauty.

"Cal."

She's by my side in an instant and we finish off the squadron that cornered us in this street. When the last body touches the soiled paving stones, we lock eyes.

If emerald is to be the last thing I see when I die, then let it be her eyes, looking back into my soul, with her guard down and her love within reach.

I cross the distance between us, reaching for her as she reaches back. Pulling her to me, I rest my forehead against hers, letting the tips of our noses touch.

"I kept my promise," I whisper.

Her hand goes to the side of my face, her gentle touch emboldening me.

"I know you're scared, but I hope you'll come to see one day that my love is no cage."

With knitted brows, her teeth seize her lips between them before releasing the reddened flesh. My heart is beating out of my chest as her glistening eyes dart to the ground before locking with mine.

The sounds of the battlefield disappear, engulfed in her silence as I wait.

"I love you."

The words leave her trembling lips as no more than a whisper, but my chest expands tenfold, unable to contain the rush of bliss coursing through my veins.

Her features remain frozen in a mask of angst as tears prickle in her beryl eyes and an irrepressible grin claims my mouth.

My lungs strain against my ribcage, near to bursting as I feel whole for the first time in my life. Her protective walls have crumbled, revealing what I always knew.

The first salty droplet rolls on her ash-coated cheek and her lips curve into a tentative smile before joy unfurls it wider, lighting up her face. Our shared future stretches out before us, limitless, illuminated solely by the radiant flare of her growing smile.

"I—"

"Forward, you bastards!"

Wyn's order fills the air as he runs past us like a madman, his scarred face a mask of rage.

Vesta pulls back as soldiers rise to their feet and follow him. We exchange a glance full of promises before focusing on our squadrons.

"Forward," I echo Wyn's call, my heart still pounding with the force of her words piercing my soul.

Savage screams resonate all around us as our soldiers push on, chasing after emerald enemies.

We're about to turn a corner when I signal the units behind me to slow. Another battle is raging ahead.

I turn back to face our soldiers, looking each one in the eyes.

Signing with my hands, I gesture for some of my men to join our forces already in battle and command the rest to cross the street.

"We encircle them."

Seeing their nods, I raise my right hand, ready to launch our attack.

"Pull back!" A soldier's scream reaches my ears a moment before I give the signal. "Pull back!"

I peer around the corner and see our soldiers running towards me. A moment later, the street is engulfed in a ball of fire and the ground shakes beneath my feet as smoke and projectiles scatter.

A warm gust of wind follows, and the echo from the blast sets me in motion. Reaching for the first soldier I find, I help them to their feet before pushing forward.

I dispatch enemies and look for survivors, joining what's left of the unit caught in the blast. Vesta follows close behind, to the end of the destroyed street.

We know what to look for; most have seen the dark powder before, but it won't be enough to prevent more bloodshed.

We haven't reached the central plaza yet, and we've lost so many already. An impending sense of doom grows in my heart, but I push it back when we join Wyn's units at the next crossroad.

Airdan's soldiers are ruthless in their disregard for civilians, slicing and killing anyone within their reach.

I engage another group of fighters, my arm tiring under the relentless assaults, my chest heaving from effort.

When the body of a woman falls at my feet, a pool of blood down her middle, my vocal cords strain, a guttural roar clawing free. These wretched souls hold nothing sacred in life.

Scattered body parts line the charred paving stones. With each step I take, each enemy I slay, I stumble upon another massacre.

With each rasping inhalation, smoke and dust climb deeper into my lungs, but we can't relent now.

Another scream of rage tears through me when I lose sight of Vesta behind enemy lines.

"Vesta," I shout, hoping my voice will carry over the sound of steel clashing.

I elbow a soldier's face and spin as I slice through a mass of bodies.

"Vesta!" I call again, trying to discern her voice in the chaos, but come up empty until a bestial growl responds.

Several emerald fighters slow to look around, and a grin blooms on my blood-covered face. It's about damn time.

I spot his two-bladed sword before his red eyes land on me, and Azran pounces on the soldiers, tearing through them like a wild animal.

Soldiers around me rush towards the enemy, victorious screams bursting from their lungs as they slice through emerald armor relentlessly.

The effect Az has on his fighters has always been beyond anything I've ever seen. Admiration, pride, and pure devotion shine in their eyes. Although he doesn't see it, or never allows himself to, they will go to the ends of this earth for him and our cause. There lies the power in fighting for equality and justice.

A familiar voice rings out above the madness and Vesta emerges from the mass of fighters, shouting orders to soldiers around her. Pride and relief swell in my heart.

We manage to push the mass of soldiers back and take another street when we finally catch a break. Airdan's soldiers are scattering through the city.

Relieved, I turn, looking for that crazy, red-eyed bastard.

"You're late," Az drawls behind me. His short hair is coated in blood, the crimson liquid dripping down his temple, and his wrathful gaze fixes on me.

"So are you."

The corner of my mouth lifts, but his remains pinched in a tight line, his jaw clenched. The prince of bloodshed eyes me, assessing the damage to my body.

Boots hitting the ground echo around us and my heart sinks. Our reprieve will be short lived.

"You look terrible."

A flicker shines in Az's crimson eyes as a small smile tugs his lips.

"I know," I answer with a wink, before looking around. "Ela?"

Az turns in the direction of enemy soldiers, the sound of their footsteps growing closer by the second, but doesn't answer.

"In formation," I command.

Our fighters take position but Azran remains still, his blade lowered.

At least two dozen soldiers in emerald armor storm onto the street, savage bellows erupting from their mouths.

"General." Wyn comes to my side, eagerly waiting for the order.

"Hold." I raise my first, my senses on high alert as I squint at the enemy.

Their screams are no battle cries. The soldiers are fleeing, their weapons hanging loosely in their hands. One of them looks over their shoulder and trips, going down with a cry.

The back of the column is engulfed in shadows, and some of the cries die down until the sound of metal hitting metal fills the air. Ela emerges from the darkness, leaving a trail of bodies behind her.

I glance at Azran, but he only has eyes for his mate, pride shining in his crimson irises. The corners of his mouth lift into a tender smile as Ela tears through another soldier.

I repress a chuckle. Made for each other doesn't begin to describe them. They were cut from the same mold.

Darkness seeps out of Ela once more, sucking the life from the soldiers around her until a dark fire engulfs five of them. Their cries die in the flames as they're called back to the void that awaits us all.

Ela unleashes another gust of fire on a group of soldiers, burning them to a crisp before our eyes, and a knot forms in my throat.

I lower my hand and Wyn charges ahead with his unit to join Ela. But in the time it takes them to close the distance, the last of Airdan's soldiers lie dead.

Ela emerges from the mass of charred corpses, a deadly resolve in her dark eyes, like a vision of hell.

The acidic smell of sulfur burns my nostrils still, seeping into my clothing and stinging my eyes.

There is no escaping it, that pungent stench of burned powder that signifies death. It overwhelms the senses, adding to the chaos and carnage of the battlefield. And in that moment, I know I will never forget that scent. It will haunt me until my last breath. Like a ghost, it will linger long after the sounds of war have faded. If they ever do.

CHAPTER 51

ELANOR

I'm walking among the living, but with each step, Death's call grows stronger. I am a wraith tasked to bring wretched souls to the darkness where they belong, with me.

Bodies lie around me but I don't see them anymore. They were dead the moment I laid eyes on them. My guilt is long gone. I don't expect it will make a comeback now, not after what they've done to me, to the humans, to my people, and to the world. Airdan's puppets deserve my wrath. They deserve their fate. They deserve worse.

My rage still boils, my power begging to be unleashed further, to burn this place to the ground.

Azran's crimson eyes, like beacons in the night, bring me back from the edge. A group of soldiers stands in front of me.

Wyn is the first to step forward, pulling me into a side hug.

"Damn, Ela. Nice skills."

His scarred face smiles at me, yet another reminder of what Airdan has done, but I return his smile, relegating the dark thoughts to another part of my soul.

"You too, Wyn," I say as I eye his blade dripping with blood. Pulling back, I turn to face the others.

"Cal," I say, with a nod.

"Good to see you in one piece, Ela," Cal says.

I give him a smile and lock eyes with several soldiers behind him, their gazes a mix of horror and admiration.

Azran steps forward, extending a hand towards me. I close the distance in a few steps and he tucks his arm around my shoulders, depositing a soft kiss on top of my head.

"Nice display of force out there, little one."

I tilt my head back to stare into his hypnotizing eyes, a hint of mischief in them.

"More are coming. We need to keep moving," he adds out loud.

Soldiers have gathered around us now, their widened eyes scanning their High Lord.

"To the central plaza." Az turns to Cal. "We're not far."

Moments later, our column is marching north through destroyed streets.

Turning a corner, an imposing archway comes into view, flanked by smooth, curved walls stretching as far as the eye can see. A bridge arches gracefully over the canal encircling the enshrouded plaza within, its white balustrades and columns topped with elaborate carvings.

"Endya," Cal intones as he raises his fist in the air. Behind him, soldiers freeze.

The arch looms tall and silent, standing immortal guard over its charge, confirming the enemy hasn't reached this entrance yet.

When we get to the bridge, shouts echo down the quay and dozens of emerald soldiers emerge onto the street, running along the canal, crushing our fleeting hope.

"Vesta." Calen steps forward. "Go back and take the side street."

Airdan's soldiers storm the avenue to try and cut us off as he dispatches troops.

"Wyn. Cover our units from behind." The moment the order is uttered, Wyn gathers his fighters. "Circle back if you can."

"Yes, General."

"Soldiers, with me." Calen locks eyes with me and Az. "You should go."

I don't think twice before making for the archway. There's still time for us to cross the bridge before the enemy covers the distance.

I'm yanked back, Az's arm tightly wrapped around my forearm.

"No fucking way." The words come out as a growl, tension radiating from his jaw. "Airdan could have entered through any of the other three entrances and be waiting for us there. Going together is reckless."

Were he not suggesting what I think he is, I would smile at his use of profanity.

"You're not leaving without me," I say through gritted teeth.

"I'll be fine. If something happens, we can't let Airdan get us both."

"I'll go. With my shadows, I can sneak past any enemy and join Keryth faster than you could."

"No. We don't even know if he's still alive."

I squint at him, knowing damn well why he's being so stubborn.

"I won't be reckless, I promise."

Stone crashes into the canal as flames engulf a building a block away, lighting Az's face in hues of red and yellow, the fire a pale comparison to his crimson eyes.

"They're aiming for the bridge," Calen warns, his voice rising above the madness.

Seconds later, the explosion reaches our ears. Another follows.

The violence of the blast sends me to the ground, coughing from the smoke burning my lungs and throat, its acrid smell filling my nose.

I climb to my knees and someone pulls me up. When the smoke clears, Calen releases his hold on my arm and I'm left to contemplate the destruction. Part of the quay has collapsed, taking the bridge with it, and debris litters the water flowing through the canal.

"Az."

My stomach drops when I find only stone and rocks. He was right there with me. A pit opens in my stomach as I dig through the rubble with my bare hands, scratching at the rocks, inhaling dust with each gulp of air.

Urgency flares in my heart and my head snaps towards the archway on the other side of the canal.

"*Azran*," I scream down the bond.

He's holding the ledge with one hand while his other still grips Dagrassaeb. His boots sway in empty air, debris-filled water raging beneath him.

Straining to hold on, he swings his arm and throws his weapon over the edge before finding purchase with both hands.

Az pulls himself up enough for his leg to find hold, and finally swings himself onto what's left of the bridge.

"*I made it to the other side.*"

I'm left heaving, my heart pounding in my chest.

"*Are you hurt?*"

"*I'm fine. I'll scout the plaza and signal you through the bond when I know more.*"

A cry tears from my throat and my fist hits the first rock I find. The zap of pain doesn't tame the flames of rage inside me.

I have no way to get across the canal, no matter how powerful I may be. The distance between us is already growing through the bond. He's gone, and it's only a matter of seconds before he'll be too far to reach me.

"Survive."

My heart shatters as I whisper the command.

"I'll see you soon, little one."

His response comes instantly, granting me a short reprieve from the torment of separation.

<hr>

The sun is ready to disappear behind the horizon by the time we finish off the last soldier in front of the destroyed bridge.

My gaze darts to the archway Azran disappeared through.

"Anything?" Cal asks as he cleans his sword on his thigh.

I shake my head in defeat. Not a word. He is out there, cut off from us, from me, wandering through the massive central plaza in the unknown.

I should have heard from him by now. I know I should have.

"We'll regroup with the rest of our forces and make for the eastern bridge."

"I'm not waiting," I say, walking past him. He doesn't argue.

My mind is made up, and he knows there's no stopping me.

I break into a run.

With Nahtar still in hand and crimson dripping from its blade, I let my rage take over, fueling it with each step and the blood of each soldier with the misfortune to stand in my path.

I'm running along the canal, my pulse pounding in my ears and my knuckles whitening around the hilt of my sword, when a unit of emerald soldiers emerges from a side street.

Unleashing my power, darkness engulfs them. I don't slow down to watch, letting their screams fill my ears as I push on.

When I reach Endya's eastern entrance, a battle is already raging on the bridge leading to the massive archway, a perfect copy of the one Airdan's soldiers destroyed. Several of our units are trying to take the crossing, paying for it with their blood as the arch towers over the dreadful scene.

"Found you," I whisper to myself.

I jump on the first emerald soldier I see, slicing through him with Nahtar. Blood splatters and he goes down with a cry. I lunge at the next soldier and unleash fire on a group to my right.

"The Unifier!" a soldier screams. "The Unifier is here."

I don't turn back to look as I cut off a guard's arm before digging my blade into her abdomen. They know I've come for them, and fear spreads like wildfire, sinking in their bones, closing around their hearts. They're now dancing with Death, and hell awaits. I bring the only certainty in this world, their demise.

Having cleared a circle around me, I move closer to the archway. I keep dancing with my blade, Savage's spirit grounding me in the back of my mind.

Another soldier falls at my feet and I push the next one off the bridge.

I break through their defense half an hour later and cross the bridge, leaving nothing but chaos in my wake.

I take off running as Azran's face overlays my vision, strengthening my resolve.

Massive platforms of various heights greet me, water cascading over their edges into streams circling all around. I pause to reorient myself. Remembering Eren's words, I make for the closest steps I find, eagerness shaking my heart.

Calling on my shadows, I wrap myself in their darkness as I climb several stairs at a time. On the landing, I emerge onto another level and look for the way up. The platform ends abruptly at a precipitous drop, the waterfall pouring over the edge the only way down, denying further ascent.

"Fuck," I mutter to myself before turning back.

I make my way down and race across the lower level until I find another staircase.

The platforms loom staggered like colossal steps for giant beings, interconnected in a layout impossible to figure out at a quick glance. Each wrong turn tightens the knot constricting my chest.

It's almost nightfall by the time I reach the highest level. Panting heavily, I turn around and dread seeps through my bones. From this vantage point, only two entrances are visible, but they're crawling with soldiers fighting and I can't make out which side is gaining terrain.

Explosions sound in the distance, but I remain focused on the cluster of domed buildings arranged in a perfect circle on the immense center platform.

Golden-roofed towers peak over the mass of construction in Endya's heart, separated by narrow streets.

I break into a run, but I'm forced to slow down at the first turn.

"Damn it."

I can't search each street and building in this maze. It will take me forever on my own, and time is the one thing I don't have.

Opting for a different strategy, I search for signs of altercations as I circle the elegant constructions, heading deeper into Endya.

My gaze darts around for landmarks, but all doors carry the same intricate designs and gold knobs, making it impossible to differentiate the buildings.

I scan the bond every few minutes, but I'm only met with deafening silence as I glide soundlessly ahead.

With my senses on high alert, I turn a corner and almost trip on a bloodied corpse wearing emerald armor.

My heartbeat accelerates as memories of the hours spent hunting game in the Dark Forest return. This is no different—I'm looking for clues and letting the terrain guide me.

Craning my neck past the edge of a building, I check for signs of the enemy before peeling myself from the wall and following the trail of bodies.

A massacre awaits me at the foot of a tower. A group of Water Fae lies dead on the ground, their blood soaking the grey stone.

Crouching by the nearest body, my fingers go to the dead Fae's face, but my fingertips meet only flesh frozen in rigidity.

My head snaps up as a fleeting shadow darts across the moonlit street, and my heart sings in response.

Savage's spirit stands in front of the tower's entrance, guarding its heavily decorated door.

I cross the distance in a few steps, carefully avoiding the corpses around me. My wolf disappears when I reach the doorstep, leaving me wondering whether I imagined him.

A flash of red catches my eye as I study the massive wood panel. A bloodied hand is printed on it.

Murmuring a silent prayer to the old gods, I slip inside, my hand tightly wrapped around Nahtar.

I step in a pool of crimson. Several bodies have been cut in two, sliced down their middles. Hope swells before a growl tears through my throat. Why the fuck did Azran go in alone? He said he would come back.

Dismissing the tug of betrayal blooming in my heart, my boots sink into plush rugs now covered in blood splatter as I cross the building's entrance.

Foreign corridors lit by sputtering torches greet me, and I'm forced to slow down and check behind each door I come across.

Expansive rooms remain pristine still, vivid carpets masking stone floors and ornate furniture untouched. Silver trays with half-finished meals or glasses of wine wait patiently on long tables, and empty divans fill neatly decorated living rooms, confirming not a single living soul remains on the ground floor.

Pushing a set of double doors open, a stairway comes into view at the end of a wide corridor. Everything is silent except for a faint gurgle. Gripping Nahtar a little tighter, I cross the hallway and reach the stairs.

An emerald soldier is sprawled over the steps, choking on his own blood. He's gone before I can question him.

I repress the curse forming in my throat and take a deep breath as I check the bond, coming up empty.

The probability of me walking into a trap is increasing by the minute, and I have a choice to make.

Turn back and find reinforcements, or keep going.

I squeeze my eyes shut as reason fights with rage, heartbreak, and panic.

A chuckle escapes my throat. The old Ela wouldn't have hesitated a second, but I'm not her anymore, am I?

I'm flooded with nostalgia when I glance at Nahtar, its blade shaking in my grip. The spirit world is at my fingertips, the barrier separating it from the living world but a thin veil in my mind. I sense a presence by my side.

"Father," I whisper.

His image appears clearly in my mind, and with him comes clarity.

I understand now. I understand why he sent me away that dreadful night he was killed. I understand his decision and sacrifice.

He didn't abandon me. He died to save me, to give me a fighting chance in this world, and I'm being presented with the same option.

Leave my mate to his fate, let him sacrifice himself so I can avenge the world, or stay.

Nahtar shines brightly in my hand, and for the first time, I feel its heat.

I can almost hear my father's voice telling me to leave as tears roll down my burning cheeks and I grind my teeth until my jaw hurts. I've known misery all my life, and the world has spared me none of its horrors, but this might be the sickest one yet, or the final one.

"I'm sorry," I say. "Where you end is where I begin, Father. You've always been the bravest on this earth."

I break into a run, climbing the stairs three at a time, and serenity washes over me. There's no going back now. I'm not my father. I never was.

I rush through corridors lined with corpses, following the trail Azran left me. I am Death, and today my judgment will be rendered.

I won't leave my mate. I can save us; I know it in my soul. We can still kill Airdan. Alone, I'm deadly, but together we're invincible. I believe in Death and her monster of war.

I slow down when I step into an empty hall with a double door at the end. The panels sit cracked open, though no sound comes from the room—the trap laid down for its prey.

Taking a deep breath, my power responds instantly, my vision darkening.

Fear rings down the bond. Only, it's not my own.

Azran is alive, and he's on the other side of this door.

CHAPTER 52

NYLREN

"There she is." Father's voice fills the air, his tongue coated in pleasure. "My devilish creature."

Elanor walks in, her dark eyes scanning the room filled with soldiers and landing on her cuffed and injured mate, now kneeling at the feet of the King. A gold collar covered in drops of blood decorates his neck. Her eyes widen slightly at the sight, our only hint the demon is about to be unleashed.

With a swift movement of her sword, she lunges at the closest guard, slicing him in half, her other hand raising and pouring a storm of fire on another guard.

The soldiers stationed by the entrance attack, but they fall one by one, slain by her wrath.

She's grown into quite a Fae since her stay at the palace. From a reckless girl to a confident warrior. Most would describe her as terrifying, but not Father. He hasn't even blinked. He's watching the scene with a smile of pure delight.

A pit of disgust opens in my stomach as he devours her from a distance, his adoration pouring from his widened pupils on a face so similar to mine. Father has never granted me such a look. Ever worthless to him, although I've always been at his beck and call.

He doesn't utter a single word until half of the men lie dying on the floor, their wails making my ears bleed.

"Tsk. Tsk. Careful now, my dear. You wouldn't want my hand to shake from terror."

Father moves so quickly I barely catch a glimpse of the blade in his hand, but Ela freezes immediately, her sword mid-air as his knife presses against Azran's throat.

Two guards grab her by the arms, seizing her sword, and she doesn't resist. A hiss escapes her lips when a familiar collar snaps around her neck. The darkness within her irises retreats, revealing a soft hazel hue.

"Let him go," Elanor says.

Father pulls back his knife as the guards bring her forward. Although she is standing several feet away from us, her hatred radiates from every fiber of her body.

Father's dark laugh sounds in the hall, but she doesn't turn to face him as sobs echo in a corner of the room.

Lord Keryth is hunched over the broken body of his mate, wracked by grief. Three soldiers stand nearby, their swords drawn and ready to strike at the slightest hint of resistance, but he is no more than another broken Fae under the King's boot.

Ela's eyes dart around as she studies the room, no doubt searching for a way out.

Father snaps his fingers until she finally meets his gaze.

"Who are you looking for? Who do you hope will come save you, now?"

"Someone ready to sink their blade into your twisted heart," she spits.

I hold my breath at Ela's defiance, but Father laughs. With another snap of his fingers, Commander Dran steps forward, a bag in his hands.

Reaching into the opening, Father pulls out a mass of blond hair and flesh.

"No one is coming, Elanor."

He throws Amrynn's head, letting it roll for everyone to see.

Ela's eye twitches, her anger barely contained as guards tighten their hold.

"And you." Airdan cocks his head towards Azran. "Won't you greet our guest of honor?"

Ela's features remain neutral, though the slight clenching of her teeth reveals the depth of her despair. She's gotten better at hiding her emotions, but no one can fool me.

Father has the talent to stir someone's deepest fears with a smile on his face, but mine is to read people better than anyone else.

"Ela, I'm—"

Airdan's fist connects with Azran's jaw the moment he opens his mouth. "That's enough."

The former High Lord's head bobs weakly against his chest before he spits blood. A growl escapes Elanor's lips when soldiers flank him.

"I understand where I failed, you know?" Father takes a step towards Ela before lifting his hands in the air, his knife now loosely held. "These emotions you have for those below you hold you back from fulfilling your true purpose. Don't you see?" His eyes widen, and his mouth opens as he waits. "I can free you of them. I can free the world. With you by my side, we will accomplish our greatest purpose. Raise our people to their rightful place, with humans crushed under the soles of our boots." Father glances towards Azran and Keryth. "And those of us too weak to see will perish."

Of course, he doesn't look at me. He doesn't need to for me to know the weakness he sees in me.

With a snap of his fingers in my direction, I move for the first time since I entered the room and took position behind him. After handing me his short blade, he leans towards Ela.

The metal handle of the knife a cool and calming presence in my palm, I barely notice when my fingers clench around the weapon. As I glance at everyone in the throne hall, the final pieces of the plan fall into place.

"Let's put all this hatred behind us, Ela." Father extends a hand towards her. "Join me."

"Set me free right now, and I'll show you what we can do together." Her voice trembling with uncontained rage, she yanks at the soldiers holding her back, widening her stance until Father retreats.

A guard closes the distance in a few steps and lands a blow on her face, busting her lips unceremoniously. Ela answers with a wide smile, her teeth reddened by the blood filling her mouth.

These reckless fools know nothing but violence, and it appears to be amusing Father. He always sounds so carefree and full of life when he laughs like this. Almost genuinely blissful. But I've been fooled by it for too long not to recognize there is no humanity left in his body.

"I could have killed both of you on sight, you know?" Father says in between chuckles. He sighs, and his tone turns dark. "But I always try to find the good in others. My biggest flaw, I must say."

When he turns his back to me to stare at the wall, I follow him on instinct. I might never be presented with an opportunity like this again.

"I'm surrounded by mad people," Father mutters to himself. "Will none of them see reason, dear?"

His question meets with the deafening silence of the room and everyone stills, even Keryth.

"No, you're right. They won't," he adds, with a shake of his head.

Madness dances in his irises as he glances around the hall, his mind ridden with paranoia.

"It has to be done, you're right."

Father's glacial tone permeates every fiber of my body as I recognize what's coming next.

My head snaps to Azran just in time to lock eyes with the fallen High Lord. I nod slightly.

Time suspends when Father snaps his fingers and guards grip their weapons a little tighter, waiting for the order.

"Kill her."

As the words leave Father's mouth, a scream leaves Azran's and he pushes to his feet. Crouching, he goes for the closest guard, knocking him to the ground.

A cry accompanies the melody of breaking bones as Ela headbutts the guard behind her. It was a mistake not to cuff her, a mistake she takes full advantage of.

Soldiers come to life, stirred from the shock of the attack, gathering around Azran and Elanor while others run to protect Father.

A sword flies at Azran and he raises his hands to meet it. The blade slices through his cuffs, earning him a cut in the process. He pulls his assailant into a neck brace with blood flowing from his forearm, and snaps their neck before jumping back. He rolls on the ground and reaches for a sword, but another guard kicks it away.

Guards close in on Ela, who's already keeping two assailants at arm's length with her fists.

Azran lunges at the nearest soldier while I remain frozen in place, assessing their every move to decide whether I should make mine.

Going low, he escapes a blow and reaches for the guard's belt. His fingers grip the handle of her knife and the blade ends in her throat a second later.

He parries a blow with his weapon and aims for his attacker's neck, having found the weakest spot in their emerald armor with a short blade.

"Seize him." Father's orders fill the hall. "Kill her. Kill her."

Seizing the split second his back turns, I lunge—plunging my small blade hilt-deep in a guard's spine. The wet crunch of shattered vertebrae gives way to frantic shouts as his body slumps—my route to freedom cleared.

Father gasps and my heart sings for the first time in ages, only I have no time to relish his surprise.

Two guards are closing in on Azran, forcing him to retreat.

"You're dead," says the short one.

"And we'll kill her next," the other adds, cocking his head towards Ela, who is still fending off attackers.

"That's right, we're—"

My blade pierces the back of the soldier's head and blood rolls down his shoulder blades as he collapses.

"What the—"

The other guard's words remain frozen on his tongue as I run the blade across his throat from behind. His hands go to his neck as he chokes on his own blood and drops to the floor.

Azran squints at me, raising his knife and no doubt debating whether to take me down or not.

Without a glance back, I turn and search the room.

Taking advantage of the guards' confusion, I make a beeline for my tormentor.

Raising my arm, I move to strike. I've hidden in Father's torturous shadows long enough.

As the blade draws close to his neck, I can picture it.

The knife stuck in his throat, blood dripping down his back, and the emerald light draining from his eyes, the accursed color stoking deeper fires of hatred.

A world without my father in it. Sitting on Nyths' throne with everyone at my feet seeing me, truly seeing me. Even I couldn't have devised a more perfect plan. This attack has made for the perfect cover.

The blade mere inches from its target, Father turns faster than I thought him capable of, and my blood freezes.

With a roar, I put all my strength in the strike until steel digs into flesh.

Blood drips down the blade, each crimson drop rolling down my wrist and forearm—a red river, its origin my father's strong hand wrapped around the knife.

My stomach drops as his fingers find purchase on my knuckles. Father grabs me by the neck with his bare hand, but my gaze is still fixed on the blade cutting into his palm.

"Foolish boy."

With these two words, I'm returned to the damp cells underneath the castle. Survival kicks in. Reaching for his shirt, I tear it open.

"No."

The word slips my tongue as panic flares.

The medallion should be around his neck. My salvation should be within reach.

I searched the entire palace of Nyths when he was busy inflicting pain on his captives. I looked everywhere and found nothing, leaving only one possibility. Father kept the pendant on him at all times and never took it off.

Terror fills my bones as the gravity of my mistake dawns on me.

"How easily you are tricked. You're nothing but a tool. A useless one." Father's words barely reach my ears as his fingers squeeze my throat. My hand goes to his.

Groaning under the pressure, my mouth drops open as I gasp for air and attempt to undo his deadly hold.

"Don't you think I noticed all these years? Even with my eyes closed, I could feel your murderous gaze on the back of my head." My eyes widen as his fingers tighten on the side of my neck, crushing my airway. "I tried my hardest to beat it out of you, but alas."

With each shallow breath I manage to steal, his pressure on my larynx strengthens. I scratch at his hand while battling to regain control of the knife, but he doesn't yield an inch. Staring back into his eyes, I lose my grip on the blade. As it clatters to the floor, Father kicks my knee and pins me down. Straddling me, both his hands press down on my neck and I see his undying hatred for me.

Clawing at his hands, I give it all I have left. I pour the same hatred into my touch, reciprocating his disgust. I manage mere scratches, the intense burn in my lungs growing stronger by the second.

So, this is how our decades-long feud ends. No more hiding behind false pretenses. No more games. One winner.

"You robbed me of my last memory of her. You're no son of mine, and certainly no son of hers."

My father's last words ring in confirmation.

My eyelids grow heavy, the pressure in my head and chest unbearable, like my heart is going to explode.

Father's mouth is still moving, but I can't hear a word as my vision clouds with black dots.

Maybe this is a victory too. Father finally gets what he's always wanted. I found a way to finally please him. I could never be worthy of his love in life, but maybe I will be in death.

CHAPTER 53

Azran

My legs are shaking, my arms burning, and with each breath, the pain in my ribs spreads further.

"Ker," I call, but he's frozen in place, still hunched over his mate's body.

I can't make out Ela in the mass of soldiers surrounding us, but I land another blow on the soldier in front of me. I take a cut to the thigh and warmth spreads, confirming it is no superficial wound.

Stars cloud my vision and I can't feel my lower body anymore. As I collapse with my knife still in hand, I get a glimpse at Nylren. My lips part, but no sounds come out.

The tip of two swords stops an inch from my face and the knife slips from my palm, clattering to the floor.

Soldiers seize me, grabbing me roughly and forcing me to my knees. Their hands grip tightly around my shoulders, confirming I'm out of options. Crimson pools underneath me, wetting my shin as blood gushes from my thigh. Guards take position in a half-circle behind me, leaving me just enough room to watch Airdan's reddened face as he crushes his son's neck beneath his palms.

Nylren's head slacks to the side revealing his bulging eyes. A short nod of acknowledgement is all I can offer.

"The best part of this ridiculous attempt is that you have betrayed your own blood and country for nothing." Airdan's pants fill the air as his knuckles whiten.

Nylren's emerald eyes settle on me, and I don't look away until life leaves his.

How could someone with such an inflated sense of worth hate such a close copy of himself?

In the weeks I spent at the mercy of Nylren's cruelty, I developed more pity than hate for him. I can't say I understand him, for I know I made a different decision for myself, but we were both dealt cards to a game we didn't know the rules of.

My head bobs to my chest when Airdan finally lets go of Nylren, and I'm tempted to close my eyes in the hopes the torment will stop. Zetrea's prince lies on the ground, his chest perfectly still.

Airdan pushes his bloodied hand against the ground to help himself up and leaves a crimson palm imprinted there.

Every part of my body throbs with pain as I kneel against the cold floor, my joints aching and the guards' fingers digging into my shoulders. I can't help but wince as each breath sends shockwaves of agony through my side. At least one of my ribs is cracked, if not fully broken. I can barely see with my swollen right eye, the skin tender and hot around the socket. Blood mixed with sweat drips down my forehead from a gash somewhere in my hairline, and a metallic taste lingers in my mouth.

Lifting my head, I bit the inside of my mouth to keep alert. I can't lose consciousness. I have to push through the fatigue permeating my muscle, and embrace the pain. Ela still needs me. She has to live and avenge us all.

A grunt tells me when Ela is kicked down. Half a dozen soldiers jump on her. She reappears moments later, still bound by a collar. Blood runs down her temple and arms, but she's still breathing.

"I'm sorry."

Her voice fills my head as her shoulders sag.

We lock eyes for a mere instant before Airdan steps between us.

Lifting my head, I stare into his beryl irises.

"I'm going to make you pay for every life you took," I grit out.

He closes the distance between us, hate deforming his features in a mask of rage, his eyebrow twitching with madness.

"I don't think so."

Coming to a halt a few feet away, he stills before leaning down and bringing his face an inch from mine.

"She's going to watch you die instead." The whisper carries his breath over my eyelashes and he straightens.

"Her sword," Airdan says, with a snap of his fingers.

Even from a distance, I can see Ela's eyes widen when a soldier hands him Nahtar.

"No!"

With a scream, she pushes on her arms to free herself, in vain. She kicks and snarl until a punch lands in her stomach and she doubles over, trying to catch her breath.

Fury infuses my blood, but I'm powerless, forced to witness her distress and our defeat.

With stars twinkling in the corner of my vision, I know there is no way out of this. Only, I'm going first and getting off easy. I'm leaving this nightmare of a place, but she's staying. She will be alone once more, with no one to help her.

Calen can't have taken Endya already. The battle is most likely still raging by the bridges. No one is coming, and I've failed her again.

"Spare him," Ela blurts out. "It's me you want, Airdan. Kill me—"

A soldier slams their first in her face, cutting her off, and a roar leaves my ravaged throat as I thrash under the restraints.

She's endured enough. Gods know, she's endured enough. A pit opens in my stomach, though it is not Death I fear. Her soul will shatter when mine leaves my body by her own blade.

"You've missed your chance, dear," boasts Airdan, self-congratulation oozing from his smug expression.

Tears roll down Ela's beautiful face, tracing a path through dried blood and dust, and I scan her features, engraving each little detail in my mind. Her full lashes trying to blink the tears away, the shape of her eyebrows, the color of her hair as it reflects the light. But also, the dips on her cheeks and her hazel eyes that sparkle when she smiles. How she closes her eyes when she laughs and the determination that settles in them when she makes up her mind. The outline of her mouth, the soft skin at the back of her neck, and every curve on her body. Wherever I'm headed, I'll take her with me.

Airdan takes position next to me, giving Ela a clear line of sight.

Nahtar flashes in the corner of my eye, but my gaze is set on Ela. If this is to be my last moment on earth, let her be the last thing I gaze upon.

"Give them hell, little one."

Her terror flares down the bond but I keep staring into her eyes, pouring in all my love in response. From the first time I saw her, to our countless verbal jousts and embraces, we've come so far and I wouldn't change a thing. I would suffer the same trials to get to her, in this life and the next. I lived through hell and found paradise in her.

"It's all right. I'm ready." A sob tears from her throat, but I keep going. She has to hear this. My silence cannot be the last she hears of me. *"Fuck this world that's always wanted us dead. I got to share a love with you that transcended all the horrors they threw at us. Nothing could ever take that away from us. They may take my body, but my soul will forever yearn for you, little one."*

She nods weakly through her tears as stars take over my eye sight. I push on.

"I'm yours, and you're mine."

When Nahtar digs into my chest, its blade sears my flesh inch by inch for what feels like an eternity before it retreats.

My only wish is for the last thing I take with me to be her beautiful face, but instead it's her scream, the battle cry of Death.

CHAPTER 54

Elanor

My voice echoes against the walls of the room, its sheer force shaking the grounds beneath my feet as a searing pain tears me apart. I pour all my emotions into the scream, all my rage at the world and the endless pit of despair opening inside me.

Acid runs through my veins, burning each cell in my body, Azran's murder carving itself into my soul. The bond disintegrates before my eyes, its luminary filament going out, like a match running out of flame.

My mind breaks, but I keep staring into my mate's lifeless eyes, even when his body hits the stone floor with a thud.

Soldiers are still holding me back when my cries die in my raw throat, but I barely feel their hands on me. There's only pain, earth shattering suffering tearing at every part of me.

I screw my eyes shut, hoping for it all to go away, but it doesn't. I couldn't do it. I couldn't save him this time. I'm drowning in an ocean of despair, surrounded by enemies, the body of my mate, and Airdan.

Sensations return to my body when I lay eyes on him. My sore abdomen, the strain in my muscles, the fire in my lungs and throat, and the cold metal around my neck.

Airdan eyes me like prey caught in his trap, a crazed smile plastered on his face. It takes a moment for his expression to register, but when it does, I see red.

"You are dead."

"No, my dear," he answers with a victorious chuckle. "But he is."

Airdan kicks Azran's body with the tip of his shoe, and a zap of energy courses through me. I snarl in response, daring him to try that again, and he does.

Anger floods my system, turning into fury, an endless rage calling for violence. The more Airdan hits Azran, the strongest it gets, and I let it, embracing my own wrath, letting it fuel my essence.

The emotion I spent my life trying to outrun proves its value in the most dire time. I engrave the sight in my brain, replaying the image over and over in my head as Airdan's laughter echoes in the hall. Each time I picture his foot coming into contact with Azran's body, my power flares, again, and again.

He did this. He helped Braern. He caged us like animals. He killed my mate. He is responsible for all the wretched things in my life, and it's payback time.

Following the thin thread of power lighting me up inside, I search for its core until the veil to the spirit world is within my grasp. In the blink of an eye, the room changes to hues of black and white, and the pain eases for a moment. Fighting against heartbreak, I search for my mate's soul.

Souls hover over the bodies of the dead soldiers. Nylren's is here too, lingering between the worlds, waiting.

Azran must be here. He must be.

My eyes dart frantically around the room until my gaze lands at the back of the room. A horned figure stands there, perfectly still, with two massive swords in hand. His features are blurred, but for some reason I know he's looking at me. No, not at me but through me and into my soul, whispering his name. War.

Fear twists in my gut when he steps forward, towering over me, his power radiating against mine that's barely more than a whisper.

"Bring her to me." Airdan's voice cuts through my connection to the dark world and my breath hitches in my throat. The searing pain returns, fully intent on ripping me apart from the inside.

My head sags heavily to my chest as the two guards bring me before Airdan.

"Come on. We've forged a connection of our own in the past months, haven't we?" His fingers find purchase around my chin, tilting my head up.

"Look at me," he barks.

A connection? I'll show this sick fuck what kind of connection we have—a connection born in Death.

A smile stretches my face as I glance up, revealing my darkened irises. He lets go instantly, although too late.

"Like I said, asshole, you're dead."

I yank my hands free of the soldiers' grip and let the embers inside me catch fire. As the collar melts off my neck, I cast ribbons of darkness around my guards' throats.

"Your artefacts can't contain me, usurper."

My captors' mouths open in silent screams and the black ribbons pierce their throats, burning through them until they drop dead.

Darkness floods my body and I let Death take over, whispering in my ear. There is no need to worry anymore. Life doesn't matter if Azran is not in it, and no one in this room deserves to take another breath.

My gaze lands on Keryth, and I find in his eyes the same pain tearing at my soul.

"Please," he mouths from a distance, begging for relief.

Extending an arm, my power reaches towards him, piercing his heart instantly. His body sags.

"Guards!"

As Airdan barks orders, the room catches on fire, starting with the doors and cutting off the exit. The smell of burned flesh fills the space and shrieks resonate all around me, but I don't turn to look. I'd rather watch the effect of their melody on Airdan.

His widened emerald eyes scan the room until his gaze lands on his son's corpse, devoured by the dark fire.

Azran's body is the only one spared, a clean circle delimited around him and leaving him untouched.

"You taught me an important lesson. You may cage my body, but no one could ever imprison my mind."

Airdan stumbles away before hurrying back to me, the flames lapping at his heels, ready to take him too. No one escapes Death, not even him.

"There it is. Terror," I intone above the screams, "permeating every fiber of your wretched soul."

I reach for his throat before he can respond, and tilt my head without breaking eye contact.

"It's time to pay for what you've done." The words leaving my lips are no longer mine. Death is here and I am her instrument. I don't belong solely to myself; I never did. We always shared this life.

The last soldier's cry dies with them as the flames surrounding Airdan and I lick at the walls and reach the arched ceiling.

"Look around," I command. "I will haunt this earth until your life's work is destroyed."

Airdan's bulging eyes dart around frantically as fire swallows the room. Sweat trickles down his forehead and his neck turns crimson from the pressure of my fingers around his throat. I hold him until smoke fills his lungs and he's choking and gasping for air. A delightful sight, but not nearly enough to quench my thirst.

The only zone left untouched by the fire forms a perfect circle around me and I still, patiently waiting for him to come to this realization.

I take a step back, and screams tear from his throat as flames lick his boots.

"No!"

He throws himself against me, and my hands go to his torso. Acid pours from my fingers, the dark ribbons trailing down his stomach until black bile pours out of his chest, melting his insides and pooling at his feet.

Gurgles escape his throat as his body is devoured by my power. With a final move, I push him back, letting the fire engulf the King's torn face.

His scream is swallowed by the flames attacking his flesh, burning his silk shirt, eating at him like a ravenous spirit trying to reach his soul. Only he doesn't have one. He never did.

I watch until his body burns to a crisp, unrecognizable, but the searing pain in my heart doesn't retreat. Every fiber of my body radiates with fury, the depth of my loss so vividly real and unbearable.

Refusing to endure it, I dive into the darkness, embracing my power at its fullest, until I'm one with Death. Without Azran, no one remains to pull me back from Death's grasp and the edge I toppled over. I was never any good at being careful, and my mate's last breath ripped the final roots binding me to compassion or conscience. To hell with the consequences.

No distant voice or crimson irises disturb the perfect killing calm settling within as I rise to lay waste to this earth.

My eyes roll in their sockets when Death takes over, leaving me vibrating from her sheer strength.

As I reopen my eyes, the world changes. I'm in one of Endya's towers and everywhere else at the same time. All-seeing, I witness everything happening in the living realm. I see the dead in hundreds, flickering souls hovering over their bodies in the central plaza, in the street, in the entire city.

Airdan's rotten soul stands before me and I stare right into it. I am all powerful in Death, and he can hear me.

"I made you a promise. You are going to watch me burn everything you represent. Everything you've ever touched, I will cleanse. Everything you've ever done, I will undo. And everyone you've ever killed, I will raise from the dead. Once I'm done, I will dump your wretched soul in the fiery pits of hell, forever a prisoner of my wrath."

My dark laughter fills the world and his soul shakes with terror.

Extending both hands, I call on my power until my body trembles and obsidian acid pours from my fingers, reaching into every corpse I find. Spreading through the city, the threads of darkness sink their claws into bodies even on streets where battles still rage.

Each dead soldier is a beacon in the night, waiting for me to find them, and I'm ready to answer their call.

When I've gathered each soul, I command the dead.

"Stand. Right your wrongs. Feel my wrath and kill all who don't."

Like puppets at my fingertips, a thousand souls rise from the dead, reuniting with their emerald-armored bodies, taking arms and turning on their own.

Each Fae that falls stands seconds later, ready to relentlessly attack Airdan's army. The streets and canals are choked with bodies, each new death filling the ranks of my army.

My chest radiates power, energy running wildly through my body and tingling in my fingertips.

Calen is still fighting among his unit. They've made it inside Endya, where he faces a sea of enemies on the plaza's platforms.

No more.

Confusion and dread spreads through the battlefield as my army grows and joins the fight, and I'm drunk on it. Each soul that lights up Death's realm is sent back, a thousand fireflies gathering more bodies for me, souls ready for harvest. With each death, my power grows.

Doors and walls are no obstacles to my sight as I contemplate the destruction.

My focus turns to the tower I'm in as a soul steps towards the door, and doubt seeps into me. The figure glows profoundly, its celestial blaze outshining all others.

As my vision adjusts to the dazzling brilliance, its feature reform and I behold Mor's stoic face as he walks up the narrow street leading to the domed construction, spine straight with fortified resolve.

Opening a path through the dark fire still raging around me, I allow him in.

My mind splits in two when I bring my consciousness back into my body. The pain stays at bay, and I keep a hold on Death's army. A part of me is in the room, attached to my physical shell, the other in the ether.

Pausing at the double doors outside, Mor undoes his braid with a swift move, before wrapping the silk ribbon around his eyes as a blindfold.

As he does, his souls expands into the brightest light, blinding me, and I let the fiery walls close in on themselves to shut the way.

When the flames take over the entire room once more, my racing heart slows.

The angst settles until an increasing pressure closes in around me. Glancing around, I search for its source, sensing a foreign presence near.

The dark flames part before my eyes, and a figure steps out of the fire.

"Death," the blindfolded healer greets me by my name and my essence sings in response, recognizing his.

I let the blaze die down, leaving us surrounded in smoke.

"Justice."

He inclines his head slightly, like he can see through the fabric covering his eyes.

"Sister. Do you know why you were sent here?"

"To avenge." The words come to me on instinct.

Justice shakes his head before answering.

"You were given a choice, a way to restore the balance of the world, but you chose to tip the scales in favor of darkness."

"I am darkness."

"You were also light once."

His words echo in my mind, forcing their way through my mental shields, and I remember.

I remember life. I remember the joy of biting into a freshly baked peach pie and riding across the plains of Averion. I remember petting Savage's warm fur, pulling Vesta into an embrace, and laughing with the twins. I remember falling asleep in Azran's arms.

As each memory spins in my head, I stumble through darkness into a brick wall.

I did have a choice, and I chose wrong. I crossed a line, blurring the boundaries between life and death.

"What have I done?"

No one should yield this much power, not even me.

"Nothing that can't be undone."

Looking through Death's eyes, I gaze upon the central plaza. Airdan's soldiers are running, dropping their weapons, surrendering, but the dead butcher them nonetheless.

Exhaustion reaches through my power's veil, letting pain back in, and with it, excruciating grief.

I screw my eyes shut and focus on each link connecting me to the rest of the world, each thread sewn into the living dead, and one by one, I let go.

Sweat trickles down my forehead, my face heating from the effort, and smoke lodges in my throat, but I keep going until the last body is laid to rest, at last.

I fall to my knees, my hands finding purchase on the ground to prevent me from collapsing. My entire body is ridden with suffering and a silent scream freezes on my lips.

Mor removes his blindfold, but I can't bring myself to look him in the eyes and endure his judgment.

"Ela."

His soft tone reaches my ears and I find the last sliver of courage in my heart to face him. The empathy I find in his gaze is more heart wrenching than his disappointment.

His forgiveness is all over his face but tears roll down mine. I don't deserve it. Certainly not from the Fae who's done nothing but help and guide me.

"He killed him," is all I manage to say before my voice breaks.

The confession has an unbearable finality, carving the reality of his loss in my bones.

"You have to let him go," Mor offers gently.

Confusion wars with anger as he suggests releasing Azran, expecting me to relinquish our bond by choice, as if I could snip such an elemental fiber of my being any more than I could stop my own pulse or peel off my skin. Azran's spirit remains fused to mine, the pain of his loss seared into my flesh.

This anguish is mine, trapping me in my own inferno of punishment for my actions, and I deserve it all. I lost myself in Death's grasp, learning the cost too late, for this power is too much for a single soul to bear.

"I can't live without him."

Water pours from my eyes still, each drop running to my chin before crashing on the ground.

I don't know how to withstand the grief. I don't know to make it stop. I don't know how to survive anymore. In fact, I don't think I want to.

"I know."

A kind smile forms on his wrinkled face, though it doesn't reach his grey eyes. With two simple words, Mor shows me the way out of this hell.

I bow to his blessing as Mor steps back, and seek my power once more.

Letting the energy flood my body, I let it extinguish my pain and mend my wounds. Slowing my breathing, I remove all barriers within me, all shields, and I open myself up entirely, seeking the light within the darkness.

As I pull on the threads, intertwining both energies in an intricate knot, I'm reminded of Azran's words.

Do you think my love for you so frail that something as elemental as Death could keep me from you?

A smile forms on my tears-dampened face as I make myself a promise.

I won't let his soul wander between the realms endlessly. Death parted us, but I will find him again.

Mor hasn't moved and I'm tempted to send him away from this tomb—he deserves better than to witness my last moments.

Perhaps sensing the silent suggestion, Mor meets my gaze, warning me from speaking foolish words as he stands vigil, confirming I don't have to do this alone, not anymore.

His smile doesn't falter when I summon the obsidian and ivory flames. Their warmth is at my fingertips and I let it spread to my arms and shoulders.

What is mere death to those already groomed in suffering's manifold shapes? Let fire take me into the darkness, unashamed at last.

I'm leaving this world, in search of the place where I come from and belong. The ruler of the spirit world and the afterlife is being called back home.

Fire spreads to my entire body and I fuel it with all my power, letting it devour the carnal envelope that's been my prison for more than two decades.

As I face Death once again, I realize I've always been fighting myself, and I'm ready to let her win.

With my last breath, I vow to find Azran.

I will find him, and then I will rest, at last.

FIRST EPILOGUE

Calen

Staring out of my bedroom window, I sigh heavily as I touch the ring on my finger, the jewel Az wore until he died and a symbol of the position I now occupy. He should be here, leading our people, not buried in the palace garden beside Ela.

I close my eyes, losing myself to the memories of our wild adventures. I can almost feel the warm air of the shitty taverns we used to go to and taste the ale on my tongue from the nights we spent celebrating a victorious battle. We were on top of the world, convinced we had eternity to fulfill our dreams.

A bittersweet longing aches in my chest at the recollection, but I roughly push the reminiscence away when my door opens.

"Hey."

Vesta's mere presence eases the heartbreak.

"Any news from Mor?" I ask, keeping my back to her.

"He and Naar are making progress towards a peaceful transition of power in Zetrea. Elections will be held in the coming months."

"Good."

"Mor must hate your guts right now, sending him there to keep an eye on things," Vesta adds in a playful tone.

"The old bastard almost volunteered. He is on his second honeymoon right now, though he'll never admit it," I say with a chuckle, before clearing my throat. "Is everything ready?"

Queen Aanor, Tharrion, and Irann should be in Averion tomorrow. Airdan's attack brought our nations closer, and although it's taken almost a year to build a solid baseline of trust with the humans, I'm hopeful. If nothing goes wrong, her visit will bring us one step closer to long lasting peace and unity.

"Yes, High Lord," Vesta answers teasingly.

"Don't call me that in here." I sigh. "Please."

She remains silent, but her footsteps fill the room until she slides her arms around my back to hug me from behind.

"It's been months, Cal." Vesta rests her head against my back. "You're more than deserving of the title."

I take a deep breath before undoing the knot of her arms around my middle and turning to face her.

"You've earned it," she continues.

I screw my eyes shut, letting her words sink in and her sultry voice chase the demons away.

"I know," I finally let out. "I just thought Az would be here for this. This was his dream."

"Our dream. We all shared it."

"Yes, but it was never meant to be me. High Lord." I huff as I utter the title I now carry.

"And yet, here you are, walking in his footsteps and finishing what he started." Her lips find mine to deposit a soft kiss. "No one else is better suited for the task, and you know it."

"He would have been." I shake my head, wishing the pit in my stomach would disappear.

"And Ela would have absolutely hated all this," Vesta says.

Laughter tears through my throat and pride shines in her eyes.

"True." I chuckle. "She really would have hated it and been a major pain in my ass."

I can almost picture it. Ela storming through the palace's corridors, going crazy from being cooped up in here, and pouring all her bottled-up frustration into her attitude or by sneaking out unnoticed, leaving chaos and panicked aides in her wake.

"There it is." Vesta touches the corner of my lips, now lifted into a smile. "This brooding High Lord act doesn't really suit you."

"And what does?"

"You're more of the charming and handsome type."

"Handsome, hm?" I cock a brow in question.

"Very."

Vesta's lips hover over mine, teasing me until I close the distance. Pressing my mouth against hers, I forget the world around us.

I devour her delicious lips, probing with my tongue as she drags her fingers down my shoulders and neck. Pressure builds at the base of my stomach when she catches the edge of my shirt and pulls the piece of fabric over my head.

We lock eyes and her gaze reveals the fire burning between her legs.

Determination sets in, and with a finger, I take the thin strap of her dress and slip it off her shoulder.

Her mouth parts slightly as her hands roam my chest and I slowly take care of the other strap. The fabric slips off her stunning body, leaving her bare before me.

A low growl leaves my lips when my gaze lands on the tiny piece of black fabric left around her hips.

"You don't like it?" Vesta bats her eyelashes at me.

"I love it, and I'll love it even more when it's on the floor."

Her chuckle fills the air as I kiss her cheek slowly before moving to her neck. When I bite at the tender skin, her breath catches in her throat.

I lower myself, covering her warm body in soft kisses until my knees hit the rug.

Caressing her legs and the backs of her thighs with my fingers, I slow down my kisses as I near her middle. Each touch finds its mark, and each touch elicits a soft moan.

When I'm on the verge of giving in to her silent demands, I look up.

"Do you enjoy the sight of me kneeling before you, Dove?"

A wide smile appears on her face, disorienting me with her beauty. Damned woman. I'll crawl to the ends of this earth for her, and she knows it.

"I love you."

I let the words roll off my tongue easily, enjoying each syllable. I'll never get tired of saying it, or hearing her say it back. I finally understand now. After losing so much, I get it. If this is all we ever share, I am perfectly content.

Acceptance rings in my heart, and something in me is unchained, set free. Pure bliss courses through my veins, setting my entire body on fire.

"I love you," she answers, tears glistening in her eyes.

With these words, she owns my entire being, body and soul.

I used to think I could never deserve such devotion, but I've grown to forgive and love myself enough to see through the web of deceit I sowed over my heart. She is the only one to whom I'd give such power over me. I'll spend the rest of my days worshipping her.

"Cal." Vesta is still smiling, a twinkle of amusement in her teary eyes as her words echo once more. *"I love you."*

My mouth drops open, for hers hasn't moved in a minute.

⸻◦⸻

Later that day, I walk into Azran's old office, left perfectly intact since we came back from Daenia months ago. I couldn't bring myself to disturb the space he's occupied for so long.

The leather couch still bears the marks of its many occupants. The bookshelves have been dusted recently. Everything is in its place, the room displaying an illusion of normalcy, except for the absence of embers in the hearth or papers on the wooden desk.

The large package I had delivered here weeks ago still rests against a wall, untouched and sealed. I glance at the rectangular shape before turning on my heels to leave.

With my hand on the door handle, I freeze. Although I hate to admit it, I know it is time.

Summoning my courage, I change course and reach for the package. Once in my hands, I know there is no turning back.

My fingers press its edge as I walk to the desk, feeling a wooden frame beneath the paper.

Putting it down, I gently remove the wrapper to reveal the artwork hiding under.

Water fills my eyes as Azran and Ela look back at me, their faces perfectly captured in the portrait. I swallow the lump in my throat as I contemplate the painting, and my stomach twists with angst.

Azran's eyebrows are relaxed, his features peaceful, looking lovingly at Ela smiling back at him. A chuckle escapes my lips. Gods know these two spent more time arguing and wielding swords than anyone else. The portrait is beautiful. Neither knew rest and ease in life, but they deserve to find it in death.

"Wherever you are, brother, may you be at peace, her soul forever entwined with yours," I whisper to the empty room, and the pressure in my chest alleviates.

A knock sounds on the door moments later.

"Come in," I answer.

"High Lord." Wyn bows to me, and for the first time, it doesn't feel so wrong. "Should I have the meeting moved to the usual room?"

I pause to look around the office before answering.

"No. Have everyone come here."

"Very well, High Lord."

"Thank you."

Wyn nods before exiting the room and I glance at the portrait.

"I'll make you proud, Az, but I can't promise I'll be as uptight as you."

The ghost of his laughter echoes in my head and a smile tugs the corners of my mouth.

SECOND EPILOGUE

ELANOR

No shroud of anxiety haunts my steps as I cross the palace court-yard. No phantom fears stir in my chest as the sole of my boot hits the paving stones. No impending doom claws at me as each step reverberates in my feet, confirming what I already know.

I'm home, where I belong.

My shoulders relaxed, I keep going as a soft breeze blows at my back, carrying Averion's afternoon heat.

The muscles in my arm tense when I push the double doors open, but my body remains free of lingering pain, as does my soul. The constant ache of regret and mourning is gone, leaving me at peace.

My gaze lands on my hands, free of scars and blood—another confirmation I'm where I intended to be.

The spirit world always left me torn, my soul split between two places as strings pulled my core in opposite directions, my memories in a haze, but this place doesn't.

As I climb the steps leading to the building's entrance, the faithful remembrance of my mortal years accompanies me. From Airdan's last moments to the dark fire devouring everyone in its path, including its host. Instead of fighting grief, I had to let it break me so I could let go, and I did. After draping myself in my rage to shield against life's assaults, I finally understood that my emotions were never my enemy. The corners of my lips lift into a smile as I picture Vesta rolling her eyes at me for taking this long to learn my lesson. I won't hear the end of it when I see her again, hopefully not for a very long time.

Keeping a steady pace, I enter the palace and make for the throne room to fulfill a promise I made.

Eagerness takes my heart as I walk through the empty corridors which once buzzed with activity. Empty chairs stand guard as the paintings' faded gazes track my steps. Life has no place in my realm, but it's the dead I seek.

Crossing the threshold of the throne room, I pause before the dais, my eyes sweeping over the tapestries lining the walls. Azran is there, victorious on the battlefield, his long hair flowing behind his back and Dagrassaeb in hand—a pale reflection of his true being that won't satisfy the urge blooming in my heart.

Turning on my heels, I make for the stairway and climb the steps two at a time, impatience flaring in every part of my being.

His office comes into view, and I swing the door open.

My breath hitches in my throat as I let my steps guide me. My fingers glide over the back of the leather couch. Everything is as we left it, except for the firewood crackling in the hearth behind the desk, casting warmth to the room. These walls witnessed my wrath more times than I can recall, but also his infinite patience with me.

Spinning around, my eyes scan each piece of furniture before halting on the fireplace where flames lick crisp logs, coals not yet formed under the fresh-split timber.

A small smile tugs my lips as I leave, following the clues he's leaving me.

Breaking into a run, I leap down the stairs, step after step, to reach his room. Resolve settles as I pause before his door, ready to end this chase.

Twisting the knob, I send the door crashing against the wall. Disappointment twists in my gut. The bed is made, its linen covers neatly arranged and pillows fluffed.

My heart pounds as doubt courses my veins, before a new theory forms.

Taking a deep breath, his scent fills my senses in confirmation.

He's making me retrace our steps, every place we were together in, every piece of furniture we painted with our love, and I know his next stop.

Hurrying out of the room, I aim for the one down the hall—my bedroom.

This time, I creak the door open and sneak in, determined not to let him escape. I'm done playing games.

I edge inside, searching for any stirring shadows offering signs of life, but the chamber remains untouched like the rest of the palace.

Blowing air out of my nose in a huff, I cross the empty room to stare out of the window and look for another clue. My heart sinks. He should be here.

My pulse quickens with the eerie silence around me as I contemplate this place, which held the only birthday celebration to ever mean something to me. My walls started crumbling that night, loneliness losing its bitter edge as he handed me his gift. Our true beginning unfurled here as I discovered another soul that could understand and heal mine.

My heart leaps to my throat when the door swings shut. Whipping my head around, I raise my shaky hands into fists as I stare at it.

Something lurks here, or someone.

"Show yourself," I say, mustering my sharpest tone to hide my nerves and the adrenaline coursing through my veins.

My heart pounds fiercely against my breastbone and my breaths emerge short and quick as a shape takes form.

Goosebumps prickle my arms when a tall warrior steps out of thin air, his face blurred.

I squint, trying to see through the illusion hiding his features before reaching for my sword.

My fingers grasp at air, and I realize too late Nahtar is not sheathed on my back. I got so used to carrying it everywhere I go, it didn't occur to me I couldn't bring it to Death's realm.

Widening my stance slightly, I lower both fists to my sides, waiting.

A draft stirs in the sealed room, though its windows remain closed, chasing away the fog covering the faceless warrior.

A horned mask of bones meets my stare, and my stomach drops.

I haven't forgotten our last encounter in Daenia, nor the dreams he used to haunt.

"War," I greet him as I ready myself, raising my arms before me.

He stalks towards me in response, his eyes still hidden behind the bone mask, and I meet each move with a step backwards, until my back touches the window.

"What are you doing here?" I ask, unable to hide the tremble in my voice as he takes atrociously slow steps.

Glancing around the room for an escape, I barely hear his answer.

"I came to find you."

I freeze, his voice penetrating the fear clouding my eyes like fire tunneling through ice.

A gasp tears from my throat as the mask disappears, revealing his chiseled face and hazel eyes.

"There's nowhere you can go that I won't be with you, little one."

Azran's strong brow and piercing eyes dispel the ether and I stand dumbstruck as his silhouette solidifies into beloved form. Relief wars with doubt as his footsteps echo off stone.

He stops a few feet from me and extends his arm towards me. Staggering reality clashes against frantic dreams as I uncurl the fingers in my palms and raise a shaky hand to meet his.

Time suspends as my fingers graze his skin, caressing his palm before wrapping around his forearm. His grip tightens on my wrist and water pools in my eyes.

"You're here," I breathe out as tears roll, tracing a cold path down my flushed cheeks.

When my gaze meets his, its familiar fiery warmth sets my soul alight and everything falls into place. My heartbeat settles, fear's desperate race giving way to calm at the devotion burning in his hazel stare, the eyes I both warred against and learned to trust. Home is no longer a place, but his presence by my side.

His other hand encircles my waist as I wrap desperate arms around his back, squeezing with all my might, fingers pressing into the woven fabric of his shirt.

Gathered in his arms, I nestle against his chest, feeling the heat radiating off his strong body.

"You found me." His scent envelops me as he answers, and I am whole again.

Azran withdraws just enough to cup my cheek and I lean into his hand.

"Both made from the same mold, we were always meant to find each other."

His breath brushes my face and I can barely tear my gaze from his lips to look into loving eyes.

"Did you know?" I ask.

"I suspected my destiny when yours was revealed, though I merely toyed with the idea at the time. All I knew was that I needed to be by your side."

His thumb caresses my skin and I press a kiss to his palm.

"I never thought it would hurt this much. Loosing you again was—"

I screw my eyes closed, unable to finish the sentence as distant echoes of the pain assault my mind.

"How did it end?" he asks, his jaw clenching tightly.

I shake my head before answering.

"Airdan is defeated and I am here now. That's all that matters."

Refusing to stir ghosts of the past, I bring my face closer to his until our lips touch. His mouth brushes over mine gently before pressing with renewed eagerness, and I sink into his kiss.

My arms wrap around his neck as his land on my hips, pulling me against him.

With a touch, the horrors of our lives disappear, leaving only our enduring bond that even mortality couldn't sever. I will never tire of his arms, and eternity won't be long enough to quench my thirst for him.

Azran leans subtly back to whisper against my mouth.

"Let's go, love."

I steal another kiss, unable to tear myself from him.

"Go where?" I ask, tightening my hold around his neck. A smile blooms on his handsome face.

"Did I not tell you I have big plans for us?"

I cock a brow, not moving an inch until I get an answer.

"The Blue Mountain. I want to show you where it all began."

Letting go, I take his extended hand, intertwining my fingers with his as I let him guide me to the stables.

Moments later, we're riding side-by-side through the vibrant plains surrounding Averion. A beaming smile hurts my cheeks. My chest expands tenfold in a useless attempt to contain the explosion of bliss coursing through my body.

Finally, I stand unencumbered—no duties, grief, or anxiety cling as oppressive shackles now.

The wind hits my face with each gallop of the horse, and I glance again and again at my mate, hardly able to believe the painful longing is over, for good.

After so much loss and heartache, so many moments I thought my world was ending, the future stretches ahead, filled with promises of passion, partnership, and the quiet moments of joy that come with a hard-won love.

The difficult choices, gut-wrenching sacrifices, and tears shed were all worth it. With him next to me as we ride the rolling plains, the hardships melt away, and instead of loneliness and uncertainty, my future now holds his wide smile, strong embrace, and absolute devotion.

My heart soars, giddiness bubbling up and spilling out in exhilarated laughter.

Destined to be one, we fought our way to each other. Side-by-side, we conquered everything life threw our way, even death, and there will be no separating us now.

A horned warrior rides alongside another made of darkness and light.

Children of War and Death.

The *Prince of Bloodshed* and the *Daughter of Darkness*.

Reunited in the afterlife and together for all eternity.

Author's Note

An immense thank you to:

- You, dear reader, for joining me on this journey. If you enjoyed the *Daughter of Darkness* series, don't hesitate to leave an online review to help other readers discover it.

- My Street Team, for being true cheerleaders and helping me cross the finish line with my sanity (relatively) intact. I appreciate each and every one of you.

- My ARC Team, for taking the time to review Prince of Bloodshed. I appreciate all your encouragements and constructive criticism.

- Claudia, Chrissy, Lauryn, and Marisa, for beta-reading and providing the most crucial feedback. Here's to making friends along the way!

- Rae, for being my number one supporter from the start. I'm incredibly grateful for you.

- Amanda, for our many late night FaceTimes and brainstorming sessions. Our friendship means the world to me.

- Katherine, for your approachability and crucial insights. It's been an absolute pleasure working with you.

- Enzo, for your responsiveness and ability to always help me see through the fog. I couldn't have done this without you.

- Ariel, for being the best friend a girl could ask for. You inspire me daily and always know how to silence the voices telling me I'm not enough.

- H, for bringing so much light into my life, even through the darkest times. Thank you for showing me what unconditional love is, even when I spend our evenings at my desk.

- HK, for your continued support. I couldn't have asked for a better chosen family.

- And finally, a slightly ironic thank you to my imposter syndrome, fear of failure, and anxiety. Your unrelenting attacks pushed me out of my comfort zone and helped me grow as a writer and person.

Thank you all.